FOR THE EMPEROR

'STAY BACK. WE'LL handle it,' I told Crassus, and leaned over the driver's compartment to call to Jurgen. 'Take us in!' I shouted.

As usual, where anyone else might have hesitated or argued, he simply followed orders without thinking. The Salamander lurched forwards, accelerating towards the blazing building as rapidly as it could.

'There! Those loading doors!' I pointed, but my faithful aide had already seen them, and a hail of bolter shells ripped them to shreds an instant before we hit.

A WARHAMMER 40,000 NOVEL

FOR THE EMPEROR

Sandy Mitchell

To Judith, for everything.

A BLACK LIBRARY PUBLICATION

First published in Great Britain in 2003 by
BL Publishing,
Games Workshop Ltd.,
Willow Road, Nottingham,
NG7 2WS, UK

10 9 8 7 6 5 4 3 2 1

Cover illustration by Clint Langley.

A CIP record for this book is available from the British Library.

ISBN 1 84416 050 5

Distributed in the US by Simon & Schuster
1230 Avenue of the Americas, New York, NY 10020, US.

Printed and bound in Great Britain by
Cox & Wyman Ltd, Reading, Berkshire, UK.

See the Black Library on the Internet at
www.blacklibrary.com

Find out more about Games Workshop
and the world of Warhammer 40,000 at
www.games-workshop.com

IT IS THE 41st millennium. For more than a hundred centuries the Emperor has sat immobile on the Golden Throne of Earth. He is the master of mankind by the will of the gods, and master of a million worlds by the might of his inexhaustible armies. He is a rotting carcass writhing invisibly with power from the Dark Age of Technology. He is the Carrion Lord of the Imperium for whom a thousand souls are sacrificed every day, so that he may never truly die.

YET EVEN IN his deathless state, the Emperor continues his eternal vigilance. Mighty battlefleets cross the daemon-infested miasma of the warp, the only route between distant stars, their way lit by the Astronomican, the psychic manifestation of the Emperor's will. Vast armies give battle in his name on uncounted worlds. Greatest amongst his soldiers are the Adeptus Astartes, the Space Marines, bio-engineered super-warriors. Their comrades in arms are legion: the Imperial Guard and countless planetary defence forces, the ever-vigilant Inquisition and the tech-priests of the Adeptus Mechanicus to name only a few. But for all their multitudes, they are barely enough to hold off the ever-present threat from aliens, heretics, mutants – and worse.

TO BE A man in such times is to be one amongst untold billions. It is to live in the cruellest and most bloody regime imaginable. These are the tales of those times. Forget the power of technology and science, for so much has been forgotten, never to be re-learned. Forget the promise of progress and understanding, for in the grim dark future there is only war. There is no peace amongst the stars, only an eternity of carnage and slaughter, and the laughter of thirsting gods.

Editorial Note:

What, for want of a better phrase, I will henceforth be referring to as the 'Cain Archive' is, in truth, barely deserving of so grandiloquent a title. It consists merely of a single dataslate, stuffed full of files arranged with a cavalier disregard for chronology, and to no scheme of indexing that I've been able to determine despite prolonged examination of the contents. What can be stated with absolute certainty, however, is that the author was none other than the celebrated Commissar Ciaphas Cain, and that the archive was written by him during his retirement while serving as a tutor at the Schola Progenium.

This would pin the date of composition to some time after his appointment to the faculty in 993.M41; from occasional references to his published memoirs (*To Serve the Emperor: A Commissar's Life*), which first saw the light of day in 005.M42, we can safely conclude that he was inspired by the process of writing them to embark on a fuller account of his experiences, and that the bulk of the archive was composed no earlier than this.

His motives for so doing we can only guess at, since publication would have been impossible; indeed, I placed them under Inquisitorial seal the moment they came to light, for reasons which should be immediately apparent to any attentive reader.

Nevertheless, I believe they are worthy of further study. Some of my fellow inquisitors may be shocked to discover that one of the Imperium's most venerated heroes was, by his own admission, a scoundrel and self-seeking rogue; a fact of which, due to our sporadic personal association, I have long been aware. Indeed, I would go so far as to contend that it was this very combination of character flaws which made him one of the most effective servants the Imperium has ever had, despite his strenuous efforts to the contrary. For, in his century or more of active service to the Commissariat, and occasional less visible activities at my behest, he faced and bested almost every enemy of humanity: necrons, tau, tyranids and orks, eldar, both free of taint and corrupted by the ruinous powers, and the daemonic agents of those powers themselves. Reluctantly, it must be admitted, but in many cases repeatedly, and always with success; a record few, if any, more noble men can equal.

In fairness, it should also be pointed out here that Cain is his own harshest critic, often going out of his way to deny that the many instances in which he appears, despite his professed baser motives, to have acted primarily out of loyalty or altruism were any such thing. It would be ironic, indeed, if his awareness of his shortcomings should have blinded him to his own (admittedly often well-hidden) virtues.

It is also worth reflecting that if, as is often asserted, courage consists not of the absence of fear but the overcoming of it, Cain does indeed richly deserve his heroic reputation, even if he always steadfastly denied the fact!

However much we may deplore his professed moral shortcomings, his successes are undeniable, and we can be thankful that Cain's own account of his chequered career has at last been discovered. To say the least, these memoirs shed new light on many of the odder corners of recent Imperial history, and his eyewitness accounts of our enemies contain many valuable, if idiosyncratic, insights into understanding and confounding their dark designs.

It is for this reason that I preserved the archive and have spent a considerable amount of leisure time in the years since its discovery editing and annotating it, in an attempt to make it more accessible to those of my fellow inquisitors who may wish to peruse it for themselves. Cain appears to have had no overall structure in mind, simply recording incidents from his past as they occurred to him, and, as a result, many of the anecdotes are devoid of context; he has a disconcerting habit of beginning in media res, and many of the shorter fragments end abruptly as his own part in the events he is describing comes to a conclusion.

I have therefore chosen to begin the process of dissemination with his account of the Gravalax campaign, which is reasonably coherent, and with which the members of our ordo will be at least passingly familiar as a result of my own involvement in the affair. Indeed, it contains an account of our first meeting from Cain's perspective, which I must admit I found rather amusing when I first stumbled across it.

For the most part, the archive speaks for itself, although I have taken the liberty of breaking up the long and unstructured account into relatively self-contained chapters to facilitate reading. The quotations preceding them are something of an indulgence on my part, having been culled from a collection of such sayings compiled by Cain himself for the apparent amusement and edification of the cadets in his charge, but I justify this as perhaps providing an additional insight into the workings of his mind. Apart from this, I have confined myself to occasional editorial interpolations where I considered it necessary to place Cain's somewhat self-centred narrative into a wider context; unless otherwise attributed, all such annotations are my own, and I have been otherwise content to let his own words do the work.

ONE

I don't know what effect they have on the enemy, but by the Emperor, they frighten me.

– General Karis, of the Valhallans
under his command.

ONE OF THE first things you learn as a commissar is that people are never pleased to see you; something that's no longer the case where I'm concerned, of course, now that my glorious and undeserved reputation precedes me wherever I go. A good rule of thumb in my younger days, but I'd never found myself staring down death in the eyes of the troopers I was supposed to be inspiring with loyalty to the Emperor before. In my early years as an occasionally loyal minion of his Glorious Majesty, I'd faced, or to

11

be more accurate, ran away screaming from, orks, necrons, tyranids, and a severely hacked off daemon-host, just to pick out some of the highlights of my ignominious career. But standing in that mess room, a heartbeat away from being ripped apart by mutinous Guardsmen, was a unique experience, and one that I have no wish to repeat.

I should have realised how bad the situation was when the commanding officer of my new regiment actually smiled at me as I stepped off the shuttle. I already had every reason to fear the worst, of course, but by that time I was out of options. Paradoxical as it might seem, taking this miserable assignment had looked uncomfortably like the best chance I had of keeping my precious skin in one piece.

The problem, of course, was my undeserved reputation for heroism, which by that time had grown to such ludicrous proportions that the Commissariat had finally noticed me and decided that my talents were being wasted in the artillery unit I'd picked as the safest place to sit out my lifetime of service to the Emperor, a long way away from the sharp end of combat. Accordingly, I'd found myself plucked from a position of relative obscurity and attached directly to Brigade headquarters.

That hadn't seemed too bad at first, as I'd had little to do except shuffle datafiles and organise the occasional firing squad, which had suited me fine, but the trouble with everybody thinking you're a hero is that they tend to assume you like being in mortal danger and go out of their way to provide some. In the half-dozen years since my arrival, I'd been temporarily seconded to units assigned, among other things, to assault fixed positions, clear out a space hulk, and run recon deep behind enemy lines. And every time I'd made it back alive, due in no small part to my natural talent for diving for cover and waiting for the noise to stop, the general staff had patted me on the head, given me another commendation, and tried to find an even more inventive way of getting me killed.

Something obviously had to be done, and done fast, before my luck ran out altogether. So, as I often had before, I let my reputation do the work for me and put in a request for a transfer back to a regiment. Any regiment. By that time I just didn't care. Long experience had taught me that the opportunities for taking care of my own neck were much higher when I could pull rank on every officer around me.

'I just don't think I'm cut out for data shuffling,' I said apologetically to the weasel-faced little runt from the lord general's office. He nodded judiciously, and made a show of paging through my file.

'I can't say I'm surprised,' he said, in a slightly nasal whine. Although he tried to look cool and composed, his body language betrayed his excitement at being in the presence of a living legend; at least that's what some damn fool pictcast commentator had called me after the Siege of Perlia, and the appellation stuck. The next thing I know my own face is grinning at me from recruiting posters all over the sector, and I couldn't even grab a mug of recaf without having a piece of paper shoved under my nose with a request to autograph it. 'It doesn't suit everybody.'

'It's a shame we can't all have your dedication to the smooth running of the Imperium,' I said. He looked sharply at me for a moment, wondering if I was taking the frak, which of course I was, then decided I was simply being civil. I decided to ladle it on a bit. 'But I'm afraid I've been a soldier too long to start changing my habits now.'

That was the sort of thing Cain the Hero was supposed to say, of course, and weasel-face lapped it up. He took my transfer request from me as though it was a relic from one of the blessed saints.

'I'll handle it personally,' he said, practically bowing as he showed me out.

AND SO IT was, a month or so later, I found myself in a shuttle approaching the hangar bay of the *Righteous Wrath*, a battered old troopship identical to thousands in Imperial service, almost all of which I sometimes think I've travelled on over the years. The familiar smell of shipboard air, stale, recycled, inextricably intertwined with rancid sweat, machine oil and boiled cabbage, hissed into the passenger compartment as the hatch seals opened. I inhaled it gratefully, as it displaced the no less familiar odour of Gunner Jurgen, my aide almost since the outset of my commissarial career nearly twenty years before.

Short for a Valhallan, Jurgen somehow managed to look awkward and out of place wherever he was, and in all our time together, I couldn't recall a single occasion on which he'd ever worn anything that appeared to fit properly. Though amiable enough in temperament, he seemed ill at ease with people, and, in turn, most preferred to avoid his company; a tendency no doubt exacerbated by the perpetual psoriasis that afflicted him, as well as his body odour, which, in all honesty, took quite a bit of getting used to.

Nevertheless he'd proven an able and valued aide, due in no small part to his peculiar mentality. Not overly bright, but eager to please and doggedly literal in his approach to following orders, he'd become a useful buffer between me and some of the more onerous aspects of my job. He never questioned anything I said or did, apparently convinced that it must be for the good of the Imperium in some way, which, given the occasionally discreditable activities I'd been known to indulge in, was a great deal more than I could have hoped for from any other trooper. Even after all this time I still find myself missing him on occasion.

So he was right there at my side, half-hidden by our combined luggage, which he'd somehow contrived to gather up and hold despite the weight, as my boot heels first rang on the deck plating beneath the shuttle. I didn't object; experience had taught me that it was a good idea for people meeting him for the first time to get the full picture in increments.

I paused fractionally for dramatic effect before striding forward to meet the small knot of Guard officers drawn up to greet me by the main cargo doors, the clang of my footsteps on the metal sounding as crisp and authoritative as I could contrive; an effect undercut slightly by the pops and clangs from the scorched area under the shuttle engines as it cooled, and Jurgen's tottering gait behind me.

'Welcome, commissar. This is a great honour.' A surprisingly young woman with red hair and blue eyes stepped forward and snapped a crisp salute with parade ground efficiency. I thought for a moment that I was being subtly snubbed with only the junior officers present, before I reconciled her face with the file picture in the briefing slate. I returned the salute.

'Colonel Kasteen.' I nodded an acknowledgement. Despite having no objection to being fawned over by young women in the normal course of events, I found such a transparent attempt at ingratiation a little nauseating. Then I got a good look at her hopeful expression and felt as though I'd stepped on a non-existent final stair. She was absolutely sincere. Emperor help me, they really were pleased to see me. Things must be even worse here than I'd imagined.

Just how bad they actually were I had yet to discover, but I already had some presentiment. For one thing, the palms of my hands were tingling, which always means there's trouble hanging in the air like the static before a storm, and for another, I'd broken with the habit of a lifetime and actually read the briefing slate carefully on the tedious voyage out here to meet the ship.

To cut a long story short, morale in the Valhallan 296th/301st was at rock bottom, and the root cause of it all was obvious from the regiment's title. Combining below-strength regiments was standard practice among the Imperial Guard, a sensible way of consolidating after combat losses to keep units up to strength and of further use in the field. What hadn't been sensible was combining what was left of the 301st, a crack planetary assault unit with fifteen hundred years of traditional belief in their innate superiority over every other unit in the Guard, particularly the other Valhallan ones, with the 296th; a rear echelon garrison command, which, just to throw promethium on the flames, was one of the few all-women regiments raised and maintained by that desolate iceball. And just to put the cherry on it, Kasteen had been given overall command by virtue of three days' seniority over her new immediate subordinate, a man with far more combat experience.

Not that any of them truly lacked that now, after the battle for Corania. The tyranids had attacked without warning, and every Guard regiment on the planet had been forced to resist ferociously for nearly a year before the navy and a couple of Astartes Chapters[1] had arrived to turn the tide. By that time, every surviving unit had sustained at least fifty per cent casualties, many of them a great deal more, and the bureaucrats of the Munitorium had begun the

---

1   A common mistake. It is, of course, virtually unheard of for an entire Astartes Chapter to take the field at once, let alone two; what Cain obviously means here is that elements from two different Chapters were involved. (A couple of companies apiece from the Reclaimers and the Swords of the Emperor.)

process of consolidating the battered survivors into useful units once again.

On paper, at least. No one with any practical military experience would have been so half-witted as to ignore the morale effects of their decisions. But that's bureaucrats for you. Maybe if a few more Administratum drones were given lasguns and told to soldier alongside the troopers for a month or two it would shake their ideas up a bit. Assuming by some miracle they weren't shot in the back on the first day, of course.

But I'm digressing. I returned Kasteen's salute, noting as I did so the faint discolouration of the fabric beneath her rank insignia where her captain's studs had been before her recent unanticipated elevation to colonel. There had been few officers left in either regiment by the time the 'nids had got through with them, and they'd been lucky at that. At least one of the newly consolidated units was being led by a former corporal, or so I'd heard.[1] Unfortunately, neither of their commissars had survived so, thanks to my fortuitously timed transfer request, I'd been handed the job of sorting out the mess. Lucky me.

'Major Broklaw, my second-in-command.' Kasteen introduced the man next to her, his own insignia

1 He'd heard wrong, or is possibly exaggerating for effect. The newly appointed colonel of the 112th Rough Riders was a former sergeant, true, but had already received a battlefield promotion to lieutenant during the defence of Corania. None of the senior command staff in any of the recently consolidated units had made the promotional jump directly from non-commissioned officer.

equally new. His face flushed almost imperceptibly, but he stepped forward to shake my hand with a firm grip. His eyes were flint grey beneath his dark fringe of hair, and he closed his hand a little too tightly, trying to gauge my strength. Two could play at that game, of course, and I had the advantage of a couple of augmetic fingers, so I returned the favour, smiling blandly as the colour drained from his face.

'Major.' I let him go before anything was damaged except his pride, and turned to the next officer in line. Kasteen had rounded up pretty much her entire senior command staff, as protocol demanded, but it was clear most of them weren't too sure about having me around. Only a few met my eyes, but the legend of Cain the Hero had arrived here before me, and the ones that did were obviously hoping I'd be able to turn round a situation they all patently felt had gone way beyond their own ability to deal with.

I don't know what the rest were thinking; they were probably just relieved I wasn't talking about shooting the lot of them and bringing in somebody competent. Of course, if that had been a realistic option I might have considered it, but I had an unwanted reputation for honesty and fairness to live up to, so that was that.

The introductions over I turned back to Kasteen, and indicated the tottering pile of kitbags behind me. Her eyes widened fractionally as she caught a glimpse of Jurgen's face behind the barricade, but I suppose anyone who'd gone hand to hand with tyranids would have found the experience relatively unperturbing, and she masked it quickly. Most of the assembled officers, I noted with well-concealed amusement, were now breathing shallowly through their mouths.

'My aide, Gunner First Class Ferik Jurgen,' I said. In truth there was only one grade of gunner, but I didn't expect they'd know that, and the small unofficial promotion would add to whatever kudos he got from being the aide of a commissar. Which in turn would reflect well on me. 'Perhaps you could assign him some quarters?'

'Of course.' She turned to one of the youngest lieutenants, a blonde girl of vaguely equine appearance who looked as if she'd be more at home on a farm somewhere than in uniform, and nodded. 'Sulla. Get the quartermaster to sort it out.'

'I'll do it myself,' she replied, slightly overdoing the eager young officer routine. 'Magil's doing his best, but he's not quite on top of the system yet.' Kasteen nodded blandly, unaware of any problem, but I could see Broklaw's jaw tighten, and noticed that most of the men present failed to mask their displeasure.

'Sulla was our quartermaster sergeant until the last round of promotions,' Kasteen explained. 'She knows the ship's resources better than anyone.'

'I'm sure she does,' I said diplomatically. 'And I'm sure she has far more pressing duties to perform than finding a bunk for Jurgen. We'll liaise with your Sergeant Magil ourselves, if you have no objection.'

'None at all.' Kasteen looked slightly puzzled for a moment, then dismissed it. Broklaw, I noticed from the corner of my eye, was looking at me with something approaching respect now. Well, that was something at least. But it was pretty clear I was going to have my work cut out to turn this divided and demoralised rabble into anything resembling a fighting unit.

Well, up to a point anyway. If they were a long way from being ready to fight the enemies of the Emperor, they were certainly in good enough shape to fight among themselves, as I was shortly to discover.

I haven't reached my second century by ignoring the little presentiments of trouble which sometimes appear out of nowhere, like those itching palms of mine, or the little voice in the back of my head which tells me something seems too good to be true. But in my first few days aboard the *Righteous Wrath* I had no need of such subtle promptings from my subconscious. Tension hung in the air of the corridors assigned to us like ozone around a daemonhost, all but striking sparks from the bulkheads. And I wasn't the only one to feel it. None of the other regiments on board would venture into our part of the ship, either for social interaction or the time-honoured tradition of perpetrating practical jokes against the members of another unit. The naval provosts patrolled in tense, wary groups. Desperate for some kind of respite, I even made courtesy calls on the other commissars aboard, but these were far from convivial; humourless Emperor-botherers to a man, the younger ones were too overwhelmed by respect for my reputation to be good company, and most of the older ones were quietly resentful of what they saw as a glory-hogging young upstart. Tedious as these interludes were, though, I was to be grateful for them sooner than I thought.

The one bright spot was Captain Parjita, who'd commanded the vessel for the past thirty years, and with whom I hit it off from our first dinner together. I'm sure he only invited me the first time because protocol demanded it, and perhaps out of curiosity to see what a Hero of the Imperium actually looked like in the flesh, but by the time we were halfway through the first course we were chatting away like old friends. I told a few outrageous lies about my past adventures, and he reciprocated with some anec-dotes of his own, and by the time we'd got onto the amasec I felt more relaxed than I had in months. For one thing, he really appreciated the problems I was facing with Kasteen and her rabble.

'You need to reassert some discipline,' he told me unnecessarily. 'Before the rot spreads any further. Shoot a few, that'll buck their ideas up.'

Easy to say, of course, but not so easy in practice. That's what most commissars would have done, admittedly, but getting a regiment united because they're terrified of you and hate your guts has its own drawbacks, particularly as you're going to find your-self in the middle of a battlefield with these people before very long, and they'll all have guns. And, as

I've already said, I had a reputation to maintain, and a good part of that was keeping up the pretence that I actually gave a damn about the troopers under my command. So, not an option, unfortunately.

It was while I was on my way back to my quarters from one such pleasant evening that my hand was forced, and in a way I could well have done without.

IT WAS THE noise that alerted me at first, a gradually swelling babble of voices from the corridors leading to our section of the ship. My pleasantly reflective mood, enhanced by Parjita's amasec and a comfortable win over the regicide board, evaporated in an instant. I knew that sound all too well, and the clatter of boots on the deck behind me as a squad of provosts double-timed towards the disturbance with shock batons drawn was enough to confirm it. I picked up my pace to join them, falling in beside the section leader.

'Sounds like a riot,' I said. The blank-visored head nodded.

'Quite right, sir.'

'Any idea what sparked it?' Not that it mattered. The simmering resentment among the Valhallans was almost cause enough on its own. Any excuse would have done. If he did have a clue, I never got to hear it; as we arrived at the door of the mess hall a ceramic cup bearing the regimental crest of the 296th shattered against his helmet.

'Emperor's blood!' I ducked reflexively, taking cover behind the nearest piece of furniture to assess the situation while the provosts waded in ahead of me, striking out with their shock batons at any target that presented itself. The room was a heaving mass of angry men and women punching, kicking and flailing at one another, all semblance of discipline shot to hell. Several were down already, bleeding, screaming, being trampled on by the still active combatants, and the casualties were rising all the time.

The fiercest fighting was going on in the centre of the room, a small knot of brawlers clearly intent on actual murder unless someone intervened. Fine by me, that's what the provosts were for. I hunkered down behind an overturned table, scanning the room as I voxed a situation report to Kasteen, and watched them battle their way forward. The two fighters at the centre of the mêlée seemed evenly matched to me; a shaven-headed man, muscled like a Catachan, who towered over a wiry young woman with short-cropped raven black hair. Whatever advantage he had in strength she could match in agility, striking hard and leaping back out of range, reducing most of his strikes to glancing blows, which is just as well, as a clean hit from those ham-like fists would likely have stove her ribcage in. As I watched he spun, launching a lethal roundhouse kick to her temple; she ducked just a fraction slow, and went sprawling as his foot grazed the top of her head, but twisted upright again with a knife from one of the tables in her hand. The blow came up towards his sternum, but he blocked it, opening up a livid red gash along his right arm.

It was about then that things really started to go wrong. The provosts had made it almost halfway to the brawl I was watching when the two sides finally realised they had an enemy in common. A young woman, blood pouring from a broken nose, was unceremoniously yanked away from the man whose groin she'd been aiming a kick at, and rounded on the provost attempting to restrain her. Her elbow strike bounced harmlessly off his torso armour, but her erstwhile opponent leapt to her defence, swinging a broken plate in a short, clinical arc which impacted precisely on the neck joint where helmet met flak; a bright crimson spurt of arterial blood sprayed the surrounding bystanders as the stricken provost dropped to his knees, trying to stem the bleeding.

'Emperor's bowels!' I began to edge my way back towards the door, to wait for the reinforcements Kasteen had promised; if they hadn't been before, the mob was in a killing mood now, and anyone who looked like a symbol of authority would become an obvious target. Even as I watched, both factions turned on the provosts in their midst, who disappeared under a swarm of bodies. The troopers barely seemed human any more. I'd seen tyranids move like that in response to a perceived threat, but this was even worse. Your average 'nid swarm has purpose and intelligence behind everything it does, even though it's hard to remember that when a tidal wave of chitin is bearing down on you with every intention of reducing you to mincemeat, but it was clear that there was no intelligence working here, just sheer brute blood-lust. Emperor damn it, I've seen Khornate cults with more self-restraint than those supposedly disciplined Guard troopers displayed in that mess hall.

At least while they were ripping the provosts apart they weren't likely to notice me, so I made what progress I could towards the door, ready to take command of the reinforcements as soon as they arrived. And I would have made it too, if the squad leader hadn't surfaced long enough to scream, 'Commissar! Help!'

Oh great. Every pair of eyes in the room suddenly swung in my direction. I thought I could see my reflection in every pupil, tracking me like an auspex.

If you take one more step towards that door, I told myself, you're a dead man. They'd be on me in seconds. The only way to survive was to take them by surprise. So I stepped forward instead, as though I'd just entered the room.

'You.' I pointed at a random trooper. 'Get a broom.'

Whatever they'd been expecting me to say or do, this definitely wasn't it. The room hung suspended in confused anticipation, the silence stretching for an infinite second. No one moved.

'That was not a request,' I said, raising my voice a little, and taking another step forward. 'This mess hall is an absolute disgrace. And no one is leaving until it's been tidied up.' My boot skidded in a slowly congealing pool of blood. 'You, you, and you, go with him. Buckets and mops. Make sure you get enough to go round.'

Confusion and uncertainty began to spread, troopers flicking nervous glances at one other, as it gradually began to dawn on them that the situation had got well out of hand and that consequences had to be faced. The Guardsmen I'd pointed out, two of them women, began to edge nervously towards the door.

'At the double!' I barked suddenly, with my best parade-ground snap; the designated troopers scurried out, ingrained patterns of discipline reasserting themselves.

And that was enough. The thunderstorm crackle of violence dissipated from the room as though suddenly earthed.

After that it was easy; now that I'd asserted my authority the rest fell into line as meek as you please, and by the time Kasteen arrived with another squad of provosts in tow I'd already detailed a few more to escort the wounded and worse to the infirmary. A surprising number were able to walk, but there were still far too many stretcher cases for my liking.

'You did well, I hear.' Kasteen was at my elbow, her face pale as she surveyed the damage. I shrugged, knowing from long experience that credit snowballs all the faster the less you seem to want it.

'Not well enough for some of these poor souls,' I said.

'Bravest thing I ever saw,' I heard from behind me, as one of the injured provosts was helped away by a couple of his shipmates. 'He just stood there and faced them down, the whole damn lot...' His voice faded, adding another small increment to my heroic reputation, which I knew would be all round the ship by this time tomorrow.

'There'll have to be an investigation.' Kasteen looked stunned, still not quite capable of taking in the full enormity of what had happened. 'We need to know who started it, what happened...'

'Who's to blame?' Broklaw cut in from the door. It was obvious from the direction of his gaze where he thought the responsibility should lie. Kasteen flushed.

'I've no doubt we'll discover the men responsible,' she said, a faint but perceptible stress on the pronoun. Broklaw refused to rise to the bait.

'We can all thank the Emperor we have an impartial adjudicator in the commissar here,' he said smoothly. 'I'm sure we can rely on him to sort it out.'

Thanks a lot, I thought. But he was right. And how I handled it was to determine the rest of my future with the regiment. Not to mention leaving me running for my life yet again, beginning a long and unwelcome association with the Emperor's pet psychopaths,[1] and an encounter with the most fascinating woman I've ever met.

1   Not the most flattering or accurate description of His Divine Majesty's most holy Inquisition, it must be admitted.

TWO

'You get more with a kind word and an excruciator than with just a kind word.'

– Inquisitor Malden.

'So what you're trying to tell me,' I said, turning the piece of crockery over in my hand, 'is that three people are dead, fourteen still in the infirmary, and a perfectly serviceable mess hall reduced to kindling because your men didn't like the plates they were served their meal on?' Broklaw squirmed visibly on one of the chairs I'd had Jurgen bring into my office for the conference – I'd told him to fetch the most uncomfortable ones he could find, as every little bit helps when you're trying to exert your authority – but the major's discomfiture wasn't due to just that alone. Kasteen was still visibly suppressing a smirk, which I was planning to wipe away in a moment.

'Well, that may be overstating it a little...' he began.

'That's precisely what happened,' Kasteen cut in acidly. I hefted the plate. It was good quality porcelain, delicate but strong, and one of the few pieces remaining intact after the mess hall riot. The regimental crest of the 296th was prominent in the centre of it. I turned to the dataslate on my desk, and made a show of paging through the reports and witness statements I'd spent the past week collecting.

'According to this witness statement, the first punch was swung by a Corporal Bella Trebek. A member of the 296th prior to the amalgamation.' I raised an inquisitive eyebrow in Kasteen's direction. 'Would the colonel care to comment?'

'She was clearly provoked,' Kasteen said, losing the smirk, which seemed to hover in the air for a moment before jumping across to Broklaw.

'Just so.' I nodded judiciously. 'By a Sergeant Tobias Kelp. Who, it says here, threw his plate down declaring that he would be damned if he ate off some...' I made a show of getting the quotation scrupulously correct. '"Mincing tart's front parlour tea service." Does that strike you as a reasonable comment, major?'

The smirk disappeared again.

'Not particularly, no,' he said, clearly wondering where this line of questioning was going. 'But we still don't know the full circumstances.'

'I think the circumstances are perfectly clear,' I said. 'The former troopers of the 296th and the 301st have cordially detested one another since the regiments were amalgamated. Under the circumstances the use of the 296th's regimental dinner service was bound to be regarded as an insult by the stupider elements of the former 301st.' Broklaw flushed at that. Good, let him get angry. The only way to salvage the situation was to make radical changes, and that wouldn't work unless I could get the senior officers to feel passionately that they were necessary.

'Which begs another question,' I went on smoothly. 'Just who was stupid enough to order the use of the dinner service in the first place?' I aimed my second-best intimidating commissarial glare at Kasteen for a fraction of a second, before snapping it round to nail the junior officer sitting at her right. 'Lieutenant Sulla. That would be you, would it not?'

'It was founding day!' she retorted. That did take me by surprise. I didn't often get people bouncing back from a number two glare, but I concealed it with the ease of long practice. 'We always use the regimental ceramics on founding day. It's one of our proudest traditions.'

'It was.' Broklaw broke in with sardonic amusement. 'But unless you've got some traditional adhesive...'

Both women bristled. For a moment I thought I was going to have to put down a brawl in my own office.

'Major,' I said, reasserting my authority. 'I'm sure the 301st had their own founding day traditions.' That was a pretty safe bet, as practically every regiment celebrated the anniversary of its First Founding in some way. He began to nod, before my use of the past tense registered with him, and then an expression curiously close to apprehension flickered across his face. I leaned back in my chair, which, unlike theirs, I'd made sure was comfortably padded, and looked approving. It's always good to keep people off-balance. 'I'm glad to hear it. Such traditions are important. A vital part of the *esprit de corps* we all rely on to win the Emperor his victories.' Kasteen and Broklaw nodded cautiously, almost together. Good. That was one thing at least they could agree on. But Sulla just flushed angrily.

'Then perhaps you could explain that to Kelp and his knuckle-draggers,' she said. I sighed, tolerantly, and placed my laspistol on the desk. The officers' eyes widened slightly. Broklaw's took on a wary expression, Kasteen's one of barely suppressed alarm, and Sulla's jaw dropped open.

'Please don't interrupt, lieutenant,' I said mildly. 'You can all have your say in a moment.' There was a definite edge in the room now. I had no intention of shooting anyone, of course, but they weren't going to like what I was about to say next and you can't be too careful. I smiled, to show I was harmless, and they relaxed a fraction.

'Nevertheless, you've just illustrated my point perfectly. While the two halves of this regiment still think of themselves as separate units, morale is never going to recover. That means you're sod-all use to the Emperor, and a pain in the arse to me.' I paused just long enough to let them assimilate what I'd just said. 'Are we in agreement on that, at least?' Kasteen nodded, meeting Broklaw's eyes for the first time since the meeting began.

'I think so,' she said. 'The question is, what do we do about it?'

'Good question.' I passed a slate across the desk. She took it, and Broklaw leaned in to scan it over her shoulder as she read. 'We can start by integrating the units at squad level. As of this morning, every squad will consist of roughly equal numbers of troopers from each of the former regiments.'

'That's ridiculous!' Broklaw snapped, a fraction behind Kasteen's far from ladylike exclamation. 'The men won't stand for it.'

'Neither will my women.' Kasteen nodded in agreement with him. So far so good. Making them feel they had common cause against me was the first step to getting them to co-operate properly.

'They're going to have to,' I said. 'This ship is *en route* to a potential warzone. We could be in combat within hours of our arrival, and when that happens they'll have to rely on the trooper next to them, whoever it is. I don't want my people getting killed because they don't trust their own comrades. So they're going to train together and work together until they start behaving like an Imperial Guard regiment instead of a bunch of pre-schola juvies. And then they're going to fight the Emperor's enemies together, and I expect them to win. Is that clear?'

'Perfectly, commissar.' Kasteen's jaw was tight. 'I'll start reviewing the SO&E.[1]'

'Perhaps it would be best if you did so with the major's help,' I suggested. 'Between you, you should be able to select fire-teams which at least have a reasonable chance of turning their lasguns on the enemy instead of one another.'

'Of course.' Broklaw nodded. 'I'll be pleased to help.' The tone of his voice said otherwise, but at least the words were conciliatory. That was a start. But they really weren't going to like what was coming next.

'Which brings me on to the new regimental designation.' I'd been expecting some outburst at this, but the trio of officers in front of me just stared in stupefied silence. I guess they were trying to convince themselves they hadn't heard what I'd just said. 'The current one just emphasises the divisions between what used to be the 301st and the 296th. We need a new one, ladies and gentleman, a single identity under which we can march into battle united and resolute as true servants of the Emperor.' All good stirring stuff, and for a moment, I actually thought

1 Slate of Organisation and Equipment. Not actually a physical dataslate, but an archaic term for the details of the disposition of troopers and equipment within an Imperial Guard unit. Still in use among many regiments with more than a thousand years of unbroken tradition.

they were going to buy it without any further argument. But of course it was that daft mare Sulla who burst the bubble.

'You can't just abolish the 296th!' she almost shouted. 'Our battle honours go back centuries!'

'If you count slapping down stroppy colonists as battles.' Broklaw rose to the bait. 'The 301st has fought orks, eldar, tyranids–'

'Oh. Were there tyranids on Corania? I guess I was just too busy with my needlepoint to notice!' Sulla's voice rose another octave.

'Shut up! Both of you!' Kasteen's voice was quiet, but firm, and stunned both her subordinates into silence. I nodded gratefully at her, forestalled from having to do the job myself, and pleasantly surprised. It was beginning to look as though she had the makings of an effective commander after all. 'Let's hear what the commissar has to say before we start inventing objections to it.'

'Thank you, colonel,' I said, before resuming. 'What I propose is to treat the date of amalgamation as a new First Founding. I've had the ship's astropath contact the Munitorium, and they've agreed in principle. There is currently no regiment designated the Valhallan 597th, so I've proposed adopting that as our new identity.'

'Two-hundred-and-ninety-six plus three-hundred-and-one. I see.' Kasteen nodded. 'Very clever.' Broklaw nodded too.

'A very neat way of preserving the identities of the old regiments,' he said. 'But combined into something new.'

'As was always the intention,' I agreed.

'But that's outrageous!' Sulla said. 'You can't just redesignate an entire regiment out of existence!'

'The Commissariat gives its servants wide discretionary powers,' I said mildly. 'How we interpret them is a matter of judgment, and sometimes temperament. Not every commissar would have resisted the temptation to discourage further dissension in the ranks by decimation, for instance.' Quite true, of course. There were damn few who'd go quite so far as to randomly execute one in ten of the troopers under their command to encourage the others, but they did exist, and if ever a regiment was so undisciplined that such a drastic measure might have been justified, it was this one, and they knew it. They were just lucky they'd got Cain the Hero instead of some gung-ho psychopath. I've met one or two in my time, and the best thing you can say for them is that they don't tend to be around long, particularly once the shooting starts. I smiled to show I didn't mean it.

'If the new designation is unacceptable,' I added, 'the 48th Penal Legion is also available, I'm told.' Sulla blenched. Kasteen smiled tightly, unsure of how serious I was.

'The 597th sounds good to me,' she said. 'Major Broklaw?'

'An excellent compromise.' He nodded slowly, letting the idea percolate. 'There'll be some grumbling in the ranks. But if ever a regiment needed a new beginning, it's this one.'

'Amen to that,' Kasteen agreed. The two senior officers looked at one another with renewed respect. That was a good sign too.

Only Sulla still looked unhappy. Broklaw noticed, and caught her eye.

'Cheer up, lieutenant,' he said. 'That would make our next Founding Day...' He paused fractionally, glancing at me for confirmation as he worked it out. '258.' I nodded. 'You'll have nearly eight months to come up with some brand new traditions.'

OF COURSE, THE changes I'd imposed didn't go down too well with the rank and file, at least to begin with, and I got most of the blame. But then I've never expected to be popular; ever since I got selected for commissarial training I've known I could expect very little from the troopers around me apart from resentment and suspicion. As my undeserved reputation has snowballed, of course, that's got to be the case less and less of the time, but back then I was still taking it more or less for granted.

Gradually, though, the reorganisation I'd insisted on began to work and the training exercises we put the troopers through were beginning to make them think like soldiers again. I instituted a weekly prize of an afternoon's downtime for the most efficient platoon in the regiment, and a doubling of the ale rations for the members of the most disciplined squad within it, and that helped remarkably. I felt we'd really turned a corner the morning I overheard one of the new mixed squads chatting together in the

freshly repainted mess hall instead of splitting into
two separate groups as they'd tended to do in the
beginning, and exulting over their higher place in the
rankings than a rival platoon. These days, I'm told,
'Cain's round' is a cherished tradition in the 597th,
and the competition for the extra ration of ale still
hotly contested. All in all, I suppose there are worse
things to be remembered for.

The one problem we still had to resolve, of course,
was the matter of those responsible for the riots in
the first place. Kelp and Trebek were for it, there was
no doubt about that, along with a handful of others
who had been positively identified as responsible for
the worst of the deaths and injuries. But for the time
being, I'd put off the question of punishment. The
wholesale reforms I'd instigated, and the subsequent
improvement in morale, were still fragile, and I
didn't dare risk it by ordering executions.

So I did what any sensible man in my position
would have done; dragged my feet under the pretext
of carrying out a thorough investigation, kept the
defaulters locked away where, with any luck, most of
their comrades would forget about them in the general upheaval, and hoped something would turn up.
It was a good plan, and it would have worked too, at
least until we arrived in a warzone somewhere and I
could quietly return them to a unit or have them
transferred away with no one any the wiser, if it
hadn't been for my good friend Captain Parjita.

Technically, of course, he was well within his
rights to demand copies of all the reports I'd been

compiling, and I hadn't thought there was any harm in letting him have them. What I'd been forgetting was that the *Righteous Wrath* wasn't just a collection of corridors, bunkrooms, and training bays; it was his ship, and that he was the ultimate authority aboard. Two of the dead had been his provosts, after all, and he wasn't about to sit back and let the perpetrators get away with it. He wanted a full court-martial of the guilty troopers while we were still on board, and he could make sure they were punished to his satisfaction.

'I know you want to be thorough,' he said one evening, as we set up the regicide board in his quarters. 'But frankly, Ciaphas, I think you're overdoing it. You already know who the guilty parties are. Just shoot them and have done with it.'

I shook my head regretfully. 'But what would that solve?' I asked. 'Would it bring your men back to life?'

'That's not the point.' He held out both fists, concealing playing pieces. I picked the left, and found I was playing blue. A minor tactical disadvantage, but one I was sure I could overcome. Regicide isn't really my game, to be honest – give me a tarot deck and a table full of suckers with more money than sense any day – but it passed the time pleasantly enough. 'There really can't be any other verdict. And every day you delay just leaves the cowardly scum cluttering up my brig, eating my food, breathing my air...' He was getting quite emotional. I began to suspect that there had been more than a simple line of command relationship between him and one of the dead provosts[1].

'Believe me,' I said. 'There's nothing I'd like better than to draw a line under this whole sorry affair. But the situation's complicated. If I have them shot the whole regiment could unravel again. Morale's just starting to recover.'

'I appreciate that.' Parjita nodded. 'But that's not my problem. I've got a crew to think about, and they want to see their comrades avenged.' He made his opening move.

'I see.' I moved one of my own pieces, playing for time in more senses than one. 'Then it's clearly long past time that justice was served.'

'ARE YOU INSANE?' Kasteen asked, looking at me across the desk, and trying to ignore the hovering presence of Jurgen, who was shuffling some routine reports I couldn't be bothered to deal with. 'If you condemn the defaulters now, we'll be right back where we started. Trebek's very popular with the...' she shot a quick glance at Broklaw, seated next to her, and overrode the remark she'd been about to make. 'With some of the troopers.'

'The same goes for Kelp.' Broklaw moved quickly to back her up. Exactly the reaction I'd been hoping for; now the regiment was beginning to function properly, Kasteen and Broklaw had begun

---

1   Cain is correct in this assumption. Strictly against regulations, of course, but boys will be boys...

to slip into their roles of commander and executive officer as smoothly as if the bad feeling between them had never existed. Well, up to a point, anyway; there was still an air of strained politeness between them occasionally, which betrayed the effort, but they were well on the way. And to be honest it was far more than I could have hoped for when I stepped off the shuttle.

'I agree,' I said. 'Thank you, Jurgen.' My aide had appeared at my shoulder with a pot of tanna leaf tea, as was his habit whenever I was in my office at this time of the morning. 'Could you get another couple of bowls?'

'Of course, commissar.' He shuffled away as I poured my own drink, and pushed the tray to the side of my desk. The warm, aromatic steam relaxed me as it always did.

'Not for me, thank you,' Broklaw said hastily as Jurgen returned, a fresh pair of teabowls pinched together by a grubby finger and thumb on the inside of the rims. Kasteen blenched slightly but accepted a drink anyway. She kept it on the desk in front of her, picking it up from time to time to punctuate her side of the conversation, but never quite getting round to taking the first sip. I was quietly impressed. She'd have made a good diplomat if she hadn't been so honest.

'The problem is,' I went on, 'that Captain Parjita is the ultimate authority aboard this ship, and he's well within his rights to insist on a court martial. If we don't let him have one he'll just invoke his command privilege and have Kelp and the others shot anyway. And we simply can't let that happen.'

'So what do you suggest?' Kasteen asked, replacing the teabowl after another almost-sip. 'Regimental discipline is supposed to be your responsibility, after all.'

'Precisely.' I took a sip of my own tea, savouring the bitter aftertaste, and nodded judiciously. 'And I've been able to convince him that I can't have that authority undermined if we're to become a viable fighting unit.'

'You've got him to agree to some kind of compromise?' Broklaw asked, grasping the point at once.

'I have.' I tried not to sound too smug. 'He can have his court martial, and run it himself under naval regulations. But once they're found guilty, they'll be turned over to the Commissariat for sentencing.'

'But that takes us right back to where we were before,' Kasteen said, clearly puzzled. 'You have them shot, and discipline goes to the warp. Again.'

'Maybe not,' I said, taking another sip of tea. 'Not if we're careful.'

I'VE SEEN MORE than my fair share of tribunals over the years, even been in front of them on occasion, and if there's one thing I've learned it's this; it's easy to get the result you want out of them. The trick is simply to state your case as clearly and concisely as possible. That, and making damn sure the members of it are on your side to begin with.

There are a number of ways of ensuring that this is the case. Bribery and threats are always popular, but generally to be avoided, especially if you're likely to attract inquisitorial attention as they're better at both and tend to resent other people resorting to their methods.[1] Besides, that sort of thing tends to leave a residue of bad feeling which can come back to haunt you later on. In my experience it's far more effective to make sure that the other members of the panel are honest, unimaginative idiots with a strong sense of duty and a stronger set of prejudices you can rely on to deliver the result that you want. If they think you're a hero, and hang on your every word, so much the better.

So when Parjita announced his verdict of guilty on all charges, and turned to me with a self-satisfied smirk, I had my strategy worked out well in advance. The courtroom – a hastily converted wardroom generally used by the ship's most junior officers – went silent.

There were five troopers in the dock by the time the trial had begun; far fewer than Parjita had wanted, but in the interests of fairness and damage limitation I had managed to persuade him to let me deal summarily with most of the outstanding cases. Those guilty of more minor offences had been demoted, flogged, or assigned to latrine duty for the

1   This is, of course, entirely untrue. As His Divine Majesty's most faithful servants, we're most definitely above such petty emotions as resentment.

foreseeable future and safely returned to their units,
where, in the unfathomable processes of the
trooper's mindset, I had somehow become the
embodiment of justice and mercy. This had been
helped along by a little judicious myth-making
among the senior officers, who had let it be known
that Parjita was hellbent on mass executions and
that I had spent the past few weeks exerting every
iota of my commissarial authority in urging
clemency for the vast majority, finally succeeding
against almost impossible odds. The net result,
aided no end by my fictitious reputation, was that a
couple of dozen potential troublemakers had been
quietly integrated back into the roster, practically
grateful for the punishments they'd received, and
morale had remained steady among the rank and
file.

The problem now facing me was that of the hard-
core recidivists, who were undoubtedly guilty of
murder or its attempt. There were five of them facing
the courtroom now, wary and resentful.

Three of them I recognised at once, from the
mêlée in the mess hall. Kelp was the huge, over-
muscled man I'd seen being stabbed, and Trebek,
to my complete lack of surprise, was the petite
woman who had almost disembowelled him. They
stood at opposite ends of the row of prisoners, glaring at one another almost as much as at Parjita and
myself, and if it hadn't been for their manacles, I
had no doubt they'd be at one another's throats
again in a heartbeat. In the centre was the young

trooper I'd seen stab the provost with a broken plate; his datafile told me his name was Tomas Holenbi, and I'd had to look twice to make sure it was the same man. He was short and skinny, with untidy red hair and a face full of freckles, and he'd spent most of the trial looking bewildered and on the verge of tears. If I hadn't seen his fit of homicidal rage for myself I would hardly have believed him capable of such insensate violence. The real irony was that he was a medical orderly, not a front line soldier at all.

Between him and Trebek was another female trooper, one Griselda Velade. She was stocky, brunette, and clearly out of her depth as well. The only one of the group to have killed a fellow trooper, she had claimed throughout that she'd only intended to fend him off; it was an unlucky blow that had crushed the fellow's larynx and left him to suffocate on the mess room floor. Parjita, needless to say, hadn't bought it, or cared whether she intended murder or not; he just wanted as many Valhallans in front of a firing squad as he could manage.

On Holenbi's other side was Maxim Sorel, a tall, rangy man with short blond hair and the cold eyes of a killer. Sorel was a sharpshooter, a long-las specialist, who snuffed out lives from a distance as dispassionately as I might swat an insect. Of all of them, he was the one who most threw a scare into me. The others had been carried away by the blood-lust of a mob, and hadn't really been responsible for their actions past a certain point, but Sorel had slid a knife through the joints of a provost's body armour simply because he hadn't seen any reason not to. The last time I'd looked into eyes like those they'd belonged to an eldar haemonculus.

'If it was up to me,' Parjita said, continuing, 'I would have the lot of you shot at once.'

I glanced down the line of prisoners again, and noted their reactions. Kelp and Trebek glared defiantly back at him, daring him to make good on the threat. Holenbi blinked, and swallowed rapidly. Velade gasped audibly, biting her lower lip, and began to hyperventilate. To my surprise I saw Holenbi reach across and give her hand a reassuring squeeze. Then again, they'd been in adjoining cells for weeks now, so I suppose they'd had time to get to know each other. Sorel simply blinked, a complete lack of emotional response that sent shivers down my spine.

'Nevertheless,' the captain went on, 'Commissar Cain has been able to persuade me that the Commissariat is better suited to maintaining discipline among the Imperial Guard, and has requested that they be permitted to pass sentence according to military rather than naval regulations.' He nodded cordially to me. 'Commissar. They're all yours.'

Five pairs of eyes swivelled in my direction. I stood slowly, glancing down at the dataslate on the table in front of me.

'Thank you, captain.' I turned to the trio of black-uniformed figures sitting at my side. 'And thank you, commissars. Your advice in this case has been invaluable to me.' Three solemn heads nodded in my direction.

This was the trick, you see. My earlier contact with the other commissars on board had unexpectedly paid off, showing me who would be the most easily swayed by my arguments. A couple of eager young pups just past cadet, and a jaded old campaigner who had lived most of his life on the battlefield. And all of them flattered from here to Terra to be taken into the confidence of the celebrated Ciaphas Cain. I turned back to the prisoners.

'A commissar's duty is often harsh,' I said. 'Regulations are there to be obeyed, and discipline to be enforced. And those regulations do indeed prescribe the ultimate penalty for murder, unless there are extenuating circumstances – circumstances, I have to admit, I have striven to find in this case to the best of my abilities.' I had them all on the hook by now. The fans in the ceiling ducts sounded almost as loud as a chimera engine. 'And to my great disappointment, I have been unsuccessful.'

There was an audible intake of breath from practically every pair of lungs present. Parjita grinned triumphantly, sure he'd got the blood vengeance he lusted after.

'However,' I went on after a fractional pause. A faint frown appeared on the captain's face, and a flicker of hope on Velade's. 'As my esteemed colleagues will undoubtedly agree, one of the heaviest burdens a commissar must carry is the responsibility to ensure that the regulations are obeyed not only in the letter, but the spirit. And it was with that in mind that I took the liberty of consulting with them about a possible interpretation of those regulations which I felt might offer a solution to my dilemma.' I turned dramatically to the little group of commissars, taking the opportunity to underline that it wasn't just me cheating Parjita out of his firing squad, it was the Commissariat itself. 'Again, gentlemen, I thank you. Not only on my behalf, but on behalf of the regiment I have the honour to serve with.'

I turned to Kasteen and Broklaw, who were observing proceedings from the side of the courtroom, and inclined my head to them too. I was laying it on with a trowel, I don't mind admitting it, but I've always enjoyed being the centre of attention when that doesn't involve incoming fire.

'A commissar's primary concern must always be the efficiency of the unit to which he is attached,' I said, 'and, by extension, the battlefield effectiveness of the entire Imperial Guard. It's a heavy responsibility, but one we are proud to bear in the Emperor's name.' The other commissars nodded in sycophantic self-congratulation. 'And that means that I'm always loath to sacrifice the life of a trained soldier, whatever the circumstances, unless it's the only way to win His Glorious Majesty the victories He requires.'

'I assume that you're eventually going to come to a point of some kind?' Parjita interrupted. I nodded, as though he'd done me a favour instead of disrupting the flow of an oration I'd been practising in front of the mirror in my stateroom for most of the morning.

'Indeed I am,' I said. 'And the point is this. My colleagues and I,' – no harm in reminding everyone again that this was a carefully contrived consensus, not just me – 'see no point in simply executing these troopers. Their deaths will win us no victories.'

'But the regulations...' Parjita began. This time it was my turn to cut him off in full flow.

'Specify death as the punishment for these offences. It just doesn't specify immediate death.' I turned to the line of confused and apprehensive prisoners. 'It's the judgement of the commissariat that you all be confined until it becomes expedient to transfer you to a penal legion, where an honourable death on the battlefield will almost certainly befall you in the fullness of time. In the interim, should a particularly hazardous assignment become available, you will have the honour of volunteering. In either case you can expect the opportunity to redeem yourselves in the eyes of the Emperor.' I raked my eyes along the shabby little group again. Kelp and Trebek, their truculence mitigated by surprise, Holenbi still bewildered by the sudden turn of events, Velade almost sobbing with relief, and Sorel... Still that blank expression, as though none of this mattered at all. 'Dismissed.'

I waited until they'd shuffled out, assisted by the shock batons of the escorting provosts, and turned back to Parjita.

'Will that satisfy you, captain?'

'I suppose it'll have to,' he said sourly.

'CONGRATULATIONS, COMMISSAR.' Kasteen raised a glass of amasec, toasting my victory, and the mess hall erupted around me. I smiled modestly, walking towards the table occupied by the senior officers, while men and women clapped and cheered and chanted my name, and generally carried on as though I was the Emperor Himself dropping in for a visit. I half expected some of them to try patting me on the back, but respect for my position, or an understandable reluctance to get too close to Jurgen, who was dogging my heels as usual, or both, held them in check. I held up my hands for silence as I reached my seat, between Kasteen and Broklaw, and the room gradually fell quiet.

'Thank you all,' I said, injecting just the right level of barely perceptible quaver into my voice to suggest powerful emotion held narrowly in check. 'You do me too much honour for just doing my job.' A chorus of denial and adulation followed, as I'd known it would. I waved them to silence again. 'Well, if you insist...' I waited for the gale of laughter to die down. 'While I have everyone's attention; and that's a refreshing novelty for a political officer...' More laughter; I had them in the palm of my hand now.

I waved them to silence again, adopting a slightly more serious mien. 'I would just like to offer some

congratulations of my own. In the short time I've
had the privilege of serving with this regiment you
have all far exceeded my most optimistic expectations. The past few weeks have been difficult for all
of us, but I can state with confidence that I have
never served with a body of troops more ready for
combat, and more capable of seizing victory when
that time comes.' With confidence, certainly. Truth-
fully? That was another matter entirely. But it had
the desired effect. I picked up a glass from the table,
and toasted the room. 'To the 597th. A glorious
beginning!'

'The 597th!' they all shouted, men and women
alike, swept along with cheap emotion and cheaper
rhetoric.

'Nicely done, commmissar,' Broklaw murmured as
I sat. The cheers were still deafening. 'I believe you've
turned us into a proper regiment at last.'

I'd done something a lot more important than
that, of course. I'd established myself as a popular figure among the common troopers, which meant
they'd watch my back if I was ever careless enough to
find myself anywhere near the actual combat zone.
Pulling them together into an effective fighting force
was just a useful bonus.

'Just doing my job,' I said as modestly as I could,
which is what they all expected, of course. And they
lapped it up.

'And not before time,' Kasteen added. I kept my features carefully composed, but felt my good mood
begin to evaporate.

'We've had our orders?' Broklaw asked. The colonel nodded, picking at her adeven salad.

'Some backwater dirtball called Gravalax.'

'Never heard of it,' I said.

Editorial Note:

Given Cain's complete, and typical, lack of interest in anything that doesn't concern him directly, the following extract may prove useful in placing the rest of his narrative in a wider context. It must be said that the book from which it comes isn't the most reliable of guides to the campaign as a whole, but it does, unlike most studies of the Gravalax incident, at least attempt to sketch in the historical background to the conflict. Despite the author's obvious limitations as a chronicler of events, his summing up of the causus belli is substantially correct.

* * *

From *Purge the Guilty! An impartial account of the liberation of Gravalax,* by Stententious Logar. 085.M42

THE SEEDS OF the Gravalax incident were sown many years before the full magnitude of the crisis was realised, and in retrospect, it may well be easy to discern the slow unfolding of an abhuman conspiracy over the span of several generations. A historian, however, has the perspective of hindsight, which, alas, cannot be said of the actual participants. So, rather than pointing an accusatory finger, with righteous cries of 'how could they have been so stupid?' it behooves us more to shake our heads in pity as we contemplate our forebears' blind stumbling into the very brink of destruction.

It goes without saying that no blame can be attached to the servants of the Emperor, particularly those concerned with the ordering of His Divine Majesty's fighting forces and the diligent adepts of the Administratum; the Ultima Segmentum is vast, and the Damocles Gulf an obscure frontier sector. After the heathen tau were put in their place by the heroic crusader fleet in the early seven-forties, attention rightly shifted to more immediate threats; the incursion of hive fleet Leviathan, the awakening of the accursed necrons, and the ever-present danger from the traitor legions not least among them.

Nevertheless, the tau presence remained on the fringes of Imperial space, and, all but unnoticed, they began once again to encroach on His Divine Majesty's blessed dominions.

Up until this point Gravalax had been an obscure outpost of civilisation, barely noticed by the wider galaxy. Enough of its landmasses were fertile to keep its relatively sparse population tolerably well fed, and it possessed adequate mineral reserves for such industry as it supported. In short, it had nothing to attract any trade, and an insufficient population base to be worth tithing for the Imperial Guard. It was, to be blunt, a backwater, devoid of anything of interest.

If Gravalax thought it was to remain undisturbed indefinitely, however, it was sadly mistaken. Within a century of their drubbing at the righteous hands of the servants of the Imperium, the black-hearted tau were back, spreading their poisonous heresies through the Gulf once more. When they first chanced upon Gravalax no one knows,[1] but by the turn of the last century of the millennium they were well established there.

It will come as no surprise to my readers, aware as we must be of the innate treachery of all aliens, that they had arrived at this pass by an insidious process of infiltration. And, shocking though it is to record

---

1   837.M41, according to surviving records. Like many amateur historians, Logar is long on rhetoric and short on actual scholarship.

it, with the willing assistance of those whose greed and thoughtlessness made them the perfect dupes of this monstrous conspiracy. I refer, as you have no doubt already guessed, to the so-called rogue traders. Rogues indeed, who would place their own interests above those of the Imperium, humanity, and the divine Emperor Himself!

[*Several paragraphs of inflammatory but non-specific denunciation of rogue traders, omitted. Logar seems to have had something of an obsession about their untrustworthiness. Perhaps one owed him money.*]

How and why these pariahs of profit first began trafficking with the tau, history does not record.[1] What is certain is that Gravalax, with its isolated position on the fringes of Imperial space, and close to the expanding sphere of influence of these malign aliens, became the perfect meeting place for such clandestine exchanges.

Inevitably, the corruption spread. As trade increased, it became more open, with tau vessels becoming a common sight at the new and expanding starports. Tau themselves began to be seen on the streets of the Gravalaxian cities, mingling with the populace, tainting their human purity with their soulless, alien ways. Heresy began to run rife, even ordinary citizens daring to use blasphemous devices

---

1   Or Logar couldn't be bothered to do the research.

unblessed by the techpriests, supplied by their insidious offworld allies.

Something had to be done! And at last it was. The rising stench of corruption eventually attracted the ceaseless vigilance of the Inquisition, which lost no time in demanding the dispatch of a task force of the Imperium's finest warriors to purge this festering boil in the body of His Holiness's blessed demesne.

And that's precisely what they got. For in the vanguard of this glorious endeavour was none other than Ciaphas Cain, the martial hero at whose very name the enemies of humanity trembled in terror...

THREE

*Old friends are like debt collectors; they have a
tendency to turn up when you least expect them.*

– Gilbran Quail, Collected Essays.

As I'VE RATTLED around the galaxy I've seen a great
many cities, from the soaring spires of Holy Terra
itself to the blood-choked gutters of some eldar
reiver charnel pit,[1] but I've seldom seen anything
stranger than the broad thoroughfares of Mayoh, the
planetary capital of Gravalax. We'd disembarked in
good order, the freshly sewn banner of the 597th
snapping proudly in the breeze that blew in gently
across the rockcrete hectares of the starport as the

---

1   Cain was part of the invasion force which cleansed Sanguia. His
account of this action is also recorded in the archive.

Valhallans formed up by company, and I resisted the temptation to lean across and compliment Sulla on her needlepoint. I doubt that she'd had anything to do with procuring it, but it wasn't that which dissuaded me. She just wasn't the kind to take a joke, and was still harbouring a germ of resentment at the organisational changes I'd instituted. We were a fine sight to behold, I have to admit, the other regiments glancing at us sidelong as they marched away; although that may just have been surprise when they realised we were a mixed unit.[1]

'All present and accounted for, colonel.' Broklaw snapped a drill manual salute, and fell into place beside Kasteen. She nodded, inflated her chest, and then hesitated on the verge of giving the command.

'Commissar,' she said. 'I think the honour should be yours. This regiment wouldn't even exist if it wasn't for you.'

I don't mind admitting I was touched. Although I have overall authority in whatever unit I'm attached to, commissars are always outside the regular chain of command; which means I don't really fit in anywhere. By letting me give the order to move out, she was

1   It was hardly unprecedented for men and women to serve together in the Imperial Guard. Notable units in which this was the norm included the Omicron Rangers, Tanith First, and Calderon Rifles. However, with women making up fewer than ten per cent of the total number under arms, and the vast majority of those serving in single-sex regiments, it wouldn't be that surprising if the 597th excited a certain amount of curiosity among the onlookers present.

demonstrating in the most practical form imaginable
that I was as much a part of the 597th as herself, or
Broklaw, or the humblest latrine orderly. The unaccustomed sense of belonging choked me for a moment,
before the more rational part of my mind started
gloating about how much that would mean in facili-
tating my own survival. I nodded, making sure I
looked suitably moved.

'Thank you, colonel,' I said simply. 'But I believe
the honour belongs to us all.' Then I filled my chest,
and bellowed: 'Move out!'

So we did. And if you think that sounds like a simple proposition, you haven't thought it through.

To put it into some kind of perspective, a regiment
consists of anything up to half a dozen companies –
five in our case, most of which had four or five pla-
toons. The exception was Third Company, which was
our logistical support arm, and consisted mainly of
transport vehicles, engineering units, and anything
else we couldn't find a sensible place for on the
SO&E. All told, that came to much the same thing in
a headcount. Factor in five squads a platoon, at ten
troopers each, plus a command element to keep
them all in line, and you're looking at nearly a thousand people by the time you've added in the various
specialists and the different layers of the overall command structure.

Just to add to the confusion, Kasteen had decided
to split the squads into five-man fire-teams, anticipating that any open conflict was likely to take place
in and around the urban areas. Beating off the

tyranids on Corania had convinced her that smaller formations were easier to coordinate in a city fight than full-strength squads.[1]

All this made for a fine martial display as we moved out, you can be sure, with banners flying, and the band thumping and parping away at *If I Should Forget Thee, O Terra*, as though they had a grudge against the composer. There hadn't really been time for rehearsals, what with all the excitement aboard the *Righteous Wrath*, but they were making up in enthusiasm for whatever they lacked in proficiency, and a high old time was being had by all. It was a fine fresh day, with a faint taste of salt in the breeze from the nearby ocean; at least until our chimeras and transport trucks started up and began farting prome-thium fumes into the air.

We intended to make an impression with our arrival, and by the Emperor, we surely did, setting out to march the ten kloms[2] or so into the city. Most of the troopers were glad of the exercise, revelling in the fresh air and sunshine after so long between decks, and swung along the highway, lasguns at the slope. Being an old hive boy myself, it was all one to me, but I was affected by the general holiday atmosphere

---

1   A widespread, though unofficial practice among units experi-enced in urban warfare. So much so that it's now become part of the standard operating procedure in many regiments, the *ad hoc* arrange-ment persisting to become a permanent feature of their organisation.
2   A Valhallan slang abbreviation for 'kilometre.' Cain served with Valhallan units for most of his life, and almost inevitably his speech became peppered with colloquialisms acquired from them.

I think, and I don't mind admitting to a general diffuse glow of well-being as we got underway.

Kasteen and Broklaw couldn't march, of course, having to look grander than the common groundpounders, and so trundled along at the front of the regiment in a Salamander, and I seized the excuse to do the same.

'Can't have the regiment's most vital officers plotting behind my back,' I'd said at the briefing, smiling to show I didn't mean it, and pouring everyone a fresh cup of recaf to show I was part of the team. So I lounged back in the open compartment at the rear of a scout variant, which Jurgen kept half a track's length behind theirs in the interest of protocol and reinforcing the impression of my generally assumed modesty, and took the opportunity to feel rather pleased with myself. The synchronised slapping of two thousand boot soles on the surface of the highway and the squarking of the band almost drowned out the throb of our engine, and we must have looked a splendid sight as we left the main cargo gate of the starport behind us and began to approach the city.

It was then that my palms began to itch again. There was nothing I could put my finger on initially to explain my gradually intensifying sense of disquiet, but something was definitely tapping my subconscious on the shoulder and whispering 'That's not right...'

As we entered the city itself my disquiet grew. I wasn't surprised to find the streets free of traffic, the local authorities having cleared the way for us; a thousand troopers and their ancillary equipment take up a lot of room, and we were far from the first regiment to have disembarked. Indeed, the occasional muffled curse from behind me which cut through the din made it all too clear that the front few ranks would have preferred it if the Rough Riders could have been held back for a while longer instead of being sent through immediately ahead of us. Come to that, I don't suppose Kasteen was too thrilled about having to gaze at a street's width of horse arses for the duration of our march either. But the broad thoroughfares were a little too quiet for my liking, and a little too open as well. I'm not agoraphobic by any means, not like some hivers who never feel comfortable under an open sky, but there was something about those wide streets that made me think of snipers and ambush.

That made me scan the buildings as we passed, and my unease grew the more I saw of them. There was nothing wrong with them as such, not like the bizarre architectural forms of a Chaos incursion which seem to twist reality and which hurt to look upon, or the brutal slapdash functionalism of orkish habitations, but there was something in their sweeping forms which seemed vaguely inhuman. I was put in mind of some eldar architecture by their elegant simplicity, and then it finally hit me: there were no right angles anywhere, even the corners having been rounded and smoothed. But beneath this strange styling, the shapes were clearly those of warehouses, apartment blocks, and manufactoria, as though the whole city had been left out in the sun for too long and had started to melt.

That alone should have been enough warning of an insidious alien influence at work here, but before we reached our destination, I was to see far more than that.

'There's something seriously wrong here,' I said to Jurgen, who looked up briefly from the road ahead to nod in agreement with me.

'Something doesn't smell right,' he agreed, without a trace of irony. 'Have you seen the civilians?'

Now that he came to mention it, there were remarkably few of them lining the route. Normally a big military parade would have brought them out in droves, waving their aquila flags and their icons of the Divine One, cheering themselves hoarse to see so many of the Emperor's finest ready to see off the foe so they could scuttle back to their meaningless lives without the fear of having to fight for themselves. But the pavements were half empty, and for every shopkeeper or habwife or juvie who cheered and waved, or smiled wanly at us with sidelong glances at their neighbours, there were just as many who scowled or glared at us. That put a shiver down my spine, awakening uncomfortable and all-too-recent memories of the mess hall riot, and the blood-maddened troopers a hair from turning on me.

At least no one was shouting, or throwing things. Yet. But I reached down unobtrusively, and loosened my laspistol and my trusty chainsword ready to be drawn in a hurry if I needed them.

And right on cue I noticed the first of the banners. 'MURDERERS GO HOME!' it said, in shaky capitals, hand lettered on what looked like an old bedsheet. Someone had strung it from a luminator pole so that it hung out across the street, comfortably above head height, but low enough to brush irritatingly over the head and shoulders of anyone riding in a vehicle.

Or on a horse, for that matter. As I watched, one of the Rough Rider officers reached up irritably and tore it down.

Bad move, I said to myself, expecting some trouble from the crowd, but beyond a little catcalling from a small knot of juvies nothing happened. But I was getting a distinctly uncomfortable feeling about all this. There was a perceptible undercurrent of tension in the air now, like a fainter echo of the incipient violence I'd felt aboard the *Righteous Wrath*.

'Go back to your Emperor and leave us alone!' a pretty girl shouted, her head shaven, apart from a single shoulder-length braid, and I felt as though I'd been doused with cold water. *Your* Emperor. The words had been unmistakable.

'Heretics!' Jurgen said with loathing. I nodded, still unable to credit it. Could the Great Enemy have a foothold here, as well as the tau? But common sense argued against it. If that were the case we'd have bombarded the place from orbit, surely, and the Astartes would have been sent in to cut out the cancer before it could spread.

Things weren't as far gone as I'd feared, however, as I turned back to look, a squad of Arbites forced their way through the crowd and began laying into the juvies with shock batons. Good order was still being maintained here, by the Emperor's grace, but for how much longer?

That, I very much feared, depended on us.

WE REACHED OUR staging area without further incident, fanning out through a complex of warehouses and manufactoria which had been set aside for our use. We weren't the only regiment quartered there, I recall, as the Imperium had been fortifying against an expected incursion by the tau for some time, and I gathered that the *Righteous Wrath's* complement (three full regiments apart from our own) brought the total up to around thirty thousand all told. That should have been more than enough to keep a backwater planet, even spread out across the whole globe, but rumour had it we could expect still more reinforcement, which worried me more than I wanted to show. With that amount of build-up it seemed the aliens wanted this place quite badly, and we'd more than likely be expected to hold it the hard way.

We were quartered next to one of the Valhallan armoured regiments – the 14th I think – but I couldn't tell you who most of the others were. There was definite evidence that the Rough Riders were still somewhere in the vicinity though, so you had to watch your feet, but apart from that I hadn't a clue.

Except for one other unit I already knew well, of course, which I'll come to in a moment.

I was still feeling spooked from our journey through town, so I was relieved to come across Broklaw posting sentries around our corner of the compound as I left Jurgen to sort out my quarters and went for a wander around to get my bearings. I haven't reached my second century by not knowing where the best boltholes and lines of retreat are, and finding them was always a high priority for me whenever I found myself somewhere new.

'Good thinking, major,' I complimented him, and he gave me a wry grin.

'We should be safe enough here,' he said. 'But it never hurts to be careful.'

'I know what you mean,' I agreed. 'There's something about this place which really gets under my skin.' The warehouses around us all had that peculiar rounded-off look I'd noticed before, and the subtle sense of wrongness left a vague apprehension hovering around me like Jurgen's body odour. The major knew his business, though, setting up lascannon in sandbagged emplacements to cover the gaps between the buildings around us, and sharpshooters on the roof. I was just admiring his thoroughness when the ground began to shake, and a couple of our sentinels appeared, clanking and humming and swivelling their heavy multilasers as they took up position in front of the main loading doors which gave access to the ground floor where our vehicles were parked.

Somewhat reassured by this, I made my way across the compound, passing into areas controlled by other units, watching the familiar bustle of troopers coming and going, and finding the familiar air of controlled chaos and the constant background hum of vehicle engines and profanity curiously soothing. I wasn't sure quite how far I'd gone when an engine note both louder and deeper than the others cut through the babble of sound around me.

For a moment, I was assailed by that formless sense of recognition that you get when something you once knew so well it never registered consciously comes back to your notice after a passage of years, and then I turned my head with a nostalgic smile. A Trojan heavy hauler, with an Earthshaker howitzer in tow, was growling its way across a vast open area which had probably once been used to park the private vehicles of the workers who toiled here in happier times, but which was now choked with equipment and supplies. I hadn't seen one of those up close in a long time, but I recognised it at once, having started my long and inglorious career in an obscure artillery unit. The flood of memories the sight brought back, a few of them even pleasant, was so overwhelming that for a moment I was unaware of the voice calling my name.

'Cai! Over here!'

Now, I've never been what you'd call oversupplied with friends, it goes with the job I suppose, but of the few I've acquired over the years only one has ever had the presumption to use the familiar form of my given name. So, despite the changes that the years since I'd seen him last had wrought, there was no mistaking the officer who was running across the compound towards me, grinning like an idiot.

'Toren!' I called back, as he sidestepped another Trojan just in time to avoid being squashed into the tarmac like a bug. 'When did they make you a major?' The last time I'd seen Toren Divas he'd just made captain, and was nursing a hangover as he saw me off from the 12th Field Artillery. I remember thinking at the time he was probably the only man in the battery who was sorry to see me go. 'And what in the name of the Emperor's arse are you doing here?'

'The same as you, I suppose.' He came panting up to me, the familiar lopsided grin on his face. 'Keeping order, purging the heretics, same old thing.' There were streaks of grey at his temples now, I noticed, and his belt was out another notch, but the same air of boyish enthusiasm still hung around him as on the day we'd first met. 'But I'm surprised to find you in a backwater like this.'

'Same here,' I said. I turned my head, taking in the bustle surrounding us. 'This seems like an awful lot of firepower to put the frighteners on a bunch of stroppy provincials.'

'If the tau mobilise, we'll need every bit of it,' Divas said. 'Some of their wargear has to be seen to be believed. They've got these things like dreadnoughts, but they're fast, like Astartes infantry but twice the size, and their tanks make the eldar stuff look like they were built by orks...'

As usual, he seemed to be relishing the prospect of combat, which is easy to do when you're kilometres behind the front line chucking shells into the distance, but not so much fun when you're facing an enemy close enough to spit at you. And if that's all they've got in mind think yourself lucky, unless they're one of those Emperor-forsaken xenos that come equipped with venom sacs.

'But it won't come to that, surely,' I said. 'Now we're here they'd be mad to attempt a landing.' To my astonishment, Divas laughed.

'They won't have to. They're here already.' This was new and unwelcome information, and I goggled at him in surprise.

'Since when?' I gasped. Now I'd be the first to admit that I'm seldom that diligent when it comes to reading the briefing slates, but I was sure I'd have noticed something that crucial to my well-being in my cursory glance through it. Divas shrugged.

'About six months, apparently. They were already deployed on the planet when the *Cleansing Flame* dropped us off here three weeks ago.'

This was seriously bad news. I'd been looking forward to a nice brisk round of target practice on civilian rioters, or, at worst, a turkey shoot against the odd renegade PDF unit. But now we were facing a foe that could give us a real run for our money. Emperor's bowels! If half of what I'd heard about the tau and their technosorcery was true, we could be the ones getting our arses kicked. Divas grinned at my expression, misinterpreting it entirely.

'So you could see some fun after all,' he said, clapping me on the back. I could have killed him.

I DIDN'T, OF COURSE. For one thing, as I've said, I don't have so many friends that I can afford to waste them, and for another, Divas had been here long enough to pick up some vital information which I currently lacked. Namely, the location of the nearest bar we could get to without attracting too much attention to ourselves.

So we set out through the streets of Mayoh together, my commissar's uniform getting us through the guard on the compound gate without any argument, although he did give us a word of caution.

'Be careful, sir. There's been disturbances up in the Heights,[1] they say.' That meant nothing to me, so I smiled, and nodded, and said we'd be careful, and checked with Divas that we'd be going nowhere near there as soon as we were out of earshot.

'Good Emperor, no,' he said, frowning. 'It's crawling with heretics. The only way you'd catch me up there is with a squadron of Hellhounds to cleanse the place.' Needless to say, he'd never seen what

---

1   The most affluent area of the city, where it began to rise up into the surrounding hills. Though tau influence on the local architecture was widespread, as Cain notes elsewhere, it was more overt here than anywhere else in Mayoh. As a result, it was popular with the most radical of the pro-tau citizens, and a natural focus of protest for the Imperial loyalists. As the political situation continued to deteriorate, clashes between the two factions became commonplace here.

incendiary weapons can do to a man, or he wouldn't have been half so keen on the idea. I have, and I wouldn't wish it on my worst enemy. Actually, there are one or two I would wish it on, come to think of it, and sit there happily toasting caba nuts while they screamed, but they're all dead now anyway, so it's beside the point.

'So where did they all come from?' I asked, as we made our way through the streets. Dusk was falling now, the luminators and the cafe signs flickering to life, and the swirl of bodies around us growing thicker as the night descended. Small knots of passers-by stood aside to let us pass, intimidated no doubt by our Imperial uniforms and the visible sidearms we carried – some with respect, and others resentful. Several of the latter had the curious tonsure the heretic juvie had sported, their heads shaved except for a long scalplock. The significance of it wasn't to dawn on me until some time later, but even then, I realised it was a badge of allegiance of some kind, and that those who bore it were liable to turn traitor if the shooting started. For now, though, they were content merely to mutter insults under their breath.

'They're local,' Divas said, not deigning to notice them, which was fine by me. Of all the ways I could have ended up dead over the years, getting sucked into a pointless street brawl would have been among the most embarrassing. 'The whole planet's infested with xeno-lovers.'

A bit of an exaggeration, that, but he was more or less right, as I was later to discover. To cut a long story short, the locals had been trading with the tau for several generations by now, which wasn't terribly sensible, but what can you expect from a bunch of backwater peasants? The end result was that most of them were quite used to seeing xenos around the place, and despite the sterling efforts of the local ecclesiarchy to warn them that no good would come of it, a lot of them had started to absorb unhealthy ideas from them. Which was where we came in, ready to guide them back into the Imperial fold before they came to too much harm, and all very noble of us too I'm sure you'll agree.

'The trouble is,' Divas concluded, downing the rest of his third amasec in one, 'the hard core are so far gone they don't see it like that. They think the tau are the best thing to hit the galaxy since the Emperor was in nappies, and we're the big bad bullies here to take their shiny new toys away.'

'Well, that might be a little more difficult now the tau are digging in,' I said. 'But I'm surprised they're prepared to risk it.' I followed suit, feeling the smoky liquor warming its way down through my chest. 'They must know we'll never allow them to annex the place without a fight.'

'They claim they're just here to safeguard their trading interests,' Divas said. We both snorted with laughter at that one. We knew how often the Imperium had said exactly the same thing before launching an all-out invasion of some luckless ball of dirt. Of course when we did it, it was true, and it was my job to shoot anyone who thought otherwise.

'One for the diplomats, then,' I said, signalling for another round. A nicely rounded waitress bustled over, full of patriotic fervour, and replenished our glasses.

One thing I can say for Divas, he knew how to find a good bar. This one, the Eagle's Wing, was definitely in the loyalist camp. The wide, smoky cellar full of Planetary Defence Force regulars were delighted to see some real soldiers at last, and fulminating at the governor for not letting them loose on the aliens years ago. The owner was a corporal in the PDF reserves, recently retired after twenty years' service, and he couldn't seem to get over the honour of having a couple of real Guard officers in the place. And once Divas had introduced me, and I'd been appropriately modest about my earlier adventures in the Emperor's name, there was no question of us having to pay the bill either. After signing autographs for some of the civilian customers – all of whom urged us to pot a few of the 'little blue bastards' on their behalf – and charming the waitress had begun to pall, we'd retreated to a quiet side booth where we could talk uninterrupted.

'I think the diplomats could be getting a little help on this one,' Divas said, tapping the side of his nose conspiratorially as he lifted the glass. I drank a little more slowly, acutely aware that we'd have to start making our way back through a potentially hostile city soon, and wanting to keep a reasonably clear head.

'Help from who?' I asked.

'Who do you think?' Divas dipped his finger in the glass, and sketched a stylised letter I with a pair of crossbars bisecting it on the surface of the table, before erasing it with a sweep of his hand. I laughed.

'Oh yeah, them. Right.' I've yet to arrive any place where the political situation's fluid without hearing rumours of Inquisition agents beavering away behind the scenes, and unless I happen to be the errand boy in question, I never believe a word of it. On the other hand, if there aren't any rumours, then they probably are up to some mischief and no mistake about it.[1]

'You can laugh.' Divas finished his drink, and replaced the glass on the table. 'But I heard it from one of the Administratum adepts, who swore he'd got it from... somewhere or other.' An expression of faint bewilderment drifted across his face. 'I think I need some fresh air.'

'I think you do, too,' I said. Leaving aside what I thought then were his ridiculous fantasies about the Inquisition, he'd still given me a lot to think about. The situation here was undoubtedly far more com- plex than I'd been led to believe, and I needed to consider things carefully.

So we took our leave of our kindly hosts, the wait- ress in particular looking sorry to see me go, and staggered up the stairway and into the street.

---

1   A reasonable assumption on both accounts. Details of Cain's sub- sequent activities as my 'errand boy,' as he puts it, can be found in the Ordo's libram if any readers care to check the official accounts; his own version of these events can be found elsewhere in the archive, but need not concern us at the moment.

The cold night air hit me like a refreshing shower, snapping me back to alertness, and I glanced around while Divas communed loudly with the Emperor in a convenient gutter. Fortunately, the bar he'd steered us to was down a quiet side alley, so no one saw the dignity of the Imperial uniform being sullied. Once I was sure there were no more eruptions to come, I helped him to his feet.

'You used to be able to hold it better than that,' I chided, and he shook his head mournfully.

'Local rotgut. Not like the stuff we used to drink. And I should have eaten something...'

'It would just have been a wasted effort,' I consoled him, and glanced around, trying to get our bearings. 'Where the frak are we, anyway?'

'Dock zone,' he said confidently, hardly swaying on his feet at all now. 'This way.' He strode off towards the nearest luminated thoroughfare. I shrugged, and followed him. After all, he'd had three weeks to get his bearings.

As we made our way through the well-lit street, however, I began to feel a little apprehensive. True, we'd been deep in conversation on our way to the bar, but none of the landmarks looked familiar to me, and I began to wonder if his confidence had been misplaced.

'Toren,' I said after a while, noticing a gradual increase in the number of scalplocks and murderous glances among the passers-by, 'are you sure this is the way back to our staging area?'

'Not ours,' he said, the grin back on his face. 'Theirs. Thought you'd like to get a look at the enemy.'

'You thought what?' I yelped, amazed at his stupidity. Then I remembered. Divas bought the myth of my purported heroism completely and without question, and had done ever since he'd seen me take on an entire tyranid swarm with just a chainsword when we were callow youths together. Purely by accident, as it happened, I'd had no idea the damn bugs were even there until I'd blundered into them, and if I hadn't ended up inadvertently leading them into the beaten zone of our heavy ordnance and saving the day, they'd have torn me to pieces. Waltzing up to the enemy encampment and thumbing our noses at them probably struck him as the kind of thing I did for fun. 'Are you out of your mind?'

'It's perfectly safe,' he said. 'We're not officially at war with them yet.' Well, that was true, but I still wasn't keen on jumping the gun.

'And until we are, we're not going to provoke them,' I said, all commissarial duty. Divas's face fell, like a child denied a sweet, and I thought I'd better put a gloss on it that would match his expectations of me. 'We can't put our own amusement ahead of our responsibilities to the Emperor, however tempting it is.'

'I suppose you're right,' he said reluctantly, and I began to breathe a little more easily. Now all I had to do was manoeuvre him back to the barracks before he got any more stupid ideas. So I took him by the arm, and turned him around. 'Now how do we get back to our compound?'

'How about in a body bag?' somebody asked. I turned, feeling my stomach drop. About a dozen locals stood behind us, the street light striking highlights from their shaven heads, a variety of improvised weapons hanging purposefully from their hands. They looked tough, at least in their own minds, but when you've been face to face with orks and eldar reiver slavers you don't intimidate that easily. Well, all right. I do, but I don't show it, which is the main thing.

Besides, I had a laspistol and a chainsword, which in my experience trumps a crowbar every time. So I laid a restraining hand on Divas's shoulder, as he was still intoxicated enough to rise to the bait, and smiled lazily.

'Believe me,' I said, 'you don't want to start anything.'

'You don't tell me what I want.' The group's spokesman stepped forward into the light. Fine, I thought, keep them talking. 'But that's what you Imperials do, isn't it?'

'I don't quite follow,' I said, affecting mild curiosity. Movement out of the corner of my eye told me that our retreat had been cut off. A second group emerged from the alley mouth behind us. I started calculating the odds. If I made a move to draw the laspistol, they'd rush me, but I'd probably manage to get a shot off. If I took out the leader with it, and ran forward at the same time, I stood a good chance of breaking through the line and making a run for it. That assumed they'd be surprised or intimidated enough to hesitate, of course, and I was able to open up a decent lead. With any luck they'd turn on Divas, buying me enough time to get away, but I couldn't be sure of that, so I continued to play for time and look for a better chance.

'You're here to take our world!' the leader shouted. As he came forward fully into the light I could see that his face was painted blue, a delicate pastel shade. It should have made him look ridiculous, but the overall effect was somehow charismatic. 'But you'll never take our freedom!'

'Your freedom is what we're here to give you, you xeno-hugging moron!' Divas broke free of my restraining arm, and lunged forward. 'But you're too brainwashed to see it!'

Great. So much for diplomacy. Still, while he was set on re-enacting Gannack's Charge,[1] I might be able to make a run for it.

No such luck, of course – the surrounding heretics drove in on us as a concerted wedge. I just managed to draw my laspistol and snap off a shot, taking out half the face of one of the group, which, I'm bound to say, didn't make much of a difference to his overall personal charm, before an iron bar came down hard on my wrist. I've been in enough mêlées to have seen the blow coming, and to have ridden it, which saved me from a fracture or worse, but that didn't

1   A famous military blunder in the Spiron campaign, which took place on 438.926.M41. Captain Gannack's sentinel troop, from the 3rd Kalaman Hussars, misinterpreted their orders and charged an ork redoubt containing an artillery battery. No one survived.

help the pain, which exploded along my arm, deadening it. My fingers flew open, and I ducked, scrabbling after the precious weapon, but it was futile. A knee drove up into my ribs, slamming the breath from my lungs, and I was down, cold, hard rockcrete scraping the skin from my knuckles (the real ones anyway), and knowing I was a dead man unless I could get away somehow.

'Toren!' I screamed, but Divas had problems of his own by now, and I wasn't going to get any help from that quarter. I curled up, trying to protect my vital organs, and tried frantically to get at my chainsword. Of course, I should have gone for that first, holding the mob at bay with it, but hindsight's about as much use as a heretic's oath, and now the bloody thing was trapped under my own bodyweight. I scrabbled frantically, feeling fists and boots thudding against my ribs. Luckily there were so many of them that they were getting in each others way, and my uniform greatcoat was thick enough to absorb some of the impact, or I'd have been in even worse shape than I was.

'*Greechaah!*' something shrieked, an inhuman scream that raised the hairs on the back of my neck, even under those conditions. My assailants hesitated, and I rolled clear, in time to see the largest of them yanked back by sheer brute force.

For a moment I thought I was hallucinating, but the pain in my ribs was all too real. A face dominated by a large hooked beak was gazing down at me, surmounted by a crest of quills that had been dyed or painted in some elaborate pattern, and hot, charnel breath washed across my face, making me gag.

'You are comparatively uninjured?' the thing asked, in curiously accented Gothic. It's hard to convey in writing, but its voice was glottal, most of the consonants reduced to hard clicking sounds. It was perfectly understandable, mind you. My stupefaction was due entirely to the fact that something that looked like that was able to talk in the first place.

'Yes, thank you,' I croaked after a moment. Whenever you don't have a clue what's going on, I've always found, it never hurts to be polite.

'That is gratifying,' the thing said, and threw the heretic in its left hand casually away. The others were standing around aimlessly now, like sulky schola students when the tutor turns up to spoil the fun. Then it extended the same thin, scaly hand equipped with dagger-like claws towards me. After a heartstopping moment, I divined its intention, and accepted the proffered assistance in gaining my feet. As I did so, it turned to the sullen group of heretics.

'This does not advance the greater good,' it said. 'Disperse now, and avoid conflict.' Well, that was a challenge if ever I'd heard one. But to my surprise, and, I must admit, my intense relief, the little knot of troublemakers slunk away into the shadows. I eyed my rescuer a little apprehensively. He (or she – with kroot it's impossible to tell, and only another kroot would care anyway) was slightly taller than I was, and still looked pretty intimidating. They're tough enough to take on an ork in hand-to-hand combat, and I, for one, wouldn't be betting on the greenskin, but if it wanted me dead, it would only have had to wait a few moments. I retrieved my fallen laspistol anyway, and tried to get my breath back.

'I'm obliged to you,' I said. 'I must admit I don't understand, but I'm grateful.' I fumbled the weapon back into its holster with some difficulty. My arm was swelling up now, and my fingers felt thick and unresponsive. My rescuer made a curious clicking sound, which I assumed to be its equivalent of laughter.

'Imperial officers murdered by tau supporters. Not a desirable outcome when the political situation is tense.'

'Not a desirable outcome at any time when one of them is me,' I said, and the xeno made the clicking noise again. That reminded me of Divas, and I staggered across to check on him. He was still breathing, but unconscious, a deep gash across his forehead. I'd picked up enough battlefield medicine to know he'd recover soon enough, but have the Emperor's own headache when he woke, and that was fine with me – serve the idiot right for nearly getting me killed.

'I have the honour to be Gorok, of the Clan T'cha,' the creature said. 'I am kroot.'

'I know what you are,' I said. 'Kroot killed my parents.' And thereby got me dumped in the Schola Progenium, and thence into the Commissariat, instead of following my undoubted true destiny of running some discreet little house of ill repute for slumming spirers and guilders up from the sump with more money than sense to splash around. I vaguely resented that, far more than the loss of my progenitors, who hadn't been all that much to have around while they were alive, to be honest. But it never hurts to grab the moral high ground. My new acquaintance didn't seem terribly concerned, though.

'I trust they fought well,' he said. I doubted it. They'd only joined the Guard to get out of the hive ahead of the Arbites, and would certainly have deserted the first chance they got, so there must be something in genetics after all.

'Not well enough,' I said, and Gorok clicked his amusement again. It was a slightly unnerving experience, feeling that something so unhuman was able to read me more readily than my own people.

'Go carefully, commissar,' he said. 'And feed on your enemies. May we have no cause for conflict.'

Well, thank the Emperor for that. But somehow I doubted that it was going to happen, and of course, I was right. I was surprised, though, by how quickly the crisis came upon us.

Editorial Note:

It is perhaps worth pointing out at this juncture that the account of his background that Cain gives during his conversation with the kroot, although superficially plausible, doesn't quite hold together on further examination. For one thing, admittance to the Schola Progenium is a privilege usually reserved for the offspring of officers. If he was indeed the son of common troopers his parents must have acquitted themselves with singular valour in the action which resulted in their demise, which, to say the least, seems remarkably at odds with his characterisation of them. Moreover, he implies that they enlisted and served together. Although mixed units are, as pointed out elsewhere, not unheard of in the Imperial Guard, it would have been extremely unusual for this to have been the case.

Cain makes frequent references throughout the archive to having spent his early years on a hive world, but never specifies which one; which, in turn, makes the verification of any such claims virtually impossible. However, no hive world of which I'm aware raised a mixed Guard regiment in the time frame consistent with his narrative.

We should also bear in mind that, by his own admission, the man was a pathological liar; given to saying anything he judged would be effective in manipulating his listeners.

FOUR

It's often remarked that diplomacy is just warfare by other means. Our battles are no less desperate for being bloodless, but at least we get wine and finger food.

– Tollen Ferlang, Imperial Envoy to
the Realm of Ultramar, 564-603 M41.

'ARE YOU SURE you're fit enough?' Kasteen asked, a faint frown of concern appearing between her eyebrows. I nodded, and adjusted the sling I'd adopted for dramatic effect. It was black silk, matching the ebony hues of my dress uniform, and made me look tolerably dashing, I thought.

'I'm fine,' I said, smiling bravely. 'The other fellows got the worst of it, thank the Emperor.' In the day or two since the brawl with the heretics, my arm had more or less healed, the medicae assuring me that I'd suffered nothing worse than severe bruising. It was still stiff, and ached a little, but all in all I thought I'd come off lightly. Far better than Divas had, anyway. He'd spent the night in the infirmary, and still walked with a stick. For all that, though, he was as irritatingly cheerful as ever, and I'd been finding as many duties as I could to keep me out of the way whenever he suggested socialising again.

Luckily for me, he'd lost consciousness before the kroot turned up, so my reputation had received another unmerited embellishment. He assumed I'd seen off our assailants single-handed, and I saw no good reason to disabuse him. Besides, the conversation I'd had with the creature had been curiously unsettling, and I found myself reluctant to think about it too hard. I noticed Divas's account had tactfully glossed over the reason why we were in the thick of the tau sympathizers' heartland, so maybe they'd finally knocked a little common sense into him. Knowing Divas, though, I doubted it.

'Well, that's what they get for picking on the Imperium's finest,' Kasteen said, eager to buy the generally accepted version of events, as the latest evidence of my exceptional martial abilities reflected well on the regiment she led. She adjusted her own dress uniform, tugging the ochre greatcoat into place with every sign of discomfort. Like most Valhallans, she had an iceworlder's tolerance for cold, and found even the mildest of temperate climates a little uncomfortable. Having spent most of my service with Valhallan regiments, I'd long become inured to their habit of air conditioning their quarters to temperatures which left the breath smoking, and tended to wear my commissarial greatcoat at all times, but they were still adjusting to the local conditions here with some difficulty.

'If I might suggest, colonel,' I said, 'tropical order would be perfectly acceptable.'

'Would it?' She hovered indecisively, reminding me again how young she was to be in such an elevated position, and I felt an unaccustomed pang of sympathy. The prestige of the regiment was in her hands, and it was easy to forget how heavily the responsibility weighed on her.

'It would,' I assured her. She discarded the heavy fur cap, disordering her hair, and began to unfasten the coat. Then she hesitated.

'I don't know,' she said. 'If they think I'm too informal it'll reflect badly on all of us.'

'For the Emperor's sake, Regina,' Broklaw said, his voice amused. 'What sort of impression do you think you'll make if you're sweating like an ork all evening?' I noted his use of her given name, the first time I'd heard him do so, with quiet satisfaction. Another milestone on the 597th's march towards full integration. The real test would come with their first taste of combat, of course, and all too soon at that, but it was a good omen. 'The commissar's right.'

'The commissar's always right,' I said, smiling. 'It says so in the regulations.'

'Well, I can't argue with that.' Kasteen pulled off the coat with evident relief, and smoothed the jacket beneath it. It was severely cut, emphasising her figure in ways that I was sure would attract the attention of most of the men in the room. Broklaw nodded approvingly.

'I don't think you need to worry about making an impression,' he said, proffering a comb.

'So long as it's a good one.' She smoothed her hair into place, and began buckling her weapon belt. Like mine it held a chainsword, but hers was ornately gilded, and worked with devotional scenes that decorated scabbard and hilt alike. The contrast with my own functional model, chipped and battered with far too much use for my liking, was striking. The holster at her other hip was immaculate too, the glossy black leather holding a bolt pistol which also gleamed from every highly polished surface and which was intricately engraved with icons of the saints.

'No doubt about that,' I assured her.

Her nervousness was quite understandable, as we'd been invited to a diplomatic reception at the governor's palace. At least I had, and in the interests of protocol, the colonel of my regiment and an appropriate honour guard would also be expected. This sort of soirée was quite beyond her experience, and she was all too acutely aware that she was out of her depth.

I, on the other hand, was well within mine. One of the many benefits of being a Hero of the Imperium is that you're regarded as a prime catch by a certain type of society hostess, which meant that I'd had plenty of opportunity to enjoy the homes, wine cellars, and daughters of the idle rich over the years, and had developed an easy familiarity with the world in which they moved. The main thing to remember, as I confided to Kasteen, was that they had their own idea of what soldiers were like, which had very little to do with the reality.

'The best thing you can do,' I said, 'is not to get sucked in to all that protocol nonsense in the first place. They'll expect us to get it wrong anyway, so to the warp with them.' She smiled in spite of herself, and settled a little more comfortably into the upholstery of the staff car Jurgen had found somewhere. Armed with my commissarial authority, which let him requisition practically anything short of a battleship without argument, he'd developed quite a talent for acquiring anything I considered necessary for my comfort or convenience over the years. I never asked too many questions about where they'd come from, as I suspected some of the answers might have complicated my life.

'That's easy for you to say,' she said. 'You're a hero. I'm just–'

'One of the youngest regimental commanders in the entire Guard,' I said. 'A position that, in my opinion, you hold entirely on merit.' I smiled. 'And my confidence is not lightly earned.' It was what she needed to hear, of course; I've always been good at manipulating people. That's one of the reasons I'm so good at my job. She began to look a little happier.

'So what do you suggest?' she said. I shrugged.

'They might be rich and powerful, but they're only civilians. However hard they try to hide it, they'll be in awe of you. I've always found it best at these things just to be a plain, simple military man, with no interest in politics. The Emperor points, and we obey...'

'Through the warp and far away.' She finished the old song line with a smile. 'So we shouldn't offer any opinions, or answer questions about policy.'

'Exactly,' I said. 'If they want to talk, tell them a few stories about your old campaigns. That's all they're interested in anyway.' That was certainly true in my case. I was sure I'd only been invited as patriotic window-dressing, to impress the tau with the calibre of the opposition they'd be facing if they were foolish enough to try and make a fight of it with us. Of course, in my case, that meant they could pretty much run their flag up the pole of the governor's palace any time they felt like it, but that was beside the point.

'Thank you, Ciaphas.' Kasteen put her chin on her hand, and watched the street lights flicker past outside the window. That was the first time anyone in the regiment had addressed me in personal terms since I joined it. It felt strange, but curiously pleasant.

'You're welcome... Regina,' I said, and she smiled.

(I know what you're thinking, and you're wrong. I did come to think of her as a friend in the end, and Broklaw too, but that's as far as it went. Anything else would have made both our positions untenable. Sometimes, looking back, I think that's a shame, but there it is.)

THE GOVERNOR'S PALACE was in what the locals called the Old Quarter, where the fad for tau-influenced architecture which had infected the rest of the city had failed to take hold, so the vague sense of unease which had oppressed me since we arrived began to lift at last. The villas and mansions slipping past outside the car had taken on the familiar blocky contours of the Imperial architecture with which I'd been familiar all my life, and I felt my spirits begin to rise to the point where I almost began to anticipate enjoying the evening ahead of us.

Jurgen swung the vehicle through an elaborate pair of wrought-iron gates decorated with the Imperial aquila, and our tyres hissed over raked gravel as we progressed down a long, curving drive lit by flickering flambeaux. Behind us the truck with our honour guard followed, no doubt making a terrible mess of things with its heavy duty tyres, the soldiers making the most of the grandstand view afforded by its open rear decking to point and chatter at the sights. Beyond the flickering firelight, we could make out a rolling landscaped lawn, dotted with shrubs and ornamental fountains – automatically, some part of my mind was assessing the best way of using them for cover.

An audible gasp from Kasteen signalled that the palace itself had come into view from her side window, and a moment later, the curve of the drive brought it into my field of vision.

'Not a bad little billet,' I said, with elaborate casualness. Kasteen composed herself, wiping the bumpkin gawp off her face.

'Reminds me of a bordello we used to visit when I was an officer cadet,' she replied, determined to match my blasé exterior. I grinned.

'Good,' I said. 'Remember we're soldiers. We're not impressed by this sort of thing.'

'Absolutely not,' she agreed, straightening her jacket unnecessarily.

There was a lot of the building not to be impressed by. It must have covered over a kilometre from end to end, although of course much of that area would be given over to courtyards and interior gardens currently hidden behind the outer wall. Buttresses and crenellations protruded like acne from every surface, encrusted with statuary commemorating previous governors and other local notables no one could now remember the names of, and vast areas had been gilded, reflecting the firelight from outside in a manner which was to prove eerily prophetic had we but known. At the time, though, it simply struck me as one of the most stridently vulgar piles of masonry I'd ever encountered.

Jurgen pulled up outside the main entrance, halting at the end of a red carpet as skilfully as a shuttle pilot entering a docking port. After a moment the truck pulled up behind us and our honour guard piled out, deploying on either side of it a full squad, five pairs of troopers facing each other across the crimson weave, lasguns at the port.

'Shall we?' I extended an arm to Kasteen as a flunkey dressed as a wedding cake bustled up to open the door for us.

'Thank you, commissar.' She took it as we emerged, and I stopped for a moment to have a word with Jurgen.

'Any further orders, sir?' I shook my head.

'Just find somewhere to park, and get yourself something to eat,' I said. Strictly speaking I could have had my aide accompany us, but the thought of Jurgen mingling with the cream of the Gravalaxian aristocracy was almost too hideous to contemplate. I turned to the noncom in charge of the honour guard, a Sergeant Lustig, and tapped the combead I'd slipped into my ear. 'You too,' I added. 'You might as well be comfortable while you wait for us. I'll contact you when we're ready to leave.'

'Yes sir.' A faint smile tried to form on his broad face before discipline reasserted itself, and he inhaled.

'Squad... Atten... Shun!' he bellowed, and they snapped to it with nanosecond precision. No surprise that they'd won the extra drink ration this week, I thought. The crash of synchronised heels caused

heads to turn all around us, minor local nobles looking mightily impressed, and their chauffeurs even
more so.

'I think we've made an impression,' Kasteen murmured as we gained the elaborately carved entrance
doors.

'That was the idea,' I agreed.

Inside, it was exactly as I'd anticipated, the kind of
vulgar ostentation too many of the wealthy mistake
for good taste, with crystal and gilt and garish tapestries of historic battles and smug-looking primarchs
strewn around the place like a pirate's warehouse.
The high arched ceiling was supported by pillars art-
fully carved to mimic the bark of some species of
local tree, and my feet sank into the carpet as though
it were a swamp. It took me a moment to realise that
the weave would form a vast portrait, presumably of
the governor himself, if viewed from the upper landing, and I noted with faint amusement that someone
had trodden on a dropped canapé making it look as
though his nose was running. Whether it was a genuine accident, or the act of a disgruntled servant, who
could say? Kasteen's lips quirked as she absorbed the
full opulence of our surroundings.

'I take it back,' she said quietly. 'A bordello would
have been done out in far better taste.' I suppressed a
smile of my own as another flunkey ushered us forward.

'Commissar Ciaphas Cain,' he announced. 'And
Colonel Regina Kasteen.' Which at least established
who we were. It was pretty obvious who the

unhealthy-looking individual sitting on a raised dais at the end of the room was. I've met a good few planetary governors in my day, and they all tend towards inbred imbecility,[1] but this specimen looked like he should take the prize. He somehow contrived to look both undernourished and flabby at the same time, and his skin was the pallor of a dead fish. Watery eyes of no particular colour goggled at us from under a fringe of thinning grey hair.

'Governor Grice,' I said, bowing formally. 'A pleasure.'

'On the contrary,' he said, his voice quivering a little. 'The pleasure's entirely mine.' Well, he wasn't wrong on that account, but he was ignoring me entirely. He stood, and bowed to Kasteen. 'You honour us all with your presence, colonel.'

Well, that was a new experience, being ignored in favour of a slip of a girl, but I suppose if you'd ever met her you'd understand it. She was pretty striking, if redheads were your thing, and I supposed the old fool didn't get out much. Anyway, it enabled me to fade out of the picture and go looking for some amusement of my own, which I did with all due dispatch.

---

1 Like many of Cain's sweeping generalisations, this does contain an element of truth. The majority of planetary governorships are hereditary positions, and many of the incumbents aren't up to the challenge of the job. However, the truly incompetent tend to be weeded out by the ceaseless round of dynastic power struggles and coups d'état which keep the aristocracy amused, and in cases where Imperial interests are directly threatened, we can always turn to the Officio Assassinorum.

As was my habit I circulated widely, keeping my eyes and ears open as you never know what useful little snippets of information will come in handy, although the main thing that caught my attention was the entertainment. A young woman was standing on a podium at the end of the room, surrounded by musicians who sounded almost as well rehearsed as our regimental band, but they could have been playing ork wardrums for all I cared because her voice was extraordinary. She was singing old sentimental favourites, like *The Night Before You Left* and *The Love We Share*, and even an old cynic like me could appreciate the emotion she put into them, and feel that, just this once, the trite words were ringing true. Snatches of her husky contralto carried through the room wherever I was, cutting through the backbiting and the small talk, and I felt my eyes drifting in her direction every time the crowd parted enough to afford me a view.

And the view was well worth it. She was tall and slim, with shoulder-length hair of a shade of blonde I've never seen on anyone else before or since, hanging loose to frame a face which nearly stopped my heart. Her eyes were the hazy blue of a far horizon, and seemed to transfix me whenever I looked in her direction. Her dress was the same colour, almost exactly, and clung to her figure like mist.

Now, I've never believed in sentimental nonsense like love at first sight, but I can say without a word of a lie that, even now, after almost a century, I can close my eyes and picture her as she was then, and hear those songs as though she's still in the same room.

But I wasn't there to listen to cabaret singers, however enchanting, so I tried my best to mingle and pick up whatever gossip I could that would help us fight the tau if we had to, and keep me out of it, if at all possible.

'So you're the famous Commissar Cain,' someone said, passing me a fresh drink. I took it automatically, turning a little to use my right hand and emphasize the sling, and found myself looking at a narrow-faced fellow in an expensive but understated robe which positively screamed diplomat. He glanced at the sling. 'I hear you nearly started the war early.'

'Not from choice, I can assure you,' I said. 'Just defending an officer who lacked the self-restraint to ignore a blatant piece of sedition.'

'I see.' He eyed me narrowly, trying to size me up. I kept my expression neutral. 'I take it your self-restraint is a little stronger.'

'At the moment,' I said, choosing my words with care, 'we're still at peace with the tau. The internal situation here is, I'll admit, a little disturbing, but unless the Guard is ordered to intervene, that's purely a matter for the Arbites, the PDF, and His Excellency.' I nodded at Grice, who was listening to Kasteen explain the best way of disembowelling a termagant with every sign of interest, although his retinue of sycophants was beginning to look a little green around the gills. 'I'm not averse to fighting if I have to, but that's a decision for wiser heads than mine to take.'

'I see.' He nodded, and stuck out a hand for me to shake. After a moment's juggling, more to put him off balance than anything, I transferred the glass to my other hand and took it. 'Erasmus Donali, Imperial Envoy.'

'I thought as much.' I smiled in return. 'You have the look of a diplomat about you.'

'Whereas you seem quite exceptional for a soldier.' Donali sipped his drink, and I followed suit, finding it a very pleasant vintage. 'Most of them can't wait for the shooting to start.'

'They're Imperial Guard,' I said. 'They live to fight for the Emperor. I'm a commissar; I'm supposed to consider the bigger picture.'

'Which includes avoiding combat? You surprise me.'

'As I said before,' I told him, 'that's not my decision to make. But if people like you can solve the conflict by negotiation, and keep troopers who would have died here alive to fight another enemy another day, and maybe tip the balance in a more important battle, then it seems to me that you're serving the best interests of the Imperium.' And keeping my skin whole into the bargain, of course, which was far more important to me. Donali looked surprised, and a little gratified.

'I can see your reputation is far from exaggerated,' he said. 'And I hope I can oblige you. But it may not be easy.'

That wasn't what I wanted to hear, you can be sure. But I shrugged, and sipped my drink.

'As the Emperor wills,' I said, a phrase I'd picked up from Jurgen over the course of our long association. Of course when he says it he means every word; from me it's just the verbal equivalent of a shrug. I've never really bought the idea that His Divine Majesty can spare some attention from the job of preventing the entire galaxy from sliding into damnation to look out for my interests, too, or anyone else's for that matter, which is why I'm so diligent about doing it for myself. 'The difficulty, I take it, being the public support for the tau in certain quarters.'

'Exactly.' My new friend nodded gloomily. 'For which you can thank the imbecile over there talking to your colonel.' He indicated Grice with a tilt of his head. 'He got so carried away counting his bribes from the likes of him...' another tilt of the head to the far corner of the room, 'that he hardly even noticed his planet slipping out from under him.'

I turned in the direction he'd indicated. A cadaverous, hawk-nosed individual dressed in unwise scarlet hose and a burgundy tabard was holding forth to a knot of the local aristocracy. Flanking him were a couple of servants in livery, who looked about as comfortable as an ork in evening dress; hired guns if I'd ever seen them. A scribe hovered next to him, making notes.

'One of the rogue traders we've heard so much about,' I said. Donali shrugged.

'So he says. But no one here is entirely what they seem, commissar. You can certainly depend on that.'

Well he was right on the money so far as I was concerned. So I exchanged a few more inconsequential words and resumed circulating.

After a few more conversations with local dignitaries whose names I never quite caught, my glass was in need of replenishment, and I headed towards the table at the far end of the room where an enticing display of delicacies had been laid out. On the way, I noticed Kasteen had managed to extricate herself from the governor's presence, and was working the room as though she'd been a habitué of high society since she could walk. The air of confidence she now radiated was remarkable, especially set against her earlier nervousness, but the ability to seem calm and in control whatever the circumstances is a vital quality in a leader, and for all I knew, she was shamming it as shamelessly as I was. It certainly looked as though she was enjoying herself, though, and I gave her a light-hearted salute as our eyes briefly met. She responded with a flashing grin, and whirled away towards the dance floor with a couple of aristocratic fops in tow.

'It looks like you've lost your date,' a voice said behind me. I turned, and found myself falling into the wide blue eyes of the singer I'd been watching before. Uncharacteristically for me, I was momentarily at a loss for words. She was smiling, a plate of finger food in her hand.

'She's, ah, just a colleague,' I said. 'A fellow officer. Nothing like that between us. Strictly against regulations, for one thing. And anyway, we're not–'

She laughed, a warm, smoky chuckle which warmed me like amasec, and I realised she was pulling my leg.

'I know,' she said. 'No time for romance in the Imperial Guard. It must be grim for you.'

'We have our duty to the Emperor,' I said. 'For a soldier, that's enough.' It's the sort of thing I usually say, and most civilians lap it up, but my beautiful singer was looking at me quizzically, the ghost of a smile quirking at the corner of her mouth, and I suddenly got the feeling that she could see right through me to the core of deceit and self-interest I normally keep concealed from the world. It was an unnerving sensation.

'For some, maybe. But I think there's more to you than meets the eye.' She picked up a bottle from the nearby table with her free hand, and topped up my glass.

'There's more to everyone than meets the eye,' I said, more to deflect the conversation than anything else. She smiled again.

'That's very astute, commissar.' She extended a hand, slim and cool to the touch, the middle finger ornamented with a large and finely wrought ring of unusual workmanship. Evidently she was extremely successful in her profession, or had at least one wealthy admirer; I would have laid money on both. I kissed it formally, as etiquette demanded, and to my astonishment she giggled.

'A gentleman as well as an officer. You are full of surprises.' Then she surprised me by dropping a curtsey, in imitation of the bovine debutantes surrounding us, the light of mischief in her dazzling eyes. 'I'm Amberley Vail, by the way. I sing a bit.'

'I know,' I said. 'And very well too.' She acknowledged the compliment with a tilt of her head. I bowed formally, entering into the game. 'Ciaphas Cain,' I said, 'at your service. Currently attached to the Valhallan 597th.' Her eyes widened a little as I introduced myself.

'I've heard of you,' she said, a little breathlessly. 'Didn't you fight the genestealers on Keffia?' Well I had, if you count hanging around drinking recaf while the artillery unit I was with dropped shells on the biggest concentrations of stealers we could find from kloms away as fighting. I'd been in at the death, so to speak, and emerged with a great deal of the credit, more by luck than good judgement. It was one of the early incidents that had laid the foundations of my undeserved reputation for heroism, but my misadventures since had tended to overshadow what most of the galaxy still regarded as a minor incident on a backwater agriworld.

'Not entirely alone,' I said, slipping easily into the modest hero demeanour I could adopt without thinking. 'There was an Imperial battlefleet in orbit at the time.'

'And two full divisions of Imperial Guard on planet.' She laughed again at my astonished expression. 'I have relatives in Skandaburg.[1] You're still talked about back there.'

---

1   The provincial capital of the smaller of the Northern continents. Most of the action in the cleansing of Keffia took place on the southern continent, where the genestealer cult was most deeply entrenched; so Skandaburg and its population would have been relatively untouched by the fighting.

'I can't think why,' I said. 'I was just doing my job.'

'Of course.' Amberley nodded, and again I got the feeling that she wasn't fooled for a moment. 'You're an Imperial commissar. Duty before everything, right?'

'Absolutely,' I said. 'And right now, I think it's my duty to ask you to dance.' It was a transparent attempt to change the subject, which I hoped she'd put down to modest embarrassment, and I half expected her to refuse. But she smiled, discarding her plate of half-eaten delicacies, and took my uninjured arm.

'I'd love to,' she said. 'I've a few minutes before my second set.'

So we drifted across to the dance floor, and I spent a very pleasant few minutes with her head on my shoulder as we spun around to an old waltz I never learned the name of. Kasteen galloped past a couple of times, a different swain in tow on each occasion, raising an eyebrow in a way which forewarned me of some relentless leg-pulling on our drive back to the compound, but just at that moment I couldn't have cared less.

Eventually, Amberley pulled away, with what seemed like reluctance unless I was succumbing to wishful thinking, and began to return to the stage. I walked with her, chatting to no purpose, intent simply on prolonging a pleasant interlude in what otherwise promised to be a dull evening, and it was thus that I noticed a quiet, vehement altercation between Grice and the hawk-faced rogue trader.

'Do you know who that is?' I asked, not really expecting an answer, but it seemed my companion was well-versed in the intricacies of Gravalaxian politics. It came with performing for the aristocracy, I supposed. She nodded, looking surprised.

'His name's Orelius. A rogue trader here to deal with the tau. So he says.' The qualification was delivered in precisely the same tone of scepticism as Donali's had been, and for some reason I found myself remembering Divas's cloak-and-dagger fantasies from our night in the Eagle's Wing.

'Why do you say that?' I asked. Amberley shrugged.

'The tau have been dealing with the same traders for more than a century. Orelius arrived from nowhere a month or two ago, and tried opening negotiations with them, through Grice. It may just be a coincidence, but...' She shrugged, her dress slipping across her slim shoulders.

'Why now, with the political situation destabilising?' I asked. She nodded.

'It does seem a little unusual.'

'Perhaps he's hoping to take advantage of the confusion to strike a better deal,' I said. Orelius turned on his heel as I watched, and marched away trailed by his bodyguards. Grice was pale and sweating, even more than usual, and reached out to pluck a drink from a nearby servitor with a trembling hand. 'He's thrown a scare into our illustrious governor, at any event.'

'Has he?' Amberley watched him go. 'That seems a little presumptuous, even for a rogue trader.'

'If that's what he really is,' I said, without thinking. Those depthless blue eyes turned on me again.

'What else would he be?'

'An inquisitor,' I said, the idea taking firmer root in my head even as I said it. Amberley's eyes widened.

'An inquisitor? Here?' Her voice became a little tremulous, as though the enormity of the idea were too huge to grasp. 'What makes you think that?'

The urge to impress her was almost irresistible, I have to confess; and if you could only know how bewitching she was, I know you'd have felt the same. So I looked my most commissarial.

'All I can say,' I told her, lowering my voice for dramatic effect, 'is that I've heard from a reliable military source,' – which sounded a lot better than 'from a drunken idiot,' I'm sure you'll agree – 'that there are Inquisition agents active on Gravalax.'

'Surely not.' She shook her head, blonde tresses flying in confusion. 'And even if there were, why would you suspect Orelius?'

'Well, just look at him,' I said. 'Everyone knows that undercover inquisitors disguise themselves as rogue traders most of the time.[1] It's by far the easiest way of travelling incognito with the rabble of hangers-on they all seem to attract.'

---

1   It is indeed regrettable that this predilection has become so widely known. Personally, I blame popular fiction for perpetuating the stereotype, although it has to be said that some inquisitors are simply woefully lacking in imagination when required to adopt a disguise.

'You could be right,' she said, with a delicate shiver. 'But it's no concern of ours.'

Well, I couldn't agree more, of course, but that's not what my heroic reputation leads people to expect of me, so I put on my best dutiful expression and said 'The security of the Imperium is the concern of all of His Majesty's loyal servants.' Well, that's true too, and it lets me out, but no one needs to know that. Amberley nodded, sombrely, and trotted back to the stage, and I watched her go, cursing myself for an idiot for puncturing the mood.

As you'll no doubt appreciate, the rest of the evening promised to be anticlimactic, so I drifted back to the food and drink. Our rations back at the compound were adequate enough, but I wasn't going to pass up the opportunity to savour a few delicacies while they were there for the taking, and it was as good a vantage point as any to enjoy Amberley's performance from. It was also, as I'd learned from uncountable similar affairs, the best spot from which to cull gossip, since everyone gravitated there sooner or later.

Thus it was that I made the acquaintance of Orelius, without the faintest presentiment of the trouble that innocent conversation would lead to.

If anything, I suppose, it was the sling that was to blame. It had seemed a good idea at the time, but now I came to fill a plate the damn thing got in the way, preventing me from reaching out for the palovine pastries perched on the opposite side of the table. If I transferred the plate to my left hand I was turned awkwardly, my centre of mass shifted, so I still couldn't reach. I was trying to work out a way of getting to them when a thin arm reached across to pick up the dish.

'Allow me.' The voice was dry and cultured. I transferred a couple of the delicacies to my plate, and found myself addressing the man I'd almost convinced myself was an inquisitorial agent. It was ridiculous, of course, but still...

'Thank you, sieur Orelius,' I said. 'You're most kind.'

'Have we met?' His eyes were shadowed, the irises were almost black, and had an unnerving piercing quality that increased his resemblance to a bird of prey.

'Your reputation precedes you,' I said blandly, letting him make of that what he would. I don't mind admitting I was less relaxed than I tried to look. If he really was an inquisitor, there was a good chance he was a psyker, too, and might know me for what I was, but I'd encountered mindreaders before and knew that they weren't as formidable as most people thought. Most of them can only read surface thoughts, and I was so long practiced at dissembling that I did so without any conscious awareness of the fact.

'I'm sure it does.' He was an old hand at this game too, I realised, an essential skill whether his profession was as it appeared or as I had surmised.

'You seem to have the ear of His Excellency,' I said, and the first momentary flicker of emotion appeared on his face. I'd got in under his guard, it seemed.

'I have both. Unfortunately, His Excellency appears to lack anything between them.' He took one of the pastries for himself. 'He's paralysed with indecision.'

'Indecision about what?' I asked ingenuously.

'Where his best interests lie. And those of his people, of course.' Orelius bit into the delicacy as though it were Grice's neck. 'Unless he starts showing some leadership, this world will go down in blood and burning. But he sits and vacillates, and hopes it will all go away.'

'Then let's hope he comes to his senses soon,' I said. The keen eyes impaled me again.

'Indeed.' His voice was level. 'For all our sakes.' He smiled then, without warmth. 'The Emperor be with you, Commissar Cain.' My surprise must have shown on my face, because the smile widened a fraction. 'Your reputation precedes you too.'

And then he was gone, leaving me curiously troubled. I didn't have long to dwell on my unease, though, because the flunkey who'd announced our arrival was back, looking a little flustered. He'd called out a number of names since Kasteen and I had made our entrance, but it was clear that this time he expected to be listened to. He pounded a staff on the polished wooden floor, and the babble of voices gradually diminished; Amberley's trailed away in mid-chorus, which was a real shame. The flunkey's chest inflated with self-importance.

'Your Excellency. My lords, ladies, and gentlemen. O'ran Shui'sassai, Ambassador of the tau.'

And for the first time since arriving on Gravalax, I was face to face with the enemy.

FIVE

Treachery is its own reward.

Callidus Temple proverb.

ONE THING I'LL say for the tau, they certainly know how to make an impressive entrance. Shui'sassai was draped in a simple white robe, which made all the Imperial dignitaries look ridiculously overdressed, and was surrounded by others of his kind similarly attired. There was no mistaking who was in charge, though, as his charisma filled the room, his entourage bobbing in his wake as he strode confidently across the polished wooden floor towards Grice like seabirds around a fishing boat. I didn't realise at the time how apt the mental image was, of course.[1]

---

1 The ambassador, like all tau diplomats, would be one of the Water caste.

What I did notice almost at once was the bluish cast of his skin, and that of his compatriots, which I'd been led to expect from Divas's gossip and the various reports I'd read. What I hadn't expected was the single braid that grew from his otherwise hairless skull, plaited and ornamented with ribbons in a variety of colours which contrasted vividly with the plain simplicity of his garment. The meaning of the bizarre hairstyle sported by their human dupes, which I'd noted many times since our landing, thus became clear to me, along with the face paint the leader of the street gang had worn, and I found myself suppressing a shiver of unease. If so many citizens had been influenced so openly by these alien interlopers, the situation was dire indeed, and my chances of keeping well away from trouble, problematic at best.

It reminded me of something else, too, and after a moment I recalled the decoration Gorok the kroot had applied to the quills on his head. Clearly the races of the tau empire saw nothing wrong in absorbing the mores and fashions of one another's cultures, eroding their very identities in the name of their union, a notion any loyal Imperial citizen would have regarded with as much horror as I did. I'd seen at first hand what happened when traitors and heretics abandoned their humanity to follow the twisted teachings of Chaos, and the thought of how fertile a soil the warp-spawned abominations would find the Imperium if it were ever to become as unwittingly open to alien influence as the tau and their dupes chilled my very soul.

Shui'sassai's flunkies also had their single tail of hair ornamented, though slightly less flamboyantly, and I found myself wondering if the pattern denoted some subtle graduations of status among them, or were merely intended to be decorative.

'Smug little grox-fondler.' Donali was at my elbow again, the words delivered through almost motionless lips as he made brief eye contact with the xeno and raised his wineglass in greeting. 'He thinks he's got the whole planet sewn up.'

'And does he?' I asked, more out of politeness than actually expecting an answer.

'Not yet.' Donali watched as the xeno delegation made its ritual greeting to Grice. 'But he's certainly got the governor in his pocket.'

'Are you sure about that?' I asked. Donali must have detected something in my intonation because his attention switched to me at once, a sensation I found mildly disconcerting.

'You suspect he might be under... other influences?' he suggested, watching my face for a flicker of reaction. Well, good luck to him – a lifetime of dissembling had left me virtually impossible to read in that way. I indicated Orelius with a tilt of my head; he was watching the exchange between Grice and the tau diplomat warily, trying not to look as though he was paying it any attention.

'Our rogue trader friend had quite a conversation with His Excellency earlier this evening,' I said. 'And neither of them seem terribly happy about it.'

'You've spoken to Orelius?' Once again, I found myself in the middle of a verbal fencing match. Emperor's bowels, I thought irritably, doesn't anyone around here ever say what they mean?

'We exchanged a few words,' I said, shrugging. 'He seems to think the shooting's about to start–'

The bark of a bolt pistol going off echoed around the ballroom, and I dived for cover behind an over-stuffed sofa even before the rational part of my mind had identified the source of the sound. I may not be a paragon of virtue, but I like to think my survival instincts more than makes up for any moral short-comings I might possess.

Donali stood, gaping, as the room erupted in panic and screams. Half the guests started running in no particular direction, while the others stared around themselves in half-witted stupefaction. Priceless crys-tal goblets shattered underfoot as drinks were dropped and swords were unsheathed, and every kind of sidearm imaginable suddenly appeared in hands on every side.

'Treachery!' one of the tau shrieked, glaring around itself and drawing some kind of handgun from the recesses of its robes. Shui'sassai was down, thick purple blood everywhere, and I knew from experience that he wouldn't be getting up again.

The bolter round had exploded inside his chest cavity, redecorating the immediate vicinity with tau viscera, which I was mildly intrigued to note was darker in colour than the human equivalent;

something to do with the colour of their skin, I assumed.[1]

'Kasteen!' I activated the combead in my ear. 'Where are you?'

'Over by the stage.' I lifted my head, scanning the room, and located her as she scrambled up next to Amberley, who was gazing at the crowd as though mesmerised.

'Did you see where the shot came from?'

'No.' She hesitated a fraction of a second. 'My attention was elsewhere. Sorry, commissar.'

'No need to be,' I said. 'You weren't to know this was going to turn into a warzone.' In truth, that looked uncomfortably like what was happening. Practically everyone with a ceremonial sidearm had drawn it in a panic-stricken reflex, except for Kasteen and myself, and was looking for someone to use it on. Which meant identifying the assassin would be virtually impossible by now.

'Gue'la animals! Is this how you respond to proposals of peace?' The gun-waving tau was getting hysterical, swinging the weapon wildly. It was only a matter of seconds, I thought, before he pulled the trigger, or, more likely, someone else shot him before he had the chance. Either way, it was going to start a massacre, and I had no intention of getting caught in the middle of it.

---

1   The tau equivalent to haemoglobin contains cobalt, rather than iron, so their blood and viscera vary from dark blue to purple, depending on the degree of oxygenation. Don't even get me started about the smell.

'Lustig,' I voxed. 'Jurgen. We're leaving now. There may be resistance.'

'Sir.' Jurgen's voice was as phlegmatic as ever.

'Commissar?' Lustig's was inflected with the query he was too well-trained to ask. But I wasn't about to let the honour guard blunder into a firefight without warning. I was going to need them if I expected to get out of here.

'The tau ambassador has just been assassinated,' I said. Then I cursed my own stupidity. The channel wasn't secured, which meant every listening post on both sides had probably picked up my transmission. Oh well, too late to worry about that now. My main priority was getting the hell out of here in one piece. Unfortunately that meant getting past the tau delegation, which looked like it was becoming a fire magnet for every Imperial hothead in the room.

There was only one thing for it. With a curious sense of déjà vu, I strode forwards, my hands held out from my sides, away from my weapons.

Please bear in mind that barely a minute had passed by this time, and the room, was far from silent. Practically everyone was shouting at everyone else, and no one was listening. The rest of the tau were babbling away in their own language. It sounded like frying grox steaks to me, but the gist of it was obviously 'put that bloody thing away before you get us all shot,' and the other guests were screaming 'drop it!' at him and each other. I realised that with the tangle of competing factions and interests in the room there would be a complete bloodbath the moment anyone pulled a trigger. Which was probably what the assassin was counting on to cover his tracks.

'Colonel. With me.' Kasteen could cover my back, at least. I saw her slip off the stage and start towards me through the milling mob; Amberley had already disappeared, sensible girl.

'You! You did this!' The tau stuck the muzzle of his curiously featureless pistol under Grice's chin. The governor seemed to lose even more colour, if that were possible, and spluttered incoherently.

'That's ridiculous! What would I have to gain–'

'More lies!' The tau shrugged off the restraining hands of his colleagues. 'The truth, or you die!'

'This does not advance the greater good,' I said, echoing the words of the kroot. I wasn't quite sure what they meant, but I hoped they had more resonance for the tau than yet another variation on 'put it down before I shoot you,' which didn't seem to be having much effect.

It worked better than I'd dared to hope. Every tau in the group, including the maniac with the gun, stared at me with something I took to be astonishment. Their faces are harder to read than human or eldar, but it gets easier the more practice you have, and these days I can usually catch even the most carefully concealed half-truth.

'What the frak's that supposed to mean?' Kasteen subvocalised into my combead, breaking through the crowd to stand beside me. I noticed with a flicker of relief that she still hadn't drawn her weapons either, which was going to make things a lot easier.

'Warped if I know,' I responded, before stepping forward to where the xenos could get a better look at me.

'What do you know of the greater good?' the tau asked, lowering his weapon a fraction, but keeping Grice covered nevertheless. His companions hesitated, clearly wondering if it was safe to disarm him yet. Grice obviously thought otherwise, sweating more profusely than Jurgen reading a porno slate.

'Not much,' I admitted. 'But adding more deaths to tonight's piece of treachery won't help anyone, surely.'

'Your words have merit, Imperial officer.' One of the other tau spoke up cautiously, an eye on his gun-toting friend.

'My name is Cain,' I said, and a whisper of voices around me echoed it. 'That's him, that's Ciaphas Cain...' The reaction seemed to bemuse my new friend.

'You are well-known to these people?'

'I seem to have acquired something of a reputation,' I admitted.

'Commissar Cain is well-known as a man of integrity,' a new voice cut in. Orelius was edging his way through the crowd, flanked by his bodyguards. At a gesture from him, they holstered their bolt pistols.

'That's right.' Donali backed him up, taking the initiative back into official hands. 'You can trust his word.' Which didn't say much for his skills as a diplomat when you come to think of it, but then he didn't know me as well as I do.

'I am El'sorath,' the conversational tau said, extending a hand in human fashion. I took it, finding it slightly warmer than I'd expected; something to do with the blue skin, probably.

'Did your friend...?' I indicated the tau with the gun.

'El'hassai,' El'sorath supplied helpfully.

'Did anyone actually see who fired the shot?' I asked, directing the question to El'hassai personally, as though we were simply having a normal conversation. A flicker of doubt passed across his features for the first time.

'We were talking to this one.' The gun came up to point at Grice again. 'I heard Shui'sassai say "What—" and then the sound of the shot. When I turned back there was no one else there. It must have been him!'

'But you didn't actually see the murder,' I persisted. El'hassai shook his head, a gesture I assumed he'd learned from his long association with humans.

'It could have been no one else,' he insisted.

'Did you see the governor with a gun?'

'He must have concealed it.' True, Grice's overly ornamented robes might have concealed almost anything in their voluminous folds, but I tried to picture this indolent lump of lard drawing a pistol, killing the ambassador, and palming it again within a matter of seconds and fought to keep a smile off my face.

'There are hundreds of people in this room,' I said calmly. 'Isn't it more likely that one of them is responsible? Maybe a servant you simply didn't notice?'

'Vastly more likely,' El'sorath agreed, holding out a hand for the pistol. After a moment, El'hassai capitulated, and handed it to him. A collective sigh of relief echoed round the room behind us.

'This will be investigated,' Donali said, 'and the murderer brought to account. You have my word.'

'We are aware of the value of Imperial promises,' El'sorath said, with the barest trace of sarcasm. 'But we will make our own enquiries.'

'Of course.' Grice wiped his face with the sleeve of his robe, quivering like a plasmoid, and failing to recover a shred of dignity. 'Our Arbites will keep you apprised of everything we're able to uncover.'

'I would expect nothing less,' El'sorath said.

'We're in position, commissar,' Lustig said in my ear. Kasteen and I exchanged glances.

'What's it like out there?' she subvocalised.

'Panic and confusion, ma'am. And there seems to be something going on in the city.'

'Perhaps you'd better return to your compound,' Donali suggested to El'sorath, unaware of the ominous messages we'd been getting. 'My driver–'

'Wouldn't get fifty metres from the gate,' Kasteen put in. I switched frequencies to the tactical net, as I was sure she had, and heard a confused babble of voices in my ear. PDF units were mobilising in support of Arbites riot squads, and unrest was spreading across the city like jam across toast.

'What do you mean?' Grice quivered, looking around for a flunkey to blame. Palace security troops were finally beginning to deploy, guarding the exits, although I didn't expect much help from them if they actually had to defend the place. Lots of ceremonial gold armour which wouldn't stop a thrown rock, and old-fashioned lasguns with the ridiculously long barrels I'd only seen before in museums, and which probably hadn't been fired in the last couple of millennia.

'There are riots breaking out all over the city, Your Excellency.' Kasteen almost sounded as though she was enjoying breaking the bad news to him. 'Mobs are attacking the Arbites sector houses and the PDF barracks, denouncing the Imperium for the ambassador's murder.'

'How could they know?' Grice blustered. 'The news hasn't had time to spread...'

For a moment I wondered if my ill-timed transmission to Lustig had been the cause of all this, then common sense reasserted itself. There hadn't been time to disseminate the information even if someone had been listening. There was only one possible explanation.

'A conspiracy,' I said. 'The murderer had confederates who were spreading the rumour even before he struck. This wasn't just meant to disrupt the negotiations, it was supposed to signal a full-scale revolt.'

'More lies!' El'hassai had been quiet for the last few minutes, staring at the ambassador's corpse as though he expected it to sit up and start giving us the answers. 'You think we'd sacrifice one of our own to seize control here?'

'I think nothing,' I said carefully. 'I'm just a soldier. But someone's orchestrating this, Emperor knows why. If it's not your people, then maybe it's some Imperial faction trying to smoke out your supporters here.'

'But who would consider such a thing?' Grice burbled. I glanced at Orelius, my suspicions about him flooding back. The Inquisition was certainly ruthless enough, and had the resources to do it.

'That's for wiser heads than mine to determine,' I said, and for a moment, the rogue trader's gimlet eyes were on me.

'Our prime concern must be the welfare of your delegation,' Donali insisted. 'Can we get a skimmer into the grounds?'

'We can try.' El'sorath was keeping it together, at least. He produced some sort of voxcaster from the recesses of his robe, and hissed and sighed a message into it. Whatever the response was, it seemed to satisfy him, and calm the others, even El'hassai seemed a little less jumpy.

'An aircar has been dispatched,' he said, tucking the vox away. 'It will be with us shortly.'

'And in the meantime, my guards will ensure your personal safety,' Grice said, beckoning a few forward. The tau looked dubious at this.

'They were signally unable to do so in the case of O'ran Shui'sassai,' El'sorath pointed out mildly. Grice flushed a darker shade of grey.

'If anyone has a better suggestion, I'd be delighted to hear it,' he snapped, grabbing a large glass of amasec from one of the servitors which continued to circle the room, oblivious to all the commotion.

'I believe the commissar arrived with an honour guard,' Orelius said. 'Surely a man of his reputation can be trusted with so delicate a task.'

Thanks a lot, I thought. But with that reputation at stake, all I could do was mutter something about it being an honour I didn't deserve. Which was perfectly true, of course.

Donali and the tau were all for it, once the idea had sunk in, so I found myself leading a small gaggle of xenos and diplomats out of the hall, and into the open air. Lustig and the others came pounding up as we emerged, lasguns primed, and took up station around us.

'Be on your guard,' Kasteen warned them. 'The assassin's still at large. So trust no one, apart from us.'

'Especially the diplomats,' I added. Donali shot me a sharp look, and I smiled to pretend I was joking.

'I don't like it here,' I said quietly to Kasteen. 'It's too exposed.' She nodded agreement.

'What do you suggest?'

'There's a shrubbery over that way.' I pointed, blessing the instinctive paranoia that had had me looking out for boltholes on our drive in. 'It'll give us some cover at least.' It was also out of the pool of light surrounding the house, less exposed to prying eyes and sensor equipment.

So we scurried over to it, the troopers double-timing, and the tau keeping up with remarkable ease. Donali kept up with difficulty, but managed to converse with El'sorath the whole way, slipping between platitudes in Imperial Gothic and the sibilant tau tongue for what I assumed to be remarks too sensitive for the likes of us.

Not that I had the time to eavesdrop on their conversation, even if I'd had the inclination. Vox traffic on the tactical band was getting more urgent, the situation deteriorating rapidly.

'The governor's declared a state of martial law,' I relayed to Donali, who took the news remarkably well, only kicking two ornamental bushes to pieces before calming down enough to respond verbally.

'He would. Cretin.'

'I take it you don't think that will be helpful,' I commented dryly.

'It's about as helpful as putting a fire out with promethium,' he said. Even I understood the logic of that. The riots on their own were bad enough, but putting several thousand PDF troopers like the ones I'd encountered in the Eagle's Wing on to the streets, itching for an excuse to bust heads, was just asking for trouble. And that was assuming none of them were secretly xenoist sympathisers.

'So long as none of the PDF trolls take it into their heads to attack the tau...' I began, then trailed off, unwilling to complete the thought. The notion of the aliens being forced to defend themselves, unleashing the wargear Divas had enthusiastically described to me, was truly horrifying; because if that happened it was credits to carrots we'd be mobilised to stop them. And, aside from my natural desire to keep as far away from the killing zone as possible, I was by no means sure that we could.

'Our enclave is surrounded by agitated citizens,' El'sorath announced after another brief and incomprehensible conversation on his own vox. 'But overt hostilities have not yet occurred.'

Well, thank the Emperor for small mercies, I thought, and stepped aside to talk to Kasteen, who was still monitoring the tactical net.

'There's a mob of rioters heading this way,' she said. 'And a PDF platoon with orders to secure the palace grounds. When they get here it'll be bloody.'

I listened to the traffic myself for a few moments, overlaying the sitreps with my still somewhat hazy mental map of the city. If I was right, we had barely ten minutes before the slaughter began.

'Then let's make sure we're somewhere else,' I said. 'As soon as our little blue friends are airborne, we're leaving.'

'Commissar?' Kasteen was looking at me, a little curiously. 'Shouldn't we stay to help?'

Help a bunch of gold-plated nancy boys hold a virtually indefensible fixed position against a mob of blood-maddened lunatics? Not if I had anything to do with it. But I needed to put it a little more tactfully than that, of course.

'I appreciate the sentiment, colonel,' I said. 'But I suspect it would be very unwise politically.' I turned to Donali for support, unexpectedly pleased that the diplomat had hung around. 'Unless I'm misreading the situation, of course.'

'I don't think you are,' he said, clearly reluctant to agree with me. In his position, I wouldn't be too happy to see the only competent soldiers in the vicinity moving rapidly away, either. 'At the moment this is still an internal Gravalaxian matter.'

'Whereas if we get involved, we run the risk of bringing the rest of the Guard in behind us,' I finished. 'Which would be just as destabilising as a tau incursion.'

'I see.' Kasteen's face fell, and I suddenly realised that she'd been hoping for a chance to prove herself and her regiment. I smiled at her, encouragingly.

'Cheer up, colonel,' I said. 'The Emperor has a galaxy full of enemies. I'm sure we can find one more worthy of us than a rock-throwing rabble.'

'I'm sure you're right,' she said, though still with a faint air of disappointment.

Well, she'd just have to get over it. I switched channels again.

'Jurgen. Get over here now,' I voxed. 'We're going to have to leave in a hurry.'

'On my way, sir.' The growl of an engine preceded him, the large military truck ploughing parallel gouges in the immaculate lawn that would take generations of gardeners to completely erase; he swung it to a halt beside us with his usual disdain for the conventional use of brakes and gears.

'Good man.' I waved to my malodorous aide, who popped the cab doors, but kept the engine running. Time began to drag now. Lustig had fanned the troopers out into a textbook defensive pattern, making good use of the available cover, and I could see that the two fire-teams had set up in mutually supporting positions as Kasteen had intended. They looked tight and disciplined, their minds on the job, and with no trace of the old rancour I'd half feared would surface the first time any of our troopers found themselves in combat together.

Of course, they still had to face that ultimate test, but this was far more than an exercise, and they were still responding well. I began to feel reasonably confident about getting back to our staging area in one piece with them to hide behind.

'Listen.' Kasteen tilted her head. I strained to hear over the thrum of our truck's idling engine, but failed to hear anything else for a moment; then I could distinguish it, the faint susurration of a nulgrav flyer approaching at speed, the humming of its ducted fans quite different from the powerful roar of an Astartes speeder or an eldar jetbike. It was the first time I'd ever encountered tau technosorcery at first hand, and its quiet efficiency was subtly unnerving.

'There.' Donali pointed, his outstretched finger tracking the curved metal hull as it swept over us and swung around to align itself on the headlights of our truck. I breathed a quiet word of thanks to the Emperor, even though I was sure he wouldn't be listening, and turned to El'sorath.

'Bring them in,' I said, and watched while Lustig's troopers moved quickly and smoothly to cover the area of lawn next to us. 'It looks safe enough.'

One day, I'm going to learn not to say things like that. No sooner had the words left my lips, and the tau diplomat raised his vox to contact the pilot, than a streak of light rose from the streets beyond the perimeter wall.

'Holy Emperor!' Kasteen breathed, and I spat out something considerably less polite. I snatched the smooth plastic box from an astonished El'sorath.

'Evade!' I screamed, not even sure if the pilot spoke Gothic. Within seconds it was academic anyway. The missile impacted on the underside of the vehicle, punching through the thin metal plating, and exploded in a vivid orange fireball. Flaming debris began to patter down around us, but the burning wreck of the fuselage carried on moving, trailing down to impact harmlessly on one of the wings of the palace. As it struck, tearing through the walls, it set off a secondary explosion, probably the fuel or the powercells. The noise was incredible, making us flinch almost as though it were a physical thing, and I was blinking the afterimages clear of my retina for some moments to follow.

'What happened?' Donali stared in bewilderment, as screaming figures erupted from what was left of the palace.

'More gue'la treachery!' El'hassai screamed, glaring around as though he expected us to turn on him any second now. To tell the truth, it was getting more and more tempting every time he opened his mouth, but that wasn't going to get my skin out of here intact. My best chance of doing that depended on keeping Donali and the xenos sweet.

'I'm inclined to agree,' I said, shutting him up through sheer astonishment. 'It seems our assassin has confederates in the PDF.'

'How can you be sure?' Donali asked, clearly not wanting to believe it.

'That was a krak missile,' Kasteen explained. 'We're the only Guard unit in the city, and we didn't fire it. Who else does that leave?'

Well, too many possibilities for my liking, but there wasn't time to go into that now. I cut into the tactical net, using my commissarial override code.

'Krak missile fired in the vicinity of the governor's palace,' I snapped. 'Who's responsible?'

'I'm sorry, commissar, that information isn't available.'

'Then find out, and have the brainless frakker shot!' I was suddenly aware that my voice had risen. Kasteen, Donali, and the little group of tau were staring at me, their faces flickering yellow in the light of the burning palace. I hesitated, more considered courses of action beginning to suggest themselves. 'No, wait,' I corrected myself, to the evident relief of the unseen vox operator. 'Have everyone in that squad arrested and held for interrogation.' I bounced off Donali's questioning look.

'We don't know yet if it was someone panicking, a deliberate attack on the surviving tau, or just sheer stupidity,' I explained. 'But if it was an attempt to finish what the assassin started, it might lead us to the conspirators.'

'If you are able to identify the assailants.' El'sorath nodded, the human gesture strangely unsettling.

'If it is a conspiracy they'll have covered their tracks,' Donali predicted gloomily. 'But I suppose it's worth a try.'

'What I don't understand,' Kasteen said, frowning, 'is why they didn't wait until the aircar took off again. Surely if they wanted to kill the other tau, downing it on the run in was pointless.'

'No, colonel. It was exactly the point.' Sudden realisation hit me like a punch to the gut. One thing to be said for being paranoid is that sometimes you begin to see patterns no one else can. 'Killing the ambassador was meant to make them run. The mobs in the streets were meant to leave them with nowhere to go. They're supposed to have only one option now.'

'Call in their military to extract them.' She nodded, following my chain of reasoning. Donali put the last link in place.

'Bringing them into direct conflict with Imperial forces. The one thing we can't allow to happen if we're to have any hope of avoiding a full-scale war over this miserable mudball.'

'Then we must die.' El'sorath said, as though he'd been suggesting a stroll through the park. 'The greater good demands it.' His companions looked sober, but none of them argued.

'No.' Donali did, though; he wasn't about to have any little blue martyrs offing themselves on his watch. 'It demands that you live, to continue the negotiations in good faith.'

'That would be preferable,' El'sorath said. I was beginning to suspect that the tau had a sense of humour. 'But I see no way to effect so desirable an outcome.'

'Colonel. Commissar.' Donali looked at Kasteen and me a moment after a sudden sinking feeling in my gut warned me that this was about to happen. 'You have a vehicle, and a squad of soldiers. Will you try and get these people home?' For a moment, I struggled with the idea of the xenos as people. I suppose Donali's diplomatic training made him think a little differently from the rest of us[1], but I couldn't think of an excuse to refuse, try as I might. 'Not just for the good of the planet. For the Emperor Himself.'

Well, I'd pulled that one on enough people in my time to be aware of the irony, but it was an appeal I couldn't turn my back on without sacrificing my hard-won reputation, and even though I'd be the first to admit it's completely undeserved, it's proven its worth to me far too often to be casually discarded.

Besides, however unhealthy trying to smuggle a truck full of xenos through a city in flames was likely

---

1 'Going xeno,' as it's colloquially known, is an occupational hazard among diplomats who spend a lot of time in contact with an alien culture. The prolonged immersion in a foreign mindset sometimes leads them to identify closely with the beings they're negotiating with. In this case, however, it seems clear that Donali was just being polite.

to be, staying here to be caught in the crossfire
between rioters and the PDF looked like being a
whole lot worse. So I smiled my best heroic smile,
and nodded.

'Of course,' I said. 'You can count on us.'

Editorial Note:

Once again, as we might expect, Cain's account of this crucial
night's events is completely self-centred and lacking in any
wider perspective. I've therefore taken the liberty of inserting
another extract from Logar's history of the Gravalax incident,
which, like the one quoted earlier, provides a moderately accurate summary of the overall situation despite his manifest
shortcomings as a historian in almost every other respect.
Hopefully it may prove useful in placing Cain's narrative into
some kind of context.

* * *

From *Purge the Guilty! An impartial account of the liberation of Gravalax,* by Stententious Logar. 085.M42

With the advantage of hindsight, we can see how the conspirators had prepared the ground carefully for their coup d'etat, spreading rumours of the assassination so far in advance of its execution that few, if any, thought to demand proof of these claims when the deed was actually accomplished. Tension between the loyal subjects of His Divine Majesty and the turncoat dupes of the alien interlopers had by now become so pervasive that only the tiniest spark was needed to ignite an inferno of lawlessness which threw the entire city into disarray.

The greatest bloodshed of the night was to occur around the governor's residence, as the heroic palace guard held off a rampaging mob of turncoats with the aid of the most loyal cadre of PDF volunteers. Despite the appalling losses they endured, which were exacerbated by the treacherous defection of those perfidious PDF units who turned their weapons against their erstwhile comrades, these brave souls were able to hold out until daybreak brought relief in the shape of a loyalist armoured unit.

By the cruellest stroke of irony, it was later to transpire that one of the guests at the governor's reception earlier that evening had been none other than Commissar Cain, the paladin of martial virtues against whom no enemy could possibly have prevailed, but he had left shortly before the fighting broke out. This was a tragedy indeed, since his inspiring leadership would surely have turned the tide of battle, routing the unrighteous in short order! But alas, it was not to be, and those gallant warriors were left to their own, far from inconsiderable, resources.

Elsewhere, the situation proved equally grave. Widespread rioting choked the city centre, overwhelming the Arbites units posted there, until they had no option but to call in PDF units for support. Some responded loyally, while others, perfidious as their fellow traitors in the Old Quarter, revealed their true colours, turning against all that they had professed to hold dear, the insidious influence of the alien corrupting them utterly. Small wonder, then, that ordinary citizens took to the streets in their thousands, incensed at the sheer magnitude of this betrayal, armed only with their faith in the Emperor and such makeshift weapons as they could lay their hands on to wreak bloody revenge on the traitors in their midst.

The worst of the fighting took place in the Old Quarter, as we have previously noted, and, predictably, in the Heights, the most poisonous nest of pro-alien sentiment in the city, but in truth, no street was safe.

As the unrest continued, one question was paramount. Where were the Guard? Why did the Emperor's finest continue to sit in their barracks and staging areas while his loyal subjects bled and died in his name?

It was, and still is, clear that some hidden cabal was directing events, hindering the decisive action the situation manifestly called for, in pursuit of their own selfish agenda. In the years since, many theories have been put forward as to the true identities of those responsible, the vast majority of them laughably paranoid, but a careful sifting of the evidence can lead to only one conclusion; the unseen hand behind so much mayhem and treachery is unquestionably that of the rogue traders.

[At this point the narrative diverges, albeit quite amusingly, from anything resembling scholarship, or, indeed, historical accuracy.]

SIX

When in deadly danger,
When beset by doubt,
Run in little circles,
Wave your arms and shout.

– Parody of the Litany of Command, popular
among Commissar cadets.

WELL, I'VE SEEN my share of city fighting over the
years, and given my choice of battlefield, an urban
area's about the last one I'd pick. The streets channel
you into firelanes, every window or doorway can
conceal a sniper, and the buildings around you frak
up your tactical awareness – if they're not blocking
your line of sight they're distorting sounds, the overlapping echoes making it virtually impossible to

pinpoint where the enemy fire is coming from. In most cases the best thing you can say for it is that at least there aren't any civilians around to get caught in the crossfire, as by the time the Guard gets sent in they're either dead or have fled from the airstrikes and the artillery bombardments.

Mayoh that night was different. Instead of the piles of rubble I'd normally expect to find in an urban war-zone, the buildings were, for the time being at least, intact. (Although the ominous orange glow in the distance suggested that wasn't going to be true for much longer.[1]) And the streets were full. Not bustling, exactly, but by no means deserted either. As the truck gathered pace, we caught sight of civilians running for cover, to join or avoid the swelling groups of shouting rioters who seemed to be congre-gating at every corner. Some wore the xenoist braids, others symbols of Imperial loyalty. Aquilae were common, of course, and several of the loudest and most militant sported scarlet sashes, like the one which marked my own commissarial authority. Regardless of their nominal allegiance, however, most of the groups we passed were energetically engaged in breaking open the nearest storefronts and looting the contents.

1 Since Cain was already aware of the fire at the governor's palace, which eventually rased approximately two-thirds of the structure, he must have noticed one of the many smaller fires which broke out across the city that night. Despite his apprehension, few of them spread very far, and much of the urban infrastructure remained intact, for a short while, at any rate.

'Not much of an advertisement for the Imperial cause,' Kasteen muttered acidly in my ear. She was crammed in the cab with me, jammed up against the passenger door, as far from Jurgen as she could get. The wind of our passage ruffled her hair, the window wide open. Well, why not? The glass wasn't going to stop a las-bolt anyway, and I was even closer to our pungent driver than she was, so I wasn't about to object.

'Or theirs.' I indicated a mob of scalplocked xenoists running from a burning pawnbroker's, their pockets bulging with currency.

'Must be something to do with the greater greed,' she joked grimly.

As we approached, the xenoists recognised our truck as an Imperial military model and began to shout abuse. A few bottles and other makeshift missiles flew in our direction.

'Over their heads, Lustig,' I ordered. The squad of troopers in the cargo space behind us fired, just low enough to make the troublemakers flinch away from the crackling las-bolts, and they scattered as Jurgen put his foot down.

'Very restrained,' Kasteen commented. I shrugged. I couldn't have given a damn if the troopers had killed the lot of them, to be honest, but I was trying to make a good impression on our little blue guests, and there was always that reputation to consider.

We'd left the governor's palace as soon as we could get the tau aboard the truck, scrambling over the tailgate in the flickering light from the burning building.

Lustig's squad split into teams again, five on each side, leaving the xeno diplomats in the middle. It wasn't exactly high security, but it was the best we could do under the circumstances, and I hoped it would be enough.

'Good luck, commissar.' Donali's sober tone told me he thought we'd need it as he grasped my hand. I shook it firmly, thankful for the augmetics that prevented the tremors in my bowels from transmitting themselves as far as my fingers, and nodded gravely.

'The Emperor protects,' I intoned with pious hypocrisy, and climbed into the cab. At least with a box of metal and glass around me I was afforded some degree of shelter, and with Kasteen and Jurgen on either side to absorb any incoming fire, I'd be safer there than anywhere else. The Emperor, as I'd noted on more than one occasion, tends to extend his protection more readily to those who take as many precautions as possible for themselves.

Donali stood and watched us leave, silhouetted in the flickering light from the flames, and turned back towards the burning building as he passed out of sight. To my vague surprise, I found myself hoping he survived the night. I don't normally have much time for diplomats, but he struck me as a decent sort, and he seemed to be going to a lot of trouble to keep me from getting shot.

At least in the abstract; preventing a war wasn't going to do me a damn bit of good if some xenoist rioter stove my skull in with a paving slab this evening, so I was alert for any potential threat as we made our way through the troubled city.

'Left here.' Kasteen was guiding Jurgen with the aid of the tactical net, hoping to avoid the worst of the trouble. We passed a couple of street brawls, but the worst of the rioting appeared to be happening else-where.

'So far so good,' I said, tempting fate once more, and, typically, fate obliged. As we turned out of the alleyway into one of those broad thoroughfares which had so excited my unease on the journey into the city from the starport, I could see figures up ahead through the windscreen. Metal barrels had been pushed into the roadway, forming the spine of a makeshift barricade, and fires had been set inside a couple of them.

'Roadblock,' Jurgen said unnecessarily, and glanced at me for orders.

'Ease off,' I said, considering the situation. 'No point drawing their fire unless we have to.' Figures were moving slowly towards us, lasguns levelled, sil-houetted against the firelight. I squinted, trying to identify them. They wore plain fatigues, of a colour I couldn't quite identify in the yellowish glow, but which looked grey or blue, and light flak armour of an even darker shade[1].

1   Cain's memory might be playing him false here, as the standard uniform colour of the Gravalaxian PDF was actually magenta, with ter-racotta body armour. On the other hand, he might just have been confused by the firelight affecting his colour perception.

'PDF,' Kasteen confirmed after a moment listening to the tactical net. 'Loyalist, supporting the Arbites.'

'Thank the Emperor for that,' I said, and voxed Lustig. 'They're friendlies. Apparently.'

'Understood.' The sergeant's voice was calm, picking up on my qualification, and I was pretty sure the troopers would be ready if we turned out to be mistaken. Call me paranoid if you like, and I'll cheerfully admit to it, but I didn't get to an honourable retirement by having a trusting nature.

A single figure was stepping out in front of the truck now, a hand raised, and Jurgen coasted to a halt. I straightened my uniform cap, and tried to look as commissarial as I could manage.

'Who goes there?' He was young, I noticed, his face still pitted with acne scars, and his helmet looked too big for his head. A lieutenant's rank insignia had been painted in the centre of it, clearly visible; typical PDF sloppiness. The last thing you want in a firefight is an obvious sign saying, 'Shoot me, I'm an officer.' But then no one in the PDF ever really expects to go into combat, unless they make the grade the next time the Guard come recruiting, and that hadn't happened on Gravalax in generations.

'Colonel Kasteen, Valhallan 597th. And Commissar Cain.' Kasteen leaned out of the cab window to talk to him. 'Order your men aside.'

'I can't do that.' His jaw took on a stubborn set. 'I'm sorry.'

'Really?' Kasteen looked at him as though she'd just found him on the sole of her boot. 'I was under the impression that a colonel outranks a lieutenant. Isn't that so, commissar?'

'In my experience,' I agreed. I leaned past her to address the young pup directly. 'Or do you do things differently on Gravalax?' He paled visibly as I raked him with the number two glare.

'No, commissar. But I've been ordered not to let anyone past under any circumstances.'

'I think you'll find my authority supersedes any orders you may have been given,' I said confidently. His jaw worked convulsively.

'But the rebels are in control of the next sector,' he said. 'The tau are leaving their enclave–'

'Lies!' El'hassai jumped up on the flatbed behind us, now clearly visible to the young lieutenant and his PDF troopers. I was really beginning to suspect that the hot-headed tau had some sort of death wish, and one I'd be happy to grant if he carried on like this for much longer. 'They remain behind the boundaries we agreed!'

'Bluies!' The lieutenant swung his lasgun up to cover us. Behind the barricade his men did the same. To my intense relief Lustig and his troopers kept their cool, keeping their own weapons lowered, or there would have been blood spilt within a heartbeat. 'What's going on here?'

'You don't have the security clearance to know,' I said calmly, hiding my jangling nerves with the ease of years of practice. 'I'm ordering you in the name of the Commissariat to let us pass.'

'Traitors!' one of the PDF trolls shouted. 'They're xeno-lovers! Probably stole the truck!'

'Check with your superiors,' I said, calmly as before, loosening the laspistol in its holster below the level of the window. 'The Guard liaison office will confirm our identities.'

'Yes.' The young lieutenant nodded, trying to sound resolute, and wavered the barrel of his lasgun between Kasteen and me, unsure of which one of us to threaten. 'We'll do that. Right after you hand over the bluies.'

'String 'em up!' someone else yelled, probably the same idiot who'd shouted before. The tau began to look agitated.

'The xenos are under Imperial Guard protection,' I said levelly, taking heart from his obvious indecision. 'And that means mine. Stand aside in the Emperor's name, or face the consequences.'

I suppose I was to blame for what happened next. I'd got so used to being around Guardsmen, who accepted my authority without question, that it never even occurred to me that the young lieutenant wouldn't back down. But I'd reckoned without the PDF's relative lack of discipline, and the fact that to them a commissar was just another officer in a fancy hat. The fear and respect that normally goes with the uniform just wasn't there so far as they were concerned.

'Sergeant!' the lieutenant turned towards one of the troopers outlined by the firebarrels. 'Arrest these traitors!'

'Lustig,' I said. 'Fire.' Even as I spoke I was levelling the laspistol. The lieutenant's eyes widened for a fraction of a second as he began to turn back to us, the glint of vindictive triumph giving way to a momentary panic, and then half his face was gone as I squeezed the trigger.

I've killed a great many men over the years, so many that I lost count about a century back, and that's not even taking into account the innumerable xenos I've dispatched. And I've barely lost a night's sleep over any of them. It's usually been them or me, and I don't suppose they'd have been unduly troubled if things had gone the other way. But the lieutenant was different – not an enemy, or guilty of a capital crime – just stupid and overeager. Maybe that's why I can still picture his expression so vividly.

The troopers in the back of the truck raised their lasguns, snapping out a burst of rapid fire while the PDF were still in shock. Only a few had time to react, diving for cover as the bolts burst around them, and Jurgen floored the accelerator.

'Warp this!' Kasteen ducked as a lasbolt from the defenders scored the cab door beside her, and drew her bolt pistol.

'Take them all,' I ordered. If there were any survivors, they'd be on the vox net in moments, betraying our position to whoever might be listening, and marking us as a target to be hunted down by either side. I was within my rights, you understand, they'd refused a direct order, which was more than enough reason for any commissar to have done the

same, but I couldn't help thinking of the lengths I'd
gone to in order to avoid executing the five troopers
aboard the *Righteous Wrath* who deserved it far more
than these fools had.

No matter. Jurgen floored the accelerator and we
burst through the barricade, a tardy PDF trooper
falling beneath our wheels with a scream and an
unpleasant crunching sound vaguely reminiscent of
someone treading hard on a thin wooden box. The
first line of barrels scattered like skittles, spinning
away across the thoroughfare, clanging into the sides
of buildings and inflicting severe dents in the body-
work of the groundcars parked nearby. By the time
they stopped moving, most of the men opposing us
were already dead. Whatever skills they'd acquired in
basic training were pitifully inadequate in the face of
veteran troopers who'd fought a hive fleet and survived. A few tried to stand their ground, snapping off
hasty and badly aimed shots before the superior
marksmanship of the Valhallans blew bloody, self-
cauterising craters through heads and body armour.
A muffled curse over the vox link told me that one of
the troopers had been hit by the ragged return fire,
but if she was able to swear like that it couldn't be all
that serious.

'Hold on, commissar.' Jurgen gunned the engine,
and a jolt bounced through the truck as he
knocked one of the burning barrels in the second
rank aside. It spilled, blazing promethium spreading across the road behind us, consuming the
bodies of the dead.

'Runner.' Kasteen tracked her target with the bolt pistol and fired. A thin trail of smoke connected the barrel with the back of a fleeing PDF man, punching through his body armour, and exploding in a rain of blood and bowel.

'Nice shooting, colonel.' I tapped the combead. 'Lustig?'

'That was the last one, sir,' he said flatly. I could tell how he felt. Gunning down a virtually defenceless ally was hardly the blooding any of us would have chosen for our new regiment. But it had been necessary, I kept telling myself.

'Any casualties?'

'Trooper Penlan caught a ricochet. Just minor flash burns.'

'Glad to hear it,' I said. I hesitated. I needed to say something now, to maintain morale, but for once in my life my glib tongue had deserted me. 'Tell them... Tell them I appreciate what they just did.'

'Yes sir.' There was an unexpected note of sympathy in the sergeant's voice, and I realised that I'd said the right thing after all. They knew what was at stake here as much as I did.

We were silent for a long time after that. There was nothing to say, after all.

I'D HOPED THAT distressing incident would have been enough of a blood price to see our mission through, but of course, I'd reckoned without the insensate mentality of the mob. The divisions between the loyalist and xenoist factions had had generations to fester here, and the animosity ran deep. As we came closer to the tau enclave, we began to see signs of bloody faction fighting that would have looked less out of place in the underhive than the prosperous merchant city we were driving through. Bodies were lying in the streets, or, in a few cases, hung from luminator poles, loyalists and xenoists alike, but most of them were in no condition to determine allegiance, or, for that matter, very much else. Kasteen shook her head.

'Have you ever seen anything like this?' she asked, more in shock than because she expected an answer. To her visible surprise, I nodded.

'Not often.' And then only in the wake of a Chaos incursion or an ork attack. Never inflicted by ordinary citizens on their neighbours. I shuddered, reflecting on how close to the surface of the mundane world such savagery lurked, and how easily everything we fought to defend against it could be swept away if it wasn't for the ceaseless vigilance of the Emperor.

'Disturbance up ahead, commissar,' Jurgen said, easing up on the accelerator again. I peered through the windscreen. A baying mob filled the street, milling around a high wall with a huge bronze gate in the centre of it, blocking the thoroughfare. Even without the distinctive curving architecture I would have been sure we'd reached our destination.

'The perimeter of the tau trading enclave,' El'sorath confirmed when I retuned my combead to his portable vox. 'But gaining entry may prove problematic.'

'Problematic be warped,' I snapped undiplomatically. I hadn't come all this way and shed all that blood to be baulked this close to our goal. 'I'll get you in there if I have to throw you over the wall.'

'I doubt that gue'la muscles are sufficiently well developed,' the tau responded dryly. I'd been right, he did have a sense of humour. 'An alternative strategy would be preferable.'

'I have a plan,' Jurgen offered. I stared at him in surprise. Abstract thinking was never exactly his forte.

'A particularly devious one, no doubt,' I said. He nodded, immune to sarcasm.

'We could go through the gate,' he suggested. Kasteen made a peculiar noise, halfway between a snort and a hiccup.

'We could,' I agreed. 'Except that there's about a thousand rioters between us and it.'

'But they're all xenoists,' Jurgen said. 'So they'll just let us through, won't they?'

Well, they might have done, I thought, if we weren't wearing Imperial Guard uniforms and driving an Imperial Guard truck. But then again...

'Jurgen, you're a genius,' I said, with a little less sarcasm than before. 'Why frak around when the direct approach might work?' I voxed Lustig and El'sorath again. 'Can we get the tau somewhere visible?'

In a moment, the xenos were standing, flanked by the troopers, and El'sorath was hissing away on his vox again. Jurgen slowed the truck to a crawl, and blew the horn loudly to attract the crowd's attention.

A few heads turned in our direction, then more, as a sullen groundswell of hostility began to build. A couple of rockcrete chunks bounced from the windscreen, leaving small starred impact craters in the armourglass. Kasteen wound her side window up, clearly deciding that Jurgen's body odour was better than concussion, at least for a short while.

'Whenever you're ready,' I suggested, thankful I wasn't out in the open in the back of the truck. Maybe this wasn't such a brilliant idea after all, I found myself thinking.

'Please desist, for the greater good.' El'sorath must have had an amplivox function built into his 'caster, because his voice rang out across the crowd. To my amazement they complied, falling silent and parting in front of us. I contrasted it with the response of the crowd in Kasamar,[1] who'd charged our lines with berserk fury as soon as the Arbites commander had tried to address them, and wondered at the degree of influence the tau were able to wield over their supporters and one another.[2]

Jurgen rolled the truck to a halt in front of the huge gates, ten metres high and wide as the thoroughfare they blocked, just as they began to swing open. Eerily, they were completely noiseless, or at least so quiet I could hear nothing over the murmur of the

1   A minor civil insurrection, at which Cain had been present a few years before.
2   Still a subject of great interest to the Ordo Xenos, although investigation of this phenomenon remains frustratingly difficult.

crowd and the throbbing of our engine, even after Kasteen and I had disembarked to see our guests safely home. I noticed she breathed deeply once her boot-heels hit the rockcrete.

'What's that?' Lustig's voice crackled in my ear. Something small and fast swooped down from over the wall, heading in our direction, then several more, wheeling and diving like birds.

'Hold your fire,' I said hastily, fighting the urge to draw my own weapon. 'They're still on their side of the line.'

Well, technically, at least. They were still above the slope of the wall, even though they'd passed the crest. I tried to focus on the nearest one, but it was small and fast-moving, and all I got was a vague impression of something resembling a large platter with a rifle slung underneath it.

'A courtesy,' El'sorath assured me, hopping down from the flatbed with remarkable dexterity. 'To ensure your departure goes smoothly.'

Well, there was more than one way to take that, of course, but I chose to interpret it as a guarantee that the crowd would continue to behave themselves.

'Much appreciated,' I assured him, as the rest of the xenos clambered down and began trooping into their enclave. Armed warriors in body armour came forward to meet them, their faces hidden inside blank-visaged helmets. I caught sight of something else moving behind the gate, and turned my head for a better look.

'Dreadnoughts,' Kasteen breathed. They were certainly large enough for that, but they moved with an easy grace far removed from the lumbering war machines I'd encountered before. Their lines were angular, topped off with headpieces which resembled the helmets of their line troopers, but the resemblance ended with their size, towering at least twice the height of an ordinary tau.

'Just battlesuits,' El'sorath said, with a faint trace of amusement. 'Nothing special.'

Kasteen and I glanced at one another. I couldn't make out much detail at this distance, but they were clearly heavily armed, and the idea of facing a foe that fielded such things as a matter of course wasn't exactly comforting. I began to suspect that this was precisely the impression we'd been meant to get.

'I'm sure they're not,' I said, radiating an easy confidence I didn't feel, and enjoying the momentary flicker of doubt in the xeno's eyes.

'Go with your Emperor, Commissar Cain. You have our gratitude,' he said at last, and followed his friends inside. The gates began to swing closed.

'Time we were gone,' I said, hoisting myself back into the cab. Kasteen decided to ride in the back this time. Can't say I blamed her after getting the full benefit of Jurgen, so I suggested the wounded trooper Penlan rode back in the cab with us instead.

'Better safe than sorry,' I said, 'until we get back to the medicae at least.' So, despite her understandable reluctance, I was able to replace my human shield and enhance my reputation for concern about the troopers under my command at the same time.

And we'd succeeded in doing our bit to prevent a full-scale war from breaking out, which was no mean feat, so all in all I could have been forgiven for feeling a little smug as we made our way back to our own staging area. So why, instead, did I keep thinking about the PDF troopers we'd been forced to kill, and wondering whose plans we'd derailed by their sacrifice?

SEVEN

*The gratitude of the powerful is a heavy weight
to bear.*

– Gilbran Quail, Collected Essays.

DAWN BROKE AT last across the wounded city,
columns of smoke cracking the porcelain blue of
the sky above the compound as the sun rose higher
and ceased to echo the glow from the scattered fires,
and my mood remained foul all morning. To my
relief, we'd managed to make it back without having to shoot anyone else, apart from a couple of
looters who'd been so high on some vicious local
pharmaceutical they hadn't even realised the truck
they were trying to hijack was full of armed soldiers
until after they were dead, and all I wanted was a

few hours' sleep. I'd been so pumped full of adrenaline since the assassin's gun went off that, when I
finally got the chance to relax, I collapsed like a
puppet with its strings cut, and even Jurgen's
appearance with a fresh pot of tanna tea hadn't
been enough to revive me. Nevertheless I made my
report to brigade headquarters as quickly as I could,
reasoning that the sooner the whole sorry mess was
someone else's problem the better, and after an
hour or so of paperwork, crawled away to my bunk
with strict orders that I wasn't to be disturbed for
anything short of a summons from the Emperor
Himself.

In the event, I got about an hour's sleep before the
next best thing.

'Frak off!' I shouted, after the knocking on my door
had finally become loud and insistent enough to
wake me, and had gone on for long enough to convince me that it wasn't going to stop unless I
responded in some way.

'I'm sorry to disturb you, commissar.' Broklaw's
head appeared round the doorframe, looking
remarkably free of regret. 'But I'm afraid I can't. There
are some people wanting to see you.'

Tired as I was, I knew there was no point in arguing. The mere fact that it was an officer of his rank
rousting me out, instead of Jurgen or some other
lowly trooper, told me that. I yawned, trying to force
my sluggish brain into gear, and reluctantly rolled
out of bed.

'I'll be right there,' I said.

In the event that turned out to be a bit of an optimistic forecast. By the time I'd thrown some clothes on, splashed some water on my face, (and for once, the Valhallan habit of washing in ice water didn't provoke a stream of blasphemy from me, which gives you some idea of how far gone I was) and got Jurgen to brew some double-strength recaf, nearly twenty minutes had passed. But I followed the directions I'd been given, picking my way carefully across the compound (the Rough Riders were still around somewhere) and entered a building I'd vaguely recalled being earmarked for the brigade-level communications specialists. That meant Intelligence, of course, and I assumed I was about to be debriefed about the events of last night by some high-level spook.

If I hadn't been so tired, I would probably have wondered about the number of high-ranking officers in the echoing marble corridors, and the increasing opulence of the furnishings in the succession of anterooms I was waved through by dress-uniformed troopers with gold-plated lasguns, but it all passed in a haze of irritation, and I never thought to question where I was and who had sent for me so peremptorily.

'Commissar. Please, come in.' The voice was familiar, but, dazed as I still was from lack of sleep, it took me a moment to recognise Donali. He smiled what looked like a genuine welcome, and motioned me towards a side table where a fresh pot of tanna tea steamed invitingly next to several large platters of food.

I smiled in return, equally pleased to see him, although his night's adventures had obviously been at least as traumatic as my own. His expensive attire was now crumpled and stained, smelling of smoke and blood, and a dressing patch was stuck to his forehead.

'This is an unexpected pleasure,' I said, spooning a large portion of salma kedgeree onto a plate, and pouring tea into the most capacious mug I could find. 'I must admit I was rather concerned for your safety.'

'You weren't the only one.' Donali fingered the dressing patch ruefully. 'Things got a little hectic after you left.'

I took a seat at the conference table in the middle of the room. Several officers I didn't recognise were already there, along with other men and women in civilian dress. The latter I assumed to be Donali's colleagues, from the cut of their garments and their general air of bureaucratic prissiness. The only one who stuck out from the crowd was a woman slightly younger than the others, who wore an elegant green gown a couple of sizes too small for her, which showed rather too much décolletage for so early in the day, and who seemed curiously distracted, twitching and mumbling to herself from time to time before snapping upright and glaring round at the rest of us as though we'd somehow insulted her. I'd have taken her for an astropath, if it weren't for the fact that she still had her eyes, which seemed to swim in and out of focus. Probably a psyker, then – I resolved to keep my mental barriers up – but as I've remarked before, I've never had much trouble dissembling in front of them despite their curse.

'Sorry I missed all the fun,' I said, playing up to the audience's expectations of me, and started in on the food. I still had no idea why I was here, but I was a seasoned enough campaigner to make the most of the rations while they were on offer. While I plied my fork, I took the opportunity to study the officers' insignia, hoping for some clue as to their identities and why I was there, and found them a mixed bunch indeed.

My gaze swept across a couple of majors, a colonel, and as I got my first good look at the man seated at the head of the table, I almost dropped my cutlery. This could only be Lord General Zyvan himself, the supreme commander of our little expedition. I hadn't seen any pictures of him, but his rank and campaign medals were clearly visible, and I'd heard enough descriptions of his steely blue eyes (actually slightly watery) and neatly trimmed beard (concealing the beginnings of a double chin) to have no doubt as to his identity. He was half turned away from me, discussing the contents of a dataslate with an aide, and Donali was able to continue our conversation as he dropped into the seat beside me.

'Don't be,' he said. 'You did us a far greater service last night than you could possibly have done by staying.'

'I'm glad to hear it,' I said. 'But you seem to have managed all right. The palace guard must be better soldiers than they look.'

'Hardly.' He shook his head in disgust. 'Half of those antique weapons of theirs malfunctioned, and the ones who did shoot couldn't hit the side of a starship. We barely held out until the PDF platoon arrived. If it hadn't been for Orelius and his bodyguards picking off the ringleaders, the mob would have rolled right over us.'

'Orelius. Hm.' I took a welcome sip of the tea, and noticed that no one else seemed to be drinking it. Well, it's an acquired taste, I admit, I'm one of the few non-Valhallans I know who likes the stuff, but the implication was flattering; they'd clearly provided it for my personal benefit. Whatever I'd been called here for they wanted to keep me happy, which was fine by me. 'You were right about him, obviously.'

'I was?' Donali looked at me curiously, and again I felt he was playing some subtle diplomatic game. Trying to gauge how much I'd surmised of what was going on behind the scenes, I supposed. I nodded, clearing the plate, and wondered if I could get away with going back for another portion.

'You said there was more to him than met the eye,' I reminded him.

'So I did.' He might have been about to say more, but Zyvan turned back to the conference table and cleared his throat. Blast, I thought, there goes my chance at a second helping of kedgeree. There was still plenty of tea in the mug, though, so I sipped at it, regarding the room through a haze of pleasantly scented steam.

'Commissar.' Zyvan addressed me directly. 'Thank you for joining us so promptly.'

'My lord general.' I nodded a formal greeting. 'If I'd known your chef was so talented I would have been even less tardy,' I added, enjoying the sudden intake of breath from around half those present. A commissar, of course, is outside the normal chain of command, so technically I didn't have to show deference to him or to anyone else, but most of us do our best not to remind the officers around us of the fact. As I like to tell my cadets these days, treat them with respect and they'll do the same to you. All frak, of course, but it greases the wheels. My status as a widely acknowledged hero allows me a bit more latitude, though, and I knew Zyvan had a reputation for bluntness himself, so I felt a bit of the bluff old soldier routine would go down well with him. I was right, too. He warmed to me at once, and we got on like a downhive bar brawl after that.

'I'll pass on your compliments,' he said with a half-smile, and the sycophants around the table decided they ought to like me too. 'If you'd care to avail your-self further before we proceed?'

'Proceed with what, exactly?' I asked, moving to refill my plate. I'd forgotten to take my mug with me, so I took the teapot back to the table and topped it up there, keeping it beside me in case I wanted another refill. Partly, I admit, for the pleasure of upsetting some of the bootlickers again. 'Anyone else, while I'm up?'

'Thank you, no.' Zyvan waited until I'd sat down again before deciding he'd like some more recaf after all, and dispatching the most disapproving-looking of his aides to deal with it. As he did so his eye caught mine, and the gleam of mischief in it was unmistakable. I decided I liked the lord general.

'I've been reading your report,' he said, once his recaf had arrived. 'And I think I speak for everyone here when I say that I'm impressed.' A chorus of mumbled assent rippled around the table, not all of it grudging. Donali smiled warmly at me as he nodded, and I reflected that I seemed to have found a friend in the diplomatic corps, which could be very useful in future. The strange woman in green met my eyes for a moment.

'Choose your friends carefully,' she said suddenly, her voice harsh with flattened vowels. I almost choked on my tea.

'I beg your pardon?' I said. But her gaze was already unfocussed again.

'There's too many out there,' she said. 'I can't hear them all.' One of the bureaucrats handed her an ornate silver box, a little smaller than her palm, and she scrabbled a couple of tablets out of it, swallowing them whole. After a moment her attention seemed to sharpen again.

'You'll have to make allowances for Rakel,' Donali murmured. 'She's useful, but can be a little difficult.'

'Evidently,' I replied.

'Not quite the envoy I would have chosen to send to this little get-together,' the diplomat went on, 'but under the circumstances I suppose they needed her talents the least at the moment.'

'Who did?' I asked, but before he could reply Zyvan called the meeting to order.

'Most of you know why we're here,' he began, with a sip at his recaf. 'But for those of you who are new to these discussions,' and he acknowledged me with a conspiratorial quirk of his mouth, 'let me reiterate. Our orders were to reclaim Gravalax for the Imperium, by force of arms if necessary.' The military officers harrumphed approvingly. 'However, the sheer size of the tau military presence here changes the situation radically.'

'We can still throw them out, my lord general.' One of the officers cut in. 'It would take longer than we'd anticipated, but–'

'We would end up mired in a protracted campaign. Maybe for years.' Zyvan cut him off dismissively. 'And, to be blunt, I doubt the planet is worth it.'

'With respect, lord general, that isn't your decision to make,' the officer persisted. 'Our orders are–'

'For me to interpret,' Zyvan said. The officer shut up, and the general turned to Donali. 'You still believe a diplomatic solution is possible?'

'I do.' Donali nodded. 'Although, with the civil unrest persisting, it may prove more difficult. Not to mention the matter of the ambassador's assassination.'

'But the tau are still willing to negotiate?' Zyvan persisted.

'They are.' Donali nodded again. 'Thanks to Commissar Cain's resourcefulness last night, we still have a residue of good faith to draw on.'

Everyone but Rakel, who seemed more interested in the underside of her recaf cup, looked approvingly at me.

'Which brings me to the assassination itself.' Zyvan tried to attract the woman's attention. 'Rakel. Has the inquisitor made any progress in the investigation?'

I suppose I should have expected it, especially after my suspicions about Orelius the previous night, but I'd still been half inclined to dismiss them as the result of Divas and his drunken fantasies getting lodged somewhere in my brain. I stared at Donali.

'You knew about this?' I murmured.

'I suspected,' he replied, sotto voce. 'But I didn't know for sure until Rakel turned up this morning with a message bearing the inquisitorial seal.'

'What did it say?' I whispered, ignoring the young psyker's attempts to reply. Donali shrugged.

'How should I know? It was addressed to the lord general.'

'The investigation continues. Yes.' Rakel nodded eagerly, forcing herself to concentrate with a visible effort, her flat, nasal voice grating against my sleep-deprived nerves. 'You will be informed. When the conspiracy is exposed.' She paused, cocking her head as though listening to something, and stood abruptly. 'Have you got cake?' She wandered over to the food table to check.

'I see.' Zyvan tried to look as though she'd made some kind of sense.

'If I may, lord general.' I spoke up, trying to sound confident. 'I suspect that there may be a faction here with an interest in provoking conflict between us and the tau.'

'So messire Donali informs me.' Zyvan seized the opportunity to return the meeting to business with barely concealed relief. 'Which is the main reason I invited you to join us. Your reasoning appears sound.'

'No cake. No frakking cake!' Rakel muttered in the background, scuffling around the food table. 'I can't eat that, it's too green...'

'Thank you.' I acknowledged the compliment, and tried to ignore her.

'Does it extend as far as to who might be responsible?' Zyvan asked. I shook my head.

'I'm a soldier, sir. Plots and intrigue aren't really my specialties.' I shrugged. 'Perhaps the inquisitor can enlighten us when his enquiries are complete.'

'Perhaps.' Zyvan looked a little disappointed, no doubt hoping I could have helped him to second-guess the inquisition. Rakel returned to her seat, clutching a cyna bun, which she proceeded to nibble at for the rest of the meeting; at least with her mouth full she kept quiet.

'The other reason I wanted to consult you, commissar, is that you've met Governor Grice. What's your assessment of his understanding of military matters?' I shrugged.

'About as good as his understanding of anything else, if I'm any judge. The man's an imbecile.' More indrawn breaths around the table, but Zyvan and Donali nodded their agreement.

'I thought as much,' the lord general said. 'Although you'll no doubt be gratified to hear that he was very impressed with you.'

'He was?' I couldn't imagine why, until Donali spoke.

'After all, you did save his life last night.'

'I suppose I did,' I said. 'I hadn't really thought about it.' Which was perfectly true; I'd disarmed the tau to save my own skin, and so much had happened since then it had driven almost everything else out of my mind. Luckily, this was exactly the sort of thing everyone expected me to say, so I had the unexpected pleasure of receiving a warm smile of approval from one of the most powerful men in the Segmentum. Of course, that would come back to haunt me in time, which only goes to prove that no good deed ever goes unpunished.[1]

'Well, he's been thinking about you,' Donali said. 'He wants to give you some sort of medal.[2]'

1   From this point on Zyvan took a personal interest in Cain's career, eventually appointing him to his personal staff. This in turn led to a number of life-threatening incidents which are recorded elsewhere in the archive.

2   The Order of Merit of Gravalax, second class. In later years Cain was to joke that if he'd let the tau shoot Grice after all, the grateful populace would probably have given him the first class decoration.

'That may have to wait,' Zyvan said. 'We've a more urgent problem to deal with right now.' He touched a control stud on the arm of his chair, and the surface of the table lit up from within, proving to be a hololithic display of a size and resolution I'd seldom seen before. If I'd realised, I'd have been a bit more careful with the teapot. I wiped the ring of beverage away with my handkerchief as the image flickered drunkenly in the air before me, finally steadying into decipherability as Zyvan leaned forward and banged the tabletop hard with a clenched fist. He must have spent considerable time with the techpriests, because it functioned perfectly after that, staying sharp and in focus more than half the time.

'That's the city,' I said, stating the obvious. Rakel nodded, spraying crumbs across the image like block-sized meteors.

'All the little people look like ants,' she said, resting her head on the tabletop. The scale was far too small to show individual people, of course, or vehicles, even ones the size of a Baneblade, but she was bonkers, after all. 'Scurry, scurry, scurry. Looking up when they should be looking down. You never know what's under your feet, but you should, 'cause you could trip up and fall.'

I ignored her, picking out the salient tactical information with the instinctive ease of years of practice.

'There's still fighting going on.' I could see a handful of hotspots across the city. 'Haven't the Arbites managed to restore order yet?'

'Up to a point.' Zyvan shrugged. 'Most of the civilian rioters have either been arrested, shot, or got bored and gone home. The big problem now is the rebel PDF units.'

'Can't the loyalists sort them out?' I asked. It seemed obvious from where we were sitting that the xenoists were outnumbered at least three to one in most cases. Zyvan looked disgusted.

'You'd think so. But they're bogging down. Half of them are refusing to fire on their own comrades, and the rest might just as well not be bothering for all the good they're doing.' He hesitated. 'So the governor has, in his infinite wisdom, petitioned the Guard to go in and clean up his mess for him.'

'But you can't!' Donali was aghast. 'If the guard mobilise in the city the tau will too! You'll spark the very war we're trying to prevent!'

'That hadn't escaped my notice,' Zyvan said dryly.

'The man's a cretin!' Donali was fuming. 'Can't he see the consequences of his actions?'

'He's panicking,' I said. 'All he can see now is the prospect of the rebellion spreading. If the xenoists in the general population join them–'

'We're frakked,' Donali said.

'Not quite.' Zyvan compressed his lips into a grim parody of a smile. 'I can still play for time. Briefly. Can you use it to convince the tau that any Guard deployment in the city is no threat to them?'

'I can try,' Donali said, without much enthusiasm. Zyvan nodded encouragingly.

'I can't ask for more than that.' He turned to me. 'Commissar. Would you say that the tau have reason to trust you?'

Well of course they didn't, but that wasn't what he wanted to hear, so I nodded judiciously.

'More than most other Imperial officers, I suppose. I did save them a bit of a walk last night.' As I'd expected, my modest joking at my own expense went down well, fitting these idiots' idea of a hero. Zyvan looked pleased.

'Good,' he said, and turned back to Donali. 'You can inform the tau that Commissar Cain will be overseeing the operation personally. That might allay their concerns.'

'It just might.' Donali looked a little happier at the prospect. Which is more than I was, you can be sure. After all I'd been through the night before, the prospect of being sent back to the firing line again was agonising.

But I was supposed to be a hero after all, so I sat there impassively sipping tea, and wondered how I was going to get out of this one.

EIGHT

*Inquisitors? They're sneaky bastards. Useful, yes,
even necessary, but I wouldn't buy a used aircar from
any of them.*

– Arbitrator General Bex van Sturm.

IN THE END, of course, I had no choice but to go along
with it. The lord general himself had picked me for
this mission, so all I could do was hope for the best
and prepare for the worst. Fortunately, Donali's
negotiations with the tau gave me a bit of a breathing space, and I was able to devise a plan of action
which gave everyone the impression of leading from
the front while staying sufficiently far back from the
firing line to appreciate the full tactical overview. Kasteen and Broklaw had been fired with enthusiasm as

soon as I took them into my confidence, certain that the lord general's special interest in me boded well for the future of the regiment, so I was able to let them take the lead without really seeming to. Between us, we'd come up with a plan which actually looked like it might work, at least, if the bluies (as the troopers had begun to refer to the tau, picking up on the local slang) could be persuaded not to take our incursion into the city in bad faith. That, of course, was a question only the Emperor could answer, and he was otherwise engaged, so I just thumbed my palm[1] and got on with the things I could do something about.

Even then, I couldn't quite shake the suspicion that we were overlooking something important, that whatever shadowy cabal was trying to ignite a full-scale war on this worthless mudball wasn't about to give up that easily, but thinking about it only worried me, so I tried to forget it. For the life of me I couldn't see what anyone could hope to gain by forcing a confrontation, and unless you know what your enemies are after, you can't devise any counter-measures to their plans. I don't mind admitting that it irked me a little. I'm used to my innate paranoia keeping me a jump ahead of most things, but even Chaos cultists generally have an agenda of sorts (even if it's just 'kill everything on the planet') which

---

1 A gesture used on many worlds in the segmentum to bring good luck or ward off misfortune. The thumb is pressed into the palm of the hand, leaving the fingers to form a stylised aquila wing.

makes itself obvious after a while. Still, that's what
we have inquisitors for, so I wished Orelius the best
of Imperial luck and gave up thinking about it in
favour of the best way to give the rebellious PDF
units a bloody nose. This was just as well, I suppose.
If I'd had a clue as to what was really going on I'd
have lost even more sleep, believe me.

'They couldn't be making it easier for us if they
tried,' Broklaw said with some satisfaction as he
looked at the hololith. I'd prevailed on the lord general to lend us the conference suite he'd summoned
me to before, citing the need to co-ordinate the input
of more than one regiment, and Broklaw was as
pleased with the tabletop display unit as a juvie with
his first set of toy soldiers. I half expected to find it
smuggled aboard the troopship when we departed.
He gestured at the disposition of the xenoist units.
'What's that phrase you artillerists use? Clusterfrag?'

'Close enough.' Colonel Mostrue of the 12th Field
Artillery nodded curtly, his ice blue eyes, as always,
regarding me with something akin to suspicion.
Throughout my posting to his unit he'd always tried
to give me the benefit of the doubt, but of all the battery officers I've come across, he'd come closest to
guessing the truth about Desolatia, and never quite
seemed to trust me after that. Which was extremely
sensible of him when you think about it. Certainly,
he'd responded with almost indecent haste on the
few occasions I'd been forced to call in a barrage
close to my own position, but, in turn, I'd preferred
to think he was just doing his job as efficiently as

possible. He hadn't changed a bit in the years since I'd seen him last, unlike the visible marks the passing of time had left in Divas. The major was with him too, still limping slightly after our brawl with the xenoist supporters a week or so ago, and grinned at me with the same unrestrained enthusiasm he always displayed.

'It'll be like shooting fish in a barrel,' he declared confidently.

'For you, maybe,' Kasteen said. 'But we'll be where the fish can shoot back.' The xenoists were lightly armed, for the most part, with nothing much stronger in terms of firepower than missile launchers, so the artillery unit wouldn't have to worry about return fire, but unfortunately they'd had enough sense to dig in, for the most part in the area around the Heights. That meant winkling the survivors of the barrage out building by building, which would be hard, bloody work if things didn't go well. Fortunately, Kasteen and Broklaw's experience of urban fighting was just what was needed here, and I hoped the men and women of the 597th would find the PDF defectors easy meat after the tyranids they'd faced on Corania.

'We'll keep their heads down for you,' Divas promised. 'All you'll need to clean them up afterwards is a mop.' Kasteen and Broklaw exchanged glances, but let it go. Divas might have had only the vaguest idea of what city fighting entailed, but he did know his artillery, and I'd spent enough time with his unit to understand his confidence. The xenoist defectors had gradually linked up as they pulled back to the Heights, packing tighter and tighter into the network of boulevards and parkland around the mansions, until they might just as well have been standing there with a big target painted around their perimeter.

'It's all a little too neat for me,' I said. 'You'd think they'd have had the sense to disperse.'

'Amateurs.' Mostrue's contempt was obvious. Like most senior guard officers, he had a low opinion of the majority of PDF regiments, although I'd come across a few in my time who could have given a Guard unit a run for their money. In this case, though, his opinion seemed more than justified. A heavy barrage would take out the majority, I had no doubt. Of course, the survivors would be well dug in and hard to shift, especially with all that fresh rubble to burrow into, but I couldn't see there being too many of them. Certainly nothing the 597th couldn't handle in pretty short order.

Even allowing for the defectors' lack of experience, though, it seemed remarkably stupid of them to offer so tempting a target, and the tingling sensation was back in my palms. I tried to concentrate on the briefing, and not think about the undercurrents of conspiracy I was sure Orelius was tracking down even as we sat here. I had hoped to set my mind at rest by interrogating the PDF idiots who'd shot down the tau aircar, and determining once and for all whether it had been a simple act of stupidity or part of a more sinister agenda, but despite my order to arrest them, the perpetrators had simply vanished. Or joined the defectors, which raised even more questions I wasn't sure I wanted the answers to.

'What do you make of this?' Broklaw asked, studying the display more closely. I followed the line of his finger, to where a platoon of loyalist PDF troopers had cordoned off a couple of blocks of an industrial zone near the Old Quarter, and shrugged.

'The local boys afraid to get their fingers dirty.' The icon at the centre of the cordon marked a hostile contact, but they didn't seem to be in any hurry to close the noose. Presumably some stragglers, too late to join the exodus to the Heights, I thought. That was followed by the sudden realisation that I could use this little anomaly to my advantage.

'I'll swing by and see if I can buck their ideas up,' I said. 'It's not far out of our way.' And by the time I'd finished the extra piece of makework I'd just found for myself, Kasteen and Broklaw should have the xenoist survivors pretty much dealt with. If all went well, most of the dust would have settled before I got anywhere near the firing line. It seemed my luck hadn't deserted me after all.

'Are you sure, commissar?' Kasteen was looking at me curiously, and that old expression was back in Mostrue's eyes. 'It doesn't seem all that important. Surely it can wait until we've dealt with the main force?'

'It probably can.' I shrugged. 'But the lord general himself is trusting me to clean up this mess. I don't want a nucleus of rebellion left to deal with after we've broken the back of the conspiracy. I'd feel a lot happier if we knew for sure they weren't going to break out before we can get to them.'

'Good point.' She nodded. I decided it was time to lighten the mood, and smiled.

'Besides,' I said, 'It's not as though any of you need your hands held. I think you know one end of a las-gun from another by now.'

Kasteen, Broklaw and Divas laughed, and Mostrue essayed a wintery grin.

'I'd rather not divide our force, though,' Kasteen added. 'If we're going to mop up the bluie-lov... The xenoist sympathisers, I want to keep our net tight.'

'Agreed,' I said. 'We'll stick to the timetable. I'll just peel off, put the fear of the Emperor into the PDF drones guarding the perimeter to make sure none of the rebels inside escape while we're busy, and catch up. I should be back with you before the fun begins.'

'I'd put money on it.' Kasteen smiled. 'I've seen the way Jurgen drives.'

She would have lost the bet, of course. I was going to make damn sure I got delayed sorting out the PDF rabble until after the shooting stopped. That was the plan, anyway. If I'd known what I was letting myself in for as a result of that little diversion, I'd have led the charge into the Heights in a heartbeat.

DONALI FINALLY CONTACTED us about an hour after noon, saying the tau weren't exactly happy at the prospect of Imperial Guard units running rampant in the city, but so long as I was there to keep an eye on things and we stuck to the plan they'd been shown, they'd let us get on with it without interference. Of course, the language was a bit more diplomatic than that, but you get the gist. I was also aware of the subtext, even before Donali helpfully spelled it out for me, that if they got so much as a sniff of treachery they'd be on our backs with guns blazing before you could say 'fubar'.

So as you can imagine, I was feeling somewhat under pressure as the force of which I was titular head left our compound and entered the city, so much so that I wasn't even able to enjoy the unique position I found myself in.[1]

As I said before, I'd had the sense to let Kasteen and Broklaw make the tactical decisions, as their experience of city fighting was rather more practical than mine, so I was pretty confident we had the right mix of resources to achieve our goal. Reasoning that the ground would be pretty chewed up by the time the artillery had finished (which I could attest to from personal experience after my time with the 12th), they'd suggested going in on foot, with a troop of Sentinels for heavy fire support. That sounded good to me, as the walkers would have a

1 Cain is mistaken in his assumption that his position was unique. It was by no means unprecedented for a commissar to be given direct command of an ad hoc task force when circumstances demanded it, although it was, and is, an extremely rare occurrence. In fact, there is at least one instance on record of a commissar being given overall command of an entire regiment for a period of several years; albeit with the dual rank of colonel to facilitate the paperwork.

devastating psychological effect on the shell-shocked survivors of the barrage, or, at least, I hoped so. Taking the Chimeras in close was right out, their tracks would be shredded in moments once they entered the rubble, but if they held back on the perimeter after debarking their troopers, their heavy bolters would certainly encourage any rebels still inclined to make a fight of it to keep their heads down.

We'd debated about bringing in an armoured unit too, but decided against it. A couple of Leman Russes would have made little difference against dug-in infantry, especially after Mostrue's Earthshakers had finished doing their stuff. And it would have meant bringing another regiment into the operation. Given the delicacy of the situation, I wanted to keep the opportunities for fouling things up to a minimum, and my paranoia was tingling again, warning me not to spread our plans any further than we needed to. Besides, tanks would have slowed us down, and the key to this operation was speed. Especially if I wanted it to be all but over by the time I arrived.

'The harder and faster you go in, the better,' I concluded my briefing speech, breaking off to glare at Sulla, who'd whispered something to her neighbour and giggled. 'Are there any questions?'

There weren't, which meant the plan was either brilliant or so fatally flawed no one could spot it, so I made one of the standard encouraging speeches I'd been trotting out by rote since the head of my old scholar had presented me with my scarlet sash and told me to get lost, and dismissed the sergeants and officers who started to trickle back to their squads. I caught Lustig's eye, and he grinned at me. I'd made sure his squad were assigned to the centre of the battle line, as I thought getting stuck into a proper stand-up fight would be good for their morale. Gunning down the PDF loyalists had left a sour taste in their mouths, I knew, although they were good enough soldiers to have appreciated the reasons for it. A couple had been to talk to the chaplain, but all in all, they'd held up remarkably well. I knew if they were left with time to brood on it, though, their morale might start to suffer, so it had seemed prudent to take steps quickly before the rot had a chance to spread.

'I take it you approve, sergeant,' I said. One of the most important things I'd found over the years, and which I try to instil in my cadets these days, is that you should always take the time to talk to the troopers as individuals. You'll never make friends of them, except possibly a couple of the officers if you're lucky, and you'll never get the job done if you try, but they'll follow you a damn sight more readily if they think you care about them. And what's far more important, at least to me, is that, if they start to think of you as one of their own, they'll watch your back when the shooting starts. I've lost count of the number of times one of the grunts around me has taken out a xeno or a traitor who would have put a round in my back before I even noticed them, and I've returned the favour, too, which is why I'm well into my second century while the graveyards are full of by-the-book commissars who relied on intimidation to get the job done.

'It's a good plan, sir.' Lustig nodded. 'My boys and girls won't let you down.'

'I'm sure of that,' I said. 'I wouldn't have asked for them otherwise.' A faint flush of pride worked its way up past his jaw line.

'I'll tell them you said that, sir.'

'Please do.' I returned his salute, and looked around for Jurgen as Lustig strode off, his shoulders set. There shouldn't be any morale problems with his squad now, I thought. My aide was nowhere to be seen, so I walked towards the door, past the row of chairs where more than a dozen officers and non-coms had been sitting a few moments before. If I knew Jurgen, he'd be in the vehicle park, conscientiously checking over our Salamander.

'Commissar.' I turned, momentarily startled by the voice at my elbow. Sulla was still seated, her face flushed with uncharacteristic nervousness. She juggled the briefing slate in her lap.

'You have a question, lieutenant?' I asked, keeping my voice neutral. She nodded rapidly, swallowing a couple of times.

'Not exactly. Sort of...' She stood, the top of her head level with my eyes, and tilted it back slightly to speak directly to me. 'I just wanted to say...' She hesitated again, then blurted it out in a rush. 'I know you haven't formed a very high opinion of me since you joined us, but I appreciate you giving me a chance. You won't regret it, I promise you.'

'I'm sure I won't.' I smiled, a warm expression cal-culated to boost her confidence. 'Your platoon was my first choice for this mission, because I know they can get the job done.' In truth, it was Lustig's squad I wanted, for the reasons I've already gone into, and the rest of the platoon just came along with them. But she didn't have to know that. 'Integrating the two old regiments into a new unit has been tough on everyone, especially those of you who were thrust into positions of responsibility you weren't prepared for. I think you've coped admirably.'

'Thank you, commissar.' She coloured visibly, and trotted out with a slightly uncoordinated salute.

Well, that was an unexpected bonus. If I was any judge, she'd be so keen to justify my non-existent confidence in her that she wouldn't be making any more trouble, at least for a while. Despite the prospect of imminent combat, there was a definite spring in my step as I went to find Jurgen.

THE FIRST PART of the plan went like clockwork. We formed up in the main vehicle park, two full pla-toons, which I thought would be enough for the job, plus the Sentinels, which hissed and clanked their way over the rockcrete to join us like vast robotic chickens. And if you think they look ungainly, try hitching a lift on one some time. I've been in boats in a storm and felt less motion sick. Mind you, when the alternative is being ripped apart by orks, I'll take an upset stomach any time. If you think that sounds a little on the puny side, remember the xenoists only numbered about a dozen squads themselves, so we had them pretty well outnumbered even so, and given the delicacy of the diplomatic situation, I didn't want to go in with any more troopers than we needed. Besides, I was counting on the artillery barrage to take most of them out, so the firepower we had seemed more than enough for mopping up with.

And before you ask, yes, I suppose dropping shells on a part of the city we'd been sent to protect did seem a little paradoxical to us at the time, but it was all a question of expediency. To my way of thinking, anyone still in the target area was there by choice, and any civilians who hadn't fled were either traitors themselves or so stupid we were doing future generations a favour by removing them from the gene pool.

I mounted the command Salamander Jurgen had procured and looked out over our expeditionary force, feeling a surge of pride in spite of my obvious trepidation. The infantry squads were mounted in Chimeras, the two platoon command ones standing out from the rest by virtue of the vox antennae that clustered their upper surfaces. Sulla's head and shoulders protruded from the top hatch of hers, a pair of earphones protecting her from the engine noise. Seeing me look in her direction, she raised the mic in her hand.

'Third Platoon ready,' she reported.

'Fifth Platoon ready.' Her opposite number, Lieutenant Faril, echoed her words. A dogged, somewhat unimaginative commander, he none-the-less had the respect and confidence of his troopers, largely due to a dry sense of humour and an earnest concern for their welfare, which meant he was unlikely to press too hard if they ran into stiff resistance. I'd selected him precisely because of this, knowing he'd wait for the Sentinels to back him up if things got sticky instead of throwing his troopers lives away taking stupid risks. Some casualties were inevitable, of course, but I wanted to keep them to a minimum. If the regiment's first clash of arms resulted in an easy victory, it would boost their confidence and consolidate morale, whereas a high body count could easily undo all the hard work we'd done getting them back into fighting trim.

'All squadrons ready.' That was Captain Shambas, head of the Sentinel troop; we had all three squadrons with us, which gave us a total of nine walkers. Considerable overkill, given the quality of the resistance we were expecting, but there's nothing like overwhelming fire superiority to give you a sense of self-confidence.

'Confirm.' Broklaw's voice joined the others in my combead. He was in another Salamander, which, like mine, had been fitted out as a command unit. I was more used to the lighter, faster scout variant, which was always my vehicle of choice (I prefer to be able to outrun trouble if I have to), but under the circumstances, I wanted to be able to keep a close eye on things. Besides, the command version had a heavy flamer fitted, which might come in handy in the brutal close-quarter fighting I expected through the rubble of the Heights.

Which reminded me...

'Artillery units commence firing,' I said. A moment later, the ground beneath our treads started to tremble as Mostrue's Earthshakers began living up to their name. I swept my gaze around, tallying the assembled task force. A dozen Chimeras, nine Sentinels, and two Salamanders. I drew my chainsword and gestured towards the gate.

'Move out!' I ordered. Jurgen gunned the engine, and we lurched into motion. Inured to his robust driving style by years of familiarity, I kept my balance with little difficulty. Broklaw's driver moved smoothly in behind us, and I could see his head and shoulders in the open rear compartment; he caught my eye and waved. Kasteen, I knew, would dearly have loved to take command herself, but had stepped down in favour of her subordinate. After all, he too deserved a chance to prove his mettle, and technically, the operation was too small to be overseen by someone of her rank anyway. I was pleased she'd given way without prompting, though, and I could tell Broklaw appreciated it. It was another example of the way the regiment was beginning to function as it was supposed to.

Kasteen was there to see us off, though, along with everyone else who didn't have pressing duties to attend to, or who thought they might get away with skiving off for a few minutes. A cheer went up from our comrades which, for a moment, managed to make itself heard above the roar of engines, the din of the Sentinels, and the rolling thunderclaps of the Earthshakers.

As we hit the streets, the city was in turmoil. We'd kept our plans secret, of course, so none of the natives had a clue what was going on; they scattered in front of us like frightened sump rats, and Jurgen gunned the engine as though it were capable of the speeds he usually drove at. Ahead of us, a plume of dust and smoke marked our destination.

I flipped vox channels to the tactical net. The loyalist PDF units were being told to stand down and let us through, which came as a relief, although ill-disciplined rabble that they were, many were arguing or demanding to know what was going on.

'Major.' I switched back. 'It's all yours for the moment. Try to save a couple for me, eh?'

'I'll do my best.' Broklaw waved as Jurgen peeled us away from the rest of the convoy, mowing down a couple of ornamental shrubs and a litter basket as we swung off the broad boulevard into a narrower cross street which would take us to the industrial area.

The muffled crump of the shells detonating was audible now, the shriek and whine of their passage presaging each explosion, and the noise cleared the street for us far more effectively than any Arbites siren could have done. After a few moments, and several lurching turns any driver but Jurgen would probably have flipped us over attempting to execute, the buildings around us were unmistakably industrial in nature. Still that Emperor-forsaken xenoist-style architecture, admittedly, but sufficiently grubby for their purpose to be obvious.

'Broklaw to command.' The major's voice was calm and competent. 'Cease barrage. We're in position.'

I was glad to hear it. I hadn't even begun my make-work errand yet, and he was already on the verge of clearing the traitors out. Jurgen began to slow the Salamander, and, with a sense of *déjà vu*, I could see a PDF officer stepping out in front of us, his hand raised. Manufactoria rose all around us, tall enough to shadow the streets, but apart from the man in uniform, there was no sign of life. That struck me as strange, as the work shifts should still have been in full swing.

'Commissar,' Jurgen said, his voice uncertain. 'Can you hear firing?'

As the engine idled down, I realised he was right. For a moment, I found myself wondering at the acoustics, assuming that what I was hearing must be echoes of the firefight up in the Heights, which a series of crisp exchanges in my combead told me had already broken out. Then I realised it was coming from somewhere ahead of us, inside the line of the PDF cordon marked on the mapslate in front of me.

'What's going on?' I asked, glaring down at the officer. He looked a little panicky.

'I'm not sure, sir. We had orders to hold, but there's dozens of them. Have you brought reinforcements?'

'I'm afraid we're it,' I said, playing for time. 'Who are you holding against?'

'I don't know. We were pulled out of barracks last night, and told to cordon off the area.' He didn't seem any older than the officer I'd shot, I noticed with a sudden flare of apprehension, and the rapid tumble of his words told me he was on the verge of panic. Whatever I'd blundered into was heading for the sump, that much was obvious, and I cursed my luck; but it was too late to back out now. 'We were just told to secure the area until the inquisitor's party got back...'

Merciful Emperor, this was just getting better and better. Clearly, whatever stones Orelius had been turning over had revealed more than the shadowy conspirators he was chasing were happy with, and they were determined to make sure no one lived to pass on their secrets.

'Did he say what he was after down here?' I asked, and the officer shook his head.

'I didn't speak to any of them. Only the captain did, and he's dead now...' His voice began to rise, hysteria bubbling below the surface. I jumped down to stand beside him, feeling the rockcrete jar beneath my boot-heels, and tried to project all the reassurance and authority I could.

'Then I take it you're the officer in charge, lieutenant.' That got through to him. He nodded, a short, myoclonic twitch. 'So report. Where did they go? When? How many? What can you tell me?' His jaw worked for a moment, as though he were trying to force it to function. Gunfire and screams continued to echo between the buildings.

'There's a warehouse. Back there.' He pointed to one of the structures. A las-bolt cracked from one of the upper windows, passing between our heads, and struck the side of the Salamander. I ducked, pulling him down to safety, while Jurgen rotated the sturdy little vehicle on its tracks to bring the hull-mounted heavy bolter in line. It roared in response, gouging away part of the wall, and reducing the sniper to an unpleasant stain.

'Thank you, Jurgen.' I returned my attention to the young officer. 'And the inquisitor went in there?'

'They all did. Just before dawn. We were told to let no one in or out until they came back.' That would have been about ten-and-a-half hours ago, by my reckoning, and something told me Orelius wouldn't be returning any time soon.

'How many of them were there?' I asked. He thought for a moment.

'I saw six,' he said at last. 'Four men and two women. One of them seemed a bit peculiar.' That would be Rakel the psyker, I assumed.

'What about the hostiles?' I prompted him. He shook his head.

'They're everywhere, dozens of them...' His head twitched nervously from side to side as he tried to keep the entire street in view.

'Where? Inside the warehouse?'

'Mostly.' He stood up, about to flee, and another las-bolt caught him in the shoulder. He fell back, shrieking like a child.

'You'll be fine,' I told him after a cursory glance at the injury. One thing you can say for being shot by a las-bolt is that they cauterise the wound they cause, so at least you won't bleed to death from a glancing hit; a fact that has saved my own miserable life on a couple of occasions. I looked back down the street, trying to spot where the fire had come from, and caught sight of some movement behind a pile of shipping crates. I pointed. 'Ours or theirs?'

'I don't know! Emperor's blood, it hurts–'

'It'll hurt a damn sight more in a moment if you don't stop frakking me around!' I shouted suddenly. 'Your men are dying out there! If you can't start behaving like an officer and help me save them, I'll finish you off myself!' That was the last thing I was going to do, of course, the way he was yelling he'd draw the enemy fire off me like a champion when we moved, but it did the trick. I could see the coin drop behind his eyes as he suddenly remembered what had happened to the last PDF unit to get in the way of a commissar.

'They're all civilians,' he gasped out after a moment. 'Anyone in a uniform is one of ours.'

'Thank you.' I pulled him into the shadow of a dumpster. 'Keep your head down and you'll be fine.' I scrambled back aboard the Salamander, grateful for the armour plate surrounding me.

'Broklaw to Cain.' The major's voice rang in my combead. 'Are you all right? We're getting some odd feedback off your frequency.'

'So far.' I checked the flamer, finding it fully charged and ready to go. Emperor bless Jurgen and his streak of thoroughness, I thought. 'It seems our PDF boys weren't holding back after all.'

'Resistance is light here...' His voice was drowned out for a moment by the crack of ionising air I associated with one of the Sentinel multi-lasers. 'But we'll be a while yet.'

'Don't hurry on my account,' I said. The renegades could only have small arms, judging by the sounds I heard, and the Salamander's armour was thick enough to afford complete protection. I switched frequencies, searching for the PDF squad's internal tactical net, but found only static; I should have known better, of course,[1] but old habits are hard to break.

A few more las-bolts from behind the crates confirmed the identities of the rebels lurking there, making a mess of our paintwork in the process, so I triggered the flamer, sending a gout of burning promethium down the alley. The results were impressive. The crates bursting into flame, and the rebels behind them got caught in the backwash. They burst into the open, their clothes and hair on fire, shrieking like the damned, and Jurgen cut them down with the bolter. Their bodies exploded under the impact, spraying the walls of the building with burning debris, and I was incongruously reminded of fireworks.

1 Unlike the Imperial Guard units Cain was used to fighting with, most Planetary Defence Force troopers on Gravalax weren't equipped with personal combeads. This lack of contact between individuals outside line of sight of one another partially accounts for the relative lack of co-ordination within a squad, which most Guard veterans disparagingly attributed to poor levels of training and discipline. Of course, most PDF units were inferior to them in this regard, in any case.

'Let's finish this,' I said, and my aide gunned the engine, rolling us forward over the pool of burning promethium which now carpeted the alleyway. As I glanced behind us, the PDF officer was gazing at the devastation we'd wrought, his eyes wide with shock.

The alley opened out into a cross street, the wall of the warehouse forming one side of it, stretching away in front of us in both directions. The distinctive crack of lasgun fire continued to echo through the roads around it, and as our field of vision widened, I could see the sparks of muzzle flashes inside the building, and the puff of vaporising rockcrete where other bolts were impacting around the upper windows. Shadowy figures were visible inside, snapping off shots before ducking back, and I could make out little of them; just that, as the wounded lieutenant had said, they were all in civilian clothes. They were a mixed bunch, too. I caught a glimpse of velvet and the crest of one of the merchants' guilds, and someone who looked like a pastry cook, before I swept the flamer over the whole façade. The results were spectacular; the firing stopped at once, the wood of the window frames igniting with a roar, and a few short-lived screams cut the air.

'That ought to keep their heads down,' Jurgen said with satisfaction, sending a burst of bolts after the promethium to make sure of the fact. Thick black smoke continued to pour from the building, and a ragged cheer mingled with the roar of the flames.

I turned to see a wary group of PDF troopers emerging from the buildings opposite the warehouse, or

whatever cover they'd been able to find among the
parked trucks and other detritus of the street. A few
ragged shots continued to echo between the buildings, indicating that not all the traitors had been
incinerated, but their sporadic nature spoke of a
panic-stricken retreat which was running into the
troopers on the other side of the cordon. The plume
of thick black smoke must have been visible from
where they were by now, and they were evidently taking heart from the sight. I jumped down from the
Salamander.

'Sergeant Crassus, 49th Gravalaxian PDF.' A tall,
grey-haired man snapped a salute, but kept his eyes
on the street; the first PDF trooper I'd seen since I
arrived on planet who actually seemed to know what
he was doing. I returned it smartly.

'Commissar Cain, attached to the 597th Valhallan.'
Once again, I had the quiet satisfaction of noting that
my name had been recognised, the low murmur of
voices among the troopers flattering my ego with its
awestruck tone.

'We're grateful for your assistance,' Crassus said.
'Did the inquisitor send for you?' I shook my head.

'Just poking my nose in,' I admitted. 'I noticed your
little sideshow on the tactical display and wondered
what was going on.' Crassus shrugged.

'You'd have to ask one of the officers.'

'I did.' I pointed back up the alleyway, where the
promethium pool had burned itself out, leaving a
scorched patch of blackened rockcrete. 'Back there.
He needs a medic, by the way.'

'Ah.' Crassus didn't seem surprised. 'I thought he'd done a runner, to be honest.' My lack of a reply seemed to confirm something for him, but after a moment, he detailed one of the troopers to take a medkit and see to the lieutenant.

'You seem to be standing up to combat better than most of the PDF,' I said.

Crassus shrugged. 'I'm a fast learner. Besides, I'm used to looking after myself.' Taking in his physique and his air of watchfulness, I didn't doubt it. 'I was in the Arbites before I joined up.'

'That seems like an odd career move,' I said. His jaw tightened for a moment.

'Office politics,' he said curtly. I nodded sympathetically.

'It's the same in the Commissariat,' I told him.[1] But before we could exchange any more words, a loud crack from behind us presaged the collapse of one of the upper stories of the burning warehouse. 'Better pull your men back,' I told him. 'That's going to go any minute.'

'I think you're right.' He summoned the squad vox operator, relayed the instruction, and led his men up the alley at a rapid trot. I turned to look at the ware-

1   This is another prime example of Cain's manipulative streak, in which he invites confidence by pretending to have shared the experiences of others. Though there are, of course, divisions within the Commissariat over matters of doctrine and procedure, they can hardly be described as anything so trivial as 'office politics.' They are also, let us note, considerably less fratricidal than similar disagreements among fellow inquisitors.

house again. It was well ablaze by now, and pieces of debris were starting to drop from the roof and outer walls. I scrambled back aboard the Salamander while Jurgen gunned the engine, and began to reverse us to safety.

Abruptly, I became aware of the sound of small arms fire, echoing from inside the building, audible even over the pop and crackle of the flames.

'Crassus,' I voxed, chafing at the necessity of relaying messages through his squad vox operator. 'Are any of your men inside the building?' He had just begun to reply when the link went dead, over-ridden by a message on a higher priority command channel. I'd done the same thing enough times to recognise what was happening, but it had been a long time since I'd been the one cut out. Still, I supposed it showed Orelius was still alive, at any rate, and I'd heard enough of the reply to be reas-sured that I hadn't accidentally killed any more loyal subjects of the Emperor. That was a relief, as I was still slogging through the paperwork on the last lot of collateral damage I'd inflicted on the PDF.

I'd just decided that the firing I'd heard was over-heated ammo cooking off, or xenoist traitors deciding they'd rather shoot themselves than be burned to death, when Crassus was back on my combead.

'Commissar. The inquisitor's team are pinned down inside the warehouse. They want immediate extraction.'

Well, what they want and what they'll get are two different things, I thought. Venturing into that inferno would be suicide. Let Crassus try if he wanted, but it looked to me as though Orelius and his cohorts were about to report to the Emperor in person, and there was damn-all any of us could do about it.

Then a truly horrifying thought struck me. I'd been the one who set fire to the building. If the Inquisition thought I'd been responsible for the death of one of their own, and had just stood by and let him burn without even trying to rescue him, I'd be a dead man – if I was lucky. I dithered for a fraction of a second, which seemed like eternity, and came to a decision.

'Stay back. We'll handle it,' I told Crassus, and leaned over the driver's compartment to call to Jurgen. 'Take us in!' I shouted.

As usual, where anyone else might have hesitated or argued, he simply followed orders without thinking. The Salamander lurched forwards, accelerating towards the blazing building as rapidly as it could.

'There! Those loading doors!' I pointed, but my faithful aide had already seen them, and a hail of bolter shells ripped them to shreds an instant before we hit. We bounced into the shadowy interior of the warehouse, billows of smoke shrouding everything, pieces of tattered door spraying from under our tracks. I coughed, tore off my sash, and tied it around my face. It didn't do a lot of good, to be honest, but my lungs felt a little less choked than before.

Las-bolts started striking the front armour of the vehicle, which at least gave us a clue as to where the enemy was, and Jurgen was about to reply with the heavy bolter again when I forestalled him.

'Wait,' I said, 'you might hit the inquisitor.' That would have been the crowning irony. Instead, he swung us over to one side, slamming into a pile of stacked crates, and bringing them crashing down. Sudden screams were abruptly cut off. I twisted my head frantically, trying to orientate us, and the whole vast space was suddenly lit in vivid orange as the roof whooshed into flame.

'Frak this!' I said, on the verge of ordering Jurgen to withdraw, then I caught sight of a small knot of figures hurrying towards us. I pointed, and Jurgen swung the Salamander round, stopping us almost dead. There were five of them, running for their lives, with an indeterminate number of shadowy figures in pursuit. Orelius I recognised at once, turning as he ran to loose off a volley from his bolt pistol. A couple of the pursuers fell, but las-bolts continued to impact around the inquisitor and his retinue. A heavily muscled man I recognised as one of his bodyguards from the governor's party was firing, too, but went down hard as one of the las-bolts caught the back of his head. Orelius hesitated for a moment, but even from where I was standing it was obvious the fellow had been dead before he hit the floor.

The rest of his party were in real trouble, so, despite my natural reservations about making myself a more obvious target, I clambered up to the pintle-mounted bolter I'd made sure was installed. Not every Salamander has them, but I've been grateful enough for their presence in the past to insist on having one available if at all possible, and I blessed that foresight now as I took advantage of the extra height the vehicle afforded me to fire over the heads of the inquisitorial party and strike home against their pursuers. A gratifying number went down, or scattered, but too many carried on firing. I'd expected them to start shooting at me, but to my relief they continued to concentrate their fire on the fleeing figures before them.

The scribe I'd seen with Orelius was out in front; long white beard flapping as he ran with surprising dexterity for a man of his age. It was only after I saw him take a las-bolt to the leg, which sparked but continued to function, that I realised his lower limbs were augmetic. Behind him were two women: Rakel, whose green dress was now heavily stained with blood, apparently from a chest wound, but who was still babbling nonsense without appearing to inhale, and another who held her up. She was swathed in a hooded cloak of the deepest black I'd ever seen, which seemed to swallow the light that fell on it, blurring her outline. I saw her flinch as a las-bolt scorched the material, but she kept coming, supporting the gibbering psyker with surprising strength.

I hosed down their pursuers again, hoping to throw off their aim at least, but for every one I felled, another seemed to replace it, moving with an eerie precision which seemed somehow familiar. There was no time to worry about it now, though. I reached down to grasp the fingers of the old scribe, which to my total lack of surprise were also augmetics, and haul him aboard.

'Much obliged,' he said, dropping into the crew compartment, and glancing around with evident interest. 'An Imperial Guard Salamander. Good solid piece of kit. Manufactured on Triplex Vall, unless I miss my guess...'

I left him to gather whatever wits he had, and turned to the others.

'Jurgen!' I shouted. 'Help the women!' Orelius took a las-bolt to the shoulder, dropping his handgun. I wasn't about to lose him now, not after going through all this, so I jumped down, drawing my laspistol, and went to help him up.

'Commissar Cain?' He looked slightly confused until I remembered my makeshift smoke mask and pulled it down; it wasn't doing a damn bit of good now anyway. The whole building around us was ablaze, the heat terrific, and I suddenly remembered the promethium tanks of the heavy flamer aboard the Salamander. Well, it was too late to worry about that now. 'What are you doing here?'

'I heard you needed a lift,' I said, hauling him to his feet, and aiming a couple of speculative shots in the vague direction of the enemy. I dragged him back to the vehicle, where Jurgen was doing his best to help the women, but Rakel wasn't exactly cooperating. She seemed terrified of him, struggling against her companion's grip in an effort to get away.

'He's nothing! Nothing!' she shrieked, which seemed a little harsh to me. All right, he wasn't the most prepossessing trooper in the guard, but once you got past the smell and the interesting collection of skin diseases, he had his good points. Then she convulsed suddenly and passed out, dribbling foam between her clenched teeth.

I hustled Orelius aboard, hefted Rakel's dead weight like a sack of tubers, and let the scribe take her. He lifted her easily with his augmetic limbs, and I climbed up myself beside the woman in black as Jurgen returned to the driver's compartment and gunned the engine.

'Jurgen! Get us out of here!' I yelled, and he opened the throttle fully.

'With pleasure, commissar.' The Salamander leapt forwards, breaking for the shattered loading door we'd come in by, and clipped the frame as we passed through, gouging a shower of sparks from it. As we gained the street, the furnace heat seemed to drop away, although it was still hot enough to raise blisters from our paintwork. I sagged with relief, trembling with the reaction, still trying to comprehend what an insanely risky thing I'd done. As if to underline how close we'd come, the building collapsed behind us with a roar of tumbling masonry.

Well, there's no point cheating death with an act of insane bravery if no one's in a position to praise you for it, so I voxed Crassus.

'Crassus,' I said. 'The inquisitor's safe.'

'So I am.' The woman in black dropped her hood, revealing a face I'd thought about often in the last few days. With blonde hair and blue eyes, she was even more beautiful than I'd remembered, and the voice I'd last heard singing sentimental ballards still had the faint edge of huskiness that had made my heart skip.

Amberley Vail gazed at me with what I took to be faint amusement as my jaw dropped open, an inquisitorial electoo flashing into visibility in the palm of her hand. 'Thank you, commissar,' she added, smiling sweetly.

Editorial Note:

Once again, it seems prudent to insert a little material from other sources here, as the Valhallans' expedition against the xenoist defectors was to have unexpected repercussions. Cain, as we might expect, has little to say on the matter himself as his attention was elsewhere.

The first is extracted from the after-action report of Major Ruput Broklaw, made on 593.931 M41, shortly after the engagement was successfully concluded.

AFTER THE PRELIMINARY bombardment ceased both infantry platoons disembarked from their Chimeras, which had been dispersed around the perimeter of the rebel-occupied zone in accordance

with the previously determined deployments. Third
Platoon was supported by First Sentinel Squadron
on the left flank, Fifth Platoon by Second Squadron
on the right, leaving Third Squadron with the company command element as a mobile reserve.

Resistance was light, as anticipated, and Fifth
Platoon rolled up their flank with little difficulty
apart from a couple of heavy exchanges of fire
with dug-in survivors of the bombardment. Lieutenant Faril called in Sentinel support for the two
squads thus engaged, which committed our reserve
squadron. The flamer-equipped Sentinel in each
group clear out the entrenchments with little difficulty after the other two laid down suppressive
fire from their multi-lasers to allow them to
approach.

On the left, things didn't run quite so smoothly.
As Fourth Squad of Third Platoon came under
crossfire from two enemy positions, pinning them
in place. The flamer Sentinel sent to assist was
struck and disabled by a krak missile, forcing its
fellows into a defensive posture which severely
attenuated the effectiveness of their suppressive
fire.

At this point, Lieutenant Sulla broke the dead-
lock by leading her command squad in a flank
attack against one of the enemy positions, while
Second Squad under Sergeant Lustig hit the other.
By luck or good judgment, both were able to carry

the positions almost simultaneously, allowing the remaining Sentinels to close and Fourth Squad to advance.

I am still undecided as to whether Lieutenant Sulla's action was bold or reckless, but it was undeniably effective.

Extracted from *Like a Phoenix From the Flames: The Founding of the 597th*, by General Jenit Sulla (retired), 097.M42.

Notwithstanding Commissar Cain's assurances that resistance would be light, as indeed was to prove the case, I felt more than a touch of apprehension as the barrage ceased and Major Broklaw gave the order to advance. Not at the prospect of combat itself – the pitiful handful of rebels we faced seeming little to fear after the tyranid hordes we'd bested on Corania scant months before – but at the realisation that my first real test as an officer was upon me, and the fact that one of the most renowned heroes in the Segmentum had reposed his trust in me was an added burden which I felt ill-equipped to bear.

All went well at first, however, with the squads in my platoon advancing swiftly to contact. My readers may well imagine the frustration I felt as I sat in my command Chimera, listening to the vox chatter, reliant on the reports from my subordinates for a full tactical analysis, for until my unlooked-for promotion, I would have been among them, facing the Emperor's enemies head-on, as a soldier should. My impatience increased as it became clear that one of my squads, women I'd served alongside and men I was beginning to know and respect, was pinned down, taking casualties and unable to advance. As the Sentinels which should have relieved them ran into trouble themselves, I could stand by no longer, regardless of the commissar's admonition to be cautious. Especially since, knowing his reputation, I was certain he would not have hesitated to put himself in danger for the good of his fellows were he to find himself in a similar position.

Calling on my troopers to follow me, and taking but a moment to switch the command channels to the combead in my ear, I jumped from the rear ramp, eager to join the fray.

The sight which met my eyes was to give me pause. The elegant buildings and thoroughfares through which we'd driven were no more, their places taken by heaps of rubble through which barely recognisable pieces of their original form could still, in places, be discerned. A thick pall of dust and smoke hung over everything, reducing the bright afternoon sun to a sullen grey, and for a moment, I couldn't still the flicker of regret which rose unbidden in my breast. Even tainted by the alien as it had been, the architecture had been undeniably elegant.

I had little time for reflection, however, as the crack of las-fire reminded me forcefully of the dire peril my soldiers were in, and with a cry of 'For the Emperor!' I led my doughty quartet to the rescue. A quick study of the tactical slate in the Chimera had shown me that I had an unengaged squad sufficiently close to the most distant of the enemy positions to flank it with a high probability of success, and after a few terse instructions to the sergeant leading it, this indeed was to prove to be the case. That left the nearest to us.

We took them completely by surprise, a couple of frag rounds from our grenade launcher bursting among them and causing great dismay, before charging home to dispatch the survivors with pistols and chainsword. Cowards all, as those who oppose the Emperor invariably are, they broke and ran, exposing themselves to the vengeful fire of the squad they'd been pinning down, who were only too keen to even the score. I'm proud to say that of the team under my direct command only one man was wounded, taking a las-bolt to the leg as we charged, while none of the traitors escaped alive.

[From which we may safely conclude that, whatever her martial abilities, Sulla was no literary stylist.]

NINE

Things are very seldom what they seem. In my experience, they're usually a damn sight worse.

– Inquisitor Titus Drake.

IT GOES WITHOUT saying that, given my profession, I've had more than my fair share of unpleasant surprises. But to find that the woman I'd spent a pleasant social evening trying to impress with my half-formed speculations about events she was privy to, and, it must be admitted, had been quite smitten by (insofar as I've ever been susceptible to such things[1]), was really an undercover inquisitor came pretty close to the top of the list. And if that wasn't

---

1 At the risk of appearing egotistical, I suspect he's protesting a little too strongly here...

bad enough, the expression of tolerant amusement on her face at my utter stupefaction increased my discomfiture a thousandfold.

'But I thought... Orelius...' I said, barely making sense even to myself. Amberley laughed as the Salamander hurtled through the streets back to the fortified compound where Zyvan had established the headquarters of our expeditionary force. Through the vox bead in my ear, I could hear the firefight in the Heights continuing. Sulla had apparently done something stupid, but we were winning comfortably with few enough casualties for things to be fine without any further interference from me, so I felt justified in ordering Jurgen to take us back to the staging area as quickly as possible. Rakel and Orelius quite clearly needed medical attention, which gave me the perfect excuse, and I supposed it was my duty to see the inquisitor safely on her way as quickly as possible.

As it turned out, of course, I was to see a great deal more of her before we left Gravalax, and even that would be just the beginning of a long and eventful association which was to leave me in mortal peril on more occasions than I care to contemplate. Sometimes I wonder whether, if I'd had some premonition of who she really was the first time I saw her, I'd simply have left the room and avoided all the horrors to come in the ensuing decades; but I doubt it. Her company, on the rare occasions I was able simply to enjoy it for its own sake, more than made up for all the times I was left fleeing for my life or facing imminent painful death. Hard as that may be to understand, if you'd met her you'd think the same, I'm sure.[1]

'Orelius?' She braced herself as Jurgen swung us around a bend most other drivers would have thought too tight at half the speed. 'He helps me out on occasion.' She smiled again. 'He seemed very impressed with you at the governor's party, by the way.'

'Then he's an inquisitor too?' I asked, my head still spinning. Amberley laughed, like water over stones, and shook her head.

'Good Emperor, no. He's a rogue trader. What in the warp made you think he's an inquisitor?'

'Just something a friend said,' I said, thinking that would be the last time I took Divas's word for anything. But I suppose, to be fair, he hadn't been all that wrong as it turned out, and he hadn't been responsible for my own febrile imaginings.

'And the guy with the beard?' I indicated the scribe, who was leaning over the lip of the driver's compartment carrying on an enthusiastic conversation with Jurgen about the finer points of Salamander maintenance.

'Caractacus Mott, my savant.' She smiled fondly. 'A mine of information, some of it useful.'

'The others I've met,' I said. I indicated Orelius, who had taken out a medkit and was tending to

---

1 Frankly, I doubt it. But we certainly seemed more at ease in one another's company than either of us were used to with anyone else. Make of that what you will.

Rakel as best he could with a damaged arm. 'What's wrong with her?'

'I'm not exactly sure,' she replied, a thoughtful frown appearing for a moment on her face. That, I was later to discover, wasn't entirely true; she had her suspicions, but the truth about Jurgen wouldn't be confirmed for some time yet.

To cut a long story short, we made it back to HQ without further incident, and dispersed to our various duties. Amberley went off with the medicae to ensure that her friends were properly patched up, although as I was to find out for myself on subsequent occasions, having an inquisitor hovering in the corner doesn't exactly help them to concentrate on stemming the bleeding or whatever. I went off for a shower and a change of clothes, but was still smelling faintly of smoke when Broklaw and the others returned in high spirits.

'You did well, I hear,' I congratulated him as he disembarked from his Chimera. He nodded, still a little high from the adrenaline.

'Cleared out the whole nest of them. Minimal casualties, too.' He broke off to return Sulla's salute; her face was shining as though she'd just been out on a heavy date. 'Well done, lieutenant. That was a tough call.'

'I just asked myself what the commissar would have done,' she said. At that point I still didn't have a clue what either of them were talking about, but I assumed she'd distinguished herself in some way, so

I tried to look pleased. It turned out later she'd
pulled some damn fool stunt that had almost got her
killed, but the troopers thought she was the hero of
the hour, so it had all turned out for the best. Besides,
it was the sort of thing I was assumed to have done
myself, so I could hardly chew her out for it when the
reports came in, could I?

'And then did the opposite, I hope,' I said, then
raised an eyebrow at her expression. 'That was a joke,
lieutenant. I'm sure whatever decision you made was
the correct one under the circumstances.'

'I hope so,' she said, saluting again, then trotting off
to check on the wounded from her platoon. Broklaw
watched her go with a thoughtful expression.

'Well, it worked, anyway. Probably saved us a heap
of casualties too. But...' He shrugged. 'She'll probably
do well in the end, if she doesn't get herself killed
first.'

Well, he was right there, of course, although none
of us could see at the time just quite how far she'd go.
Like they say, it's always the ones you least expect.[1]

After a few more words of little consequence,
Brocklaw went off to report to Kasteen, and I went to
look for a drink.

I FOUND IT in a quiet booth at the back of the
Eagle's Wing. The place was almost deserted, in an

---

1   For further details of Sulla's illustrious career see Dragen's biogra-
phy *Valhallan Valkyrie*, a populist but accurate work, and *Like a Phoenix
From the Flames*, if you can tolerate her prose style.

eerie contrast to my visit here with Divas, but I supposed it was still a bit too early in the evening for things to be lively, and anyway the solitude fitted my mood. I'd noticed, on my short walk to the bar, that the streets were unusually quiet, too, and the few civilians I'd seen had seemed nervous, scuttling away from me as they caught sight of my uniform. Our show of strength against the rebels in the Heights had put everyone on edge, and if anything, anti-Imperial sentiment seemed to be gaining ground.

I can't say I blamed them entirely, either. If I'd been a Gravalaxian, I'd probably be thinking that the tau might be blue, bald, and barmy, but at least they hadn't blown up part of the city. My opinion of Grice would have fallen even further for ordering us to intervene, if that were possible.

As the amasec started to kick in, I found myself brooding over the events of the afternoon: a hairsbreadth escape from death does that to me, I start to contemplate my own mortality, and wonder what the hell I'm doing in a job where I'm liable to be killed pretty much all of the time. The answer, of course, is that I didn't have a choice – the assessors at the Schola Progenium decided I was commissarial material, and that was that.[1]

---

1 A decision which, on the face of it, seems remarkably perverse, given Cain's manifest character flaws. However, it's a decision his subsequent career triumphantly vindicates. We can only speculate how he would have fared if directed into some other branch of Imperial service, such as the Navy, or, Emperor help us, the Arbites.

I was just working myself into a perversely comforting mood of gloom and despondency when a shadow fell across me and a mellifluous voice asked, 'Do you mind if I sit here?'

Normally, I'm never averse to feminine company, as you'll know if you've read much of these memoirs, but right then all I wanted was to be left alone to contemplate the unfairness of the universe in a self-pitying haze of alcohol. However, it never pays to be impolite to an inquisitor, so I gestured to the seat across the table and masked my surprise as best I could. She'd found the time to change and freshen up too, I noticed, into a mist-grey gown which showed off her colouring to the best advantage.

'Feel free.' I gestured to the waitress, who looked vaguely disappointed as she delivered our order. 'Two more, please.'

'Thank you.' Amberley sipped delicately at the drink, a faint *moue* betraying her opinion of its quality, before replacing the glass on the tabletop and regarding me quizzically. I tried to pull away from her depthless blue eyes, then decided I didn't really want to after all. 'You're a remarkable man, commissar.'

'So I've been told.' I waited a heartbeat before smiling. 'Though I can't say I see it myself.' The corner of Amberley's mouth twitched, with what looked like genuine amusement.

'Oh yes, the modest hero routine. You've got that one off pat, no question.' She knocked back the rest of her drink in one, and signalled for another, leaving me gaping like an idiot. Her smile widened. 'What's next? "I'm just a humble soldier," or "Trust me, I'm a servant of the Emperor?"'

'I'm not quite sure what you're insinuating–' I began, but she cut me off with a chuckle.

'Ooh, honest indignation. I haven't seen that one in a while.' She picked at the bowl of nuts on the table, some local variety I didn't recognise, and flashed a grin of pure mischief at me. 'Lighten up, commissar, I'm only pulling your leg.'

Yes, right, I thought. And letting me know you can see right through every little manipulative trick in my repertoire in the process. Something of this must have shown on my face, because her eyes softened.

'You could just try being yourself, you know.'

The thought was terrifying. I'd spent so long hiding behind masks I was no longer sure there was a genuine Ciaphas underneath them any more, just a quivering little bundle of self-interest. Then an even more terrifying thought hit me; she could tell what I was thinking! Everything I'd tried to conceal about my fraudulent reputation would be open to her, and the inquisition... Emperor's bowels!

'Relax. I'm not a psyker. Just very good at reading people.' She watched me sag into my seat with relief, not even trying to conceal it, the faint amusement still dancing in the back of her eyes. 'Whatever you're afraid I'll find out is still safe. And it'll stay that way. Unless you give me a reason to start looking for it.'

'I'll do my best not to,' I promised, picking up my own drink with a shaky hand.

'I'm glad to hear it.' Her smile was warm again. 'Because I was hoping you could help me.'

'Help you with what?' I asked, already sure I wasn't going to like the answer.

THE CONFERENCE SUITE was less crowded this time, although since two of the others present were Lord General Zyvan and an inquisitor who was already making it perfectly clear that she was in charge here, it certainly seemed full enough to me. The only other person present was Mott, the elderly savant, who sat bright and alert, occasionally poking at the dent in his leg left by a hasty techpriest who hadn't quite finished patching him up when the summons to the meeting had arrived.

'Thank you for joining us, commissar.' Amberley flashed me a smile which looked genuinely warm, although as an experienced manipulator myself, I wasn't quite sure how far I could trust it. Zyvan nodded a greeting, also pleased to see me.

'Hello again.' Mott smiled, surprisingly clear brown eyes flickering behind his excess of beard. He evidently hadn't found the time to wash the smell of the fire out of his hair and robes, or simply didn't care. 'You've caused us a great deal of inconvenience, young man. Although I suppose you weren't to know.'

'Know what?' I asked, trying not to snap. I'd grabbed a couple of sandwiches to try and mop up the alcohol I'd drunk, and got Jurgen to find me some recaf, but between the amasec and the reaction from the day's adventures, my head was still buzzing.

'All in good time.' Amberley smiled indulgently at the wizened sage. 'Caractacus does tend to skip the dull bits given half a chance.'

'When you get to my age, you don't have the time to waste on them,' he responded, smiling in return. I realised that this was all part of an easy familiarity between them, which spoke volumes for the trust the inquisitor placed in him, and the length of their association. He turned back to me. 'Which reminds me, thank you for coming to our assistance. It was most timely.'

'My pleasure,' I said.

'Then you have an extremely perverse idea of what constitutes fun. You should get out more.'

Amberley shook her head, and raised an eyebrow at me, in an exaggerated mime of exasperation.

'You just can't get the help these days,' she said. I couldn't think of any adequate response to this, so I said nothing. I'd never had a really clear idea of what an inquisitor was supposed to be like, although like most people, I had a vague impression of some scary psychopath who slaughtered their way through the Emperor's enemies. Amberley, on the other hand, seemed to be the complete antithesis of this. She had her ruthless streak, of course, as I was to find out during our long association, but back then, the cheerful, slightly whimsical young woman with the strange sense of humour seemed about as far removed from the general preconception of her profession as it was possible to get.[1] Zyvan cleared his throat.

'Inquisitor. Perhaps we could get to the matter at hand?'

'Of course.' She activated the hololith, thumping it in just the right spot to bring the image into focus. 'It goes without saying that everything you see and hear is completely confidential, commissar.'

'Of course.' I nodded.

'Good. I'd hate to have to kill you.' She smiled again, and I wondered if she was joking or not. These days, of course, I know she meant every word of it.

'In case you haven't been paying attention,' she went on, 'I'm an agent of the Ordo Xenos. You know what that means?'

'You deal with aliens?' I hazarded. Back then, I had only the vaguest idea that the inquisition was divided into multiple ordos with specific areas of interest and responsibility, but it was a pretty easy deduction to make. Amberley nodded approval.

'Exactly,' she began.

'For the most part, anyway,' Mott chimed in helpfully. 'There was that Chaos cult on Arcadia Secundus, and the heretics of Ghore–'

'Thank you, Caractacus,' she said, meaning, 'shut the warp up,' so he did. As I was soon to discover, being a savant meant being obsessed with detail and trivia, and all the pedantry that went with it. Imagine the worst barroom know-it-all you ever met, who

---

1 Which was, of course, the whole point...

really does, and is cursed with a tourette-like compulsion to spill out everything relevant on any topic that comes up, and you're about halfway there. Although he could be incredibly annoying at times, I found him good company in his own way once I got to know him. Especially as his gifts included an uncanny intuitive grasp of probability which we put to good use in a number of gambling establishments over the years.

Amberley pulled up a star chart on the hololith, which I recognised without too much difficulty, as it had been reproduced in far less detail in the briefing slate I'd skimmed through before we made planet-fall.

'The Damocles Gulf,' I said, and she nodded.

'We're here.' She pointed out the Gravalax system, seemingly alone and isolated on the fringes of Imperial space. 'Notice anything about the topography of the region?'

'We're close to the tau border,' I said, playing for time as I studied the images. She wouldn't be alluding to anything that obvious, I was sure. Several of the neighbouring systems were tagged with blue icons, marking them as tau-held worlds. In fact they almost engulfed our present position, with only a thin chain of friendly yellow beacons connecting us to the welcoming haven of Imperial space. 'Too close,' I concluded finally. 'If we had to fight a war here, our supply lines would be far too thin for comfort.'

'Precisely.' Zyvan nodded approval, and indicated a couple of choke points. 'They could cut us off here, and here with no trouble at all. We'd be blockaded and swallowed up in months. While they could reinforce at their leisure from at least four systems.'

'Which is why we're so desperate to avoid a full-scale war over this miserable mudball,' Amberley said. 'Keeping it would tie up our naval assets from at least three sectors just to secure our supply lines, and we'd be funnelling Guard and Astartes units in from all over the Segmentum. Putting it bluntly, it's not worth the effort.'

To say that I was astonished would be putting it mildly. It had been an article of faith for as long as I could remember that the sacred domains of His Majesty's Imperium should never be polluted by the alien no matter the cost. And here was an inquisitor no less, and the lord general himself, apparently quite happy to let the tau just walk in and have the place. Well that was fine with me, of course, especially if it kept me out of the firing line, so I nodded judiciously.

'I can sense a "but" coming,' I said.

'Quite right.' Zyvan nodded, clearly pleased by my astuteness. 'Just letting the little blue grox-lovers walk in and take the place isn't acceptable either. It would send entirely the wrong message to them. They're already popping up on worlds all over the sector and arming to keep them. If they take Gravalax without a fight, they'll think half the Segmentum is up for grabs.'

'But we could beat them in the long run,' I said, trying not to picture the decades of grinding attrition that would ensue as the overwhelming might of the Imperium met the technosorcery of the tau. It would be the biggest bloodbath since the Sabbat Worlds crusade.

'We could. Eventually.' Amberley nodded soberly. 'If they were the only threat we had to face.' She widened the view, systems falling into the centre of the hololith, new ones coalescing at the fringes of the projection field. Several systems were tagged in red. I recognised one of them as Corania, and then, a moment later, I picked out the Desolatia system where I'd first been blooded against a tyranid horde over a decade before.

'In the last few years, tyranid attacks have been increasing in this region of the galaxy,' Zyvan said. 'But you'd know all about that.'

'I've seen a few,' I admitted.

'There's a pattern,' Mott butted in. 'Still not clear, but definitely beginning to form.[1]

'Our greatest fear is that they could be the harbingers of a new hive fleet,' Amberley said soberly. I tried to envision such a thing, and shivered involuntarily. The hordes I'd encountered before had been weak, the scattered survivors of hive fleet Behemoth which had been shattered centuries before, but still dangerous shards of poison in the body of the Imperium. Even attenuated as they were, they could still overwhelm a lightly defended world, growing in strength

---

1   In hindsight, these were clearly the precursors of Hive Fleets Kraken and Leviathan, the bulk of which had still to be detected at this time.

with each one they consumed. The prospect of facing a fresh fleet with almost limitless resources was, quite simply, terrifying.

'Then let's pray you're wrong,' I said. Unfortunately, as we now know, she was right twice over, and the reality was far worse than even my craven imaginings.

'Amen.' Zyvan made the sign of the aquila. 'But if she's not, those ships and men will be needed to defend the Imperium. And it's not just the 'nids...' He trailed off as Amberley shot him a venomous look. Clearly I wasn't supposed to be let in on everything.

'Necrons,' I said, jumping to the obvious conclusion. I pointed out the tomb world I'd been lucky to escape from a couple of years before. 'Not the friendliest of xenos. And cropping up more frequently of late, if these contact icons are anything to go by.' I indicated a couple of others in the same purple script.

'That would be pure speculation, commissar,' Amberley said, a clear warning tone entering her voice, but Mott nodded enthusiastically.

'A two hundred and seventy-three per cent increase in probable necron contact over the last century,' he said. 'Only twenty-eight per cent fully confirmed, however.' That would be because the majority of contacts left no survivors, of course.

'Be that as it may,' Amberley said, 'the fact remains that the resources we would expend fighting a war for Gravalax are likely to be needed elsewhere, and if we're forced to use them now, we would be fatally weakened.'

'Which still begs the question of who would be insane enough to try to provoke such a war, and what they could hope to gain by it,' I said, eager to show I was paying attention.

'Precisely what the inquisitor was sent here to find out,' Zyvan assured me.

'Not exactly.' Amberley killed the hololith display, probably to stop me from making any more uncomfortable guesses about what might be lurking in the outer darkness. 'Our attention was drawn to the increase in tau influence on Gravalax, and the activities of certain rogue traders who seemed to be profiting from it. I came to look into that, and assess the loyalties of the governor.'

'That's why you had Orelius pressuring him for trade concessions,' I said, the coin suddenly dropping. 'You wanted to see if he had any influence with the tau.'

'Quite right.' She smiled at me, like a schola tutor whose least promising pupil has just recited the entire catechism of abjuration. 'You're really quite astute for a soldier.'

'And your decision?' Zyvan asked, carefully not taking offence at the remark.

'I'm still considering it,' she admitted. 'He's certainly weak, probably corrupt, and undeniably stupid. He's let the alien influence take root here far too deeply to be dislodged without considerable effort. But he's no longer our primary concern.'

'You mean the conspirators?' I asked. 'Whoever's trying to provoke a war over this?'

'Precisely.' She nodded, favouring me with another smile, which, perhaps due to wishful thinking, looked remarkably like praise. 'Another astute deduction on your part.'

'Do you have any clue as to their identities?' Zyvan asked. Amberley shook her head.

'There's no shortage of enemies who would stand to gain from weakening the Imperial presence in this sector,' she said, with a warning glance at Mott, who seemed on the verge of listing them. 'Not least the tau themselves.' He subsided with visible disappointment. 'But whoever it is is undoubtedly working through the xenoist faction here, and the PDF units they control. Fortunately, the Guard seem to have drawn their teeth without dragging the tau into it, for which we can all be thankful.'

Zyvan and I took the implied compliment without comment.

'How is the investigation into the ambassador's murder going?' I asked. 'If you find the assassin, you find the conspirators, don't you?'

'Probably.' Amberley shook her head. 'But so far we don't have a suspect. The autopsy showed he was killed by an imperial bolt pistol at close range, but we already knew that, and half the guests at the party were carrying one. Our best lead is still the xenoist connection.'

'Or it was,' Mott chimed in with a censorial glare at me. 'Until this young man set fire to it.'

'I'm sorry?' I gazed at him in confusion.

'So you should be,' he said, without rancour. Amberley sighed.

'The local Arbites have been keeping tabs on the most vocal xenoist groups. One of them used to hold meetings at that warehouse, so we went to check it out.'

'And found a bit more than you bargained for,' I chipped in helpfully. She nodded.

'That we did. We found a way down to the under-city.'

'Definite surprise there,' Mott chipped in helpfully. 'Although given the amount of relatively new tau-influenced architecture in the city as a whole, finding one wasn't totally unexpected.'

I suppose I must seem naive, but up until this point it had never occurred to me that there wasn't an undercity – part and parcel of growing up in a hive, I suppose. You see, most imperial cities are millennia old, each generation building on the remains of the last, leaving a warren of service tunnels and abandoned rooms under the latest level of streets and buildings, often tens, or even hundreds, of metres thick. Mayoh, being so sparsely populated in imperial terms, didn't have anything like so thick a layer beneath it, but I'd just taken it for granted that it was bound to have the same labyrinth of sewers and walkways below its citizens' feet as any other urban area I was familiar with.

'Seems like a good place to plot sedition,' I conceded.

'Ideal,' Amberley agreed. 'As we found to our cost.'

'We were ambushed,' Mott said, 'though not before determining that the tunnel system is extremely extensive.'

'Ambushed by who?' Zyvan asked.

'Ah. Well, that's the question.' Amberley cocked her head quizzically. 'Whoever they were, they were well armed, and well trained. We barely got out alive.'

'Tomas and Jothan didn't,' Mott reminded her, and her brow darkened for a moment.

'Their sacrifice will be remembered,' she said, in the reflex way people do when they don't really mean it. 'They knew the risks.'

'More PDF defectors?' Zyvan asked. I shook my head.

'I don't think so. My aide and I got a good look at several of them. They were definitely civilians.'

'Or in civilian clothes,' Mott suggested. 'Not necessarily the same thing.'

'In either case,' Amberley said decisively, 'we need more information. And there's only one place we can get it.' I began to develop a familiar sinking feeling in the pit of my stomach.

'The undercity,' Zyvan said. The inquisitor nodded.

'Precisely. Which is why I require your assistance.'

'Anything at all, of course.' Zyvan spread his hands. 'Although I don't quite see—'

'My retinue is out of action, lord general. And I'm not stupid enough to undertake an expedition of this nature entirely alone.' Well, anyone could see that. 'I'd like to request the use of some of your Guard troopers.'

'Well, of course.' Zyvan nodded. 'You can hardly rely on the loyalty of the local PDF.'

'Exactly.' She nodded again.

'How many do you want?' Zyvan asked. 'A platoon, a company?' Amberley shook her head.

'No. We'll need to move fast, and light. One fire-team. And the commissar to lead them.' She turned those dazzling eyes on me again, and smiled. 'I'm sure a man of your formidable reputation will be up to the challenge.'

I wasn't, you can take my word for it, but I couldn't refuse a direct request from an inquisitor, could I? (Although if I'd known what I was getting into, I'd probably have given it a damn good try.) So I nodded, and tried to look confident.

'You can rely on me,' I said, with all the sincerity I could fake, and from the grin which quirked the corner of her mouth, I could tell she wasn't fooled for a second.

'I'm glad to hear it,' she said. 'I gather your regiment has had a great deal of experience in city fighting, so I'm sure they'll be ideal.'

'I'll ask for volunteers,' I said, but she shook her head.

'No need.' She skimmed a dataslate over the table-top to me. I stopped it, a premonitory tingle beginning in the palms of my hands. 'You've already assigned some.'

I glanced at the list of names, already knowing, in the way you can see the avalanche start even before the rocks begin to slide, what I'd read there. Kelp, Trebek, Velade, Sorel and Holenbi. The five troopers on the planet I'd least trust to watch my back, unless it was to stick a bayonet in it. I lifted my head.

'Are you sure, inquisitor? These troopers are hardly the most reliable–'

'But they are the most expendable.' She grinned at me, the mischievous light back in her eyes. 'And I'm sure you can keep them in line for me.'

It was official, then. This was a suicide mission. I swallowed, my mouth suddenly dry.

'You can count on it,' I said, wondering how in the name of the Emperor I was going to get out of this one.

TEN

'Trust? Trust's got nothing to do with it. I just don't want them out of my sight.'

– General Karis, after promising full access to his command bunker to the local PDF commanders on Vortovan.

'ARE YOU SURE about this, commissar?' Kasteen asked, clearly as troubled by the prospect as I was. She and Broklaw had joined me in my office at my request, and I'd filled them in on as much of the assignment I'd been handed as Amberley would permit. I sighed deeply.

'No, I'm not,' I admitted. 'But the inquisitor was quite insistent. These are the troopers she wants.'

'Well, we'd better give them to her,' Broklaw said. 'At least they'll be off our hands at last.' Kasteen nodded, clearly cheered by the prospect.

'That's true,' she conceded. Despite my best efforts to arrange their transfer to a penal legion, the Munitorium was proving as slow and obstructive as usual, and didn't seem the least bit inclined to send a ship all the way out here just to pick up a handful of cannon fodder. Normally, that wouldn't have been a problem, I'd simply have found space on the next outbound freighter or something, but Gravalax wasn't exactly the hub of the Segmentum, and even what little shipping there normally was had almost dried up as the political situation deteriorated. Even if the worst-case scenario I'd been shown on the hololith didn't come to pass, it looked as though we were going to be stuck with the five defaulters until we returned to Imperial space, which was going to be months away at this rate.

Which, in turn, had meant they were our responsibility for the foreseeable future, which wasn't exactly what I'd had in mind when I cheated Parjita out of his firing squad back aboard the *Righteous Wrath*.

'And on the plus side,' Broklaw went on cheerfully, 'at least we won't be losing anyone we'll miss.' He stopped suddenly, realised what he'd just said, and floundered in a way I would have found comical under any other circumstances. 'Not you, commissar, obviously. I mean, we would miss you, but I'm sure we won't. Have to, I mean. You'll be back.'

'I certainly intend to be,' I said, with more confidence than I felt. I still hadn't been able to think of a plausible reason to wriggle out of the assignment, so I'd bowed to the inevitable and started trying to find

ways of ensuring my own survival instead. None of
the troopers could be trusted, that much was certain,
but Amberley seemed confident enough so my best
bet was to stick close to her and hope she had a plan
of some kind. On the other hand, chances were that
Orelius's luckless bodyguards had thought the same
thing. Like most hivers, I was comfortable enough in
a tunnel complex unless someone was actually
shooting at me, so maybe the most prudent thing
would be to get conveniently lost at the earliest
opportunity and make my way back to the compound after a reasonable interval had passed. Then
again, if I did that and Amberley survived she would-
n't be terribly pleased with me to say the least, and
the prospect of hacking off an inquisitor wasn't one
to contemplate lightly.

The upshot of all this was that I'd spent a largely
sleepless night vacillating about my non-existent
choices until sheer exhaustion had tumbled me into
old nightmares of fleeing from gleaming metal killers
down endless corridors, heaving grey masses of
tyranid chitin roaring in towards me like a tide of
death, and a green-eyed seductress trying to suck the
soul from my body in the name of the Chaos power
she worshipped.[1] And probably others too, which I
was glad not to recall on waking.

1   These dreams would appear to refer obliquely to some of Cain's
earlier experiences. The last one in particular can certainly be matched
to a specific incident recorded elsewhere in the archive, although the
others are a little more problematic. He had encountered both necrons
and tyranids on more than one occasion prior to this date.

Jurgen appeared at my elbow, presaged by his usual miasma, and poured me my habitual bowl of tanna leaf tea. Instead of withdrawing as he normally did, though, he hesitated next to my desk.

'Was there something else, Jurgen?' I asked, anticipating some routine query about paperwork I couldn't be bothered to deal with. If I was going to die today, I wasn't going to waste my final hours filling out forms in triplicate. And if I didn't, which I swore to the Emperor I was going to do my damnedest to achieve, he could sort it out for me while I was gone. That was supposed to be an aide's job, after all. He cleared his throat stickily, and a faint expression of nausea ghosted across Broklaw's face.

'I'd like to go with you, sir,' he said at last. 'I wouldn't trust any of those frakheads further than I could throw a Baneblade, if you don't mind me saying so, and I'd feel a lot better if you'd let me watch your back.'

I was touched and I don't mind admitting it. We'd been campaigning together for the best part of thirteen years by that point, and faced innumerable perils together, but his loyalty never ceased to amaze me. Probably because the nearest I've ever got to the concept myself is looking it up in a dictionary.

'Thank you, Jurgen,' I said. 'I'd be honoured.' A faint flush crept up from behind his shirt collar, which, as usual, was open at the neck and stained with something that probably used to be food. Kasteen and Broklaw looked suitably impressed, too.

'I'd best go and get ready then.' He sketched a salute, about turned with the closest I'd ever seen him get to precision, and marched out, his shoulders set.

'Remarkable,' Broklaw said.

'He has a strong sense of duty,' I said, feeling cautiously optimistic about my chances of survival for the first time since Amberley dropped her bombshell. We'd been in some pretty tight spots together over the years, and I knew I could rely on him completely, which is more than I could say for anyone else in the team.

'He's a brave man,' Kasteen said, seemingly surprised by the idea. Most people tended to avoid him, put off by his appearance and body odour, and the vague sense of wrongness he exuded, but I'd been close to him for so long I'd got used to seeing past that to his well-hidden virtues. Though I was the last person you'd normally expect to appreciate them.

'I suppose he is,' I said.

'WELL, THERE THEY are,' I said. 'They're all yours.' Amberley nodded, and walked along the line of troopers, meeting their eyes one by one. They were as sullen a bunch as I remembered, gazing back at us in silence.

I'd had them marched to one of the storage sheds in our sector of the compound at the double, and was pleased to note that none of them seemed particularly out of breath, so their weeks of confinement hadn't left them as out of condition as I'd feared; but then, I don't suppose they'd had much to do except exercise anyway. They'd looked vaguely surprised when I dismissed the guards, except for Sorel, whose expression never seemed to change whatever happened, and stared at me as I sat casually on a nearby crate.

'I promised you a chance to redeem yourselves,' I said. 'And that chance has now come.' That got their attention. Velade looked vaguely apprehensive, Holenbi baffled as always, and even Sorel seemed to take slightly more interest than usual. Kelp and Trebek just stared at me, but at least they didn't seem inclined to go for one another again. Perhaps it was my personal charisma, or my unmerited reputation, but it was most likely the laspistol in the holster at my hip which I'd visibly left unfastened for a quick draw. I gestured to Amberley, who stepped forward from the shadows, the black cloak she'd worn before rendering her almost invisible until she moved. 'This is Inquisitor Vail. She has a little job for us.'

Velade gasped audibly as Amberley raised her hand, and her electoo flashed into visibility. Dressed in black as she was, she fit the popular conception of an inquisitor far more closely than the sultry lounge singer that I'd first encountered, or the cheerful young woman I'd been getting to know, and I could tell that most of them, at least, were properly intimidated.

'What kind of a job?' Trebek asked. I waited for Amberley to reply, but after a moment I realised she was leaving the briefing to me. Not that I knew much more than the rest of us, of course, but I'd pass on everything I could. The longer they survived, the longer I could hide behind them from whatever was waiting for us in the tunnels below.

'Recon,' I said. 'Into the undercity. Resistance is expected.'

'Resistance from who?' Trebek asked. I shrugged.

'That's what we're supposed to find out.'

'I take it we aren't expected to survive,' Kelp cut in. Amberley met his eyes, staring him down.

'That rather depends on you,' she said. 'The commissar certainly intends to. I suggest you follow his lead.'

'It's not going to make any difference to us anyway, is it?' Velade asked, with surprising vehemence. 'Even if we get through this one alive, we've only got another suicide mission to look forward to.'

'I'd worry about that later if I were you,' I said. But Amberley was nodding slowly, as though she was being perfectly reasonable. I certainly wouldn't have mouthed off to an inquisitor in her boots, but I suppose she felt she had nothing to lose in any case.

'Good point, Griselda,' she said. Velade and the others looked a little taken aback at the use of her given name. I recognised the technique as a subtle piece of psychological manipulation, quietly enjoying the chance to watch an expert at work. Amberley smiled, suddenly, the full force of her capricious personality manifesting itself again. 'All right, you need an incentive. If you make it back in one piece, you have my word you won't be transferred to a penal legion. How's that?'

A total pain in the fundament so far as I was concerned. The paperwork alone would be a nightmare, not to mention the morale and disciplinary problems which would undoubtedly ensue from trying to integrate such an insubordinate rabble back into a line company. I wasn't about to undermine my own authority by having it verbally overridden by an inquisitor in front of them, though, so I stayed quiet. Maybe I could get them transferred to another command, or assigned somewhere relatively harmless after she'd gone. The local PDF could certainly use a professional training cadre to bring them up to scratch once this mess was sorted out, and we were hardly likely to be coming back to Gravalax...

'All of us?' Holenbi asked, clearly not quite believing his own ears. Amberley shrugged.

'Well, she did ask first. But I suppose so. Wouldn't be much of an incentive for the rest of you otherwise, would it?'

No one answered, so I resumed the briefing.

'An undetermined number of hostiles are holed up down there. Our job is to find out how many, their disposition, and what they're up to.'

'Do we have a map of the tunnels?' Kelp asked. For what it was worth, they seemed to be focussing on the mission at least. I turned to Amberley.

'Inquisitor?' I asked. She shook her head.

'No. We didn't penetrate very far the first time before we were forced to retreat. We have very little idea of their extent, or what's down there.'

'Who's we?' Trebek asked.

'My associates,' Amberley replied. Trebek glanced pointedly around the shed.

'I can only see you.'

'The others were injured. That's why I need you.' No mention of the dead ones, I noticed, which was probably just as well. It wouldn't fool the troopers anyway, they knew enough about firefights in confined spaces to realise that not everyone she'd gone down there with would have made it out.

'So, to recap,' Kelp said, 'you want us to go into an unmapped labyrinth, looking for something you think might be down there, but you don't know what, protected by an indeterminate number of heavily armed guards, and the last time you tried you were the only one who made it out in one piece.'

'That about sums it up, yes,' Amberley admitted cheerfully. 'But you are forgetting one thing.'

'Which is?' I asked, already sure I wouldn't like the answer.

'They know I'm on to them now.' She smiled, as though it were a tremendous joke. 'So this time they'll be expecting us.'

'Another question.' Sorel spoke up for the first time, puncturing the sombre silence. 'Your generous offer notwithstanding , you've obviously chosen us because we're expendable.' His voice was as flat and colourless as his eyes. 'I assume you're not expecting many survivors from this little excursion.'

'As I said before, that rather depends on you.' Amberley nailed him with her eyes. 'I certainly intend to come back. So does the commissar.' She'd got that right, at least. 'And your question is?'

'What's to stop any of us putting a las-round through your head and disappearing over the horizon the first chance we get?' His wintry gaze swept the other prisoners. 'Don't tell me you're not all thinking about it.'

'Good point.' Amberley smiled, the amused expression I'd seen before back on her face. If it disconcerted Sorel he gave no sign of the fact, but it certainly worried the others. She jerked a thumb in my direction. 'There's always the commissar to get past before you can reach me, of course.'

'And I'll execute any one of you who even looks like they're thinking of making a run for it,' I promised. I would, too, because they'd have to kill me as well if they were to have a hope of getting away with it, and that would be a highly undesirable outcome from my point of view.

'Even if you could take us both,' and the amusement was abruptly gone from her voice, 'and I sincerely doubt that, I've lost count of the number of people I've met who thought they could outrun the Inquisition. But you might as well give it a try if you really want to.' Then the undercurrent of mirth was back in her voice. 'After all, there's a first time for everything.'

I smiled too, to demonstrate my confidence in her, but none of the others did. Sorel nodded, slowly, like a debater conceding a point.

'Fair enough,' he said.

* * *

No one had anything constructive to add, so after a few more desultory questions about the mission parameters (the answers to which all boiled down to 'Emperor only knows' in any case), I led them outside to where Jurgen had a Chimera waiting, its engine running, and tried to look confident. I would have preferred my usual scout Salamander, given the choice, but there wouldn't have been room for the entire team aboard it, and besides, the fully enclosed passenger bay would discourage any last-minute attempts at desertion, or so I hoped.

'Your equipment's already aboard,' I told them, standing well back until they'd embarked, like an ovinehound shepherding a flock through a gate. (Although the canines tend not to use laspistols to emphasise the point, of course.) Five bundles of kit were waiting for them, each one wrapped in a carapace vest with a name stencilled on it, and they all picked out their own as they boarded.

'Check it carefully,' Amberley told them. 'If there's anything missing you won't get a chance to come back for it.'

'Discharge papers?' Trebek said, raising a tension-relieving laugh from Velade and Holenbi.

'Something's wrong here,' Kelp said, shrugging into the body armour. 'It fits. Quartermaster must be slipping.' It was an axiom among the Guard that kit only came in two sizes – too large and too small.

'I had a word with him,' Amberley said. 'He assured me that there wouldn't be any complaints.'

'I'll just bet he did,' Kelp muttered.

'Hellguns. Shady!' Velade hefted her new weapon, looking incongruously like a juvie on Emperor's day morning. As a regular line trooper, she was only used to handling a standard-issue lasgun, the more powerful variant normally being reserved for storm-troopers and other special forces. At least her evident enthusiasm for her new toy seemed to be keeping her apprehension in check.

'Nice,' Kelp agreed, snapping a powercell home with practiced precision.

'We thought the extra punch might come in handy,' I said. Amberley had suggested I replace my battered old laspistol with the handgun version of the heavier weapon, but after some hesitation, I'd demurred. I'd got so used to it over the years that it was more like an extension of my own arm than a weapon, and no amount of added stopping power would compensate for the different weight and feel of a replacement throwing off my instinctive aim. In a firefight, that could mean the difference between life and death.

I'd grabbed a set of the body armour, though, and wore it now, concealed beneath my uniform great-coat. It felt a little heavy and uncomfortable, but a lot less so than taking a las-bolt to the chest.

'It just might,' Trebek agreed. She was busily hanging frag grenades from her body harness. Most of them had a couple, along with smoke canisters, luminators, spare power packs, and all the other odds and ends troopers carry into the field. The exception was Holenbi, who carried a medpack in place of the grenades, but his expertise in battlefield medicine made him more valuable patching the others up if the necessity arose. And if it came down to grenades in a confined space, we were pretty much fragged in any case, so a couple more or less wouldn't make any difference.

'You can take the brute force approach if you like.' Sorel sighted along the length of his long-las, and made a minute adjustment to the targeter. I'd taken the trouble to find the weapon that used to be assigned to him, knowing that a sniper gets as attached to his weapon as I was to my old pistol, and that he would have customised it in a dozen subtle ways to improve its accuracy. 'I've got all the edge I need right here.' He must have realised the strings I'd had to pull to obtain it for him, because he met my eyes at that point and nodded, a barely perceptible thanks. I was astonished. Up until then I'd been convinced he had no emotions at all.

'Just make sure you keep it pointed in the right direction,' I said, with enough of a smile to take most of the sting out of the warning. It was still there, though, and an expression I couldn't quite identify came close to surfacing on his habitually impassive face.

'I could use a few more pressure pads,' Holenbi said, inventorying the medkit with the speed of long practice. I gestured to the primary aid box bolted to the Chimera's inner bulkhead.

'Help yourself,' I invited. He burrowed rapidly through it, scavenging several items which made the bag on his belt bulge, and stowed a few more in other pouches and pockets, discarding a couple of ration bars to make room for them.

'Better eat that,' Velade advised, taking the seat next to him. 'You'll only get hungry later if you leave it.'

'Yeah, right,' he agreed, breaking one in half and offering the rest to her. She took it with a smile, their hands touching for a moment as her fingers closed around it, and Amberley grinned at me.

'Aww,' she mouthed, her back to them. 'How sweet.'

Maybe to her, I thought, but to me it was little more than another potential complication in a catastrophe just waiting to happen. I quelled my irritation, and picked the remaining bar off the bench.

'She's got a point.' I split the bar with Amberley. 'Better stock up with carbohydrates while you can. You'll be burning a lot of energy soon enough.'

'You're the expert,' she said, as though anyone else's opinions mattered a damn on this foolhardy expedition. She sniffed at the grey fibrous mass, and bit into it cautiously. 'You people actually eat this frak?'

'Not if we can help it,' Velade said.

'Then I'm definitely surviving this.' Amberley swallowed the remains of her ration bar with a grimace of distaste. 'No way that's going to be my last meal.' The troopers all laughed, even Sorel, and I marvelled again at her powers of manipulation.[1] By playing the civilian outsider, she'd reinforced their sense of

---

1 Coming from Cain, that's a real compliment.

identity as soldiers with great subtlety. I doubted whether it would be quite enough to weld them into a cohesive unit, but that wasn't really an issue on this assignment. All that was necessary was that they work well enough together to get Amberley the intelligence she required. And me out in one piece, of course.

There were still far too many weak links for my liking, though. Kelp and Trebek were professional enough to put their rivalries aside for long enough to get the job done, I hoped, especially with an inquisitorial pardon up for grabs, but the way they kept avoiding eye contact with each other was a far from encouraging sign. And whatever was going on between Velade and Holenbi might just be enough for them to put their concern for each other ahead of the mission objective, or the survival of anyone else. Like me. And as for Sorel; well, he flat out gave me the creeps, and I was determined not to let him get anywhere I couldn't keep an eye on him. I'd met psychopaths before, and he had all the hallmarks. He wouldn't hesitate to sacrifice the rest of us to save his own skin, of that I was sure.[1]

And then there was Amberley. Charming as I found her, she was still an inquisitor above all else, and that meant that all we were to her was a means to an end. A noble and important one, no doubt, but that

---

1 An old expression about pots and kettles springs to mind at this point, as well as the saying about taking one to know one...

would be of little comfort to me when the black bell tolled.[1]

So it was little wonder that my palms were tingling as I closed the tail ramp and activated my combead.

'All right, Jurgen,' I said. 'We're ready to go.'

THIS TIME, THERE were no waves and cheers as we left the compound, although I had no doubt that the rumour mill had spread the news of our departure just as far as before. I was quietly relieved by that, to be honest, as this was to be no easy victory for our newly forged regiment to take pride in and celebrate. This would be a desperate struggle for survival, I didn't need my itching palms to tell me that. Although how desperate, and against how terrible a foe, I still at that time had no inkling. (And that was a mercy, let me tell you. If I'd known then what awaited us in the undercity of Mayoh, I would probably have broken down in hysterics from sheer terror.)

As it was, I masked my concern with the ease of long practice, and kept a stern eye on the troopers, hoping any agitation I felt would be mistaken for vigilance. To my relief they seemed to be settling, focussing more on the mission now that it was underway, and if they weren't exactly on the same wavelength yet, at least they weren't jamming each other.

1   He is speaking figuratively here, the tolling of the Black Bell of Terra being a well-known soldier's euphemism for death in action. I hardly think he would have expected such an accolade in actual fact!

That reminded me I hadn't reported our departure to Kasteen yet, so I retuned my combead to the command frequency and exchanged a few words with her. As I'd expected, her mood was sombre, and she wished me luck as though she thought I might actually need it.

I was beginning to find the tense atmosphere inside the vehicle a little claustrophobic, not to mention being rattled around like a pea in a can by Jurgen's habitual driving style, so I popped the turret hatch and stuck my head out for some fresh air. The sudden rush was invigorating, almost taking my cap with it as I emerged, and I checked the heavy bolter so I'd have an excuse for staying out there for as long as I could. It was primed and ready, of course, Jurgen having done his usual thorough job, so I was able to settle back and enjoy the spectacle of the local civilian traffic swerving out of our way. There seemed to be a lot of it, I noticed, particularly in the main boulevards; but there was no obvious pattern to the movement. There was just as much going in each direction, and when I glanced down the crossways, they all seemed choked as well.

'Inquisitor,' I subvocalised, switching to the channel Amberley had given me earlier. I hadn't seen any sign of a bead in her ear, but that didn't surprise me. For all I knew, she'd disguised it in some way, or was stuffed with augmetics that did the same job. (And a great many others, as I was to discover over the course of our association.) 'There seems to be a lot of civilian activity. Anything we should be aware of?'

There was actually a great deal we should have been aware of, of course, the conspiracy we tracked was far more extensive and dangerous than we had imagined, but at that point, I was still blissfully ignorant of how much trouble we were in.

'Probably lots of things.' Amberley sounded wary, though not particularly concerned. 'But we'll just have to make do with what we know, and proceed with caution.'

Easier said than done with Jurgen driving, I thought, but she was the expert. I watched as he swerved us around a slow-moving cargo lifter, its flatbed jammed with civilians carrying hastily assembled bundles of possessions. Probably just spooked by our raid on the Heights, but the implications troubled me. I began to look out for similar sights, and found several in the space of a handful of seconds. I voxed Amberley again.

'It's looking like refugee traffic up here,' I said.

'Intriguing,' she responded, a note of curiosity entering her voice. 'What would they be fleeing, I wonder?'

'Nothing good,' I said, speaking from bitter experience, although in truth it wouldn't be that unexpected for anyone who could to be leaving the city by now. The political and military situation was still balanced on a knife-edge, and it wouldn't need someone of Mott's intellect to deduce that things would be a lot healthier somewhere else if it all boiled over. No harm in checking everything, I thought, so I hopped through the tactical frequencies, finding a lot of garbled traffic on the PDF net. Very little of it seemed to be making sense, though.

'Commissar.' Kasteen's voice cut in suddenly. 'I think you should know. We've just had instructions to go to combat readiness.'

'Who from?' Amberley interrupted before I could respond. I suppose I might have resented her butting in, let alone monitoring my supposedly secure messages, but right then I was too busy swinging the bolter round and taking the safety off. A thick column of smoke was visible ahead of us, rising from a burning truck in the middle of the road, and the traffic was beginning to stall and gridlock as panicked drivers tried to find a way around it or turn back. Bright las-bolts were scoring the air, but who was shooting and what they were aiming at remained obscured behind the smoke.

'By order of the governor,' Kasteen said.

'Imbecile!' Amberley said, along with some qualifying adjectives which I'd last heard in an underhive drinking den when someone turned out to have more than the conventional number of emperors in their tarot deck. I began to suspect that Governor Grice's political future was going to be short and uncomfortable. 'We'll have the tau on our arses like flies round a corpse.'

'I think we already have,' I said. Something was moving inside the smoke, fast and agile, twice the height of a man. It wasn't alone, either. There were more of them moving back there, and the whole pack of them was surrounded by little darting dots. I suddenly remembered the flying platters we'd seen at the tau enclave, and that they were armed too.

Abruptly, unnervingly, the leading dreadnought (the same type El'sorath had called battlesuits) swung its head in our direction, and turned, a pair of long-barrelled weapons mounted on its shoulders coming to bear. We were still a long way away from being an easy target, but I've always been cautious, so I hailed our driver.

'Jurgen!' I shouted, 'get us out of here!'

By way of reply, he swung us abruptly towards a narrow alleyway, crushing a raised bed of ornamental shrubs beneath our left-hand tread, and barging a small, sleek groundcar out of the way. The driver's volley of profanity was drowned out by a sudden thunderclap of displaced air as something hit the front of an omnibus right where we'd been a moment before, reducing its entire nose to metallic confetti before raking the length of it, blowing a tangled mass of wreckage, blood and bone out of the back. Before I could see anything more, we were behind the shelter of a building, our hurtling metallic shell gouging lumps out of the walls, our tracks leaving a trail of burst and flattened waste containers in our wake.

'Emperor's bowels!' I said, stunned by the narrowness of our escape.

'What was that?' Amberley asked, her voice almost drowned out by the complaints of the troopers around her. I tried to explain the best I could, still shaken by the range and accuracy of the weapon deployed against us. 'Sounds like a railgun,' she said, apparently unperturbed. 'Nasty things.'

'Could it have damaged us?' I asked, making sure the spare ammo boxes were in easy reach. There was nothing ahead of us now except more panicking civilians, but I wasn't planning on being taken by surprise twice, you can be sure.

'Easily,' she replied cheerfully. 'Even at that range it could have gutted us like a fish.'

'The Emperor protects,' Jurgen said piously. Well He hadn't done a hell of a lot for the bus passengers, I thought, but decided it wouldn't be tactful to say so. He'd only take it as a sign that we were important to His ineffable plan anyway.

'Who were the tau engaging?' I asked.

'The PDF,' Kasteen said. 'Who else? We're getting reports in that some of the loyalists have mutinied, and opened fire on the tau compound. The diplomats are trying to calm things, but the bluies are claiming they have a right to retaliate, and have entered the city. They're engaging every PDF unit they come across.'

'What about the Guard?' I asked, already sure I wouldn't like the answer.

'The governor's orders are to contain the situation by any means necessary. The lord general is asking for clarification.' Playing for time, in other words. If the Guard units entered the city, they'd be caught in the middle; with half the PDF unreliable, they'd become a target for both sides. My stomach lurched, and for once, it wasn't due to Jurgen's driving.

'Well, that's it then,' I said, the words like ashes in my mouth. 'We've run out of time.' The war so many people had sacrificed so much to avoid was upon us at last, and it seemed there wasn't a damn thing we could do about it.

Editorial Note:

It goes without saying that the unrest which Cain noticed breaking out across the city was being duplicated to a lesser extent across the whole of Gravalax; although with the bulk of both the Imperial and tau expeditionary forces based around the capital, the situation deteriorated further and faster in Mayoh than anywhere else on the planet. Minor clashes did take place around several of the starports, as both sides realised keeping them open or denying them to the enemy would be vital in either reinforcing or evacuating their forces. For the most part, the warfare was internecine, pro- and anti-xenoist factions within the PDF turning on one another with the terrible ferocity unique to civil war.

The following extract may prove useful in appreciating the wider picture.

From *Purge the Guilty! An impartial account of the liberation of Gravalax,* by Stententious Logar. 085.M42

Thus it was, spurred by the workings of a vast, malign conspiracy, the entire world was rent asunder in an orgy of fratricide which shames the survivors and their descendents even to the present day. If anything at all can be said to have been learned from these terrible events, it must surely be this; that however benign they may appear, the alien is not to be trusted, and that turning aside from the word of the Emperor in even the smallest respect is the most certain route to damnation for us all.

It must have been the belated realisation of this which spurred the loyal cadre of Planetary Defence Force regulars into turning on the traitors in their midst, taking heart from the salutary way in which the Imperial Guard had dealt with the alien-lovers who had dared to desecrate the streets of an Imperial city with open rebellion. Their patriotic fervour at last aroused, His Divine Majesty's most loyal servants began to cleanse the hideous stain on their honour in the only way possible; by shedding the blood of those whose craven panderings to the aliens

in their midst had led the whole planet to the very
brink of the abyss.

At first, the renewal of martial spirit was sporadic,
beginning with the arrest of those unit commanders
whose loyalties were, for one reason or another, suspect. Inevitably, however, faced with the threat of
exposure, those whose souls were stained with the
guilt of collaboration resisted, proving their black-
heartedness by opening fire on the heroic defenders
of Imperial virtue. The rot spread exponentially after
that, until almost every PDF unit was engaged on
one side or the other; indeed, such was the confusion
that many were unable to tell friend from foe and
simply engaged every other unit they encountered
indiscriminately.

Under these circumstances, it was hardly surprising that the most fervent of the loyalists lost no
time in placing the blame squarely on the shoulders
of those ultimately responsible, the xenos themselves, and resolved to rid our world of the taint of
their presence without further delay. These heroes
of legendary proportions, whose names would
undoubtedly ring down the ages of Gravalax forever
more if enough of their bodies had remained intact
to identify, turned on the corruption at its source
and threw themselves against the very citadel of the
invader.

Alas, faced with the overwhelming firepower of
this redoubt of the unholy, they were cut to pieces,

but the damage had been done. Aware for the first time of their own vulnerability, the tau advanced into the city to slaughter the righteous, and the very future of Gravalax hung in the balance.

Throughout these events, one question remains unanswered. Why did the Imperial Guard take so long to respond? Accusations of cowardice are clearly ridiculous, if not treasonous, the lord general's reputation alone being sufficient to belie them without a moment's thought. Once again, the only credible explanation is that of conspiracy, some dark machination hindering their deployment for reasons we can only guess at. As to the hand behind that conspiracy, a careful sifting of the evidence once again points us firmly to the shadowy presence of the rogue traders...

[And after a reasonably concise summary of events up to that point, he veers off on his personal obsession once more. Perhaps it's just as well, though; if anyone were to deduce the real enemy we were facing, we would have to take steps to obscure the truth.]

ELEVEN

Whatever happens, we have got
The Emperor's blessing. They have not.

– From 'The Guardsman's Duty,'
a popular ballad. (Trad.)

THE WAREHOUSE WAS just as we'd left it, which is to say it was a tangled mess of collapsed rubble and gently smoking debris. As we disembarked from the Chimera, the scent of old burning caught at the back of my throat, making me cough. We hadn't seen any more of the supernaturally fast tau dreadnoughts before we reached our destination, but I remained cautious nevertheless, ordering the troopers to consider the area enemy territory as we left the relative safety of the armoured carrier. What little I'd been able to glean from the vox traffic was less than encouraging, and my attempts to get through to someone more senior at divisional HQ for clarification were futile; no one there seemed to have a clue what was going on either. Besides, this was the inquisitor's little expedition, and she showed no sign of calling it off, so I gave up after a while and just let her get on with it.

'It seems clear enough,' Amberley said, consulting an auspex she'd produced from somewhere, and for a moment, I wondered what else the dark cape concealed. Nevertheless, the troopers debarked with commendable precision, covering each other as they moved. Kelp on point, while the others remained protected by the vehicle's armour plate until he'd reached the cover of a nearby heap of rubble, then Trebek, who headed for a tumbled wall on the opposite flank. Once they were established, Velade followed, taking up a position behind them, then Holenbi, who, I noticed, picked a spot where he could cover her as effectively as possible despite leaving a small blind spot in his coverage of Trebek. After a moment's hesitation, I decided to let it go just this once. After all, they weren't the most cohesive team I might have wished for, and it could have been an honest mistake. Sorel swept the area with the targeter of his long-las, and raised a hand.

'It's clear, commissar,' he said. 'You can move.'

'After you,' I said. He shrugged, almost imperceptibly, and was gone, crouching low, hurrying over the uneven ground to a point about fifty metres ahead of

Kelp, where a fallen structural beam lay across a tumbled internal wall. He scrambled up it, worming his way into a gap between the chunks of masonry, and froze, scanning the rubble around us through his magnifying sight. If I hadn't been keeping an eye on him the whole way, I would barely have known he was there.

Amberley raised a quizzical eyebrow at me.

'Wouldn't it have been more prudent to have moved out while he kept you covered?' she asked.

'Any other sharpshooter, yes,' I said. 'But after what he said at the briefing–'

'Better safe than sorry,' she finished for me. I nodded, and indicated the open ramp.

'Whenever you're ready, inquisitor.'

'After you,' she said, and I almost missed the grin that accompanied her echo of my own words. I wouldn't have been all that surprised if she didn't trust me, mind you; I wouldn't have trusted me either, but then I suppose I know myself better than most.

So I smiled in return, to let her think I thought she was joking, and dropped to the ground, my boots crunching on the scattered ash. Jurgen had left the driver's compartment by now and I was joined by his odour, followed an instant later by the man himself. In spite of myself, my eyebrows rose.

'Are you sure you're not a little lightly armed for this?' I asked, and a momentary frown of concern flashed across his face before he realised I was joking.

Like the rest of us, except for Amberley (for all I knew, she might just have concealed hers the way I

had), he was wearing a carapace jacket, but in a reassuring nod to the Guard I knew, his was definitely
one of the standard sizes – too big – although most
of his kit looked like that at the best of times. He had
a hellgun like the others, but it was slung across his
shoulders. In his hands was the unmistakable bulk of
a meltagun, a heavy thermal weapon normally used
to give tanks a hard time in close terrain, which was
about the only time you stood a chance of getting
near enough to use one without being spread across
the landscape. Emperor alone knew where he'd got it
from, but it was a reassuring sight nonetheless. He
shrugged.

'I thought if we were tunnel fighting we might want
to clear a path quickly,' he said. Well, it would certainly do that, I thought, whether our path was
blocked by rubble or enemy troopers.

'Good idea,' I said. On this kind of mission there
was no such thing as overkill.

'Did you remember the marshmallows?' Amberley
asked, appearing at my elbow. Jurgen looked a little
worried.

'I don't think so...' he began.

'She's joking, Jurgen,' I reassured him. A slow grin
spread across his face.

'Oh, I get it. It's a thermal weapon, and you toast–'

'Quite.' I turned to see Sorel signal the all-clear, and
Kelp begin the next step in the complex game of
leapfrog which would get us to our objective.

* * *

I'D HALF EXPECTED us not to find it, what with the building having collapsed and all, but Amberley's auspex pointed us in the right direction, and after a few moments of alternately dashing forward, ducking for cover, and trying to keep an eye on five former mutineers I didn't trust for a second, we assembled again in the shadow of a wall. Or what was left of one, at least.

'It should be around here,' Amberley said, sweeping the little instrument around so its guiding spirit could get a better view. Something on the readout seemed to satisfy her, and it vanished into the recesses of her cloak as deftly as it had appeared in the first place. She indicated a small heap of rubble, and smiled. 'Under that, if I'm not mistaken.'

'Kelp, Sorel,' I said, indicating the debris, and the two men stepped forward, Kelp with a scowl and the sniper with his usual lack of expression. They slung their weapons and began the onerous task of shifting the rubble. 'The rest of you keep watching our perimeter,' I ordered, diverting their attention from the work. Somewhat shamefaced, Trebek, Velade, and Holenbi stopped gawping at the rapidly growing hole and resumed their guard duties.

'Not good,' I muttered to Jurgen. They shouldn't have let themselves get distracted that easily, even if the inquisitor's little gadget had assured them there were no hostiles in the area. He nodded.

'Sloppy,' he agreed, unconscious of the irony.

'Is that what you're looking for?' Kelp asked, after a few more moments of heavy lifting. What looked like a maintenance hatch of some kind had been revealed, bent and twisted by the heat and the pounding it had received from the falling rubble. He wiped a grimy hand across his sweating face, leaving a streak of soot and masonry dust. Sorel, more fastidious, wiped his hands against the knees of his trousers.

'I think so,' Amberley said. Kelp nodded, grasped the handle, and pulled, every one of his overdeveloped muscles standing out as he strained against it. After a moment he gasped and let go.

'We'll need a demo charge to shift that.'

'Maybe if I...' Jurgen took a step forward, and aimed the melta at it. Kelp and Sorel scrambled back with almost indecent haste, and even Amberley looked a little disconcerted as she raised a hand to forestall him.

'We just want the hatch open, not the whole building down.'

'Right idea, though,' I added, seeing his crestfallen expression. 'Velade, Holenbi, front and centre. Five rounds rapid.' The twisted metal flashed into vapour under the combined power of the hellgun volley, and I clapped Jurgen on the back encouragingly. 'Good thinking.' Which, by his standards, it had been.

'Or that might do it,' Kelp conceded, staring down into the darkened hole which had opened up at our feet. I aimed my trusty pistol at it, but it was a pointless precaution; anyone waiting in ambush would have been vaporised along with the inspection panel, and anyone outside the hellguns' area of effect would have been shooting back by now.

'Good.' Amberley looked satisfied. 'I was hoping they'd think this way down had been blocked off.'

I wasn't about to take anything for granted, though, so I assembled the squad quickly.

'Kelp,' I said, 'you're on point.' He nodded, but didn't look happy. 'Then Sorel, Velade, Jurgen, me, the inquisitor, Holenbi. Trebek has the rear.' That ought to keep the biggest potential troublemakers as far apart as possible, and separate the two lovebirds just enough to keep their minds on the job instead of each other. I hoped. Amberley caught my eye and nodded. Good, she wasn't going to undermine my authority by contradicting me.

'Whatever happened to "ladies first"?' Kelp grumbled, and dropped into the dank-smelling darkness below.

WELL, IT MIGHT have been a consequence of my upbringing, but the labyrinth of service ducts we found ourselves in felt almost reassuring. I was careful not to let myself get too comfortable, though, as in my experience complacency is just a shortcut to a body bag. No one was shooting at us, and the auspex, now back in Amberley's hand, remained reassuringly free of hostile contacts.

Or, indeed, contacts of any kind. Our footsteps echoed back at us, despite every attempt at stealth, and the beams of our luminators picked out nothing more threatening than the occasional rodent.

After a while, I noticed that the dust in the corridor ahead of us was undisturbed, a thick layer which puffed up under our footfalls before settling slowly back down again. I felt the residue tickling my eyes and the back of my throat, and fought the impulse to sneeze.

'This isn't the way you came before, is it?' I asked, and Amberley shook her head.

'No,' she admitted. 'I thought a detour might be prudent, given the welcome we got the last time.'

'But you do know where we're going, right?' I persisted. She repeated the gesture.

'Haven't a clue,' she said cheerfully. Something of what I felt must have shown on my face, because she smiled then, and qualified the remark. 'I mean we should be heading roughly south-west, but all these corridors look alike to me.'

'Then we need to bear off more in that direction,' I said, indicating a side corridor that intersected the one we were in about thirty metres ahead.[1] Kelp flattened himself against the wall next to it, and signalled the all clear.

I was beginning to pick up a clearer idea of Amberley's destination, which, despite her claims of uncertainty, she manifestly had. If I still had my bearings we were heading in the general direction of the

1   Cain's sense of direction underground was indeed remarkably good, as I had the opportunity to observe a number of times, a fact which adds some plausibility to his claim to have been native to a hive world. Although it should be noted that he could become as lost as anyone else on occasion, particularly when under fire or attempting to move closer to the enemy, a minor discrepancy over which I have tended to give him the benefit of the doubt.

old quarter, which made some kind of sense. The tunnels would be closer to the surface there, making them more accessible to whoever else was down here. Who they might be, and what they might be hoping to achieve was still a mystery to me, however.

We proceeded in silence for some time, until Sorel held up a hand, warning us to stop. Amberley and I padded over to join him.

'What is it?' I asked. Kelp's face, a pale disc in the gloom, stared back at us, waiting for the signal to proceed.

'Movement,' he said, pointing away into the darkness ahead of us. Amberley checked the screen of her auspex.

'Nothing on this,' she said. I didn't care what the box said. Techpriests might have complete faith in their machines, but I'd been let down by them too often in the past. Sorel had a sniper's instincts, and was as much a survivor as me, and if he was feeling spooked, then so was I.

'Kelp?' I asked. The point man made a negative gesture. No contact.

'I didn't see anything,' he added verbally.

'OK. Proceed,' I said. Then quietly I added to Sorel, 'Keep your eyes open.' He nodded an acknowledgement and moved out, his gun at the ready. The others followed, a little more nervous now, and I waited until they'd all passed before dropping into line behind Trebek.

'Taking the rearguard now?' Amberley asked, falling into step beside me. 'Isn't that dangerous?'

It was, of course, the second most dangerous spot in the column, vulnerable to being picked off by an ambusher or a pursuer. But if Sorel was right, the enemy was definitely ahead of us now. I shrugged.

'As opposed to the position of perfect safety that you're in at the moment?' I asked, and was rewarded with another throaty chuckle, which lifted my spirits in spite of myself. The mood didn't last long, though; as we passed the mouth of a service duct, I noticed the dust around it had been disturbed, and not long ago, either. I pointed it out to Amberley, my voice low so as not to alarm the others. 'What do you make of that?'

The duct was a good two metres above the floor, but the dust beneath it showed only the marks of our own boots. My palms tingled, and I swept the beam of my luminator across the tangle of pipework that hung from the ceiling over our heads. It was possible someone had lurked there, but why had they moved just as we approached? And how had they got up there in the first place?

'Remind you of anything?' Amberley asked quietly. Now that she asked, it did – a maddening sense of familiarity that refused to gel. The only thing I was certain of was that it had been something bad, but with all the horrors I'd faced up to that point, it didn't help much in narrowing it down. I was about to say something sarcastic to Amberley about another clue helping when my attention was firmly distracted.

'Commissar.' Kasteen's voice hissed in my ear, hazed with static. 'Can you hear me?'

'Barely,' I said. The metres of masonry and rockcrete over our heads were attenuating the signal, and if we went much further, we would be out of contact entirely. 'What's happening?'

'The governor has ordered the arrest of Lord General Zyvan!' Even through the static the outrage in her voice was palpable. 'And he's demanding the Guard move into the city right away!'

'On what charge?' Amberley said. Whatever vox gear she had was evidently a little stronger than mine, because Kasteen recognised her voice.

'Cowardice!' Kasteen sounded even more outraged than before. 'How he has the nerve–'

'Will be determined by the proper authorities.' Amberley's voice was crisp and commanding now. 'Until such time as that can be arranged the armies of the Imperium will remain under the command of the lord general, and if the governor objects to that, he is more than welcome to take the matter up with the Inquisition.'

'I'll relay that message,' Kasteen said, evidently relishing the prospect of the governor's reaction.

'Colonel,' I added, before she could cut the link. 'What's the situation with the tau?'

'Grim,' Kasteen admitted. 'They're still engaging PDF units all over the city. Civilian casualties are already up in the thousands, and we have rioters choking the streets. But so far they've held off from attacking us. If the lord general and the diplomats can buy us a little more time–'

'They'll have to,' Amberley cut in. 'Whatever happens, the Guard must not get sucked into an open war with the tau.'

'Understood,' Kasteen said. It must have been galling for her, though, and the strain was clear in her voice. Being forced to stand by and do nothing while an imperial city burned, and xenos massacred the citizens with impunity was probably the hardest thing she ever had to do.

'Well, that's something,' Amberley said, as the vox link went dead. 'At least there's still hope.'

'Hope for who?' I asked, trying not to think of the civilians who, even as we stood here, were losing their homes and their lives. I'd be the first one to admit that I'm a self-centred hedonist, but even I felt a surge of sympathy for their plight.

'For half the segmentum,' Amberley replied, sounding suddenly weary, and for the first time, I had an inkling of the terrible weight of responsibility her calling imposed. 'You need to focus on the big picture, Ciaphas. Emperor knows, sometimes that's hard.' Moved by an impulse I couldn't explain, I took her hand for a moment, imparting what moral support I could through simple human contact.

'I know,' I said. 'But someone has to do it. And today that someone is us.'

Amberley laughed, only slightly forced, and squeezed my palm for a moment before letting go.

'That was completely ungrammatical, you realise.'

'Never my strong point,' I admitted. It was strange, now I come to recall it, but her use of my given name seemed so natural I never thought to be surprised.

SHORTLY AFTER THAT, we lost contact with the surface entirely. Or at least I did, and if Amberley was still able to get a signal through she wasn't saying. Even though we were beyond all realistic hope of reinforcement in any case, I found the sensation profoundly dispiriting, and tried to concentrate on the job at hand. It was in one of these moments of distraction that I collided with Trebek, who had stopped suddenly in the tunnel ahead of me.

'What is it?' I asked, knowing that she wouldn't just freeze like that for no reason.

'I thought I heard something,' she said. I cocked my head, listening hard, but couldn't make out anything over the scuff of our footfalls and our breathing. We were moving stealthily enough – these troopers had been hunting tyranids less than six months before in conditions not dissimilar to this, don't forget, and if there's anything in the galaxy more calculated to teach you caution than that, I've yet to come across it – but the multiplicity of hard surfaces around us magnified every sound we made, however slight, with dozens of overlapping echoes. And, paradoxically, the quieter we moved the louder we sounded to our own ears, straining all the harder to hear over it.

So I issued the order to halt, and we waited tensely for the echoes to die away.

'There,' Trebek breathed after a moment. 'Hear that?'

I could. It was the sharp crack of lasguns, and a similar, deeper note which sounded both familiar and slightly wrong. At the time I put it down to the echoes, but we were to discover the real reason soon enough.

'Gunfire,' I confirmed. 'About half a klom that way.' I indicated the direction without thinking, before realising it lay almost dead on to Amberley's preferred route. Just great. Trebek looked a little puzzled.

'Are you sure, sir?'

'Absolutely,' I said, before realising that no one else here would be quite so at home in these tunnels as me.[1] Valhalla has its cavern cities, of course, but they're quite different to the average hive, with wide open spaces under well-lit roofs of rock and ice. It was perishingly cold too, the way the locals like it, but it takes all sorts to make a galaxy, and you can always turn up the heat in your hotel suite. (Not too much, though, as I discovered once, or you can end up with bits of the wall dripping onto your belongings.) Amberley took another look at her auspex, which was as quietly unhelpful as before.

'If you say so,' she said. After a moment, the firing stopped, and a deeper, more unnerving silence

---

1   Again, I can vouch from personal experience that Cain did have an almost uncanny ability to disentangle sounds from echoes in a confined space, his estimates of their sources being remarkably accurate in most cases.

descended. We listened for a little while longer, but it soon became apparent that we would learn nothing more by remaining where we were, and Amberley urged us to proceed. Not having a plausible reason to go back, I agreed, and we moved on as before, though not without a considerable amount of trepidation on my part.

It was about five minutes later that Kelp, who was still on point, held up his hand and halted.

'What is it?' I asked.

'Bodies. Lots of them.' Well, that was a bit of an exaggeration, but there were at least half a dozen spread out across the large open space which the corridor had eventually led us into. It seemed to be a junction point of some kind because a number of other tunnel mouths led away from it, to all points of the compass, and by my estimation it had been used for storage or something quite recently. About a dozen stacking units had been broken open, though what they had contained was now a mystery, and the smashed remains of a glow globe showed that someone had been working here not too long ago.

'Recognise this?' I asked Amberley, who was looking around with obvious signs of familiarity. She nodded.

'This was as far as we got before,' she said. 'We came in through that corridor there.' She pointed to one of the other entrances. 'We took them by surprise, but there were more of them than we'd anticipated, and then the reinforcements showed up.' I spotlighted the nearest corpse with my luminator, a stocky fellow in work overalls with most of his chest missing.

'Was he among them?'

'I wasn't waiting around to be introduced,' she said. 'But I don't think so.' Her eyes glazed over for a second with the effort of recall. 'Rakel was having some kind of seizure, and then she took a las-bolt to the stomach. After that it got a little confusing.'

The troopers were acting like proper soldiers, I noted absently, spreading out to secure our perimeter as best they could without waiting for orders, which was something at least, so I returned my attention to what the inquisitor was saying. This was the most she'd let slip about her previous excursion into these tunnels since we started, and I hoped to find out a little more.

'What kind of a seizure?' I asked. 'Like the one she had when she saw Jurgen?' Amberley shook her head.

'No,' she said slowly, 'that was something quite different. I'm still not sure what it means.' But she had her suspicions, I could tell, even if she wasn't about to share them with me. She moved on rapidly, in a transparent attempt to change the subject, which vaguely surprised me, as I'd come to expect more subtlety from her than that. 'We were standing over there.' She pointed. 'Rakel had been getting more agitated the deeper we came, sensing something, but not really able to tell me what it was. Then as we got closer to the people here, it got worse.'

'They were psykers too?' I asked, feeling even more uneasy, if that were possible. I'd encountered those

before, and it had never ended well. Amberley
shrugged, a delicate ripple of her shoulders.

'Possibly.' Whether she was uncertain, or just being
non-committal, I couldn't tell.

'Sir. Inquisitor.' Holenbi gestured diffidently from
the side of one of the corpses. 'I think you should see
this.'

'What?' I moved to join him, Amberley at my side.

'This one was killed by something else.' He indicated the body, a young woman with a shaved head
and a xenoist braid, who had apparently been eviscerated by a close combat weapon of some kind. I'd
seen a lot of people killed the same way over the
years, but the wounds the weapon had left were unfa-
miliar. That didn't necessarily mean much, of course;
there are plenty of ways of mounting a blade, but
there's usually a fair degree of consistency within a
culture, and I hadn't seen anything here which
looked that unusual.

'I'm still trying to work out what killed the others,'
I said. The wounds were too heavy for lasguns, even
the hellguns we carried. I'd heard them being fired
though, I was sure about that. By the insurgents,
then; there were several lying around close to the
corpses, so it didn't need an inquisitor to join those
dots.

'It looks like plasma rounds to me,' Jurgen volun-
teered. The doubt in his voice told me how unlikely
he thought it, though; plasma weapons were big,
bulky, and unreliable, and took an age to recharge
between shots. You'd have to be mad to arm an

entire squad with them. Not to mention being rarer than an ork with a sense of humour. 'Plasma pistols, maybe?'

'Maybe,' I conceded. Those were even rarer, but suppose someone had found a whole cache of them from the fabled Dark Age of Technology? That would be worth going to almost any lengths to protect, wouldn't it?

'There's... something else,' Holenbi said, redirecting our attention to the dead woman. He looked a little green for a medic, I thought, then I noticed it myself. A large chunk of flesh had been ripped from her torso, as though by teeth.

'Merciful Emperor!' I made the sign of the aquila almost without thinking. I hadn't seen wounds like that since my last encounter with the tyranids. Even then, though, a small dispassionate part of my mind recognised that this was different, something I'd never seen before. 'What in the galaxy could do that?'

'Whatever it was, it didn't like the taste,' Amberley said, directing her luminator beam to a detached chunk of bloody flesh lying a few feet from the corpse. Holenbi turned greener, and eating his discarded ration bar earlier turned out to have been a bit of a waste of time for him.

'I've got movement!' Sorel called from the entrance to one of the tunnels.

'Are you sure?' Amberley was looking at that bloody auspex again, and the screen was still blank. 'I'm getting no human lifesigns at all.'

'What about abhuman ones?' I asked, and she shrugged.

'It's only calibrated for–'

A ball of light, eye-achingly bright, shot from the mouth of the tunnel Sorel was guarding, and exploded against an empty crate. Whoever the enemy was, they were upon us.

Editorial Note:

With the situation in the city deteriorating by the moment,
Lord General Zyvan and the troops under his command were
growing increasingly impatient to do something, notwithstanding the explicit instructions I had given to the contrary.
Governor Grice's heavy-handed attempt to seize control of
the imperial expeditionary force had tried their patience to
the limit, and, as a man of honour, Zyvan clearly felt the
slight of the accusations levelled against him. His subsequent
actions may therefore be understood, if not entirely con-
doned.

What follows is a summarised partial transcript of the
meeting he held with the senior officers of the expeditionary
force, taken from the hololithic recording made by the

equipment in the conference room, supplemented by a few personal observations subsequently gleaned from some of those present: most notably savant Mott, who represented the Inquisition in my absence, Colonel Kasteen of the 597th Valhallan, and Erasmus Donali of the Imperial Diplomatic Service.

The lord general is clearly irritated at this point, but keeping his temper by focussing on the issue at hand. He begins by asking Colonel Kasteen to confirm the instructions I gave her over the vox link regarding the governor's demands.

'That is correct, sir,' Kasteen replies, seeming cool and efficient despite being the youngest regimental commander present. Only someone very skilled at the interpretation of body language could detect her nervousness. 'You have complete command of this army by the express order of the Inquisition.'

'Good.' Zyvan's voice is clipped and decisive. 'Then I propose to calm the situation by removing the primary cause of the problem.'

'The inquisitor was also quite explicit that we cannot engage the tau under any circumstances.' Kasteen is clearly nervous here about appearing to contradict her commander, but her sense of duty outweighs the prospect of any personal consequences – a commendable trait which stood her in good stead throughout her career. Zyvan concedes the point.

'I wasn't referring to the tau,' he reassures her, and everyone else at the table. 'I meant that cretinous excuse for a governor.'

There is general approval of this proposal. Several of the officers present suggest courses of action ranging from arrest to assassination. Eventually, the mood calms as Mott outlines the Inquisition's position on the matter.

'It does indeed appear that Govenor Grice is ultimately responsible for this situation,' he agrees. 'But there is still some ambiguity as to the degree of his culpability.' He begins to quote legal precedent at length, until Donali, who is familiar with the savant's peculiar mental processes, is able to steer him back to the topic at hand. 'In short,' he eventually concludes, 'we would rather have him available to account for his actions.'

'If the Inquisition wants him, they can have him,' Zyvan says. 'But in my opinion, his removal is a necessary prerequisite to restoring the situation to any kind of stability,' Donali agrees.

'The tau are also in agreement with this proposition,' Donali adds, which throws the meeting into turmoil for a few moments until Zyvan is able to restore order.

'You've discussed it with them?' he asks.

'Informally,' Donali admits. 'We still have a residue of goodwill, thanks to the actions of Commissar Cain, and I've been attempting to build on this. If we send troops to remove the governor, I believe they won't interfere.'

'Tell that to the PDF!' someone shouts. 'Or the civilians they're butchering!' Donali stares him down.

'They recognise the distinction between us and the local militia,' he says. 'By their logic, the PDF attacked them first, so they're fair game, and the civilians merely collateral damage. They can be persuaded that it's in everyone's interests to back off, I'm sure.'

'I'd like to see how,' Colonel Mostrue of the 12th Field Artillery cuts in. Mott begins to explain.

'Tau psychology is very peculiar by human standards. They crave stability, and are terrified at the prospect of any loss of order. In fact, it would be no exaggeration to say that, for them, it's as disturbing as we would find an eruption of Chaos.' This casual reference to the Great Enemy creates considerable consternation. Zyvan restores order with some difficulty.

'So you're saying that the situation in the city right now is essentially their worst nightmare come true?' he asks. Mott agrees.

'Anarchy, rioting, civil war between rival imperial factions, nothing fixed or reliable. If someone wanted to goad them into reckless behaviour, they could arrange nothing better.' A few of the more astute officers, Kasteen among them, pick up on the unspoken assumption behind those words.

'If they're so panicked and disorientated,' Zyvan asks, 'what makes you think they'd give us the benefit of the doubt?'

'They have this dogma they call the Greater Good,' Donali explains. 'If we can promise them that the governor's removal will improve the situation, they're as bound to let us try as we would be to accept an oath sworn in the Emperor's name.' The audio recording is swamped for a few seconds by sharp intakes of breath, and mutterings about heathen heresies. Zyvan brings the meeting back to order.

'Very well,' he concludes. 'Make overtures to them, and see if they'll swallow it.' Donali bows and leaves, making the sign of the aquila. Zyvan turns to Kasteen.

'Colonel,' he says. 'The 597th have been more deeply involved in these events than any other regiment, and your commissar seems to have the confidence of the inquisition as well as the xenos. If we can cut a deal with the tau, you'll supply the troops to carry the operation out.'

Kasteen salutes, looking stunned, and manages to respond in the affirmative.

TWELVE

*My enemy's enemy is a problem for later. In the
meantime, they might be useful.*

– Inquisitor Quixos (attributed)

I'M PROUD TO say that, despite the suddenness of the
attack, my intellectual faculties remained undimmed.
Which isn't to say that I didn't dive for the nearest piece
of cover the instant I realised we were under fire, of
course. A level head is a fine asset on the battlefield, but
not when it's been shaped like that by a fragment of
shrapnel. As I drew my faithful laspistol, the analytical
part of my mind was already assessing the positions of
the troopers, and the nearest lines of retreat, but my
chances of making it to one of the tunnel mouths without being blown halfway to golden throne seemed on

the slim side of pitiful, so I decided to stay put behind the nice solid piece of piping I'd found. More enemy fire was pouring in on us by now, and to my horror, I realised that Jurgen was right. These were plasma weapons we were facing, and even the heavy body armour we were wearing would be all but useless against it. I'd doused the luminator at once, of course, the others following suit, but the sun-bright flashes of the enemy weapons lit the space around us in a dazzling strobe that made my eyes ache.

A bolt of incandescent energy burst against the metal piping close to my head, just missing my face with a spray of molten metal. If profanity was a weapon our assailants would all have been dead in seconds at that point, believe me. Stray pieces of debris ignited from similar accidents, suffusing the chamber with a flickering orange glow that only intensified my sense of disorientation.

'Jurgen!' I shouted. 'Can you get a shot?'

'Not yet, commissar!' He was tucked in behind a barricade of crates, the melta gun rested across it, covering the tunnel entrance. When they burst through he'd be able to catch them, but they didn't seem in any hurry to assault us, probably anticipating just such a contingency.

'I have movement,' Sorel said calmly, sighting carefully down the barrel of his long-las. I noticed with some distaste that he'd concealed himself behind one of the corpses, lying prone and resting the barrel of the weapon across its chest as though it were a sandbag.

'What are they waiting for?' Amberley asked. 'Last time they were on us like a rash by now.' She'd taken cover behind an upturned table a few metres away. My palms tingled. In my experience, people didn't change their strategies that radically, that quickly. Especially if they'd seemed to work the last time...

'Kelp, Velade,' I ordered. 'Watch the cross corridors. They're trying to flank us!' Both troopers waved an acknowledgement, and began scanning the dark openings around us. I was suddenly uncomfortably aware of just how many there were to keep track of. Trebek and Holenbi kept their hellguns aimed at the entrance the enemy were firing from, sending an occasional las-bolt back in the vague hope of keeping their heads down.

'I have a shot,' Sorel said, his voice as emotionless as ever, and pulled the trigger. This one was undoubtedly effective, resulting in a screech of pain from deep in the tunnels that raised the hairs on the back of my neck.

'What the hell was that?' Velade asked, her face ashen. I was equally shocked, I have to admit, but for a very different reason; even despite the echoes and the gunfire, I'd recognised it.

'That was a kroot!' I said, in stunned amazement. Now it was Amberley's turn to look taken aback.

'Are you sure?' she asked. I nodded.

'I've spoken to one.' I expected her to query it, but instead she stood.

'Cease fire!' she yelled, with more volume than I would have thought her capable of. Although, come to think of it, her voice wasn't as loud as all that. It was the authority behind it which made it cut through the noise, and the troopers responded at once, even though every instinct they possessed probably told them to keep fighting. Of course, our assailants were under no such inhibition, and the volume of fire continued to pour into our makeshift barricades with undiminished vigour. Despite having made herself the most obvious target in the vicinity, however, Amberley seemed quite unperturbed. (At the time, I wasn't sure whether I was more impressed with her coolness or amazed at her recklessness, although, as I was to find out later, she had less reason to fear the plasma bolts than the rest of us. She could still have been hurt or killed, though, don't get me wrong – they're a tough-minded breed, inquisitors, make no mistake.)

She shouted again, her voice magnified by some amplivox device she produced from inside the robe, but this time, to my amazement, it was the hissing speech of the tau that came from her lips.[1]

I clearly wasn't the only one to be astonished by this, as the incoming fire ceased immediately. After a

---

1 To understand an enemy, you have to understand how they think; and language, according to the magos of the Ordo Diologus, shapes perception. Accordingly, many inquisitors of the Ordo Xenos take the time to learn the languages of the species they expect to encounter in the course of their duties. Without wishing to appear immodest, I can claim reasonable fluency in the most common forms of the tau and eldar tongues, and communicate quite effectively in orkish (which is not that impressive an accomplishment, to be honest, as this particular 'language' consists largely of gestures and blows to the head.)

tense pause, she was answered in the same tongue, and gestured to me.

'Stand down and show yourselves,' she said. 'They want to talk.'

'Or shoot us more easily,' Kelp said, keeping his hellgun aimed.

'They can do that anyway,' I said. I gestured to the corpses surrounding us as I stood, flinching involuntarily from the anticipation of a plasma round impacting on my chest. Nothing happened, of course, and if I'd seriously expected it to I would have stayed huddled behind my nice, cosy pipes, and to the warp with the Inquisition. 'These heretics were pinned down in exactly the same position as us, and they tried to make a fight of it.'

'Can't argue with that.' Sorel stood, holding his sniper rifle by the barrel, arm outstretched from his body, making it obvious that he wasn't going to use it. One by one, the others revealed themselves, stepping out from behind whatever concealment they'd been able to find. Kelp was the last to move, complying at last with ill grace.

'Stay where you are.' Amberley moved forward, taking up a station in the middle of the largest open space she could find, and reactivated her luminator. She'd been visible before, of course, silhouetted in the flickering firelight, but now, if the xenos intended treachery, she might just as well be holding up a sign saying, "Shoot me, I'm here!" Once again, I found myself marvelling at her courage, and having to remind myself that this attractive young woman was actually an inquisitor with far more resources at her command than I could begin to imagine.

'Something's moving,' Sorel said. Thanks to his sharpshooter training, he'd kept his eye on the tau position ever since he'd first spotted them, even despite the order to disengage. As I strained my eyes through the murk, and the drifting smoke which was beginning to make them itch and to catch at my chest, I could see vaguely humanoid figures begin to take form.

At first, there were only the tau, their distinctive fatigues and hardshell body armour dulled with black and grey camouflage patterns ideally suited to blending into the shadows of this dusty labyrinth. Their faces were obscured by visored helmets – ocular lenses where the features should have been – which gave them a blank, robotic look. That brought back uncomfortable memories,[1] and I shuddered involuntarily. Usually, even xenos have expressions you can read, but those impassive visages gave nothing away about either their mood or their intentions.

Behind them padded a trio of kroot, three faces I would have been quite happy to have had obscured. As they entered the cavern, one of them sniffed the air, its head turning in my direction, then to my distinct unease, walked directly towards me.

Amberley continued to hiss and aspirate at the tau, one of whom had stepped out at the head of the half-dozen troopers. I conjectured, rightly, as it later turned out, that this was the leader of the group. I

---

1 Presumably of his past encounters with the necrons.

knew nothing of the language, of course, but I'd heard enough of it spoken to realise that things weren't going well.

'Inquisitor?' I asked, raising my voice slightly and trying to sound calm as the kroot padded closer, 'is there a problem?'

'They seem reluctant to trust us,' Amberley said shortly, and returned to the negotiations.

'Anything I can do to help?' I persisted. The kroot was almost on top of me now, and I couldn't help noticing the combat blades attached to its peculiar long-barrelled weapon were stained with blood. A vivid mental picture of the eviscerated woman we'd discovered, and how those wounds had been caused, rose up in my mind.

'None of them speak Gothic,' Amberley snapped, not needing to add, 'so shut up and let me get on with it,' because her tone did it for her.

'Then how were they expecting to interrogate any prisoners?' Velade asked, before reaching the obvious conclusion, and trailing off with a sudden 'Oh!' of realisation.

'That would be my function, should the situation require it,' the kroot said, in the familiar combination of clicks and whistles I'd heard before. 'I'm pleased to find you in good health, Commissar Cain.'

Well, you're probably thinking I'm pretty dense not to have recognised Gorok straight away, but you should bear all the circumstances in mind. It was dark, we'd just been in the middle of a firefight, and why in the galaxy should I have expected him to be there in the first place? Besides, unless you're very close to them, kroot look remarkably alike. At least with orks you've got the scars to help tell them apart, in the unlikely event that you'd ever have to.

His use of my name had an immediate, and somewhat gratifying, effect on the tau, whose heads snapped round to stare at me. Then the leader turned back to Amberley, and asked something. Gorok made the peculiar clicking laughter-equivalent I'd heard before.

'The shas'ui is asking if it is really you,' he translated with evident amusement. I gathered that 'shas'ui' was some sort of rank, roughly equivalent to a sergeant or officer, and he meant the tau in charge.

'I was the last time I looked,' I said. Gorok clicked again, and translated the remark into tau, which he seemed to have mastered as thoroughly as Gothic. (I found it curious that so feral a creature should appear to be so educated, and questioned him about it later. He claimed to have learned both during his career as a mercenary in order to facilitate negotiations with his employers. Needless to say, I found the notion that he'd served alongside imperial troops somewhat hard to believe.[1])

---

1 Difficult, but not impossible. Although kroot mercenaries are generally associated with the tau, and their homeworld appears to be a tau fiefdom, there have been sufficient reports of kroot fighting alongside other races to raise the possibility that they may not be quite so faithful servants as their patrons appear to believe. It's not entirely beyond the bounds of possibility that this particular one found employment on a backwater human world somewhere, or, more likely, had been part of a temporary alliance with Imperial forces against a mutual foe.

Amberley said something, apparently confirming my identity, and the shas'ui looked in our direction. His next words were clearly addressed to me. I bowed formally to him.

'At your service,' I said.

'He states that your service to the greater good is remembered with gratitude,' Gorok translated helpfully. 'El'sorath remains in good health.'

'Pleased to hear it,' I said, tactfully refraining from hoping out loud that El'hassai wasn't. Amberley seized on the opening, and began speaking rapidly again. After a few more exchanges, the tau fire-team, or 'shas'la'[1] as they called themselves, withdrew to confer together in muttered undertones. Quite pointless really, as only Amberley had a clue what they were saying and she'd already heard it, but it was an oddly human gesture which I found vaguely reassuring.

'That was a lucky break,' she said. 'They weren't inclined to believe me at first. But apparently they think they can trust you.'

Well, more fool them, I thought, but of course I had more sense than to say it out loud. I just nodded judiciously.

'That's all well and good,' I said. 'But can we trust them?' Amberley nodded slowly.

1 Generally rendered into Gothic as 'pathfinders,' these are reconnaissance specialists roughly equivalent to Imperial Guard storm-troopers or the forward observers normally attached to an artillery battery. Cain would no doubt have had some pertinent observations on the topic had he been able to speak to them.

'That's a good question,' she said. 'But right now I don't think we've got the option.'

'Begging your pardon, miss,' Jurgen coughed deferentially to attract her attention. 'But did they happen to mention what they're doing down here?'

'The same as us,' Amberley said. 'Following a lead.' My paranoia started twitching at that one, you can be sure.

'What kind of a lead?' I asked. But it was Gorok who answered.

'The intelligence reports provided by Governor Grice, as he agreed after the assassination of Ambassador Shui'sassai, made mention of a violent pro-Imperial group meeting in these tunnels. It was felt that further investigation was merited.'

'Did they indeed?' Amberley looked thoughtful, and in a way which boded ill for the governor.

'I take it that this is the first you've heard of it,' I said. She nodded.

'You take it correctly. But it's not entirely out of the question that such a group exists.' Her eyes went back to the dead woman with the xenoist braid, and clouded thoughtfully.

'I don't understand,' Jurgen said, frowning with the effort of concentration. 'If the governor knew about something like that, why tell the tau and not the Inquisition?'

'Because the tau could eliminate them for him without having to admit to his own weakness in allowing such a group to get established,' I suggested. Amberley nodded.

'Or to consolidate his position with the xenos if he really was planning to hand the planet over to them.' She shrugged. 'Doesn't really matter. Incompetence or treachery, he's dead meat now whatever his motives.' The casual way she said it dripped ice water down my spine.

While we were talking, the tau had concluded their own deliberations, and came over to join us, the other two kroot in tow. The shas'ui said something, and Gorok translated it.

'Your proposal is acceptable,' he said. 'It would appear to serve the greater good.'

'What proposal?' Kelp asked, an edge in his voice. Amberley stared at him for a moment until he subsided.

'It appears our objectives are the same,' she said. 'So we're joining forces. At least until we know what we're up against down here.'

'Makes sense,' I agreed. 'I'd rather have those plasma guns on our side than shooting at us.' Now I came to look at one close up they were surprisingly compact, no larger than a lasgun, but the amount of firepower they could put out wasn't to be sniffed at.

'Team up with the bluies?' Kelp was outraged. 'You can't be serious! That's... That's blasphemy!'

'That's what the inquisitor wants. Live with it.' Trebek exchanged glares with him for a moment, until Amberley intervened.

'Thank you, Bella. As you so helpfully point out, my decisions are not requests.' She raised her voice a little, so all the troopers could hear. 'We're moving out. Anyone who objects is welcome to stay behind. Of course, the commissar will have to execute them before we leave to maintain operational security.' She smiled at me. 'I think it's very motivating for people to feel they have a choice, don't you?'

'Absolutely,' I said, wondering just how many more ways she'd find to surprise me before the day was over.

So we formed up, the tau leading, which was fine by me – let them soak up any fire from the ambushers I was sure would be lurking in the dark ahead of us – then our motley group of troopers. Jurgen took the whole business as phlegmatically as he did everything else, but I could see Kelp wasn't the only one with reservations about our new alliance. Warp only knows, I had my share too, but then I'm paranoid about everything (which in my job is the only prudent state of mind.) Velade and Holenbi kept a wary eye on the xenos, particularly the kroot, which really spooked them. Hidden under their armour, and their faces concealed by helmets, the tau might almost have passed for human if it hadn't been for the finger missing from each hand, but the kroot just looked like bad luck waiting for someone to happen to. Trebek professed to be entirely comfortable with the inquisitor's decision, but I suspected that was more to bait Kelp than from any sense of conviction. Only Sorel seemed completely at ease.

I turned to Kelp as we began to file out of the chamber.

'Coming?' I asked, my hand resting lightly on the butt of my laspistol. After a moment he fell in with the others, his eyes burning, but I've been glared at by experts, so I just returned the favour and waited for him to blink.

To my surprise, Gorok joined me at the rear of the column, but then I don't suppose there would have been much point in the interpreter being out of earshot of the monoglots. His companions were at the front, loping along next to the shas'ui, and as I watched their easy gait something struck me.

'I can't see a wound,' I said. 'Which kroot did Sorel shoot?'

'Kakkut,' he said, 'of the Dorapt clan. A fine tracker. Died quickly.' He seemed remarkably matter-of-fact about it. 'Your marksman is commendably skilled.'

Sorel, overhearing, looked quietly pleased at the compliment.

WE PROCEEDED ONWARDS and downwards in an uneasy silence, weapons at the ready, although truth to tell, I suspect both parties would have been just as happy to use them on each other than on the mysterious enemy we still seemed no closer to identifying. We were making better time now, though, the tau appearing to have some way of seeing in the dark. They certainly had no visible luminators, so I assumed the lenses on the front of their helmets enabled them to see in some way I couldn't quite comprehend. The kroot had no need of visual aids of any kind, slinking through the dark as though they were born to it. Maybe they were, who knows.

A muffled whisper from the lead tau brought everyone else to a halt – or to be more accurate, the tau stopped, and the rest of us ran into the back of them.

'What is it?' I asked. Amberley listened for a moment.

'Turn off your luminators,' she ordered. I complied, but not without some misgivings. I didn't trust our own troopers where I could see them, let alone in the dark, and as for the xenos... But she was an inquisitor after all, and I assumed she knew what she was doing.

I'd closed my eyes before dousing the light, so I knew they'd adjust quickly when I opened them again, but even so, the few moments it took were unnerving. I waited in the shrouding darkness, listening to the rapid beat of my heart, and tried to distinguish the other sounds around me: the scrape of boot soles against the floor, the muffled clinking of weapons and equipment, and the susurrus of a dozen pairs of lungs. The air felt warm and thick against my face, and I remember being obscurely grateful for Jurgen's distinctive odour, which was no more pleasant than usual but at least felt reassuringly familiar.

Gradually, I began to distinguish shapes in the gloom around me, and became aware of a faint background glow in the distance ahead of us.

'Lights,' Jurgen whispered. 'Someone's down here.' One of the tau said something in an urgent undertone.

'There are sentries,' Amberley translated quietly. 'The kroot will deal with them.'

'But how can they see?' Velade asked, confusion obvious even in the undertone.

'We don't have to,' Gorok assured her, and a swirl of displaced air at my elbow told me he was gone. With my eyes now adjusted to the darkness, I could see three faint shadows against the faint light in the distance, and abruptly, they vanished.

A moment later there were a few muffled cries abruptly cut off, the sounds of a scuffle, and the unmistakable crack of snapping bone. Then the silence descended again, to be broken by a muffled whisper from the tau sergeant.

'All clear,' Amberley assured us, and we scurried forward towards the light, which now seemed cosy and welcoming despite the potential threat it represented. It wasn't all that bright really, just the first in a chain of low-powered glowglobes embedded in the ceiling with long stretches of shadow between them, but after the darkness it seemed positively effulgent.

Just beyond the first of them, a makeshift barricade had been erected across the corridor, which gave on to a slightly wider chamber beyond, narrowing the way to the width of a single man.

'It looks like a checkpoint,' Trebek said, and Kelp snorted loudly.

'What was your first clue?' he asked.

She was right, though, the obstruction was clearly meant more to regulate traffic than to keep intruders out; presumably that had been the job of the contingent further back, until the tau had relieved them of the responsibility. Otherwise it would have been sited with a great deal more care, and I mentioned as much to Amberley.

'What do you mean?' she asked, which told me that whatever else they know, inquisitors tend not to think like soldiers.[1]

'It's in the illuminated area,' I pointed out. 'If they were seriously expecting intruders, they would have placed their pickets forward, in the dark, where their eyes would adjust and they'd be able to see down the corridor. As it is, they can't see anything from here outside the pool of light.'

'Which greatly assisted us in gaining the element of surprise,' Gorok added helpfully. Reminded of his presence, I turned just in time to see him bend down and take a large bite out of the human corpse lying at his feet. Bile rose in my throat, and the troopers muttered anxiously, or vented expletives of disgust. Kelp started to bring his hellgun to bear, then thought better of it.

The tau, I noticed, all seemed to be looking somewhere else as their allies began their obscene meal, as though they were equally disgusted but too polite to mention it. Then, to my even greater surprise, Gorok spat the gobbet of meat out, and I was reminded of the similar thing we'd seen before. He rattled off something in his native

1   And why should we, when we can call on our own Astartes chapters for that kind of thing?

tongue, and the other kroot dropped their potential snacks too.

'What in the Emperor's name was all that about?' I whispered to Amberley, but she just shrugged.

'Sorry, I don't speak kroot.' Gorok's hearing must have been preternaturally acute, though, at least by human standards, because he answered me.

'Tainted, like the others.' He made a sound I took to be indicative of disgust.

'Tainted, how?' Amberley asked. Gorok spread his hands, a curiously human gesture for an alien, which I assumed he'd picked up from whoever had taught him Gothic.

'It is the...' He lapsed into kroot for a few whistles and clicks. 'There's no exact equivalent in your tongue which I know. The twisted molecules which replicate...'

'The genes? DNA?' Amberley asked. Gorok cocked his head on one side, apparently considering it, and asked one of the tau a question in that language. 'Something similar,' he said at last. 'The tau know of it too, but not as we do.'

'You're trying to tell me you can taste their DNA?' I asked incredulously. Gorok cocked his head again.

'Not exactly. As you lack the ability, it would be like describing colour to a blind man. But I am a shaper, and I can perceive such things.'

'And their genes are tainted.' Amberley nodded to herself, as though it confirmed something she suspected, and a terrible realisation hit me. The nagging memories of some previous campaign, our conversation at the palace the first time we met; suddenly I knew what she expected to find down here, and it was all I could do not to turn on my heels and run, screaming, for the surface.

Editorial Note:

Despite my misgivings about the style, or, more accurately, lack of it, I feel it would be helpful to insert the only eyewitness account of the mobilisation of the 597th I've been able to locate at this point. Readers with a refined appreciation for the Gothic language may prefer to skip this section. For those of you who wish to persevere, my apologies.

Extracted from *Like a Phoenix From the Flames:
The Founding of the 597th*, by General Jenit Sulla
(retired), 097.M42

Imagine, if you can, the awful sense of futility which
hung over us in those darkest of days. As the city we
were here to protect burned around us, the flames of
our impatience blazed no less furiously in our
breasts. For here we were, sworn warriors of the
Blessed Emperor, enjoined we knew not why to step
back from the fray which every woman and man of
us yearned to enter. Yet we stayed our hand, grim
duty no less inflexible for being unwelcome, for had
we not sworn to obey? And obey we did, despite the
anguish we all felt at our enforced inaction, until at
last the lord general gave the order to mobilise.

I think I can truly speak for all when I say that at
the news that our regiment, newly born, all but
untried, was to take the lead in this magnificent
endeavour, our hearts swelled within us, borne aloft
on the wings of pride, and a determination to show
that the lord general's confidence had not been
bestowed upon us in vain.

As I led my platoon to our Chimeras, I could see
the whole regiment lined up and battle-ready for the
first time, and a sight to stir the blood it truly was.
Dozens of engines rumbled, and our sentinels
formed up alongside us. I noticed that Captain
Shambas was smiling broadly as he checked the

heavy flamer mounted on his doughty steed, and I paused to exchange a few words with him.

'I love the smell of promethium in the morning,' he said, and I nodded, understanding the urge he felt to unleash the cleansing fire of retribution against the Emperor's enemies.

As I mounted my command Chimera and took my accustomed place in the top turret, I kept turning my head hoping for a glimpse of the legendary Commissar Cain, the man whose courage and martial zeal was an inspiration to us all, and whose dedication and selflessness had turned us from an ill-disciplined rabble into a crack fighting unit that even the lord general deemed worthy of notice; but he was nowhere to be seen, no doubt even then bestowing the benefit of his wisdom on those entrusted with ensuring our final victory. Indeed, as the Emperor willed it, I wasn't to set eyes on him until that final climactic confrontation which lives on in the annals of honour to this day. At length, Colonel Kasteen took to her own Chimera, and gave the eagerly awaited order to advance.

A stirring sight we must have been as we moved out, to the cheers and envious glances of less fortunate regiments. Beyond the perimeter, however, I must admit that my spirits were somewhat dampened by the devastation which met our eyes. Hollow-eyed civilians gazed at us from the ruins of their homes, and curses and lumps of masonry were

frequently thrown in our direction. Fruitless to
protest that this wilderness of desolation was none of
our doing, for they had every right to expect protection from the tau invaders, and we had left them
bereft. Everywhere wreckage burned, and the bodies
were scattered in profusion – many in the uniform
of the PDF, some modified with strips of blue cloth
to proclaim their allegiance to the alien despoilers.
Naught had it benefited them though, and they had
reaped the just reward of all turncoats; but whether
at the hands of their more loyal fellows or the interlopers they had sought to appease, His Divine
Majesty alone knew.

Of the tau themselves we saw little sign, save, on
occasion, a rounded tank hull hovering ominously at
the end of a street, or a swiftly darting dreadnought
keeping pace with us for a block or two. For the most
part, however, they seemed content to watch us
through the eyes of their aerial pictcasters, which
floated like flying plates above the rooftops or flitted
around our vehicles like flies around grox. Had it not
been for our orders, I'm certain that many would have
been downed by our sharpshooters; but however
intolerable they found this provocation, not one of
our stout-hearted cohort broke faith by opening fire.

It was only as we approached the precincts of the
governor's palace that the resistance we'd expected
truly began, and it was of a kind we were ill-prepared
to face, and had no reason to expect.

THIRTEEN

Taking the long view is all well and prudent, but take care that you don't become so preoccupied with it that you miss what's right under your nose.

– Precepts of Saint Emelia,
Chapter XXXIV, Verse XII.

WE PRESSED ON, even more warily now if that were possible, because it was obvious from the presence and layout of the checkpoint that we were somewhere deep inside the perimeter of the enemy encampment. The tau took the lead again, which was fine by me, as whatever sensor gear they had inside those odd-shaped helmets of theirs seemed a good deal more reliable than Amberley's auspex. She'd consulted it a few more times since it had failed to detect our alien

307

companions, but after Gorok's announcement and my panic-stricken deduction of what we truly faced, I wasn't expecting anything more from it. Of course, some of the enemy down here might still be sufficiently human to register on the thing, but I'd be a damn sight more worried about the ones that weren't. So I relied on my eyes and ears, and dropped back far enough to voice my fears to Amberley where the others were unlikely to overhear us.

'This isn't what you were expecting to find, is it?' I asked, trying desperately to keep my voice calm. Even so, it seemed to be rising in pitch to an alarming degree. Amberley looked at me with her usual appearance of cheery good humour, which I was beginning to suspect was as much a mask as my own attempt at professional detachment.

'To be honest, no,' she admitted. 'I thought we were just after some run-of-the-mill insurrectionists when we came down here. If we're right, this changes things a bit.'

A damn sight more than a bit so far as I was concerned, but I wasn't about to be out-cooled by anyone, so I just nodded agreement as though I was considering our options carefully.

'I can't get a message back to command,' I said. 'We've come too deep.' All I'd been able to raise on my combead for some time was static. I looked at her hopefully. 'Unless you've got something more powerful?'

"Fraid not.' She shook her head, apparently only mildly put out by the inconvenience. 'So I guess we're on our own.'

'I could take Jurgen and backtrack a bit,' I suggested. 'Try to get a message through at least. The lord general should be informed of our suspicions right away. If we're right, we need a couple of regiments down here, not half a squad and a handful of xenos.'

'I appreciate the offer, Ciaphas.' She looked at me with those wide blue eyes, a twinkle of amusement in the back of them, and I felt suddenly sure that she could read my true intentions with ease. 'But at the moment, suspicion is all we have. If we're wrong,' and I hoped to the Emperor we were, 'mobilising that number of troops would only undermine our truce with the tau.'

'And if we're right, chances are none of us will survive to warn him,' I said. 'I've done this before, remember?'

'I've had a little experience with aliens too,' she reminded me, and I suddenly realised I was all but arguing with an inquisitor. That was a sobering thought, and I shut up fast. Amberley smiled at me again. 'But you do have a point. As soon as we have confirmation one way or the other, we'll pull back.' That was something at least. I nodded my agreement.

'I think that would be prudent. Even with the xenos' firepower we wouldn't stand much of a chance otherwise.'

'Oh, I don't know.' She smiled again, to herself this time, as though she knew something I didn't. (Which she did, of course, but she was an inquisitor after all, so I guess she was supposed to.) 'We might have a bit of an edge ourselves.' She was glancing at Jurgen as she said it, and I remember thinking one melta gun wasn't going to make all that much of a difference. But of course, it did in the end, and that wasn't the edge she'd been thinking of in any case.

WE'D GONE ON for maybe another three kilometres when the shas'ui held up his curious malformed hand for silence. Over the last couple of hours we'd become quite adept at reading the non-verbal signals of our alien companions, although none of us were really at ease with them. Kelp at least looked as though he was just waiting for an excuse to open fire, and much as I disliked the man, I had to admit that he probably had a point. Xenos were xenos after all, and even though we were supposed to be on the same side at the moment, I knew from bitter experience that any such alliances could only be temporary, and were liable to be bloodily severed without warning at any time.

'He says he's picking up life forms ahead, in large quantities,' Gorok said quietly, translating the flickering finger signs. The tau all had voxcasters and Emperor knew what else built into their helmets, but their kroot allies had no such aids to communication, and, I was beginning to suspect, would have spurned them if they'd been offered anyway. So they used this peculiar semaphore to pass orders and information silently, in much the same way that Guard units did when the troopers didn't have individual combeads, or the enemy was so close they might have overheard a verbal transmission.

'How large?' Amberley whispered, taking a final look at the screen of the auspex, which, for once, actually seemed to be displaying some life signs that weren't ours or the six troopers with us. The answer seemed to perturb her slightly, as I could see far fewer blips than the number Gorok translated, but then that worried me too as it seemed to confirm our worst fears.

'We're going to have to confirm this visually, aren't we?' I asked, not because I expected an answer, but because asking the question gave me the comforting illusion of some measure of control over my destiny. Which, at that point, I thought was all too likely to be short, bloody, and messily terminated. Amberley nodded, looking grimmer than I would have thought possible, and it suddenly struck me that even an inquisitor could feel fear under the right circumstances (and if ever the circumstances were right to be terrified, these were the ones).

'I'm afraid so,' she said, sounding as though she actually meant it.

I've often wondered since if things would have worked out any differently if we'd warned the troopers in advance what we were getting into. After all, they were all veterans, and had fought a tyranid invasion to a standstill, so they weren't likely to have flown into a panic at the news. But on the other hand, I didn't trust them, and that was the plain, honest truth. For all I knew, if I told them what we'd surmised, they'd simply desert, killing Amberley to cover their tracks as Sorel had suggested. And me too, of course, which was the really important issue so far as I was concerned.

So, rightly or wrongly, I kept my mouth shut, and let them go on thinking we were simply after an insurrectionist cell; and if that left their blood on my hands I can live with it. It's not like I haven't done far worse, to far less-deserving people over the years, and I haven't lost any sleep over them either.[1]

After a few more moments of consultation, which Amberley and Gorok helpfully translated, we moved on, more cautious than before. A few metres ahead, the corridor seemed to open out into a wider chamber, as we'd seen several times already on our journey through the undercity, and I expected this one to be little different – like the one we'd discovered the checkpoint in, or the larger one where the tau had slaughtered the outer guards. So as I reached the opening, and peered cautiously round it, my breath left my body in an involuntary gasp.

The chamber was huge, vaulted tens of metres over our heads, like the schola chapel where I'd spent many dull and draughty hours as a juvie listening to old Chaplain Desones droning on about duty and loyalty to the Emperor, and furtively swapping salacious holopicts with the other cadets. The atmosphere here was about as far from musty piety as it was possible to get; however, palpable danger seeped from every corner.

---

1   I suspect this isn't entirely true; I've certainly known him to be woken by nightmares on several occasions.

We'd come out on a mezzanine gallery some twenty metres above the floor, and, Emperor be praised, there was a waist-high balustrade around it which afforded us a measure of concealment. We crouched behind it, humans and aliens alike, equally appalled at the sight which met our eyes.

The space below us was vast, receding into the distance like a forgeworld manufactoria. I'd seen a Titan maintenance bay once, where Warhounds were rearmed and readied for battle, and the huge echoing space had bustled with the same sense of martial purpose. Instead of towering metal giants, however, this space held only people, scurrying to and fro in their hundreds, tending to vast machines of great antiquity whose purpose I could only guess at.[1] Of rather more immediate interest to me, though, were the ones carrying, drilling with, and maintaining with a meticulousness which would have done credit to a member of the Imperial Guard, more small arms than I was happy to see in the hands of anyone other than His Majesty's most loyal servants.

'Emperor's bones!' Trebek muttered. 'There's an entire army of them down here!' A few short, sibilant exclamations from among the tau were enough to confirm that they were as unpleasantly surprised as we were.

---

1   Subsequent study of the city records leads me to believe we were in one of the primary distribution centres of the water purification system. Like many examples of technology from the early days of settlement on human worlds, it had apparently been functioning undisturbed for several millennia, and would no doubt have continued to do so indefinitely if we hadn't started blowing holes in it shortly thereafter.

'It's worse than that,' Kelp muttered. Amberley and I exchanged concerned glances, already aware of what he'd noticed, but then we'd been expecting it, and had known what to look for.

'How do you mean?' Holenbi whispered, his habitual frown of puzzlement back on his face.

'They're mutants,' Sorel told him, scanning the chamber through the magnifying optics of his sniper scope. 'Some of them, anyway.' A ripple of unease stirred the troopers, an atavistic loathing of the unclean rising to the surface despite their training and discipline. Now that someone had pointed it out, the contamination was obvious: though many of the cultists below us were human, or could pass for it, others were unmistakably something else. In some cases, it was as subtle as a wrongness of posture, a peculiar hunching of the back, or an elongation of the face, but in others it was far more pronounced. In these individuals the taint of the alien was obvious, their skin hardened almost to armour, their jaws wide and filled with fangs; a few sprouted extra limbs, tipped with razor-sharp claws.

'No they're not,' Jurgen chipped in helpfully, blissfully unaware of my frantic 'shut up!' hand gestures as he shaded his eyes for a closer look. 'They're genestealer hybrids. We saw plenty just like them on Keffia, and...' His voice trailed off lamely as he finally turned his head in my direction, and saw the expression on my face.

'And we wiped them all out,' I finished, trying to sound decisive and confident. Kelp's jaw clenched.

'You knew.' It was a flat statement, an accusation, and the others all hung on his words. 'You knew what was waiting down here all along, and you led us right into it to get slaughtered!'

'No one's getting slaughtered unless I do it,' I snapped back, realising that if I lost the initiative now I'd never regain it, and that would mean the end of everything – the mission, me, Amberley, and probably Gravalax too, although the welfare of the planet wasn't exactly at the top of my priority list. 'This is a recon mission, nothing more. Our objective was to identify the enemy, which we've done, and get back to report that information. We're pulling back to the surface now, to call in reinforcements, and we'll only engage in self-defence. Satisfied?'

He nodded, slowly, but the truculence remained on his face.

'Works for me,' Sorel said. Velade, Trebek, and Holenbi nodded, following his lead.

'Not for me.' Kelp raised his hellgun, aiming squarely at Amberley. Sibilant whispers of consternation rippled through the tau, but the shas'ui gestured the ones who'd begun to raise their weapons to stand down, and to my relief, they complied. The last thing we needed now was to start killing each other; there were plenty of 'stealers around to do that job, and attracting their attention was right up there with challenging an ork to an arm-wrestling contest so far as really bad ideas went. 'I'm out of here. And I'll kill her if you try to stop me.' I reached for my pistol, but she shook her head.

'No, commissar. He's not going to shoot, are you, Tobias?' She tilted her head towards the bustling throng of half-human monsters below. 'The noise would bring them all running, and you wouldn't get a hundred metres before they ripped you to pieces.'

The same thing would apply to my sidearm, I realised, as I let it slip back securely into its holster.

'You'll never get away with this,' I said levelly, absurdly conscious of sounding like a character in a holodrama. A sneer of derision crossed his face.

'Like I've never heard that before.'

'Get out of here.' Amberley's voice was stiff with contempt. 'I've no use for cowards. You had a second chance, and you pissed it away.' For the first time, a flicker of unease moved across his face, and he took a step backwards.

'You'd better hope the 'stealers find you first,' I added, with all the bravado which comes from issuing an empty threat you know you'll never have to back up. 'Because if I ever catch up with you, you're in for a world of hurt.'

'Dream on, commissar. I've taken my last order from you.' He looked at the others, hoping for some show of support, but they just stared back, their faces set. I was surprised, I don't mind admitting it, but when you came down to it, they were still soldiers of the Emperor before anything else. After a moment, Kelp stepped back into the shadows and turned, and we heard the sound of running feet receding down the tunnel.

'I reckon I've still got a shot,' Sorel offered, raising the long-las and sighting carefully in the direction of the sound. 'And this thing's silenced.' I shook my head.

'Let him go,' I said. 'At least he's still good for drawing their fire.' The sniper nodded, and lowered his weapon.

'Your call,' he said.

Amberley was still engaged in earnest conversation with the tau, though how she was hoping to retain their confidence after this was beyond me, so I did my best to rally the troops with a few quiet words of praise for their loyalty.

'The shas'ui is saying it would be most prudent to divide our forces again,' Gorok translated helpfully. Big surprise there, I thought. If I was the shas'ui and I'd just seen one of our allies pull a gun on his commander, I'd be having second thoughts about our little arrangement now too.

'We both need to report this to our own forces,' Amberley said, breaking off just long enough to meet my eye, then returning to her sibilant dialogue.

'No question of that,' I agreed. 'So what's taking so long?'

'The tau were unaware of this ability of the creatures you call genestealers,' Gorok said. 'They knew them only as a warrior form of the tyranid overmind. Your inquisitor is attempting to enlighten them as to their true nature.'

'They're infiltrators,' I explained. 'They worm their way into a planet's society, and weaken it from within before the hive fleets arrive. Wherever they go they sow disorder and anarchy.'

'Then they are indeed a potent threat,' the kroot agreed.

'Sir,' Velade whispered urgently, trying to attract my attention. I turned towards her, and she gestured down towards the chamber floor. 'Something's happening down there.'

'Time to leave,' I said, tapping Amberley on the shoulder. She glanced up at me and nodded.

'I think you're right.' One of the hybrids, an ugly fellow who might have passed for human in a bad light if it wasn't for a complexion which looked as though he'd recently showered in acid, was running into the chamber. He was carrying something under his arm, and after a moment I realised it was the head of the kroot Sorel had shot.

'Oh frak,' I said. They were on to us now, and no mistake. As he moved further into the cavern, more and more of the cultists stopped what they were doing and crowded around him. The most eerie thing about it was that none of them said anything, just clustered together in silence and stared at the grisly trophy.

'What are they doing?' Trebek asked quietly.

'Communicating,' Amberley responded, turning to lead us back up the corridor we'd entered by.

'They've all got this hive mind thing, remember?' Velade was tense but determined. 'You just have to shoot the big ones.'

'It's not like the tyranid overmind,' Amberley said. 'They're all individuals. They're just linked to each other telepathically, at least up close.'

'Like psykers,' Jurgen added helpfully.

'I hope so,' Amberley said, though what she meant by that I still didn't know at the time.

'Pull back slowly,' I ordered. 'They haven't noticed us yet. We've still got time to make it back to the surface before they realise where we are.' And we probably would have done too, if it hadn't been for the bloody kroot.

'They taint the flesh,' Gorok said. 'And they must not taste ours.' Before I had a chance to react, or even realise what the hell he was on about, he shouted something in his own tongue to his compatriots.

My bowels froze. As that avian screech echoed round the chamber, every head turned in our direction as though tugged by the same string. I was uncomfortably reminded of a Hydra battery coming to bear. Uncounted eyes stared at us for a moment, then they broke and ran, as Gorok and the other kroot aimed their long-barrelled weapons at the centre of the group and opened fire.

'What the hell do they think they're doing?' Holenbi asked.

'Who cares? Run!' I ordered. Looking back I could see they'd felled the hybrid carrying the kroot head, and another volley pulped the trophy to mush.

I'm still not sure why that was so important to them. All I can assume is that they'd grasped some of what Amberley had been saying about the genestealers' peculiar ability to overwrite the genetic code of their victims and had thought possession of the severed head would have let them infect other kroot in some way. Palpable nonsense of course. Genestealers need live victims to infect so that when they have children of their own, they unwittingly spread the taint, but I suppose it got mixed up in some way with their religion, or whatever else it is that makes them go around chewing lumps out of corpses. At the end of the day a xeno's a xeno, and who knows why they do anything?[1]

One thing I was sure about, though, was that the tau were as surprised as we were. The shas'ui was shouting something I could make a pretty good guess at the gist of without an interpreter, but the kroot weren't listening, and he gave up in favour of trying to organise his own squad. Not a moment too soon either, because the amount of noise from the corridor we'd entered by told me we were about to have company.

A volley of plasma fire from the tau guns ripped down the corridor, almost blinding me with its brightness, and I turned away. We wouldn't get back out the way we'd come in, that was for sure, and our only hope was to move off along the gallery and hope to find a clear route through one of the other tunnel mouths.

Incredibly, the enemy kept coming, although I half expected that after my adventures on Keffia, where they'd just kept leapfrogging the pile of their own

---

1 For a rather more accurate and informed analysis of kroot psychology, see Zigmund's *Warriors of Pech: The Savage Sophisticates*, which is readily available from the restricted stacks of any Ordo Xenos libram.

dead in their eagerness to close. A ragged volley of las-bolts and autogun fire thundered in reply, and one of the tau went down, his armour shredded by multiple impacts.

'Tell them to pull back before they're slaughtered,' I said to Amberley, and she nodded before shouting something in tau. Not that I cared, of course, but the longer the xenos kept firing the further away we'd get. I hoped.

'There's another tunnel up ahead,' Velade called excitedly, then turned back to face us, raising her hellgun. I flinched, anticipating treachery after all, but the high-powered las-bolt went wide of us, impacting on the thorax of the first of the enemy to emerge from the tunnel behind us.

'Emperor's bowels!' Trebek said, following suit. My heart froze with terror. I'd seen too many, on Keffia, and as part of the screeching mass of a tyranid army, to mistake it for anything else.

A purestrain genestealer. One of the deadliest creatures in creation. And it wasn't alone.

FOURTEEN

Never take a gamble you're not prepared to lose.

– Abdul Goldberg, rogue trader.

MY ORDER TO pull back had bought us a little time, at least. The horde of mutant crossbreeds vomited out of the tunnel between us and the tau, forcing the two parties apart, taking punishing casualties, but still laying down a withering volley of fire as they came. I recognised the tactic from the cleansing of Keffia, and Jurgen evidently, did too, as he raised the melta before falling back. The blast of superheated air roared against my face, vaporising the oncoming stealer and chewing a chunk out of the front few ranks.

The firing continued, with las-bolts and bullets chewing up the masonry around us, and I felt a sudden blow against my chest. I glanced down; a las-bolt had impacted against the borrowed armour beneath my greatcoat, and I blessed the foresight that had impelled me to requisition it. We were all shooting continuously now, the troopers retreating in good order by fire and movement, much to my relief. Amberley had produced a bolt pistol from the depths of her cloak, and wielded it with a skill no less greater than my own, bringing down two more of the bounding monstrosities with carefully placed shots. The explosive bolts detonated inside their chitinous shells, blowing their thoraxes to bloody mist.

'Keep your distance!' I shouted. The hybrids were hoping to pin us, allowing the purestrains to close, and if that happened it would all be over. They bounded forward eagerly, claws scything, and if you think that's not intimidating to a man with a gun, then all I can say is count yourself lucky you've never been close to one. I was there when the Reclaimers boarded the *Spawn of Damnation*,[1] and saw the purestrains which infested it tearing open their Terminator armour as though it were card-board to get at the Astartes within. After that you can be sure I never wanted to be within arm's length of those killing machines again. And since they

1   A space hulk which drifted into the Corolian Gap in 928; Cain was liaising with the Astartes Chapter in question at the time, as a member of the Brigade command staff, and went in with the Imperial Guard unit detailed to mop up after the initial Astartes assault.

have four of the damn things, that can be harder than it sounds.

'You don't have to tell me twice!' Trebek placed a couple of accurate shots, downing a purestrain and a hybrid with a flamer. Thank the Emperor she'd spotted that, I thought, or it would have been the end of us for sure. Sorel followed up, putting a round through the promethium tank, and the width of the gallery erupted in flame.

'Good shooting,' I said. He acknowledged the compliment with a nod, and turned to retreat.

He'd bought us some time, I noted with gratitude, the inferno blocking us off from our assailants, and consigning many of them to an agonising death. The most terrifying thing, though, was that they burned in silence, trying to walk towards us through the flames until their musculature gave out and they collapsed, consumed by the imperative to kill the swarm's enemies no matter what the cost.

On the other side of the blazing barrier, the kroot were overwhelmed in seconds, despite their phenomenal skill in close-quarter combat, swinging the blades of their curious polearm/rifle hybrids to tremendous effect. But for every eviscerated cultist that fell, another stepped forward, and then the purestrains tore into them, and it was all over in less than a second. Gorok was the last to fall, standing alone and defiant on a pile of the dead, until a frenzied flurry of blows shredded his body in a shower of blood.

What happened to the tau I couldn't see, but they'd stopped firing, so they'd either managed to disengage or they were all dead by now. My money was on the latter, but even if I was wrong we'd never be able to rejoin them now so the question was merely academic in any case.

I swear I'd only glanced back for a second, but when I looked round I was alone; the others had retreated as I'd ordered, but which of the half-dozen tunnel mouths they'd disappeared down was anybody's guess. The terror of isolation gripped me for a moment, then I pulled myself together. The pool of promethium wouldn't burn forever, and the cultists presumably knew this labyrinth well enough to circumvent it without too much difficulty in any case, so if I stayed where I was any longer, I was a dead man.

'Jurgen!' I shouted. 'Inquisitor!' There was no answer, so I picked the nearest tunnel, and started to run.

As I entered the welcoming darkness, the panic I'd tried to force down resurfaced, stronger than before, and try as I could to make myself slow down and get my bearings, fear had control of my limbs now. I ran as hard and as fast as I could, heedless of the dangers that might be lurking in the darkness around me, or the hidden obstacles which were likely to be lying in wait for an unwary shin or an ankle to turn, and didn't stop until my breath was rasping my lungs like sandpaper and my legs had begun to tremble from the exertion.

Panting hard, I sat on a convenient heap of rubble, and tried to take stock of my situation, which was undoubtedly grim whichever angle I looked at it from. For one thing, I was still deep underground, in a labyrinth I didn't know how to get out of, infested with slavering monsters. For another, the only allies I had down here probably thought I was dead, and even if they didn't, they weren't likely to waste any time searching for me. The information we'd gathered about the true nature of the threat gnawing away beneath our feet was too important to risk, and Amberley would insist on returning to the surface as quickly as possible to warn the lord general. At least, if our positions were reversed, that's what I would have done.

On the plus side, however, I was quietly confident of finding my way back to the surface given enough time, provided I didn't run into any more company on the way, and my solitude was a positive advantage in that regard, as a man moving alone will always be more stealthy than a group. Corridors like these had been my playground as a child, and I'd never quite lost the knack of finding my way around them; despite my panic-stricken flight, I still had a vague idea of which direction our compound lay and how far we'd come. In fact, if my guess about us being somewhere under the old quarter was accurate, I might even be closer to the surface than I realised. And once I'd made it back to the open air, returning to the compound shouldn't prove at all difficult. (And in case you were wondering, the irony of genuinely experiencing what I'd briefly considered feigning the previous night wasn't lost on me.)

Fleeing in terror, I'd just like to note in passing for those of you who have so far been lucky enough to avoid the experience, generally leaves you both hungry and thirsty. At least that's been the case with me on most occasions, and I've done it frequently enough to qualify as something of an expert on the topic, so I hope you'll take my word for it.

Anyhow, I decided to take advantage of this relatively peaceful interlude to replenish my energy, so I sat for a while longer sipping water from my canteen and chewing a ration bar, the flavour of which, as usual, hovered just outside the range of identification. The impromptu picnic raised my spirits somewhat, and I took advantage of the quiet moment to still the thudding of my heart and try to distinguish the sounds in the darkness around me. I briefly considered turning the luminator back on, but decided against it, as it would give my position away, besides which, my eyes had adjusted to the gloom as well as they were going to by now, and I could quite readily distinguish vague shapes of lighter or darker shadow. My other tunnel-rat senses had come into play too: I could tell by the echoes how close I was to a wall, for instance. I've often tried to explain it, but the only way you could really understand is if you'd spent a large part of your early life in the lower levels of a hive somewhere.

It was while I was gradually recovering my wits that I first heard the faint scrape of something moving in the dark. Now, I daresay most people's reaction under those circumstances would have been to call out, or snap the luminator on, neither of which was a particularly attractive option given my current situation, as I'm sure you'll appreciate. Besides, I wasn't particularly concerned as to what it might be. As I've said before, the environment was one I knew well, and I'd be happy to match my experience of blind fighting in tunnels against almost any foe. I was also pretty confident that any 'stealers or hybrids in the vicinity wouldn't have bothered lurking either, just charged straight in, so I simply waited, and was rewarded a moment later by the faint skittering sound of a small piece of rubble falling away.

That was a sound I could identify with some confidence, and I concluded that I was sharing my refuge with some kind of vermin. (An accurate assessment, as I was soon to discover, but not quite in the way I'd imagined.) Before I could consider the matter further, however, I was distracted by a faint tinnitus in my ear, which gradually rose in volume until I was able to distinguish an almost inaudible wash of static. My combead was active, and that could mean only one thing – someone was transmitting on the command frequency reasonably close by. Moreover, there was only one person it could possibly be, a conclusion confirmed by the faint voice, unmistakably feminine, which ebbed in and out of audibility.

'… can you hear… commissar… respond…'

The breath sighed from my lungs as relief punched me in the gut. They might have moved out, as the mission demanded, but it seemed they hadn't given up on me entirely after all.

'Inquisitor?' I asked cautiously.

'You wish.' The voice was close and harsh, and if Kelp had been able to resist the taunt, the rifle butt which followed it would probably have stove my skull in. As it was, he'd been considerate enough to warn me, so I ducked it easily, and drove my fist into the pit of his stomach – which was still protected by his hardshell body armour, of course, so much good it did me apart from bruising my knuckles. (The real ones anyway, the augmetics were rather more robust than that.) He was still off balance, though, so I drove my hip in and tried to throw him, but he twisted out of the way just in time. For a big man he was a pretty fast mover, I'll give him that.

A vivid memory of the brawl in the mess hall flashed across my mind, so I ducked again, and sure enough, he'd tried the same spinning kick he'd almost managed to bring Trebek down with. Advantage to me, I thought, that'll teach you to play tag with a hiver in a tunnel, and I began to draw my chainsword to finish this quickly.

Consequently, I was completely unprepared for the low-level sweeping kick that followed, cracking into the back of my knee, and pitching me to the floor.

'You were almost right,' he sneered. 'I am in a world of hurt. But it's not mine, is it?' He kept trying to kick me while I was down, but the armour under my greatcoat protected me for the second time that day, and the impacts against my ribs were merely annoying rather than crippling. Then again, I suppose he might have done a better job if he'd concentrated on what he was doing instead of talking about it. I stayed silent, masking all but my general position in the darkness, and rolled aside, drawing the chainsword at last.

'If you're going to fight, fight,' I said, using the sound of my voice to draw him in, and mask the whine of the blade as it powered up. 'Don't make speeches.' He must have thought he had me, because he charged in with a roar of triumph, striking down with the rifle butt at where he must have thought my head was, but I'd already moved by then, rolling aside and slashing at his legs with the weapon. I'd hoped to take the treacherous mongrel off at the knees to be honest, but the keening of the blade must have warned him, and he turned aside at the last second, so all I got was a good cut across one of his calves.

'Emperor's guts!' It must have done the job though, because he was backing off, and the chamber was suddenly bright with half a dozen luminators, bobbing in hands or utility-taped to the barrels of hellguns.

'Commissar.' Amberley nodded to me, a casual greeting, as though we'd just met in the street.

'Inquisitor.' I rolled to my feet, advancing on Kelp, who limped backwards, his expression panicky. A trail of blood followed him. 'Excuse me a moment. I'll be right with you as soon as I've finished this.'

'Stay back.' He raised the hellgun, aiming it at my chest. Incredibly, he still didn't seem to realise that I'd concealed armour there, or he'd have gone for a

head shot I'm sure. 'One more step and I'll kill you.'
I stopped, still a couple of metres too far to finish
him off with the chainsword, and he smiled mali-
ciously. 'Or do you still think you can do something
from there?' I shrugged.

'Jurgen, kill him,' I said. The expression on Kelp's
face was almost comical for the half-second or so
that he still had one, then he exploded into a small
pile of gently steaming offal. I turned to my aide,
who was lowering the melta, and nodded an
acknowledgement. 'Thank you,' I added.

'You're welcome, sir,' he replied, as though he'd
rendered me no greater service than pouring my tea,
and I turned back to Amberley.

'This is a pleasant surprise,' I added, playing the
unflappable hero for all it was worth. 'I didn't
think I'd see you again until I got back to the barracks.'

'Neither did I,' she admitted, with a slight smile.
'But I picked up the carrier wave from your combead,
and we just headed in the direction the signal was
strongest in.'

'I'm glad you did.' I glanced across to where Trebek
was scraping a gooey piece of Kelp residue from her
boot. Amberley's smile broadened.

'You seemed to have the situation well in hand.' I
shrugged.

'I've faced worse odds.'

'No doubt. But he did you a favour, in a way.' I
must have looked puzzled at that point, because
she explained as though pointing out something

obvious. 'He made you a lot easier to find. Once we got close enough we just had to follow the noise.'

Her words hit me like a bucket of ice water. (Or a Valhallan shower, which I don't recommend to the unwary, by the way.)

'Form up,' I said to the troopers. 'We're moving out.'

'Just a moment, sir.' Holenbi was rummaging in his medkit. 'I'd like to get you patched up first.' I swear that was the first time I realised I'd taken any damage from the scuffle, or possibly the firefight in the big chamber, my knuckles were smeared with blood. My first thought was that it served me right for punching a suit of carapace armour, but they hadn't been skinned all that badly (and the augmetic ones not at all); most of it had come from the large graze on my forehead, which, now that I'd finally noticed it, had begun to sting abominably. I fended the young medic off as he sprayed it with something.

'We don't have time for that,' I said. 'If you heard something, you might not have been the only ones.'

That got them moving, let me tell you. The thought of facing another horde of hybrids and purestrains was enough to motivate anyone. We moved out in good order, though, I was pleased to note the surviving members of the team actually seemed to mesh together as soldiers should. Now Kelp was gone, the friction which had marred the mission since it started had dissipated, seemingly along with his molecules, and Trebek took point without needing to be ordered to. If she kept this up, I found myself thinking, I might even consider letting her have her corporal's stripes back.

'We were lucky back there,' I said, falling in beside Amberley again. She raised an eyebrow.

'How so?'

'When they attacked before. Most of them went for the tau rather than us.'

'And you found that curious?' I nodded.

'When I fought 'stealers before, on Keffia, they didn't prioritise. Just went for the nearest targets.'

'Intriguing,' she said. 'Mind you, after that promethium tank went up they could only get to the xenos anyway.'

'It was before then,' I said. 'Right at the start. They only seemed to come after us once we'd started to retreat.'

'And you say this isn't typical genestealer behaviour,' she prompted.

'Not in my experience,' I confirmed.

'I see. Thank you, commissar.' She looked thoughtful, and, once again, her eyes were fixed on Jurgen.

WE PUSHED ON quickly, following a run of piping which seemed to be tending upwards, but I couldn't shake the sense of unease that settled over me as we trotted through the dark. I'd suggested dousing the luminators again, but Amberley overruled me, insisting we make the best time we could, so I left my own off and hurried along at the rear of the group; that way I got the benefit of the others' lights without making myself quite so obvious a target. I didn't like it, though, my palms were tingling again, and my scalp crawled with the anticipation of a sudden shot

from the shadows, or an eruption of purestrains from
the darkness. One thing I'd learned from my previous encounters with the creatures, they were
remarkably stealthy and preferred to strike from the
shadows, as the Astartes I'd boarded the space hulk
with had learned the hard way. The hybrids weren't
so worrying, their human genes making them both
more conspicuous and easier to kill, even if they were
able to use ranged weapons against us.

'So far so good,' Amberley muttered, which was
tempting fate if ever I heard it. We'd been remarkably
lucky so far, but I knew that couldn't be expected to
last.

'They won't be too far behind,' I reminded her. In
fact, given the speed at which they moved, I was
vaguely surprised that they hadn't caught up with us
yet...

Sudden understanding hit me like a blow to the
stomach. They didn't have to comb an entire
labyrinth to try and find us – they had sentries posted
on the main routes in and out. All they had to do was
wait, and reinforce their perimeter guards, and we'd
walk right into them in our own good time.

'Wait,' I said. 'We could be running into an
ambush.' I thought rapidly, calculating our most
probable position, and the distance we'd penetrated
after finding the cavern full of the tau's victims. We
were still comfortably short, but–

The sudden detonation of a las-bolt ahead, blowing shards of rockcrete from the wall beside Trebek,
derailed my chain of thought at once. I'd missed a

trick; they were combing the corridors from their outer perimeter, tightening the noose around us–

'Pull back! Consolidate!' I yelled, as Trebek crouched low to return the fire. Running figures could be seen beyond her, picked out by the beam of the luminator taped to the barrel of her gun, and she squeezed the trigger, felling a young man in the uniform of the PDF. For a moment, I wondered if we'd made a horrible mistake, and were opening fire once more on our own allies, but some of the other figures beside him were unmistakably hybrids. One young woman, who might have been attractive if it wasn't for the third arm growing from her right shoulder blade, tipped with a gen-estealer's razor-sharp claws, flicked the tip of a xenoist braid from her eyes with the monstrous appendage (a surprisingly delicate gesture, I remember thinking at the time), and levelled the heavy stubber cradled in her other two hands. Before I could cry a warning, Sorel punched a hole through her head with his usual unerring accuracy. A second PDF trooper, his uniform embellished with a blue towel tied round his upper arm for some reason, cried out in anguish, dropping his lasgun, and cradled the body.

'I don't think we can, commissar.' Jurgen was his usual phlegmatic self, seemingly as unconcerned as if he was asking me to approve a routine piece of paperwork. 'They're behind us as well.' He was right, too, the sounds of scurrying feet echoing down the tunnel in the direction from which we'd come.

'We have to punch through,' Amberley said decisively. Velade and Holenbi nodded grimly to one another, and opened fire on the cultists in support of Trebek, hugging the walls to present the lowest target profile.

'Better do it fast!' I shouted. I'd shone my luminator back down the corridor, and my heart nearly stopped – instead of more ragged cultists, the narrow passage was choked with purestrains, jaws gaping, their teeth dripping slobber, as they charged forward at what looked like the pace of a landspeeder. I drew my laspistol and fired a futile volley at them. The lead one fell, and was instantly trampled to goo by the weight of the others as they ran right over it, the snapping of chitin and the squish of its bodily fluids turning my stomach. (And you really don't want to know about the smell.) 'We're running out of time!'

Jurgen sent a melta blast down the corridor, but it barely slowed them; for every one that fell there seemed to be an army in reserve.

'We're doing our best,' Trebek called, aiming and firing in one smooth motion. Every time she squeezed the trigger, another cultist died, and her torso armour was scored with las-bolt impacts. Whatever crimes she'd committed aboard the *Righteous Wrath*, she'd more than atoned for, and the flush of satisfaction I felt at this vindication of my decision to prevent her execution almost managed to drive out the rising terror I felt at the onrushing tide of chitinous death which by now was almost upon us.

Abruptly Trebeck took a bolt to the chest, the explosive tip bursting through her ribcage, spattering the wall next to her with viscera. She just had enough time to look surprised before the light faded from her eyes.

'Bella!' Holenbi lowered his hellgun, and scrabbled for his medkit. I grabbed his shoulder.

'Keep firing!' I shouted. 'She's beyond help!' And so would we be in a few more seconds, if we couldn't punch a way out of here. He nodded, and brought the weapon back on aim, squeezing the trigger reflexively. Amberley's bolt pistol barked in my ear, and another former PDF trooper died as messily as Trebek had done.

'This could be it,' I said, feeling the peculiar lightheaded fatalism that often kicks in when death looks inevitable. The tight knot of fear dissolved, replaced by the calm certainty that nothing I did now would make any difference, but I was damn well taking as many of the bastards with me as I could. The inquisitor turned to answer me, but before she could say anything a las-bolt burst against the side of her head.

'Amberley!' I yelled, but to my astonishment she was suddenly gone, vanishing without a trace apart from the sudden thunderclap of displaced air rushing in to fill the sudden vacuum in the space which she'd occupied. 'What the hell–'

'Commissar.' Her voice was suddenly in my combead. 'Tell Jurgen to shoot the wall, about three metres back from his current position. Hurry!' Sudden hope flared, and I did as I was bid, though as you'll appreciate, I wasn't in any position to understand what had happened to her or why she would issue so strange an instruction.

To his credit, Jurgen complied as quickly and efficiently as he obeyed any order, and to my astonishment, a large hole appeared instantly, about a metre across. The wall there was barely the width of my forearm, and I dived through before the sides had even had a chance to cool.

'This way!' I shouted. Velade and Holenbi started to fall back, while Sorel took a final shot at the onrushing purestrains. Jurgen turned to do the same, unleashing another blast of ravening energy, and then the masonry over the gap started to crumble. 'Hurry!' I yelled, but it was too late; with a grinding roar the wall collapsed behind me, raising a cloud of choking dust, and sealing my companions in with the creatures, which would surely kill them all.

Now, under any normal circumstances, the idea that I was safely sealed away from a genestealer horde behind tons of fallen masonry would just leave me feeling intensely relieved. I can only assume I got hit on the head or something, because without a second's thought I started scrabbling at the rubble, trying to clear the way back to the corridor which, by now, would undoubtedly be decorated with the internal organs of the others. I only desisted when I felt a hand on my shoulder.

'Leave it, Ciaphas.' Amberley shook her head regretfully. 'They're past helping now.' I stood, slowly, brushing the dust from my clothes, and wondered how I was ever going to manage without Jurgen. Thirteen years was a long time to serve together after all, and I was going to miss him. 'What happened?' I asked, blinking dust from my eyes. It felt as though my brain was full of it too. 'Where did you go?'

'Here, apparently.' Amberley looked around at the chamber we were in. It wasn't very prepossessing, but at least it was free of genestealers. 'The displacer field dumped me here when I got shot.'

'The what?' I shook my head, dazedly. My hair was full of dust too, and I couldn't find my cap. For some reason that seemed very important, and I kept looking round for it, even though it was almost certainly buried under piles of debris.[1]

'Displacer field. If I take a strong enough hit, it teleports me out of the way.' She shrugged. 'Most of the time, anyway.'

'Useful toy,' I said.

'When it works.' She glanced around the chamber. 'Shall we go?'

'Go where?' I asked, still trying to take it all in.

'Away. Fast.' She swung her luminator beam over a darker shadow in the corner of the room. 'This looks like a way out.' I nodded.

'I can feel an air current.'

'Good.' She looked at me curiously, and I realised that she couldn't. What is it they say? You can take the boy out of the hive... 'Let's go then.'

---

1 A common symptom of shock. Hardly surprising under the circumstances...

Well, I didn't have any better ideas, so I trailed along after her. Although if I'd known what we were heading into, I might just have decided to stay put after all.

Editorial Note:

Once again, I must apologise for this, but it really is the only eyewitness account I've been able to find.

(Actually, there are the official after-action reports, too, which might yield a more coherent picture if someone were to go through them and collate the various viewpoints of a dozen different officers, but to be honest, I haven't the time or the patience.)

Extracted from *Like a Phoenix From the Flames:
The Founding of the 597th*, by General Jenit Sulla
(retired), 097.M42.

By the time we had reached the old quarter, we had
almost grown used to the shadowy presence of the
tau, flitting about us like malign ghosts, and it is
greatly to the credit of the troopers I was honoured
to serve with that not one of them gave way to the
temptation to exact retribution for the destruction of
the city, despite the presence of an obvious target on
more than one occasion. However strong this urge
might become, and strong it was, we remained mind-
ful of the injunction placed upon us, and focused our
minds on the delicate mission with which we had
been entrusted. Truly, there can be no foe more
despicable than an imperial servant who has betrayed
the trust of the Emperor, and we were, if anything,
even more eager to call the wretched governor to
account for his perfidy than we were to wreak
deserved vengeance on the alien interlopers whose
presence he had tolerated for so long, with such dire
consequences.

We had anticipated little difficulty in achieving this
end, for what forces could he possibly have had at
his disposal to defy His Divine Majesty's most loyal
servants? A handful of palace guards, if that, whose
martial abilities had been found sorely wanting when
they were called upon to defend his residence from

no more than a street-brawling mob. So it was with ever-rising confidence that we swept through the desolated streets on our errand of vengeance; a confidence which was soon to seem gravely misplaced.

My first warning that all was not well was the sound of an explosion, as a krak missile detonated against the hull of one of the Chimeras ahead of us. From my position in the turret of my command vehicle, I could see the bright blossoming of the explosion, an unfolding red rose of destruction that scored the armour plating on one side. It evidently failed to penetrate, however, as the dauntless gunner swung the turret round, unleashing a hail of heavy bolts at the importunate enemy. My sense of satisfaction at seeing the building from which the attack came scoured with the Emperor's retribution was short-lived, however, as a number of other missiles followed it, hissing from positions concealed in the rubble around us.

Inevitably, some found their mark, penetrating armour and shattering tracks, bringing several of our Chimeras to a halt; and the chatter on the vox channels told me that our company was not alone in being so treacherously defied. The other elements of our regiment, strung out along many of the adjacent roads in an effort to surround the palace, were under similar attack, and a glance at my tactical slate was enough to tell me that this was a well-planned operation, executed with a meticulous precision greatly at

odds with the bedraggled and dispirited force we had
expected to meet. Without further thought I
dropped back inside the Chimera, where the spe-
cialised sensoria and vox equipment would let me
direct my subordinates to greater effect, and began to
plan our response.

'Halt and dismount!' I ordered, realising that our
advance would be stalled indefinitely unless we
closed with the enemy on foot, our lumbering vehicles being easy targets for the dug-in missile teams,
and our drivers made haste to obey.

It was then that I took to my feet myself, for the
whole vehicle rang with a sudden impact, and we
slowed to a halt, thick smoke billowing through the
crew compartment. Swift enquiry made it obvious
that our driver was dead, so I lost no time in forming
up my command team and bailing out of our now
crippled Chimera.

A scene of sheer pandemonium met my appalled
gaze as we pounded down the ramp. Two of the
armoured carriers were on fire, and a handful of others immobilized; the rest were manoeuvring into
what cover they could find. I followed suit smartly as
a flurry of las-bolts erupted from the enemy positions, impacting around us as we took whatever
shelter presented itself.

'Third Platoon, report.' Major Broklaw's voice was
strong in my combead, his calm demeanour reassuring despite the confusion surrounding us. I

responded as crisply as I could, as befitted a warrior of the Emperor.

'We're immobilised, and taking fire,' I reported. 'The enemy seems well dug in.'

'They were waiting for us,' he said. That was my opinion, too; the positions they occupied had to have been prepared some time in advance. The implications of this were staggering. The governor had obviously realised the game was up, but where had he found the troops we were facing? I levelled my optical enhancers, and inhaled sharply.

'The enemy are PDF elements,' I reported. A couple of the lurking figures still had blue rags tied around an arm, but the squad leader, confusingly, bore the makeshift insignia of the imperial faction in the recent civil disturbances.

'Loyalist or xenoist?' Colonel Kasteen cut in. For a moment I was at a loss as to how to answer.

'Both,' I said at last. 'Both factions seem to be working together now–'

'That doesn't make sense!' Broklaw said, an edge of frustration beginning to enter his voice. But Kasteen remained unruffled, fine commander that she was.

'Nothing about this Emperor-forsaken rathole makes any sense,' she pointed out reasonably. But the major was right about one thing.

'There are no loyalists any more,' he said. 'Take them all.'

That was an order we could obey with enthusiasm, and we went to it with a will, of that you may be sure. All the frustration we had endured since our arrival on Gravalax came boiling to the surface, transmuted into true martial zeal, and I vowed that the blood of the traitor would surely be shed this day.

As I urged my troopers forward, and watched the sentinels move up to suppress the first line of resistance, a flash of motion in the corner of my eye drew my attention skyward. Sure enough, it was one of the tau's aerial pictcasters, and a momentary shiver of apprehension passed through me as my mind became crowded with questions. What were the enigmatic aliens making of all this? And, more to the point, what, if anything, were they intending to do about it?

FIFTEEN

It's never too late to panic.

— Popular Valhallan folk saying.

I DON'T MIND admitting that the aftermath of the fight in the corridor had left me completely drained, both mentally and physically. I washed the worst of the dust from my throat with a couple of swallows from my canteen, but I couldn't shake the gritty feel of it from my skin, or my hair, or the inside of my clothes, and I wouldn't be able to, either, until about the third shower. As it turned out, by the time I got the opportunity for that, the dust would be the least of my worries.

And Jurgen was dead. I still couldn't quite believe it, after so many years and so many dangers faced and bested together. The sense of loss was numbing, and quite unexpected. Somehow I'd always assumed we'd meet our ends together, when fate finally pitched me into something my luck and finely-honed survival instinct couldn't get me out of.

So, for an indeterminate time, I said nothing, and trailed after Amberley, who at least seemed to have some kind of plan. All this time, I remember, I kept my pistol in my hand, a curious thing to do as we were in no apparent danger, but I'd somehow kept hold of it when the wall collapsed and felt strangely reluctant to return it to its holster. Later, I found bruising on my palm where I'd been grasping it, so tight was my grip.[1]

We'd gone some distance in silence before Amberley spoke again, the pressure in my ears telling me that the tunnel we were in had begun to descend gradually, but there didn't seem to be any obvious route back to the surface, so I guessed this was as good a direction as any. I suppose I should have mentioned it, but it never occurred to me that she wouldn't have noticed. If I'd realised that she hadn't, and thought we were still moving on the level, I certainly would have mentioned it, believe me, especially if I'd known what was waiting down there on the lowest tier.

---

1 As I said before, he seemed to be suffering from shock for some time after we lost our companions. He was, however, remarkably robust, and recovered far more quickly than I would have believed possible; no doubt the many perils he'd faced and escaped before had inured him to some extent to psychological traumas most men would have found incapacitating.

'Well, I guess that answers the main question anyway,' she said.

'Which question?' I asked. By now, the whole situation had become so bizarre that none of it seemed to make any sense. I was beginning to feel that the only thing I could truly rely on was the prospect of more treachery and confusion to come, and in that I was far from disappointed. Amberley looked momentarily surprised, and then pleased that I'd responded.

'The main one,' she repeated. 'Who would have something to gain by provoking a war with the tau?'

'The hive fleet,' I said, and shuddered despite the clammy warmth of the tunnel. If the 'stealers were indeed the harbingers of a fresh tyranid onslaught, then they were working to a more grandiose strategy than any I'd heard of before, and the implications of that were far from comforting. She nodded, clearly pleased with my response, and intent on prolonging the conversation. I assume she was trying to keep me centred on the mission,[1] and prevent me from dwelling too much on what had happened to our companions .

'The 'stealer cult has obviously been active here for several generations already. Lucky it's such a backwater, or the contagion might have spread halfway across the sector by now.'

'That's something,' I agreed. I know from my subsequent contacts with her that she followed up the

---

1   He assumes correctly; right then I needed a warrior with me, not a basket case.

possibility anyway, and managed to eradicate a couple of small subcults which had made the hop to neighbouring systems before they got properly established, but the danger did indeed seem to have been contained; at least, until the hive fleets showed up in person, and we realised we were facing a war on two fronts. I thought for a moment, then added, 'They've obviously been here long enough to infiltrate the PDF pretty thoroughly.'

'Among other things,' the inquisitor agreed. I nodded too, beginning to be drawn into the conversation in spite of myself.

'It looks like they managed to get involved in the local political groups too. The xenoist faction...'

'And the loyalist.' She smiled grimly. 'Raising the tension between the two, splitting the PDF. It's currency to cabbages it was cultists in both factions who started them shooting at each other, and got the loyalists to attack the tau.'

'Hoping to draw us into a war, so we'd chew each other to pieces, and let the hive fleet walk into the sector practically unopposed.' I shuddered again. 'It's diabolical. And it came so close to succeeding...'

'It still might.' Amberley's voice was grim. 'We're the only two left who know about this. If we can't tell the lord general...'

'They might still succeed,' I finished for her. The prospect of that was almost too grim to be contemplated, and we walked on together in silence for some time.

Perhaps it was just as well that we did, for, after a while, I began to detect a faint murmur up ahead over the scuff of our boot soles through the thick dust which carpeted the corridor ahead of us. I had found that reassuring, since it would muffle our footfalls, and indicated quite clearly that no one else had been this way in decades; which meant we were unlikely to be running into any more ambushes. The presence of other sounds down here, though, might be a cause for concern. I held up my hand and doused my luminator, waiting again for my eyes to adjust, the last remnants of my torpor dropping away like a blanket at reveille, replaced by a sudden surge of adrenaline.

'What is it?' Amberley asked, following suit and plunging us into even deeper darkness.

'I'm not sure,' I admitted. 'But I think I can hear something.' To my pleased surprise, she didn't ask for more details, evidently trusting me to provide them if I had them, so I concentrated my energies on listening. It wasn't even a sound, as such, more of a vibration in the air, The nearest I can come to explaining it is by saying that it was akin to the way I could tell roughly how close I was to a wall in the dark by the way the echoes changed. Bottom line is you either know what I'm talking about, in which case you probably grew up in the underhive, too, or you'll just have to take my word for it.

In any event, there was nothing to be gained by staying here, so we moved on at last, trusting my dark-attuned senses rather than activating the luminators again. My palms were tingling in that old familiar way, and Amberley seemed to trust my instincts, at least in this environment. The corridor continued to be relatively open ahead of us, so moving in the dark was less taxing than you might think, and I gradually became aware of a faint luminescence ahead of us in the gloom.

'Is that light ahead?' Amberley murmured, confirming my thought, and I whispered an agreement. The sounds were getting louder too, but still too faint to discern. There was an organic quality about them, though, which raised the hairs on the back of my neck.

'About half a klom,' I added, still keeping my voice low, and hefting the pistol in my hand.

'Maybe it's a way up to the surface,' she whispered hopefully. I shook my head, not sure whether she would be able to see the movement yet against the gradually intensifying glow.

'We've come too deep for that. We must have gone down at least three levels in the last couple of hours–'

'And you didn't think to say anything?' Her voice was a furious hiss, and for the first time I realised she hadn't noticed the change in depth. 'We were supposed to be looking for a way out, in case you'd forgotten!'

'I thought you knew,' I snapped back, feeling oddly defensive. 'You're the one in charge of this expedition, remember?'

'Am I? Oh yes, now you come to mention it, I suppose I am!' There was a petulant edge to her voice which I found incongruously at odds with her rank and power, and all at once, I felt an overwhelming urge to laugh. It was probably just the tension, but the full absurdity of the situation suddenly hit me. Here we were, the only two people left alive to warn the Imperium of a terrifying threat, lost, alone, outnumbered, surrounded by an army of monsters, bickering like a couple of juvies on a disappointing date. I bit my lower lip, but the harder I tried to suppress it the more the laughter effervesced inside my chest, until it finally escaped with an audible snort.

That did it. She lost her temper completely.

'You think that's funny?' she snapped, all thoughts of concealment now completely forgotten. I should have been terrified, of course, the wrath of inquisitors not being something to be lightly invoked, but hysteria had me now, and I simply howled with glorious, tension-relieving laughter.

'Of... Of course not,' I managed to get out between rib-shaking paroxysms. 'But... This whole thing... It's just... So ridiculous...'

'I'm glad you think so,' she said frostily. 'But if you think I'm just going to forget...' a brief hiccup interrupted her flow of invective. 'Forget this... Oh Emperor damn it all...' and it infected her too, the throaty chuckle I'd found so appealing before erupting from her chest like magma. After that, there was no stopping either of us, and we simply held each other up until we could finally force the air to remain inside our aching ribs.[1]

---

1 I would just like to point out here that this is a perfectly normal reaction to severe stress, which can in no way be interpreted as irresponsible behaviour under the circumstances.

Afterwards, we both felt more like ourselves again, and were able to press on with renewed vigour. We'd resumed moving stealthily, though, as the mere fact that more cultists and 'stealers had failed to boil out of the walls at us probably meant we were alone down here, but we'd made enough noise between us to attract any search parties in the vicinity. Having nothing else to aim for, we kept moving towards the mysterious glow in the distance, and the closer we got, the brighter it became.

'That's definitely artificial,' Amberley said, the yellowish tinge of electrolumination unmistakable from this distance. By the backwash of light it gave, I was able to make out more of our immediate surroundings, and was surprised to note that the stonework surrounding us was now carefully dressed, the vaulted roof being supported by well-crafted columns.

'I think we're in a cellar of some kind,' I hazarded in an undertone. Amberley nodded.

'I think you're right.' She had the auspex out again, and was studying the display. 'And there are people down here. Not many according to this, but...'

She didn't have to finish the sentence. Hybrid cultists might not register on it, and any purestrains in the vicinity certainly wouldn't. Advancing would be a terrible risk, but turning back, trying to find another route to the surface through a tunnel complex swarming with 'stealers and their dupes would be almost as bad. And there was the time factor too. The longer we took to report back, the longer the conspirators would have to provoke their war; assuming it hadn't broken out already.

'Only one way to find out,' I agreed, and we started cautiously forward again.

The light was coming from a huge chamber, a high vaulted ceiling supported by columns similar to the ones I'd noticed in the corridor, but far higher and thicker. Like the chamber we'd seen before, where the cultists had attacked us, there was a wide gallery running around the edge of the room, with a number of smaller tunnel mouths opening onto it, but to my relief I couldn't see anyone or anything up there.

This time, however, there was no humming machinery filling the space. It was light and airy, with braziers burning incense on marble plinths, and littered with antique statuary. Dusty boxes were everywhere, and I surmised we'd stumbled across some long-forgotten depository which the cultists had appropriated for their own purposes. We slunk into it like thieves, and took shelter behind one of the pillars holding the roof up. It was as thick as a cathedral column and almost as wide as I am tall, and concealed the pair of us with ease.

'Stairs.' Amberley nudged me, and pointed. Off to one side, a wide stone staircase rose to the gallery, from where another flight rose, cut into the stonework, rising out of sight.

'Great,' I whispered back. But getting to them would be another problem entirely. I could see figures moving around in the distance, some of them armed. There was the usual mixture of civilian clothing and

PDF uniforms I'd grown used to seeing among the cultists, and something else; a bright flash of crimson and gold. I nudged Amberley and pointed. 'Palace guard.' She nodded in response.

That was a real surprise. From what Donali had said, I'd assumed they were all dead by now, but the cultists, as I'd seen on Keffia, would always try to look after their own. I began to suspect that their defence of the governor hadn't been quite as inept as they'd wanted us to think, forcing the situation to escalate by bringing the PDF onto the streets where their brood brothers could begin to work their insidious mischief. Instead of the antique longarm he'd been issued with, he was carrying a modern lasgun, looted, I assumed, from the PDF armoury.

'We'll have to get past them,' she whispered. I nodded. Not an appealing prospect, by any means, but one we would have to attempt. If we kept to the cover of the pillars and the other detritus, we might just make it, at least most of the way, before we were spotted. When that happened we'd just have to make a run for the stairs as best we could.

As we moved off, I glanced around again, more by reflex than anything, trying to fix a sense of the space in my mind – disorientation can be a killer in a firefight. And then it struck me.

'This is a shrine,' I murmured. Amberley didn't seem in the least surprised, but then I suppose she'd realised that the moment we'd walked in here.

There were tapestries on the walls, which, now I came to look at them, I found myself recoiling from in horror. Blasphemous things they were, holy images of the Emperor profaned and debased, the Father of All depicted as a hunched hybrid with too many arms, or a monstrous purestrain 'stealer which seemed to tower over its adoring acolytes. I resolved to send a squad down here with flamers the moment we reported back. It seemed almost intolerable to me that such things should be allowed to exist.

'Ready?' Amberley asked at my shoulder, and I nodded, making the sign of the aquila for luck. My pistol was already in my hand, as I've said, and I drew my chainsword quietly with the other, thumb poised over the activator. Amberley drew her bolt pistol, checked that the first round was chambered, and nodded grimly. 'Right. Go.' We scuttled as far as the next pillar and went to ground again, my heart pounding in my ears. I was acutely aware of the background noise now, the sound I'd noticed in the corridor; the hum of activity as the cultists moved to and fro, but in eerie silence, as they had done in the chamber full of machinery.

Praise the Emperor, none of them had spotted us. We moved again, making it to the shelter of the next column, and then on to the one after that. I was just beginning to hope that we would make it all the way to the stairs, and whatever lay beyond, when the crack of a las-bolt against the stonework close to my head told me we'd been spotted.

I turned, in time to see the palace guard levelling his lasgun for another shot, and brought up my pistol, but Amberley was faster and her bolt pistol spat first. His chest exploded in a rain of red entrails and shredded gold armour, and before you know it we were in the middle of a serious firefight. Two more armed cultists appeared, attempting to catch us in a crossfire, and we took one each; another chest shot for Amberley, and a head shot for me, blowing the fellow's brains out through the back of his skull.

'Showoff!' Amberley grinned at me, and I didn't have the heart to tell her it had been a fluke. I'd aimed for the chest as well, and he'd ducked at just the right moment. More shots were being aimed at us from behind other pillars, but they were as well protected as we were, and our return fire had little effect beyond persuading them to keep their heads down. 'Looks like a standoff. What'll they do now?'

'Rush us,' I said, not relishing the prospect. Sure enough, a moment later we could discern a scuttling in the shadows, and my heart fell. 'Merciful Emperor, it's purestrains!' A swarm of them, about a dozen strong, was hurrying towards us across the stone floor of the vault. A couple went down to our bolts and las-shots, more by luck than judgment, I suspect, and in another moment I knew they'd be on us. I gripped my chainsword, determined to fend them off for as long as I could, clinging to the last desperate hope that I could somehow cut my way through to the stairwell, which right then looked about half the segmentum away.

Suddenly, an explosion rocked their ranks, then a couple more. Dazed and uncomprehending I glanced upwards, expecting I knew not what, perhaps the

Emperor himself since only divine intervention looked like saving us now. What I saw was almost as unexpected; the familiar shambling form of Jurgen, even grubbier than usual, lobbing frag grenades over the balustrade of the gallery. A small explosion of joy and relief shook my chest, and I grabbed Amberley's arm.

'Look!' She glanced up and nodded, as though she'd half expected something of the sort, and stood.

'Time to run,' she said, cool as you please. She headed for the stairs, and I followed, waving an acknowledgement to Jurgen. He waved back, grinning, and chucked another grenade into the milling mass of 'stealers for luck. Most of them were down by now, leaking foul-smelling ichor, but one was up and running, inhumanly fast, heading straight for Amberley.

'Amberley!' I shouted, and she half turned towards it, but I could see the warning had come too late. Her bolt pistol would never come up to aim in time, and I was too far away to intervene. The claws I'd seen tear open Terminator armour as though it were a crusty meat pie were already slicing at her cape when its head exploded, showering her with an unpleasant organic residue, and leaving the body to topple to the floor. I looked up at the gallery again and saw Sorel already seeking a fresh target for his long-las.

'Emperor be praised!' I breathed, my head still reeling with incomprehension, but grateful for this apparent miracle. I should have known better, of course; that moment of distraction almost cost me my life, and surely would have done if Jurgen hadn't shouted a warning.

'Commissar! Behind you!'

I turned, expecting another foe to be charging in, and swung the chainsword in a reflexive defensive pattern. That surely saved my life, for instead of a cultist or a purestrain, which would have been bad enough, I came face to face with a creature from the worst of nightmares. (Or, to be more accurate, face to belly, as it was at least twice the height of a man.) It was a twisted, grotesque, vast, bloated parody of a genestealer, and the whining blade bit deep into the arm which would surely have ripped my head off if it hadn't been for Jurgen's shouted warning. It howled then, in anger and pain, and I was fighting desperately for my life.

'It's the patriarch!' Amberley yelled, as though I didn't know; from the corner of my eye, I could see her levelling the bolt pistol, waiting for an opening, but I was blocking her shot. I tried to twist out of the way, leaving room for her to aim, but the flailing multiple limbs of my bloated antagonist had me boxed in, and it was all I could do to keep parrying frantically with the chainsword as it swung one talon-tipped arm after another at me. This, then, was the source of the cancer which had infected Gravalax, the centre of the brood mind which the cultists shared, the instrument of the will of the tyranid overmind which had sought to devour the sector unopposed by playing us off against the tau.

'Die, damn you!' I tried to bring my pistol to bear, but couldn't spare the concentration from the more urgent requirement to stay alive for the next few seconds, my entire attention on ducking, blocking, searching for an opening–

Amberley's bolt pistol barked at last, and for an instant I thought I was saved, but the patriarch fought on unharmed, and I realised she was keeping the cultists off my back. They were swarming out of the shadows now, desperate to help their sire, and closing fast. The only mercy was that the ones with guns couldn't use them, for fear of hitting the monster I battled.

Sorel had no such inhibitions, however; a chunk of chitin on the creature's head suddenly burst into bloody fragments, and it roared again, but barely staggered, its natural armour proof against a conventional las-bolt. It was momentarily distracted, though, and I was able to get a good cut across its belly at last. It staggered, thick, foul-smelling ichor beginning to leak from the wound, then came at me again with renewed fury. Seeing that the creature was invulnerable Sorel switched his aim, and began taking down the cultists who were trying to get to me, while Amberley continued to do the same.

'Hold on, commissar!' Jurgen was running down the stairs, his melta readied, and I prayed to the Emperor that he wasn't going to try a shot from there as I'd never survive it. But he had more sense than that, at least.

'Sorel!' Amberley called. 'Clear a path for Jurgen!' The two of them began to concentrate their fire on the cultists between my aide and the desperate battle I still fought. I sprang back a fraction too late and felt talons scrape my ribs, ripping through the armour beneath my coat and burning like fire. I swore, and struck back at the thing, taking the hand which had wounded me off at the wrist. Ichor pumped from it like a fire hose, spraying me and everything else in the vicinity, and if anything, it redoubled its efforts.

I turned my head reflexively, trying to keep my eyes clear, and thus got a clear view of Jurgen as he raced across the floor towards me. For a heart stopping instant, I thought a couple of purestrains were about to eviscerate him, but for some reason they hesitated for a fraction of a second as they were about to close, and Sorel and Amberley dropped them both with well-aimed shots in the nick of time.

I turned back to the patriarch, encouraged by my success in wounding it, and swung the chainsword again. It never even flinched, batting the humming blade aside, and I ducked a wild swing of its lower left arm.

'What does it take to kill you, you bastard?' I snarled, carried away by my own anger and disgust.

'How about this?' Jurgen asked, appearing at my elbow. As he approached the creature, it staggered back, like the purestrains had done, momentarily disorientated, and he jammed the barrel of the melta into the wound I'd cut into its belly. As he pulled the trigger, its entire midsection flashed into steam and foul-smelling offal; it staggered back, its eyes glazing, and swung its head in confusion. Then, slowly, it toppled over, vibrating the stone floor with the violent impact of its fall.

'Thank you, Jurgen,' I said. 'Much obliged.'

'Don't mention it, sir,' he said, turning the weapon to seek other targets, but the cultists were scattering back into the shadows. For the first time, some of them gave voice, a keening wail that sent shivers down my spine. We sent a few shots after them, but I, for one, had had my fill of combat for the time being, and was more than happy to leave them for the follow-up teams. Without the patriarch to focus and direct them, they would be easy enough to pick off, but they would have to be eradicated eventually; otherwise one of the surviving purestrains would grow to take its place, and the whole vile cancer would start to take root again.

'I thought you were dead,' I said. Jurgen nodded.

'So did I, to be honest,' he said. 'They were almost on us when the wall collapsed. Then I thought it might be just as thin on the other side, so I took a shot at it on the off chance.'

'I take it you were right,' I said. He nodded again.

'Lucky, that,' he said.

'What about the others?' Amberley asked, as we began to climb the stairs. Jurgen looked sombre.

'Sorel made it through with me. We didn't see what happened to anyone else.' But then, he didn't have to. They would have been overwhelmed in seconds.

'Lucky you found us when you did,' I said.

'Not really.' Sorel had come to join us as we reached the level of the gallery. 'We found your tracks in the dust, and just followed along.'

'How did you know it was us?' Amberley asked. The marksman shrugged.

'One pair of Imperial Guard boots, one pair of lady's shoes. Didn't need an inquisitor to work that one out.'

'I suppose not.' She looked at him with something like respect.

'Once we heard shooting, we just moved to flank the position,' Jurgen added. 'Standard operating procedure.'

'I see.' She nodded, and pointed to the solid wooden door we'd reached at the top of the staircase. 'Jurgen, if you'd be so kind?'

'My pleasure, miss.' He grinned, like a schola student picked out to answer a question he knows the answer to, and vaporised it with a single blast from the melta, along with a generous section of wall.

'Emperor's teeth,' I breathed, as we entered the passageway beyond. It was paneled in burnished wood, a thick carpet on the floor, and delicate porcelain stood on occasional tables of unmistakable antiquity.

Bright afternoon sun stabbed our eyes through mullioned windows, and a dreadful suspicion began to form in my mind.

'I think I know where we are,' I said. Amberley nodded, her jaw set.

'Me too,' she said grimly.

The silence was shattered by the bark of a bolt pistol and Sorel fell, chunks of his brain spattering an expensive-looking tapestry and staining it beyond repair.

'Commissar Cain. And the charming Miss Vail.' Governor Grice was standing at the end of the corridor, gun held firmly in his hand, the air of vapid imbecility now totally dispelled. 'You really are most annoyingly persistent.'

Editorial Note:

My apologies for this, once again – if it's any consolation it really is the last time...

Extracted from *Like a Phoenix From the Flames: The Founding of the 597th,* by General Jenit Sulla (retired), 097.M42.

The renegades resisted doggedly, with a determination I could scarcely credit, and despite the faith I had in the women and men under my command, I must confess I began to doubt that our eventual inevitable victory could be won other than at a terrible cost in the blood of these noble warriors. The traitors had prepared their positions well, and we could make little progress other than by fire and movement, scurrying from one piece of cover to the next. I gathered from the transmissions I could overhear that I was far from the only officer who found these delays unconscionable. Colonel Kasteen had already requested support from one of the armoured regiments among the expeditionary force, and some vigorous debate ensued as to whether the tau would regard this as a provocation. Why anyone would care about the aliens' feelings was beyond me, I must confess, but much of what had transpired since our landing had left me in a state of some confusion, and I comforted myself with the knowledge that my understanding was not a requirement in any case. Duty and obedience was enough, as it should be for anyone privileged to wear the uniform of the Emperor. In the event the lord general had acceded to her request, and the knowledge that a troop of Leman Russes from the 8th Armoured was on their way had bolstered the spirits of our heroic forces to no little degree.

In the meantime, we were still pinned here, and the certainty that our reinforcements, however formidable, were still half an hour away was, I must confess, taking a tithe of the exhilaration we might otherwise have felt. I had no doubt that we could hold on until relieved, but even with the spirit of the Emperor burning within us, it could prove to be a close-run thing if fate had any more surprises to throw at us.

It was while I was reflecting thus that fate did indeed surprise me, and in a fashion I could never have anticipated. My first presentiment was a vox message from Sergeant Lustig, the doughty leader of Second Squad, who broke into my command frequency with some degree of urgency.

'We have movement on our flank,' he informed me. 'Tau units, closing fast. Requesting instructions.' To his great credit, it must be said that, despite the trepidation he no doubt felt, his report was never anything less than wholly professional. A few more exchanges, equally crisp, flew between us, during which time we established the presence of a handful of battlesuits and at least one of the grav tanks our intelligence analysts had tagged 'Hammerheads.'

'Hold position,' I ordered, despite the doubts which rose unbidden to my mind. Our rules of engagement had been clear, and despite the treachery we could no doubt expect from the inhuman, they had done nothing overt so far to break our incomprehensible truce. Lustig acknowledged, and we both waited tensely to see if the gamble we were taking with our soldiers' lives would be won or lost.

I must confess that, for a brief moment as that sinister hull rose over the crest of the hillock of rubble my command squad had concealed itself behind, I had cause to curse myself for an overcautious fool; for as they came into sight, the cannon mounted atop it spoke, a thunderclap of sound which rolled over us like a physical wave, and I apprehended treachery afoot at last. But the ensuing explosion erupted in the centre of the insurrectionist fortifications, silencing their guns in a single display of sorcerous fury that left us all momentarily breathless.

The tank moved on, humming quietly with the energies keeping it aloft, and the battlesuits bounded after it, spraying the enemy positions with a prodigious amount of firepower. Rapid-fire plasma rounds burst and scorched among them, and salvos of missiles from the bulbous pods over the leader's shoulders poured into them in rippling waves, bursting in gouts of flame and shrapnel, shredding and pulping the bodies of those who defied retribution. Bewildered as I was at this sudden turn of events, for I could conceive of no reason for the xenos to turn against their erstwhile allies, I still had no doubt of my duty.

'Follow up!' I ordered. 'After the tau!' Bounding to my feet I led the troopers under my command forward, towards the hole they'd punched for us through the enemy defences. 'For justice! For vengeance! For the Emperor!'

SIXTEEN

*Life's so much easier when you've got
someone to blame.*

– Gilbran Quail, Collected Essays.

'TRAITOR!' JURGEN RAISED the melta and took a determined pace forward, placing himself between Amberley and myself and the turncoat governor. Grice winced visibly as my aide moved closer to him, although his ever-present bouquet was no stronger than usual so far as I could tell, then squeezed the trigger again. The bolt exploded against the oversized helmet protecting Jurgen's head, flinging him backwards in a shower of shattered carapace; but thanks to the Emperor, or sheer good fortune, it hadn't penetrated this time, the sturdy armour protecting him from Sorel's grisly fate. He staggered back into us, and we both moved instinctively to catch him, dropping our weapons as we did so. My pistol and Amberley's miniature bolter thudded into the spongy carpet, and my chainsword, still activated, spun into a corner where it began chewing energetically through the skirting board.

'He's still alive,' I told Amberley, feeling for the pulse at Jurgen's neck, and taking his weight fully into my arms. After all, I thought, if Grice fired again I should be all right behind that amount of protection.

'Not for long, if you don't keep him away from me,' Grice threatened.

'You're one of them,' Amberley stated flatly, as though this merely confirmed her suspicions. She took another step towards him, and Grice shifted his aim to cover her. I watched, with some trepidation, for although she was still protected by the miraculous displacer field, she had told me herself that it was not to be wholly relied upon, and even if it worked its magic again, her sudden absence would leave me wide open to a follow-up shot.

I sagged a little, as though Jurgen's weight was greater than it was, and tried to work my hand towards the hellgun still slung across his shoulder. The governor grimaced, his mouth working in a manner not entirely human now I came to study it closely, and I berated myself for not having seen the truth sooner. The excessive bulk beneath his robes had not, as I'd assumed on our first meeting, resulted from over-indulgence and the commonplace inbreeding of most noble families,[1] but from a far more sinister source.

'The brood will survive,' he said. 'A new patriarch will arise–'

'But not in your lifetime,' I said, swivelling the hellgun under Jurgen's pungently damp armpit and squeezing the trigger. The supercharged las-blast screamed through the air between us, blasting a smoking crater through the left side of the governor's chest, and for a moment I felt the exultation of victory. It was short-lived, however, because to my horrified astonishment he didn't drop, just twisted aside with inhuman speed, and switched the aim of the bolt pistol back to me. Thick plates of chitin were visible beneath the ruin of his robes now, and a third deformed arm emerged from the rent in the garment. Through my nausea a sudden shaft of understanding lit up my synapses. 'You were the assassin!' I gasped.

A vivid mental picture of the events of that fateful night reeled through my brain. With a weapon concealed in that hidden extra hand, he could have shot the tau ambassador before anyone had even the faintest suspicion of his murderous intent, and whatever disarray withdrawing it might have left in his clothing would be put down to the turmoil of the moment. Certainly all I'd seen was two empty hands, and a hysterical El'hassai who, I must reluctantly concede, had been right all along.

---

1   Something of an exaggeration, but widely believed nevertheless.

'What was your first clue?' Amberley snapped, diving for her discarded weapon. I tried to take aim with the hellgun again, but the strap was tangled in Jurgen's armour, and the dead weight of my unconscious aide was hindering me. As Grice's bolt pistol came up I already knew I wasn't going to make it.

Then, for a blessed second he hesitated, still moving with preternatural speed, and pointed the gun back at Amberley. I suppose he realised that she would get to her bolt pistol and drop him if he didn't take her down first. I tried to shout a warning, but the first syllable of her name had barely made it through my horror-constricted throat before he fired.

The bolt detonated against the floor, twisting the gun her fingertips had almost reached into scrap and sending splinters of wood flying into the air, but once again, she was suddenly somewhere else. Some highly unladylike language and the crash of falling china a few metres further up the corridor told me that she'd collided with one of the little tables and its display of porcelain.[1]

Grice looked astonished just long enough for me to tug the recalcitrant hellgun around far enough to take another shot at him, which made a terrible mess

1   The displacer field, as those of you who've used one can no doubt attest, will readily teleport you out of immediate danger. Unfortunately, you rematerialise moving at the same speed and in the same direction as when the field activates, and, as Cain points out, I was diving for a gun on the floor at the time. And it was a stupid place to put a table in any case.

of that tasteful wood panelling but unfortunately did nothing worse to the tainted governor. He turned, following the sound of Amberley's landing, just in time to see her roll to her feet with the dextrousness of an accomplished martial artist.

'Consider yourself relieved of your position,' she said, pointing an accusing finger at him like a schola tutor admonishing an unsatisfactory student. He actually started to laugh, bringing the weapon round to bear on her again, when a bright flash erupted from the ornate ring I'd noticed at our first meeting. Grice staggered, falling back, and two hands went to his throat. The third continued to clutch his bolt pistol, which discharged again randomly as he sank to his knees. His face worked, as though gasping for air, and darkened with clotting blood. Pale yellow foam frothed over his engorging lips.

'Digital needler,' Amberley explained, stepping delicately over the now spasming corpse. 'The toxin's excruciatingly painful, I'm told.'

'Good,' I said, aiming a bad-tempered kick at the erstwhile governor, and hoping he was still conscious enough to feel it before he expired.

'How's Jurgen?' She took the weight of his other shoulder, and helped me to get him laid out on the floor. I began to remove the remains of his helmet carefully.

'Not good,' I said, a surprising amount of concern entering my voice. There was a lot of blood, but most of it seemed to be from superficial wounds caused by the shattered armour. Rather more worrying was the clear fluid mixed in with it. 'I think his skull's fractured.'

'I think you're right.' She began administering first aid with a speed and competence I found astonishing. 'Better call for a medicae unit.'

Cursing myself for my own stupidity, I activated my combead, realising belatedly that I'd be able to get a message through to Kasteen now we'd returned to the surface. To my astonishment, however, the command channels were choked with traffic, and I turned back to Amberley with the bitter taste of failure burning in the back of my throat.

'We're too late,' I said. 'It sounds as though the war's already started.'

'Then we'll just have to stop it,' she said, matter-of-factly, her attention still on Jurgen. At the time, still not realising his significance, I was simply grateful for her concern for his welfare, even as I found the time to marvel at her indefatigable spirit. If ever a woman seemed capable of stopping an all-out war single-handedly, it was her. I was just on the verge of replying when the wall blew in, throwing me to the floor yet again, and showering what was left of the elegant decor with rubble.

'What the frak...' I began, scrabbling for my fallen laspistol. I'd just managed to grab it when human figures in flak armour burst through the new gap, lasguns levelled. Behind them, I noted absently, someone was making a hell of a mess of the garden. I just managed to prevent myself from squeezing the trigger in the nick of time as I recognised the armour as Imperial Guard issue.

'Stand up! Slowly!' a familiar voice barked, then took on a tinge of astonishment. 'Commissar! Is that you?'

'Right now I'm not entirely sure,' I said. Kasteen looked at me, for a long, searching moment, before taking in the dishevelled state of the inquisitor; then her gaze moved on and down to the prostrate figures of Jurgen and the governor. I indicated my aide. 'He needs a medic,' I said, then for some reason my legs gave way beneath me.

'THERE'S NO DOUBT at all, then?' Kasteen had listened to our story in silence, or at least to as much of it as Amberley felt like telling her, and I'd spent the last half hour or so alternately nodding, saying 'yes, really,' and similar helpful remarks, and scrounging the largest mug of tanna leaf tea I could find. It was not the most obvious thing to find on a battlefield, you might think, but these were Valhallans after all, and it didn't take me long to discover a fire-team brewing up once the immediate danger was past.

Broklaw was running around like the good second-in-command he was, detailing troopers to secure the perimeter and clear out the tunnels beneath what was left of the palace, and once I'd seen Jurgen safely on his way back to the aid station, I relished the chance to simply enjoy the feeling of sun on my face and the astonished realisation that, against all the odds, I'd survived again.

'None,' Amberley said. 'The body's all the proof we need. Grice was a 'stealer hybrid, and killed the ambassador to try to provoke a war. All the death and destruction in the city was just part of the same agenda.'

'Merciful Emperor,' Kasteen breathed, appalled at the thought. 'His own people, sacrificed in their thousands... The bastard.'

'His own people were the genestealers,' I said. 'The rest of us, humans, tau, even the kroot, were never anything more to him than fodder for the hive fleets.'

'Exactly.' Amberley looked sober for a moment, before the familiar carefree smile was suddenly back on her face; but it was there with an effort, I found myself thinking. 'And if we hadn't kept our heads, things might have turned out very differently.'

'They still might,' I said, indicating the hulking figures of the tau dreadnoughts around the perimeter, and the curiously rounded vehicles hovering over the surface of the grass. Tau troopers were beginning to deploy from some of them, eyeing our own soldiers suspiciously, but so far, at least, the two forces were keeping well apart. 'Can we trust them now we don't have an enemy in common?'

'For the time being, at least,' Amberley said. She might have said more, but we were interrupted by a sudden shout from the direction of the ruins.

'They've found some survivors!' Kasteen hurried off, to where a small knot of figures was emerging from the wreckage of the palace. Amberley and I exchanged glances, an unspoken presentiment sparking between us, and trotted after her as best we could. Now we were safe the exhaustion of our exertions had crashed in on us like a landslide, and I felt my calf muscles cramping as I tried to keep up.

Even before we reached them I caught a glimpse of red hair, so it was little surprise to me when the search team (one of the squads from Sulla's platoon, I seem to recall, but I couldn't tell you which one) parted to reveal Velade and Holenbi, each supported by a trooper with an arm around the shoulders, holding hands like a pair of courting teeners. It's no exaggeration to say they both looked like hell, but that's precisely what you'd expect I suppose, their uniforms ragged, and bandages leaking blood where the squad medic had applied field dressings to the worst of their wounds. Holenbi stared at me in numb confusion, but that was nothing new.

'Where did you find them?' I asked the sergeant in charge, and he saluted me smartly.

'Down in the tunnels, sir. Lieutenant Sulla told us to spread out and secure the perimeter below ground, and they were about half a klom in. They must've been in a hell of a fight, sir.'

'Velade?' I asked gently. She turned her head towards me, her eyes unfocussed. 'What happened?'

'Sir?' Her brow furrowed. 'We were fighting. Tomas and me.'

'They were everywhere,' Holenbi cut in, his voice distant.

'Then the roof came in, and we lost the others. So we fought our way out.'

'I see,' I said, nodding slowly, and glanced across at Amberley. The same doubt was clouding her eyes, I could see. I turned back to the bedraggled troopers, then brought up my laspistol and shot them both through the head before either of them had a chance to react.

'What the hell...?' Kasteen shouted, her hand moving instinctively towards the bolt pistol on her hip until common sense reasserted itself and aborted the gesture. She glared at me, her jaw tight, and the troopers around us froze in shock, anger and confusion in their eyes. I had a sudden flash of *déjà vu*, an unbidden memory of the mess room aboard the *Righteous Wrath*. For a moment, I was horribly unsure of myself, afraid I'd made a terrible mistake, then I glanced again at Amberley for reassurance. She nodded, a barely noticeable acknowledgement, and I felt a little better. At least if I was wrong, an inquisitor was, too, which wouldn't help much with rebuilding morale in the regiment, but at least I wouldn't be the only one left feeling embarrassed.

'I've seen this before,' I said, addressing Kasteen directly, but keeping my voice loud and clear enough to be heard by everyone. 'On Keffia.' I took the combat knife from the sergeant's harness and knelt beside Holenbi's body, ripping one of the dressings away to reveal a small deep wound slanting up under the ribcage. I sliced it open, ignoring the horrified gasps from those around me, and felt around with blood-slick fingers. After a moment I found what I'd expected to be there, and yanked out a small fibrous bundle of organic material.

'What the hell's that?' Kasteen asked, over the sound of Sulla being violently sick.

'A genestealer implant,' Amberley explained. 'Once it takes root in a host, it gradually subverts their own genetic identity, turning any offspring into hybrids. A generation or two after that you start to get pure-strains showing up, along with hybrids almost indistinguishable from humans, and the taint continues to spread.' She indicated an identical wound on Velade's torso. 'They were both infected when the 'stealers overran them.'

'The disorientation was the real giveaway,' I added. 'The implant messes with the brain chemistry, so the host remains unaware of being infected. All they recall is a confused impression of fighting, and assume they've escaped.'

'It's often mistaken for combat fatigue,' Amberley finished. 'Luckily, the commissar could tell the difference, or your regiment would have been leaving hidden stealer cults behind wherever you were deployed.'

'I see.' Kasteen nodded once, crisply, and turned to the sergeant. 'Burn the bodies.'

'A wise precaution,' Amberley said as the three of us turned away, and the sergeant went looking for a flamer.

'Colonel! Commissar!' Broklaw was waving from the ramp of a command Chimera. 'One of our patrols found some tau down there too. They're on their way back to the surface now!'

Amberley and I looked at one another, and went to meet the survivors of the shas'la we'd met in the tunnels. Trepidation churned in my gut as the little group, reduced to three now, staggered into the sunlight. One had lost his helmet, and squinted at the sudden brightness. I shivered, finding myself plunged into shadow as a Devilfish troop carrier swept overhead and grounded to receive them. They looked disorientated, it was true, but they would have been as exhausted as we were, and I just couldn't be sure what the cause might be. These were xenos, after all, and I just couldn't read them the way I could my own kind.

So I stood there, paralysed with indecision, while they staggered up the ramp and into the transport, aided by their fellows, and by then it was too late anyway. As I turned away, sick with apprehension, I found Amberley watching me with what I can only describe as a smile of satisfaction.

For some reason, that failed to raise my spirits. If anything it had quite the opposite effect.

Editorial Note:

Once again we need to turn to other sources for a wider perspective on the aftermath of the affair than Cain's typically
self-centred account gives us.

From *Purge the Guilty! An impartial account of the
liberation of Gravalax,* by Stententious Logar.
085.M42.

And thus it was that the world we so dearly love was
saved from the depredations of the alien by the heroism of the warriors of His Divine Majesty and the
martial fortitude of heroes whose names live on in
the glory of their deeds. Even those of the calibre of

the celebrated Commissar Cain, who, though his own contribution to this campaign was never more than peripheral, was no doubt proud to have been associated with so noble an endeavour. It is indeed a pity that, like most of the Imperial Guardsmen deployed in this most glorious of enterprises, he was able to do no more than remain on the sidelines, but he was at least in at the death, so to speak, having been present when the treacherous Governor Grice at last met deserved retribution at the hands of the Inquisition. Indeed, some even assert that he witnessed the celebrated duel to the death between the wretched traitor and the inquisitor herself, although like most conscientious historians I must reluctantly concede that this is, in all probability, nothing more than a charming myth. After a thorough examination of the evidence, it seems far more likely that an officer of his calibre would have been in the thick of the battle for control of the palace, especially once the perfidious tau had moved in to try to protect the puppet their insidious rogue trader accomplices had installed on the throne there.

Be that as it may, the Battle of the Palace was undoubtedly the true turning point in the history of our fair globe, when the grip of the xenoist interloper was finally broken, and the relieved and grateful populace brought back at last under the protection of the Divine Emperor and his tireless servants. Broken and dispirited, the tau departed,

slinking away like the vagabond thieves they were,
having failed to seize the fair world of Gravalax for
their own. Within hours of their defeat at the hands
of the Imperial Guard, they withdrew, not only from
the city, but from the planet itself. One by one they
fled aboard their starships, retreating back into the
hinterland of space from whence they'd come, never
to trouble us again.

For you can be sure that we, the generations that
followed, have been careful not to make the mistakes
of our ancestors, and remain ever vigilant against the
hour of their return. Even now, our PDF units stand
ready, at a moments' notice, to defend the sacred soil
of His Majesty's most holy dominions to the utter-
most drop of their blood, and it is our most fervent
hope that one day the cream of these doughty warriors may be found worthy to take their place in the
blessed ranks of the Imperial Guard itself.

As to the rogue traders, we must be equally on our
guard, for they remain among us, spreading their
insidious web of treachery...

[And so on, and so on...

From which you might fairly deduce that the genestealer
infestation remains a secret known only to a few; and since
those few are either servants of the Inquisition or members of
an Imperial Guard unit never likely to return to the wretched
place, it's a secret which will remain secure. As to why this
should be so important...]

EPILOGUE

Stories are much tidier than real life. Stories
have neat, happy endings, but all you ever
really get is unfinished business.

– Janni Vakonz, holo director.

I'D SEEN LITTLE of Amberley in the week that followed
our adventures in the undercity, but we both had
plenty to keep us occupied over those few days, so I
hardly found her absence surprising. Jurgen was still
recovering slowly, so I'd lost my principle buttress
against most of the tedious minutiae of my job, and
found my workload drastically increased as a result.
Add to that the fatigue and minor injuries I'd sustained, and I did little else apart from eat, sleep, and
shuffle datafiles. Divas dropped round one evening

with a bottle of amasec, which provided a pleasant enough diversion, and filled me in on the latest gossip (which, after the last time, you can be sure I did my utmost to ignore; no point in taking any chances).

'No one can understand it,' he said at one point. 'The tau are just pulling out.' I'd heard as much from other sources, most of them a good deal more reliable thanks to my connections in the lord general's office, but I nodded nonetheless as I poured us both refills.

'Well, that's xenos for you,' I said helpfully. 'Who knows why they do anything?' It still didn't make much sense when Donali explained it to me, but he seemed to know what he was talking about, and Amberley confirmed it later, so it's the best I can do.

You see, peculiar little devils that they are, they don't seem to value the objective of the fighting purely for itself, the way we do. As best as I can understand it, they reckoned that if we were that determined to pitch into a meat grinder war to hang on to this worthless mudball, we might as well have it. They'd go off and do something more productive until we got bored or complacent or distracted, and come back for it later when we couldn't put up a decent fight for the place.[1] And in the meantime,

---

1   A little vague, but substantially accurate. Tau tacticians tend to take the long view, withdrawing to regroup whenever they meet stronger resistance than they were expecting, or, as in this case, the situation proves to be more complex than anticipated.

there was the hive fleet to worry about, assuming it was actually out there. (Which, as we were subsequently to discover, it most certainly was.)

So, as you can appreciate, I was pleasantly surprised when a message arrived from Amberley inviting me to dinner at a discreet waterfront restaurant in a quarter of the city which seemed to have escaped the worst of the fighting; even more so, given that I'd never expected to see her again. (Just how far off the mark that assumption was you'll find ample evidence of elsewhere in this memoir, as I've already mentioned.)

'How's Jurgen?' she asked, over a mouthwatering smoked vyl crêpe. Touched by her solicitude, I filled her in on his recovery, and asked how her associates were getting on in return. (Reasonably well, as it turned out: Rakel was up and about and as bonkers as ever, and Orelius had already returned to his ship.)

She nodded at the news. 'I'm glad to hear it. He's a remarkable man.'

'He's certainly unusual,' I agreed, savouring the local vintage she'd obtained from somewhere – light and piquant, it complimented the food wonderfully. She smiled at that.

'More so than you realise.' Something about the way her tone changed alerted me, and I began to pay more attention to her words. This was more than mere small talk. 'I don't think we'd have made it out of the tunnels without him.' I thought back to my desperate duel with the patriarch.

'If he hadn't scrounged that melta from some-where–' I agreed, but she cut me off before I could finish.

'That isn't what I meant. Do you know what a blank is?' I must have looked baffled, because she went on to explain. 'They're incredibly rare; about as rare among psykers as psykers are compared to the rest of us.'

'You think Jurgen's a psyker?' I asked, laughing in spite of myself, and inclining my body slightly to the left to give the waiter room to remove my plate. The idea was so ridiculous I just couldn't help it. But Amberley shook her head.

'No. Quite the reverse. He's a blank, I'm sure of it.' I echoed the gesture.

'You've lost me,' I admitted.

'Blanks are like anti-psykers,' she explained. 'They can't be affected by psykers or warp entities. They block telepathic communication. You saw how the patriarch reacted to him...'

'It seemed to get disoriented when he got close to it,' I said, remembering. 'And Grice was desperate to keep him away.' Amberley nodded.

'Exactly. His presence disrupted the brood telepathy.'

'That explains a lot,' I said, recalling a number of incidents over the years which had seemed no more than mildly puzzling at the time, but which I now realised formed a pattern, confirming my aide's resistance to psychic attack. 'How long have you known?'

'Since the first time I saw him,' she admitted. 'When Rakel had a seizure while he was trying to help her into the Salamander.' A terrible suspicion began to form.

'You're going to recruit him, aren't you?' I said. 'If he can face down daemons and sorcerers you're not going to leave him buried in an obscure Imperial Guard unit.' She was smiling again, as though something amused her.

'The Inquisition is an odd organisation, Ciaphas,' she said. 'Not like the Guard, where everyone's united against a common foe, and you can rely on your comrades and your command structure.' I wasn't sure what she was driving at then, but I've had rather more dealings with the Inquisition since than I'm comfortable with, and believe me, it makes sense. Just take my word for it, and hope you never have cause to find out. 'We're not very big on sharing our sources and resources, because we never really know who else in the ordos we can trust.' As you'll appreciate, astonishment barely begins to cover what I felt listening to those words. 'So, no, I think for the time being I'd rather leave him where he is. It's safer that way.'

'Safe? In a front line Guard unit?' I thought she was joking at first, until I got a good look at her eyes. Blue and guileless, they shone with a sincerity that would have been impossible to fake. (Believe me, I'm an expert at that.) She nodded again.

'I'll be able to find you again if I need you. Either of you.' And I was so caught up in the moment that the full implication of those words never struck me at the time. 'But if I take him on as one of my staff he'll attract attention. The sort I'd rather avoid.[1]'

'I see.' I didn't really, but the main point seemed to be that I wouldn't have to worry about losing my aide after all, at least in the short term. And it also hadn't escaped my notice that while he was around I wouldn't have to worry about any passing psykers ferreting out secrets I'd rather leave buried. I started in on my toffee cream dessert with well-deserved enthusiasm.

'Good.' Amberley grinned again, the mischievous expression I found so appealing back on her face. 'Besides, Rakel's hard enough to deal with at the best of times, without passing out on me every five minutes.'

'I'm sure,' I said. The silence stretched awkwardly for a moment, so I made an attempt to change the subject. 'You've heard about the tau withdrawal?' She nodded.

'El'sorath still insists that the world is theirs by right, but they're agreeing to respect the status quo for the time being. I guess they blinked first.' She shrugged. 'Besides, they're spooked by the idea of a hive fleet moving in, even if they don't want to admit it. They've had a few skirmishes with splinter fleets in the last couple of centuries, and they're under no illusions about what a full-scale invasion would

1   Like Radicals with an agenda, or Ordo Malleus fanatics looking for daemon-fodder for their next crusade. Not my department, thank the Emperor.

mean.' Neither was I, and I shuddered at the thought. 'Hanging on to one small planet doesn't mean much in the face of that, especially if it would weaken their response to the greater threat.'

'Speaking of which...' I coughed delicately. 'I'm still not entirely sure those pathfinders... You know...'

'Who cares?' Amberley sipped at her wine appreciatively. 'If they were, then at least it'll draw the hive fleets down on them instead of us a few generations down the line. And in the meantime, we can exploit the chaos in the tau empire for our own ends.'

'Good for us, then,' I said. I raised my own glass. 'Confusion to our enemies.'

'And kudos to our friends.' Our glasses clinked together, and Amberley grinned at me again. 'Here's to the beginning of a beautiful friendship.'

Not to mention half a lifetime of running, shooting, and bowel-clenching terror, of course. But looking back, I have to say she made it well worth the effort.

[*And on that somewhat ego-boosting note, this extract from the Cain Archive comes to a natural conclusion*].

ABOUT THE AUTHOR

Sandy Mitchell is a pseudonym of Alex Stewart, who has been working as a freelance writer for the last couple of decades. He has written science fiction and fantasy in both personae, as well as television scripts, magazine articles, comics, and gaming material. His television credits include the high tech espionage series *Bugs*, for which, as Sandy, he also wrote one of the novelisations.

Apart from both miniatures and roleplaying gaming his hobbies include the martial arts of Aikido and Iaido, rifle shooting, and playing the guitar badly.

He lives in a quiet village in North Essex with a very tolerant wife, their first child, and a small mountain of unpainted figures.

**Coming soon
from the Black Library**

CAVES OF ICE

A Commissar Cain novel
by Sandy Mitchell

WARP KNOWS I'VE seen more than my fair share of
Emperor-forsaken hell-holes in more than a century
of occasionally faithful and dedicated service to the
Imperium, but the iceworld of Simia Orichalcae
stands out in my memory as one of exceptional
unpleasantness. And when you bear in mind that
over the years I've seen the inside of an eldar reiver
citadel and a necron tomb world, just to pick out a
couple of the highlights (so to speak), you can be
sure that my experiences there rank among the most
terrifying and life-threatening in a career positively
littered with hairs-breadth escapes from almost certain death.

Not that it seemed that way when our regiment got its orders to deploy. I'd been serving with the Valhallan 597th for a little over a year by that point, and had managed to settle into a fairly comfortable routine.

I got on well with both Colonel Kasteen and her second-in-command Major Broklaw, who in turn seemed to consider me as much of a friend as it was possible to be with the regimental commissar, and the kudos I'd earned as a result of our adventures on Gravalax stood me in good stead with the men and women of the lower ranks as well. Indeed most of them seemed to credit me, not entirely wrongly, with having provided the inspirational leadership that had allowed them to prevail against the vile conspiracy which unleashed so much bloodshed on that unhappy world, and providing them with an initial battle honour to which they could all point with pride.

At the risk of seeming a little full of myself, I did have some cause for satisfaction on that score at least: I'd inherited responsibility for a divided, not to say mutually hostile regiment, cobbled together from the combat-depleted remnants of two previously single-sex units who had disliked and distrusted one another from the beginning.

Now, if anything, I was faced with the opposite problem, maintaining discipline as they became comfortable working together and the new personnel assignments started bedding in. Quite literally in a few cases, which only made matters worse of course, particularly when acceptable fraternisation spilled over into lover's tiffs, acrimonious partings, or the jealousy of others. I was beginning to see why the vast majority of regiments in the Imperial Guard were segregated by gender.

Fortunately there were very few occasions when anything harsher than a stiff talking-to, some quick rotation of the protagonists to different squads, and a rapid palming-off of the problem to the chaplain were called for, so I was able to maintain my carefully-constructed facade of concern for the well-being of the troopers without undue difficulty.

Being iceworlders themselves, of course, the Valhallans were overjoyed at the news we were being sent to Simia Orichalcae. Even before we made orbit the viewing ports were crowded with off-duty troopers eager for a first sight of our new home, at least for the next few months, and a chatter of excited voices had followed Kasteen, Broklaw and myself through the corridors towards the bridge. My enthusiasm, needless to say, was rather more muted.

'Beautiful, isn't it?' Broklaw said, his grey eyes fixed on the main hololith display.

The flickering image of the planet appeared to be suspended in the middle of the cavernous chamber full of shadows and arcane mechanisms, surrounded by officers, deckhands and servitors doing the incomprehensible things starship crewmen usually did. Captain Durant, the officer in charge of the old freighter that had been hastily pressed into service to transport us from our staging area on Coronus Prime, shook his head.

'If you like planets I suppose it's fine,' he said dismissively, his optical implants not even flickering in that direction. Of indeterminate age, he was so patched with augmetics that if it hadn't been for his uniform and the deference with which his crew treated him I might have mistaken him for a servitor. It had been courteous of him to invite the three of us to the bridge, so I was prepared to overlook his lack of social graces. It wasn't until some time later that I realised that doing so was probably the only way he would ever get to meet his passengers at all, as he showed every sign of being as much a part of the ship's internal systems as the helm controls or the navigator.

Cynical, as I usually was about such things, I had to concede that Broklaw had a point. From this altitude the world below us shone like an exotic pearl, rippled with a thousand subtle shades of grey, blue and white. Thin veils of cloud drifted across it, obscuring the outlines of mountain ranges and deep shadowed valleys that could have swallowed a fair sized city.

Despite knowing the resolution was far too low to show it, I couldn't help searching for some sign of the impact crater where a crudely hollowed-out fragment of asteroid had ploughed into that serene-looking vista, vomiting its cargo of orks out to sully the surface of this pristine world.

'Breathtaking,' Kasteen murmured, oblivious to the exchange. Her eyes were wide, and like her subordinate she seemed lost in a haze of nostalgia. I could readily understand why: the Guard sent its regiments wherever they were needed, and the Valhallans all too rarely got the chance to fight in an environment they felt completely at home in.

Simia Orichalcae was probably the closest thing to their homeworld either officer had seen since they joined up, and I could almost feel their impatience to get down there and feel the permafrost beneath their boot soles. I was rather less eager, as you can imagine. I've never been agoraphobic like some hivers, and quite enjoy being outdoors in a comfortable climate, but where iceworlds are concerned I've never seen the point of weather, as we used to say back home.

'We'll get you down as soon as possible,' Durant said, barely able to hide his satisfaction at the thought of getting nearly a thousand Guardsmen and women off his ship. I can't say I altogether blame him. The *Pure of Heart* wasn't exactly a luxury liner, and the opportunities for recreational activities had been few and far between.

The crew clearly resented their own facilities being swamped by bored and boisterous soldiers, and the training drills we'd devised to keep our people busy in the few remaining cargo holds which weren't already stuffed with vehicles, stores and hastily-installed bunks hadn't been enough to let them blow off steam completely, so there had been some inevitable friction.

Luckily the few brawls which had broken out had been swiftly dealt with, Kasteen being in no mood for a repeat of our experiences aboard the *Righteous Wrath*, so I'd had relatively little to do about it beyond telling the freshly-separated combatants that they were a disgrace to the Emperor's uniform and dish out the appropriate penalties. And of course, when you have several hundred healthy young men and women cooped up in a confined space together for weeks on end many of them will find their own ways of amusing themselves, which raised the whole range of other problems I've already alluded to.

Be that as it may, despite the constant irritation of dealing with a host of minor infractions, I wasn't particularly eager for our voyage to end. I'd fought orks before, many times, and despite their brutishness and stupidity I knew they weren't to be underestimated. With numbers on their side, and the orks always had superior numbers in my experience, they could be formidably difficult to dislodge once they'd gained a foothold anywhere. And by luck or base cunning, they had found a prize on Simia Orichalcae worth fighting for.

'Can we see the refinery from here?' Kasteen asked. Durant nodded, and apparently obedient to his will, a section of the gently flickering planet in front of us expanded vertiginously as though we were plummeting down in a ballistic re-entry.

Despite knowing that it was only a projection, my stomach lurched instinctively for a second before habit and discipline reasserted themselves and I found myself assessing the tactical situation laid out before us. The slightly narrowed eyes of my companions told me that they were doing the same, no doubt bringing their intimate knowledge of the environment below us into play in a fashion that I never could.

Within seconds we were presented with an aerial view of the installation we'd been sent here to protect.

'That valley looks reasonably defensible,' Broklaw mused aloud, nodding in evident satisfaction. The sprawling collection of buildings and storage tanks was nestled at one end of a narrow defile, which would be a natural choke point to an enemy advance. Kasteen evidently concurred.

'Place a few dugouts along the ridgeline and we can hold it 'til hell thaws out,' she agreed. I was a little less sanguine, but felt it best to seem supportive.

'What about the mountain approaches?' I asked, nodding in apparent agreement. The two officers looked mildly incredulous.

'The terrain's far too broken,' Broklaw said. 'You'd have to be insane to try coming over the peaks.'

'Or very tough and determined,' I pointed out. Orks weren't the subtlest tacticians the forces of the Emperor ever faced, but their straightforward approach to problem solving was often surprisingly effective. Kasteen nodded too.

'Good point,' she said. 'We'll set up a few surprises for them just in case.'

'A minefield or two ought to do it,' Broklaw said, nodding thoughtfully. 'Cover the obvious approaches, and one here, on the most difficult route. If they try that they'll assume we've fortified everywhere.'

They might not care, of course. Orks are like that; casualties simply don't matter to them, and they'll just press on regardless as like as not, especially if there are enough of them surviving to boost each other's confidence. But it was a good point, and worth trying.

'How far have they got?' I asked. By way of reply Durant swept the hololith display round to the west, apparently skimming us across the surface of the barren world with breathtaking speed. The broken landscape of the mountain range swept past, the higher peaks dotted with scrub, lichen, and a few insanely tenacious trees, apparently the only vegetation which could survive here. Just as well too, or there wouldn't be an atmosphere you could breathe. Beyond the foothills was a broad plain, crisp with snow, and for a moment I could understand the affection my colleagues had for this desolate but majestic landscape.

Abruptly the purity of the scene changed, revealing a wide swathe of churned-up, blackened snow, befouled with the detritus and leavings of the savage horde that surged across it. A couple of kilometres wide at least, it seemed like a filthy dagger-thrust into the heart of this strangely peaceful world. The resolution of the hololith wasn't enough to make out the individual members of this savage warband, but we could see clumps of movement within the main mass, like bacteria under a microscope. The analogy was an apt one, I thought; a disease infected Simia Orichalcae, and we were the cure.

'Seems like we got here just in time,' Kasteen said, putting the thoughts of all of us into words. I extrapolated the speed of the ork advance, and nodded thoughtfully. We should have the regiment down and deployed roughly a day before they reached the valley where the precious promethium plant lay open and defenceless before them.

'I'll get everyone moving,' Broklaw promised. 'If we get the first wave embarked now we can launch the shuttles as soon as we make orbit.'

'Please yourselves.' Durant somehow managed to make his immobile shoulders convey the impression of a shrug. 'We'll be at station-keeping in about an hour.'

'Are the datafeeds set up?' I asked, while we still had some measure of his attention. He repeated the gesture.

'I don't know.' He inflated his lungs, or whatever he used instead of them. 'Mazarin! Get up here!' The top half of a woman almost as encrusted with augmetics as her captain, the cogwheel icon of a techpriest suspended from a chain around her neck, rose on a humming suspensor field to join us on the command dais. As we spoke she kept herself hovering roughly at my own head height, the tunic she wore stirring unnervingly at what would have been level with her knees, if she'd had any, in the faint current from the air recirculators. 'The soldier here wants to know if you've wired up his gadgets.'

'The Omnissiah has blessed their activation,' she confirmed, in a surprisingly mellifluous voice, with a hard stare at the captain that told me his irreverence was an old and minor annoyance. 'They are all functioning within acceptable parameters.'

'Good.' Kasteen, to my mild surprise, was looking distinctly uneasy, her eyes flickering away from the techpriest whenever she thought she could politely do so. 'We'll have full sensor coverage of the planet's surface then.'

'So long as this old blasphemer remembers how to keep his collection of scrap in orbit,' she agreed. Once again the two of them exchanged a look that spoke of an old association, confirming my initial suspicion of an easy intimacy between them. A waving mechadendrite reached forward across Mazarin's shoulder, clutching a dataslate, which she thrust towards the colonel. Kasteen took it with every sign of reluctance, all but shying away from the mechanical limb. 'The appropriate rituals of data retrieval are on this.'

'Thank you.' She handed the slate to Broklaw as though it were contaminated with something. The major took it without comment, and began scanning the files it contained.

'Waste of a perfectly good starship if you ask me,' Durant grumbled. 'But the money's good.'

'We're most grateful for your co-operation,' I assured him. A troopship would have been equipped to deploy a proper orbital sensor net, which would have been infinitely preferable, but the battered old freighter's navigational array would just have to do. Our deployment was a hurried one, in response to a frantic astropathic message from the staff of the installation below us, and we'd just had to make do with what we could grab instead of waiting for the right equipment for the task at hand.

'At least you've got the easy job,' Broklaw assured him. This much was true; the *Pure of Heart* was just supposed to stay in orbit over the refinery, feeding her sensor data into our tactical net, so we could keep an eye on our enemies from above.

'You call this easy?' Durant asked rhetorically. A sweep of his arm took in the humming activity of the bridge. 'Having half my systems rewired, trying to hold it all together...' His voice trailed off as Mazarin floated away with a faint tchah! of disapproval, and something a little softer entered his body language.

'Your techpriest seems efficient enough,' I said, trying to sound encouraging. He nodded.

'Oh, she is. Far too good to waste her time on a tub like this really, but you know. Family ties.' He sighed, some old regrets coming to the surface in spite of himself, and shook his head. 'Would have made a good deck officer if she hadn't got religion. Too much of her mother in her, I suppose.' Startled, I tried to make out traces of a family resemblance, but the predominant feature they had in common seemed to be an abundance of augmetics rather than anything genetic.

I TOOK THE first shuttle down, of course, as befitted my entirely unwarranted reputation for preferring to lead from the front, but at least that meant I'd be well under cover before the orks arrived and should have my pick of the quarters planetside. I wasn't expecting much in the way of comfort in an industrial facility, but whatever there was to be had I meant to find. In this, at least, I'd have a valuable ally, my aide Jurgen having an almost preternatural talent for scrounging which had made my life (and no doubt his own, although I was careful not to enquire about that) considerably more comfortable than it might have been in our decade and a half of serving together. He dropped into the seat next to me, preceded as always by his spectacular body odour, and fastened his restraint harness.

'Everything's in order, sir,' he assured me, meaning our personal effects had been stowed in the cargo bay to the rear with his usual efficiency. I had no doubt of that. Despite his unprepossessing exterior, and his apparent conviction that personal hygiene was something that only happened to other people, he possessed a number of positive qualities and few people, apart from me, had ever spent sufficient time with him to appreciate.

Perhaps the most important from my point of view was his complete lack of imagination, which he more than made up for with a dogged deference to authority and an unquestioning acceptance of any order he was given. As you can imagine, having someone like that as a buffer between me and some of the more onerous aspects of my job pretty much amounted to a gift from the Emperor Himself. Add to that the innumerable perils we'd faced and bested together, and I can honestly say that he was the only person apart from myself I ever fully trusted.

The familiar kick of the shuttle engine igniting cut any further possibility of conversation short. It went without saying that, rather than the military drop-ships we were used to, the *Pure of Heart* was equipped with heavy-duty cargo haulers which had been quickly converted on the voyage to meet our needs as far as possible, which was better than I could have reasonably expected, but still far from ideal. The front third of the cargo space had been partitioned off with a hastily welded bulkhead, and then subdivided into half a dozen decks with metal mesh flooring. Somehow Mazerin and her acolytes had managed to cram some five score seats and their crash webbing into this space, so that we could disembark a couple of platoons at a time. The rest of the hold had been left open, to take our Chimeras, Sentinels and other vehicles, along with the small mountain of ammo packs, rations, medicae supplies, and all the other stuff necessary to keep an Imperial Guard regiment running at peak efficiency.

Looking around I could see men and women hugging their kitbags, lasrifles held across their knees, faces half hidden by the thick fur caps they wore in anticipation of the bone-biting cold that awaited us on the planet's surface. Most had fastened their uniform greatcoats too, mottled with the blues and whites of iceworld camouflage, and I was suddenly acutely aware of what an obvious target my black uniform and scarlet sash would make me out in that icy waste. No point worrying about it so I gritted my teeth and forced a relaxed smile to my face.

'Pilot's making the most of it,' I said, half joking, and raising a few grins from the troopers around me. 'Must have been watching *Attack Run* in the mess hall.' Jurgen grunted something, swathed in his greatcoat, which, like everything else he ever wore, somehow contrived to look as though it were intended for someone of a slightly different shape.

He suffered from motion sickness on almost every combat drop I ever made with him, but that never seemed to affect his fighting ability once he was back on terra firma. I suspected that he was so relieved to be back on solid ground he'd take on the enemy with a sharpened stick rather than have to face the possibility of retreat and getting back into the air again.

This time, though, he wasn't the only one. The thickening atmosphere was buffeting the overloaded shuttle, and pale, sweating faces were everywhere I looked. Even my own stomach revolted on a couple of occasions, threatening to spray the narrow compartment with the remains of my lunch, and I swallowed convulsively. I wasn't going to compromise the dignity of my office, not to mention becoming a laughing stock among the troopers, by throwing up. Not in public, at any rate.

'What the hell does he think he's playing at?' Lieutenant Sulla, the commander of third platoon, and a sight too over-eager for my liking, scowled, looking even more like a petulant pony than usual. Nevertheless, the distraction from my somersaulting stomach was a welcome one, so I invoked my commissarial privileges and retuned the combead in my ear to the frequency of the cockpit communicator in the hope of finding out.

'Say again, shuttle one.' The voice was calm and methodical, undoubtedly the ground controller at the refinery landing field. The answering voice was anything but; a civilian suddenly in the middle of a war zone without a clue as to how to survive in it, and clearly not expecting to. Our pilot, without a doubt.

'We're taking ground fire!' The edge of hysteria in his voice was unmistakable. Any moment now he was going to panic, and if he did we were all likely to die.

There was nothing else for it. I unbuckled my seat restraints and lurched to my feet, conscious of Sulla's eyes on me as I grabbed the nearest stanchion for support. It was embossed with an Imperial eagle, which I found reassuring, and with its aid I was able to take a couple of halting steps towards the cockpit.

'Is that wise, commissar?' she asked, a faint frown of puzzlement appearing on her face.

'No,' I snapped, not having time to waste on courtesy. 'But it's necessary.' My body weight slammed into the narrow door to the flight deck, propelling it open, and I staggered inside. The pilot stared up at me, his knuckles white on the control yoke, while his navigational servitor carried on regulating the routine functions of the ship with single-minded fixity of purpose. 'What's the problem?' I asked, trying to project an air of calm.

'We're under attack!' the man shouted, raw panic edging into his voice. 'We have to pull back to orbit!'

'That wouldn't be wise,' I said, keeping my voice level and grabbing the servitor's shoulder to steady myself. It just kept on adjusting controls with a complete lack of concern. Beyond the thick armourcrys vision port the bleak and frozen landscape hurtled past beneath us. I could see no sign of enemy activity anywhere. 'We'd take hours to rendezvous with the ship if we abort on this trajectory, and we only have limited life support. You'd probably suffocate along with everyone else.'

'We have a safety margin,' the pilot urged. I shook my head.

'The rest of us do. You don't.' I let my right hand brush the butt of my las pistol, and he turned even paler. 'And I don't see any immediate danger, do you?'

'What do you call that?' He pointed off to starboard, where a single puff of smoke burst briefly. A moment later a small constellation of bright flashes sparkled for an instant some distance below and to the left. Bolter shells detonating against the ground, after some trigger-happy greenskin took a hopeless potshot in our general direction.

'Nothing to worry about,' I said. 'That's small arms fire.' The analytical part of my mind noted that the main bulk of the ork advance was still some distance away, which meant we ought to be on alert for a small scout force attempting to infiltrate the refinery (now looming reassuringly large in the viewport), or reconnoitre our lines. 'The chances of anything actually hitting us at this range are astronomical.'

One day I'm going to have to stop saying things like that. No sooner had the words left my mouth than the shuttle shuddered even more violently than before, and pitched sharply to port. Red icons began to appear on the dataslates, and the servitor began punching controls with greater speed and abhuman dexterity.

'Pressure loss in number two engine,' it chanted. 'Combustion efficiency dropping by sixteen per cent.'

'Astronomical, eh?' Strangely enough the pilot seemed calmer now his fears had been realised. 'Better strap in, commissar. It's going to be a rough landing.'

'Can you make the pad?' I asked. He looked tense, his lips tight.

'I'm going to try. Now get the warp off my flight deck and let me do my job.'

'I've no doubt you will,' I said, boosting his confidence as best I could, and staggered back to my seat.

'What's going on?' Sulla asked as I buckled in and tensed for the impact.

'The greenies put a dent in us. There's going to be a bump,' I said. I felt strangely calm. There was nothing I could do about the situation now except trust in the Emperor and hope the pilot was more competent than he sounded.

The waiting seemed to take forever, but could only have lasted a minute or two.

I listened to the chatter in my combead while the pilot read off a number of datum points, which meant nothing to me but sounded pretty ominous, and the conviction began to grow that we weren't going to make it as far as the pad. In fact the traffic controller seemed pretty insistent that we avoid the installation altogether, which I could well understand, as dropping an unguided shuttle into the middle of the promethium tanks would end our mission pretty effectively before it had even begun.

The pilot responded with a couple of terse phrases which managed to impress me even after fifteen years of exposure to the most imaginative profanity of the barrack room, and I began to think we were in safe hands after all, and might just make it.

That impression lasted all of twelve seconds, until a violent impact jarred my spine up into the roof of my skull, driving the breath from my lungs, and a sound uncannily reminiscent of an ammunition dump exploding rang through the hull. I gasped some air back into my aching lungs, and tried to clear my blurring vision as the screech of tortured metal set my rattling teeth on edge. I became gradually aware, through the ringing in my ears, that Jurgen was trying to say something.

'Well that wasn't so...' he began, before the whole ghastly cycle repeated itself another couple of times.

At last the noise and vibration ceased, and I gradually became aware of the fact that I was still alive. I struggled free of the seat restraints, and wobbled to my feet.

'Everybody out!' I bawled. 'By squads. Carry the wounded with you!'

In the back of my mind a lurid picture of overheated engines exploding into flame tried to ignite a little beacon of panic, and I fought it down. I turned to Sulla, who was trying to stem a nosebleed. For that matter I suppose we all looked a bit the worse for wear, except possibly Jurgen, as with him it was hard to tell. 'I want casualty figures ASAP.'

'Yes sir.' She turned to the nearest NCO, Sergeant Lustig, a solid and competent soldier I had a lot of time for, and started snapping out orders in her usual brisk fashion.

The door to the cockpit burst open, and the pilot staggered out, looking at least as bad as I felt.

'Told you we'd make it,' he said, and threw up on my boots.

**The frankly preposterous saga
of Ciaphas Cain continues in
CAVES OF ICE, coming soon
from the Black Library!**